DEAD MAN TALKING

Also by T. M. Simmons

A Dead Man MysteryDead Man Talking

Dead Man Haunt

Dead Man Hand

Dead Man Ohio

Dead Man Series Collection 1: Dead Man Mysteries Books 1, 2 and 3

DEAD MAN TALKING

A DEAD MAN MYSTERY
BOOK ONE

T. M. SIMMONS

ePublishingWorks!
love what you read.

Book and cover design by eBook Prep
www.ebookprep.com

August 2022
ISBN: 978-1-64457-340-2

ePublishing Works!
644 Shrewsbury Commons Ave
Ste 249
Shrewsbury PA 17361
United States of America
www.epublishingworks.com
Phone: 866-846-5123

ACKNOWLEDGMENTS

A lot of people helped in varied ways with this book. I'll probably forget someone, and I apologize if I do. First and foremost, Deputy Dave Nelson, of the Morris County Sheriff's Department, patiently explained the various local agencies, their available facilities, and how they worked together. Dave also kept me on track as to what they could and could not do within their jurisdictions, what had to be entrusted to larger cities, and how that worked. I could have listened to Sergeant Donnie Vallery of the Jefferson Police Department for hours, and do thank him again for finding that handcuff key so I could get out of the jail cell, despite what my husband wanted! The ladies at the Jefferson Chamber of Commerce answered my questions without blinking an eye. I guess they're used to dealing with ghosthunters and writers. Officers Ron Jones and Ken McKeown of the Terrell Citizen's Police Academy, as well as the great speakers they brought in, were so very willing to answer anything, no matter how sane or insane. See, guys and gals, I told you my curiosity was for my book, not any illegal activities! Thanks to Louise Harper for the wonderful title and the great Louise'isms. Thanks to my first readers, Louise, Alice, Tracy, and Lynn. Thank you, Lynn, for the web site. Thanks to OurLoopers for enjoying my scary stories even if they did give them nightmares and for encouraging me to write more of them. Sorry, Pam, about the gorgeous ghost who crawled in bed with you in our shared room—not!

To Belle and Terry, especially Belle for being my own real life Aunt Twila; Trucker and Miss Molly, for inspiration.
To Brandon and Ransom with hugs and kisses. Memaw said it would be a real book someday, huh, Ransom?
To all my ghosthunting buddies. May we have many more happy hunts!

CHAPTER 1

Weird things tend to happen when you live in a haunted house. I see ghosts. I talk to ghosts. Unlike people who scream and race hell-bent for leather the opposite direction at the first sight of a specter from another dimension, my aunt, Twila Brown, and I actually hunt down rumors of ghosts. I found my very own haunted house completely by accident—or with the help of Fate. Doesn't matter. After two years, it suits me just fine, and my paranormal residents abide by the rules—most of the time.

Two years earlier, however, all I wanted to do was curl up in my New Orleans apartment and hide from both worlds, real and supernatural. Then all the way from Yankee-land, Twila showed up on my doorstep the afternoon after the final court hearing on Jack's and my divorce. She caught me halfway through a bottle of Crown Royal and had me in the car and on the road before I sobered up. Patiently, at first, she listened to my maudlin musings.

"I thought we were being so...adult about the whole thing." I snuffled and wiped the back of my hand under my nose, and Twila sighed and shoved the box of tissues off the console into my lap. I ignored that in favor of the soggy bunch of fast-food napkins knotted in my fist.

"I didn't think it would be this hard," I continued in a self-pitying whine. "But walking out of the courthouse—Jack didn't even show up for the hearing! Did I tell you?"

"Several times," Twila answered.

"Oh. Well, I was remembering how Jack and I talked that first year. That log cabin we were gonna build with the porch all the way around it. Rocking chairs where we'd sit and watch our grandkids catch lightning bugs in the yard. It just all went so damn wrong!"

Westbound on I-10, we hit one of the miles-long stretches of causeway across a swamp, and the tires clickety-clanked on steel girders separating the asphalt sections. Twila accelerated and changed lanes to pass a pickup pulling a candy-apple red bass boat decked out with padded swivel seats and a huge Mercury motor. Boxes and suitcases filled the pickup bed. Before we reached the trailer brake lights, I ducked and buried my face, nose in the sodden napkins.

"What in the world are you doing?" Twila asked.

I turned my head sideways, but stayed crouched in a near-fetal position. "Jack. That's Jack's truck and the new boat he bought. He's moving to Longview. Remember? I told you."

"No," Twila mused. "I don't recall you mentioning that news."

"I've had a few other things on my mind," I pouted. "He has a new job. Detective on the Longview force. In Texas. Longview's about a tenth the size of New Orleans."

We were still beside the truck. I could hear matching clickety-clacks from it, and Twila glanced out the passenger window. Then she lifted one hand in a friendly wave. "Yeah, Jack."

"For God's sake, don't get his attention!" I hissed.

"We're in your car, Alice. I assume he recognizes it. You've had it for two years."

I bobbed up like an apple in a water barrel and swiveled around. Twila flipped on the blinker and smoothly slid into the right-hand lane —leaving me a clear view of Jack in the pickup. Leaving Jack a clear view of me through the rear window of my Buick Regal. Jack nodded and lifted his hand to favor me with a wave. I managed a sickly grin and a finger-wiggle reply, then snapped forward. "I'm trading off this darn car when I get my next royalty check!"

Unfortunately, the sunshade was down and the mirror on the back reflected my face. Half-moon mascara smudges coated beneath red-veined eyes and streaked my pale cheeks in zebra stripes. I moaned and yanked a gob of tissues from the box crushed on my lap.

We hit the end of the causeway, and Twila sped up. Another mile or so down the road, she glanced in the rearview mirror and said, "He's way behind us now. There's a rest area up ahead. Want to pull off?"

"No!" I spat. "What if Jack decides to stop there, too?"

Twila shrugged and continued on past the blue and white exit sign. "There's some baby-wipes in my satchel in the back seat."

I turned to reach for the satchel, but my eyes glued to that back window and searched the line of traffic behind us. I thought I saw a flash of red far back. Of course, there are lots of red vehicles on the road. Finally I unzipped the satchel and dug out the baby-wipes.

"I guess I don't blame Jack for moving to a smaller town," Twila said. "That last case he had...he finally caught that child murderer. The story was even in our paper back home."

"After six months...and three dead children. It burned him out. But he wouldn't even talk to me about it! He just brooded whenever he did happen to stop by to shower and shave."

"Seems to me you were on a book tour part of that time," she reminded me.

"Not all the time," I defended myself. "Where are we going?" I finally thought to ask as I faced the mirror again and scrubbed. Or maybe I just wanted to change the subject.

"I heard about this little forgotten-time town over in East Texas," she replied. "Six Gun, Texas. It's supposed to be crawling with ghosts."

"It's not close to Longview, is it?"

She shook her head. "At least a couple hours away. From the looks of the map."

"It'll be dark by the time we get there."

"Yeah," she said with a grin. "Neat, huh?"

I nodded in eager agreement. Nothing like a scary nighttime ghosthunt to lift a new divorcee's spirits. There were probably a few old graveyards, too, in Six Gun. Twila and I delight in roaming graveyards, daytime or in the full and dark of the moon. Ghosts and spirits congregate there, perhaps hoping for a glimpse of family members who visit their gravesites.

Two stops for directions later—Twila and I aren't known for our attention to road signs when we get to chatting about ghosts—and an hour after sundown, the headlights skimmed past a faded real estate sign along a back country, two-lane road. Twila slammed on the brakes, glanced at me, and said, "I've got a feeling about that place."

"Go for it," I agreed. We'd had lots of adventures when Twila got one of her feelings.

We were alone on the road, so she backed up until we could see the sign in the headlights again. Overgrown weeds nearly obscured it; the place had been on the market a while. Untrimmed yupon branches scratched the Buick as we drove down the sandy driveway, but it wasn't more than a hundred feet before the sprawling log cabin came into view. Security lights burned, one in front, another through the trees behind. It had a deck across the front, no doubt high enough to provide a view of the lake I'd noticed across the road just as we saw the sign.

Twila parked and we both slid out of the car. Landscaping had grown wild, but it could be tamed with a pair of clippers. Instead of climbing the steps to the deck, we wandered around the side, to the back yard. Ancient live oaks, pecan, and native cedar trees interspersed at least an acre, which stretched back to where the famed East Texas Piney Woods encroached. Spots of color indicated rose bushes and azaleas, two of my favorite plants.

"Beautiful," I breathed.

"Could be, with some work," Twila agreed.

We walked across the back patio and tried to peer in the glass doors, but curtains prevented us. So we headed back to the front deck—and smiled at each other when the little old man visualized at the top of the steps and shook his fist.

4

"If he only knew," Twila whispered with a chuckle.

"Yeah," I agreed *sotto voce*. "What better place for a writer and ghosthunter? All this privacy, and ghosts I don't have to hunt."

"Plenty of room for a few pets, too," Twila said. "You've always dreamed of having a dog and cat, but never had the room to take care of them."

We climbed the steps, and the elderly man backed up, a startled look on his face. No sense offering to shake hands. My grip would pass through his. Instead, I greeted, "Nice place."

"There's ten of us here already." He propped his fists on pudgy hips. "No more room!"

A month later, I moved in. The jittery real estate lady in Six Gun caved in immediately when, after a night in a nearby motel, Twila and I informed her that we preferred to examine the cabin alone. Inside, hardwood floors lay under a film of dust, and rustic beams outlined high ceilings. There were two beautiful stone fireplaces, one in the living room and one in a room I knew immediately would be my study. The kitchen was modernized—not that I do that much cooking, since I have a tendency to even burn water. We met four more of the ghosts, but they weren't inclined to welcome us either. That didn't bother me; they could be handled over time.

"Above all, ghosts need discipline," Twila always insisted. And she'd taught me the rules for dealing with recalcitrant souls who hung around, refusing to cross through the light for various reasons of their own. Still, with the closing behind me, and before my furniture arrived, Twila returned. A ghost or two were within my fledgling realm of powers, but ten called for someone with a tad more experience in supernatural territory.

The little old man turned out to be Howard, the ghost-in-charge. Once Howard and his band of cohorts realized their scare tactics wouldn't work on us, we drew up The Howard and Alice Ghost Agreement. A copy of that all-important document is tacked up in each room now.

* * *

Tonight, two years later, well past midnight and all alone except for the ghosts and the pets I'd acquired, I toiled away on my latest novel amidst another self-imposed deadline hell. Only a twenty-five-watt desk lamp, computer monitor glow, and slow-smoldering embers in the fireplace lit the study. Miss Molly, Siamese and queen of the six cats who deign to live with me, curled on the loveseat beside the fireplace. Trucker, my hundred-and-fifty-pound Rottweiler, lay on the faded orange and brown braided rug, chin propped on crossed paws, brown eyes closed. The ghosts, aware of the number one rule of The Ghost Agreement— Never, EVER mess with Alice when she's writing, under no circum- stances!—prowled...well, wherever ghosts prowl. But they were quiet and avoided my study under penalty of that discipline I can mete out with no qualms.

Puzzling over a tricky word, I stretched kinks from my shoulders and debated whether or not to call it a night. Then the desk phone pealed. Great granny's knickers! Why are phones so much louder at night?

"Damn," I muttered. On the fireplace mantle, the clock face in Casper's belly read a minute after two a.m.—definitely accurate. Casper hasn't lost a second since my neighbor, Granny Chisholm, presented him to me for one of those birthdays I'd rather have counted down than added up. Turned out Granny enjoys chatting with ghosts as much as I do, and that shared interest formed the basis for our friendship. Granny's eighty-year-old wrinkles had smoothed into a face that lit up like a sixty-year-old's when I placed Casper in that spot of honor among my collection of German beer mugs. I've never had the heart to take him down.

I checked caller ID, not that I wouldn't answer. Late-night phone calls aren't to be ignored. Bright white letters in the plastic window spelled out Katy Gueydan. Katy, my cousin and childhood friend, lives two hours away in Jefferson, Texas, about a half-hour from Longview. She inherited Esprit d'Chene, the family plantation, by default when our Uncle Clarence moved out. Katy also knows I don't tolerate interruptions during deadlines. I grabbed the receiver in mid-third ring, prepared to remind her. Instead—

"Alice, pack your damn ghosthunting equipment right now!" Katy shrilled before I could say hello. "I'm not taking this any longer. This—this—ghost person has to go!"

"Are we talking Sir Gary Gavin again?" I grumbled.

"He's the only damn ghost I've got, isn't he?" Katy snapped. "And I want him gone. Gone, gone, gone! Yesterday!"

Katy never swears. Southern Belles learn the word "ladylike" in diapers. However, I'd already smirked a few "I told you so's" over the last month during Katy's calls to complain about Esprit d'Chene's resident ghost, so I reluctantly held my tongue while Katy raged on. Evidently, Sir Gary closed the fireplace flue in the Master Suite when she'd decided to relax one chilly evening. A ghost in my cabin did that once—only once, after I threatened her with sea salt, which is a well-known disciplinary device among ghosthunters. Something about the salt keeps the ghosts at bay. It took me hours to clean the soot off the shelves, though.

"Katy, you have to discipline ghosts if you decide to let them hang around," I tried to interrupt with the same Twila-reminder I'd given her months earlier when she first reported Sir Gary's presence.

She ignored me. "...and he poured salt in the sugar canister! My black velvet cake tasted like I'd made it with gumbo roux!"

"Katy!" More forcefully—same result. She veered into a gripe about the ghost watering down her julep syrup to the point where her mint juleps tasted sour.

Sensitive ears reacting to my voice and probably Katy's shrill tone from the phone, Miss Molly opened her blue eyes and yawned. She jumped down and touched noses with Trucker, who woke and stretched, a long, luxurious expanse of black and tan. They ambled over to my desk, Trucker's weight shivering the hardwood floor planks even with the rug padding. Used to people not respecting my writing time, even those who should know better, I saved my precious book to the hard drive while Katy fussed on. The backup disk lay six inches beyond an arm's reach, and I left the nearly completed manuscript on the screen.

"Katy, Sugar, dig your panties out of your crack and hush!" That halted her rant on a huff of suspended breath. "I told you I was under deadline three days ago when you called. Sir Gary died two hundred years ago, and he's been at Esprit d'Chene for months, maybe years. Probably haunted the house before you moved in. You'll have to put up with him a few days longer."

Katy set off again down the complaint path. "I can't! Do you know what he did a while ago? Waggled his finger and un-alphabetized my library! It'll take me days to reorganize!"

I chuckled—a mistake given Katy's fury. Her teeth gritted as Miss Molly sailed onto my desk and settled down, hoping I'd stroke her now that the keyboard wasn't clacking. Trucker leaned against my leg, head on my knee, liquid gaze fastened on my face.

"If you won't help me, Alice," Katy said in a deadly voice, "I'll see what I can find in that chant book you published a while back and get rid of him myself. I...am...*not*...putting up with Sir Gary another minute!"

Uh oh. The uninitiated shouldn't mess around with those chants. My audience for that book was a specialized circle, ghosthunters and Wicca friends.

"Katy," I soothed. "Soon as I Fed Ex this manuscript—"

"The heck with your manu—what? What now?" Katy shrilled.

Her voice faded as she mumbled to someone else. Sir Gary, evidently, since she'd informed me only the week before—during another phone rant—that she wasn't entertaining any more until she decided what to do with her resident ghost. I really couldn't blame her. It must have taken some tall explaining on Katy's part to convince Senator Wilson-Jones that a draft in Esprit d'Chene floated a half dozen pair of sexy panties down the formal stairwell as the senator bid Katy adieu after a cocktail hour. Katy had decided. Sir Gary had to go.

"Katy?" I asked, confused at a strange tone amid her mumbles. "What did you say?"

"It wasn't me!" Katy snapped. "Gary said it. Excuse me! *Sir* Gary! He said you're the only one who can help. He's been reading your books in my library—the ghost stories mostly, but he likes the mysteries, too."

"Tell him I'm flattered—" I began, then recalled another one of Twila's training sessions: Never trust a ghost who hasn't proven his honesty. Since I had yet to meet Katy's paranormal housemate, I switched tactics. "On second thought, ask Sir Gary which book he liked best."

"She wants to know which book you liked best," Katy said in another aside. Then she screamed in my ear, "Put those back!" I could still hear her when I jerked the phone away and she shouted, "You can't use my bras for bookmarks! You'll ruin the book spines!"

I moved the phone close again, since her voice now held more frustration than piercing irritation. "Darn it, Alice! He wiggle-waggled that finger and floated all eighteen of your books off the shelf! You've got to come. He says you're the only one he can trust."

"I might work him into my schedule early next week," I conceded. "Sir Gary's obviously not leaving on his own, but I can't drop everything and hightail it over there to talk to a ghost."

"Oh, he's *obviously* not leaving! He claims he has as much right here as I do!"

"Do you have any sea salt? Sprinkle it in the corners of the rooms where you don't want Gary. At least you'll get that much peace." A canister of sea salt resides near The Ghost Agreement in every room of my cabin, just in case a stranger from the other dimension happens by. Which does happen once in a while, because the atmosphere here attracts wandering souls like buzzards around Texas road kill.

"I used the last of my sea salt in a bath yesterday." Katy's voice crescendoed again. "Trying to relax from all this stress! But I'll darn sure go to the health food store in the morning—what?" A second later Katy continued with a resigned sigh, "He says his death was murder, but not deliberate murder. That he can't find eternal rest until the deed is exposed."

That got to me. The ghost must have known it would. How can you have an undeliberate murder? I never could ignore a murder mystery with a death riddle attached.

"Interesting," I mused.

"Are you coming then? In the morning, not next week?"

I chewed my lip and contemplated. Katy's the type who insists a person respond to a request with "certainly," "I can't possibly," and preferably *not* "maybe." From what she's told me, she and Sir Gary match that way, both of them raised with a Miss Manners Primer. Sir Gary rises when Katy enters a room and opens doors for her with a wiggle of his mischievous spiritual finger. Katy issues handwritten invitations for even simple gatherings such as drinks before an evening at a local theater and never fails to send thank-you notes or bring hostess gifts. One drawer in my bedroom bureau overflows with Katy's "thank you for your hospitalities." Still, no matter how many times I remind her that I'm allergic to peanuts, she always forgets and sends the nut mixture instead of soft centers when the gift is my beloved Russell Stover candy. Chocolate always helps me through a writing marathon—

"Alice!"

"Ask Sir Gary why he doesn't come over here and talk. I'll leave a light on."

"I've already told him that," she ground out. "Hell, I even got out a map and showed him where you live! But noooo. He insists you come here!"

A stubborn ghost. He'd probably been that way in life, because Twila and I firmly believe a person's living personality follows into death. One crotchety old man—

"Alice!"

"Ummm, sorry, Katy. I —" Her shriek burst against my eardrum, and I dropped the phone. Trucker and Miss Molly stared as it bounced on the paper-strewn desk and clattered to the floor amidst my now-displaced piling system. When I scrambled around and found the phone—Trucker pawed it from under the desk—the line was still miraculously open. I could hear Katy busy with a new disaster. She uttered another uncharacteristic curse. A muffled thump set my heart thudding before Katy's strained voice came back on the line.

"He levitated Great-Grandpere's Confederate sword from above the mantle, over to the portrait of Great-Grandmere Alicia," she gasped. "I thought he was going to slash the painting, but when I dashed for him, he only cut the braided cord it's hanging on."

That did it! I'm Grandmere Alicia's namesake, the woman I admire most in our Southern family branch. Strong women who stood beside their men as they settled the Louisiana coast and spread northwest into Texas, carving lives and homes for themselves and their children out of swampland and brushy timber. Making, losing, and regaining fortunes in the cotton and timber industries. Who stayed behind and kept the home fires, children, and businesses safe while their men marched off to play macho war games. I salvaged that portrait from the Esprit d'Chene attic myself and had it restored.

Suddenly my computer monitor brightened. Above the silent keyboard, letters flew willy-nilly out of nowhere like a swarm of black gnats, slithered across the screen, curled a merry-go-round dance, and strung into sentences after my last keystroke. When I finally shook off my astonishment and snapped my mouth shut, the words didn't make sense at first: *Flatterers be like cats—they lick just a'fore they scratch. That Gary Gavin's not your usual ghost.*

Experience told me immediately what was going on. Some spiritual being had manipulated the computer! Damned prankster. I re-read the message. *Flatterers be like cats.* How true. *They lick just a'fore they scratch!* Sir Gary followed his flattery about my books with a scratch! But who the heck typed it? And how did this ghost know Sir Gary?

As that thought faded, bright green phosphorescence flashed in a corner above the fireplace, catching me off-guard. Miss Molly arched her back and spat one of those weird "meow-sers" that sets your teeth on edge. Trucker growled, a low vibration, and headed for the flash. Their psychic powers rival mine, a fact I'd found out after I adopted them.

Grabbing Trucker's collar, I whispered, "Don't antagonize a ghost when I'm busy on the phone!" Heeding the command, Miss Molly settled down, but both animals stared at the corner.

"Are you still there, Alice?" Katy demanded. "And are you coming? Now?"

On the lookout for the invisible intruder, I answered calmly. No sense upsetting Katy even more by telling her what had just happened. I'd never get her off the phone, and right now, the being infiltrating the cabin demanded discipline.

"Given the circumstances, I'll have to come. Your darn ghost evidently knows what that portrait means to me." I kept glancing back and forth from the fireplace to the computer screen. "But tell him I'm highly ticked at his manipulations, and I'm not gonna be real sympathetic about his problems. Or inclined to help him out after that trick!"

There. Twila insisted we could get into trouble if we showed our natural fear of ghosts. Still, sometimes we *did* find trouble. I groped among the papers on my desk for the Celtic Cross that Twila had blessed a few years back, and slipped the gold chain over my head.

"What have you told Sir Gary about me?" I asked Katy.

"Not much, I swear. Well...I did threaten that you could make his life miserable—I mean, his death—I mean—oh, hell, Alice. Just get here as fast as you can."

Whap! "Ouch!" I rubbed my ear as I replaced the receiver. That wasn't Katy-like either—slamming the phone down without a cordial good-bye. Heaven forbid she forget her manners like that. Maybe Sir Gary's undeliberate murder would be an interesting quest, fodder for another book. I stared at the sentences again, smack dab after the interrupted paragraph on page 437. No doubt about it; a strange ghost prowled around nearby. None of *my* ghosts ever dared break that sacrosanct number one rule in The Ghost Agreement. A ghost who ignores the rules can stir up all sorts of mayhem. I couldn't possibly leave for Esprit d'Chene until I got rid of it, no matter how upset Katy was.

Too, I really should finish this current novel before researching another one. It had been going along so well. Barely fifteen minutes ago, my heroine, Annie May, and I were deep in the heart of the wild depravity of nighttime N'awlins Bourbon Street. Jumping and dodging hell-bent through half-naked and naked bodies, silly and serious drunks, transvestites and gays, out-of-state tourists, college kids whose parents had no idea where their offspring were spending their vacation money, and just plain revelers, all with enough beads around their necks to choke a draft horse. Chasing a glimpse of Rex, the Mardi Gras King, who was either Rex or somebody who had *cojones* enough to steal the costume from the sacred Fat Tuesday symbol. Now some being from another dimension roamed around just the other side of visible. A ghost who didn't even offer a decent Texas howdy first!

Anyway, previous paranormal encounter notes already stuffed an overflowing file in my desk. Sometimes ghosts I meet relate stories that foster a book idea. Like the man who lost three wives and still didn't know who murdered them, even after vigilantes hung him for the death of his last wife. The lonely woman who sought solace from an abusive husband in the arms of a lover and desperately wanted to know if her husband had killed her lover. The teenager, paralyzed from a water tower fall one night and left to die by his friends, who thought him already dead and hightailed it out of there, scared silly of the consequences. And the Lady in Red, a saloon girl who followed me home from a haunted hotel. One day I'll tell her story. So many stories. So little time to write. No need to add another to the list.

Trucker whined, and I loosened my grip. The hair at the nap of his neck bristled, and Miss Molly emitted another cat-growl of animosity. I'd brought them here as just-weaned babies, although the other five cats in my menagerie wandered in over time. None of them were bothered by our paranormal residents. This stranger, though, was a different story. Since I'd bought the cabin, three of the residents had gone on through the veil, but three others arrived to take their place. Ten was the limit, and Howard and I kept track of them. No ghost had left recently, so there darned sure wasn't a vacant room in this spiritual boarding house!

I casually filtered my gaze across the room. Maybe by the time it crawled back, the words would be gone. I wasn't in the mood tonight to mess with a disobedient ghost. Several plants scattered around the study —droopy, I noticed, stifling a yawn and adding another chore to my mental to-do list. Miracle Gro could wait. No sense stumbling around the kitchen measuring the proper amount of green, gunky particles into a plastic milk jug at this hour. Especially not until I figured out who'd dropped by from across the veil.

The message still gleamed on the screen, type bolder than the manuscript words.

The next room search stalled on the bar refrigerator beneath shelves of well-handled highball and souvenir hurricane glasses from Pat O'Brien's Bar in New Orleans. Come to think of it, a beer would hit the spot, an icy-cold Bud Lite in a frosty mug. A hasty decision wasn't a good idea when dealing with a ghost, though. The situation called for careful consideration.

Thirsty, I groped for my thermal cup of ice water and lemon slices. Took a sip. Spit it back. Darned sure wasn't beer. It tasted like lukewarm lemon. Given the marathon writing hours, the ice was probably puddled between the Mardi Gras parade on St. Charles Avenue and the chase on Bourbon Street.

Howard and I had come to another agreement. When we do have a vacancy, he passes muster on any hopeful new spiritual arrival before we decide whether or not to let it hang around. He'd be especially welcome now, but I hadn't seen him since this morning while I cleaned off Spanish moss from the live oaks and we chatted about those medieval torture devices he'd called medical tools in his lifetime.

"Howard?" I whispered, but he didn't respond. Probably off in my rowboat, fishing. He likes to do that now and then, although sometimes a property owner mistakes the boat for empty except for a cane pole dangling a bobber and worm, and tows it to my dock. Howard has better sense than to reveal himself to anyone else besides Granny Chisholm.

Ticked off at the ghost's refusal to visualize—frankly, on the verge of pissed off—I muttered, "Okay, you nasty little piece of sixth-dimensional protoplasm. Show yourself."

The ghost didn't answer—obviously rude, on top of being an interfering busybody. I glanced at Casper's red digital numbers, spread across a white belly that looked like he'd been on the wrong end of a fertility drug. Ten minutes had elapsed. Fingering the cross, I wandered my gaze back to the bar. But I'd have to expose this interloper before I dared venture across the study. More than once, even here in my home, a suddenly materializing specter has spasmed my nerves.

Since this intruder refused to cooperate, I yanked open a desk drawer and pulled out a blue and white canister of sea salt. *"En garde!"* I whispered.

A pop shattered the silence, and I jumped as my eyes swiveled to the fireplace. An ember glowed bright, and a piece of wood flared, then crumbled. The burst of energy sent a gray ash feather up the flue. Sea salt canister aimed like a can of roach killer, I chuckled and thumb-flicked the pour spout open.

"Look," I muttered, waving the canister. "Show yourself or leave. I've got work to do! This book's scheduled for release just before next Samhain." Still no response. This ghost evidently didn't care about deadlines or Sabbats my Wiccan friends held dear.

Nut-brown drapes on either side of the glass patio doors frame the view into the now neat back yard. At times I stare out there, working out a plot point. Then a squirrel chases a blue jay away from the bird feeder, chitter and squawks of "thief, thief," a pandemonium. Or one of the cats will slink in hunting mode across the lawn, intent on disobeying the don't-chase-the-birds law despite a full belly from a never-ending supply of cat chow. At night the cats, birds, and squirrels leave the yard to an old hoot owl, which sits on a rose trellis and swivels its neck around at impossible angles.

Tonight a ground fog, spawned from the cooling lake, filtered across the lawn, wisps trickling here and there like wandering water snakes along the brick paths and through the flowerbeds. As I watched, the fog thickened and billowed into waist-high vapor clouds, as dense as a smoke screen. Above the mistiness, light from a full moon silvered the treetops.

Full moons are ripe atmosphere for ghosts or spirits to transcend that thin veil between the two worlds. And with Samhain, what most people call Halloween, less than a month away, there were numerous preparations in the works for such an important Sabbat. It pays to keep things like that in mind when you fool around on the other side of the veil like Twila and I do.

Wind from an autumn storm last week had broken off a large pecan limb. It still waited to be chopped into barbecue wood, although the squirrels had rescued most of the pecans from the laden branch, easier pickings than hauling their fat tummies up and down the tree trunk. If I didn't gather a few soon, the squirrels would pick the rest of the tree clean, too. Time for Granny to bring her pecan-picker-upper over. She bakes a pecan pie to die for, and just the smell of it cooling on her kitchen windowsill adds a pound or two to the hips.

No four-legged or winged critters prowled the yard tonight, though, at least that I could *see*. Not even one of my other usual nocturnal visitors, which include a family of raccoons and occasional deer or armadillo. No owl. Maybe they were hiding? So I sent a mental query: *Anybody prowling around out there?* Ghosts communicate without spoken words if they choose. Only a bat responded as it dove for a fluttering moth. Lore maintains bats are messengers from the Underworld, but this bat only swooped off over the roof.

A high hedge marks the end of the yard, and beyond it, jack pines, dogwoods, and live oaks shoulder together. Above the treetops, blazes of diamond-bright stars scattered across the sky. I couldn't imagine my visitor sitting in misty splendor in one of my patio chairs or Humpty-Dumpty style on the hedge, but you never knew.

A breeze swayed a tendril of Spanish moss on a low live oak limb. Only a glimpse, then it disappeared. That shouldn't be. Not in that oak, that close to the ground, floating just above the fog line. Plus, this moss was whitish rather than the pale gray of Spanish moss. The ghost!

CHAPTER 2

My chair crashed against the wall and toppled a cast-iron lamp. Trucker and Miss Molly surged to attention. The snarl in Trucker's throat and Miss Molly's irritating meow mingled in the air, and a chalkboard screech shudder crawled up my spine.

"Shush!" I ordered. Not that it did much good. "Look." I pointed at the patio doors, gripping the sea salt tight. They looked. Nice when they obey.

A white shape floated from behind the live oak, through the fog, towards the woods. It wasn't in any hurry. It stopped and smelled a late-blooming Tyler rose—then snipped the rose off and let it fall to the ground! "Damn trespasser!"

Cautiously I crept toward the patio doors. The ghost disappeared behind a young magnolia, bushy, to-the-ground branches invisible in the ever-thickening mistiness. Tense as I was, the unexpected squawk of a glider in need of WD-40 startled me when I slid the patio door open. Jumping back and stumbling over Trucker, I landed flat on my butt—lucky for my tailbone, on the braided rug. The sea salt flew from my hand, scattering a river of white crystals.

"Now look what you did!" I barked at the dog. He barked right back and slurped a drool-wet tongue across my lips. While I rubbed and scrubbed my face, Miss Molly fastidiously bathed salt granules from her fur and flicked out a pink tongue in distaste.

Rubbing my tailbone, I clambered upright. "At least we probably scared off that darn ghost, so maybe we'll get some sleep."

The white shape flittered near a lilac bush. This ghost hadn't scared. Another rose bloom bit the ground, and the culprit glided onward. This called for action! Gathering handfuls of sea salt, I clenched them in my fists. "You both come with me," I growled at my pets.

Miss Molly slit her blue eyes in disdain, shivered to shake off the last salt vestiges, then padded off, no doubt headed for her water dish in the kitchen. Trucker eagerly wagged his stubby tail and whined.

"What changed your attitude? You're never that darned eager to meet a prankster ghost."

The misty shape emerged from the lilac bushes, but disappeared immediately behind a rose trellis. "Hey," I called. "You better hie yourself back to your own dimension!"

The ghost didn't answer—or reappear, so I eased out the patio door. Cold concrete curled my bare toes, and a shroud of mist enveloped my comfortable caftan. Past the protective cabin, a lake breeze carried a hint of water and the night-blooming jasmine beside the patio.

"Hey, ghost!" I muffled an "ouch" when I stepped on a half-eaten pecan shell and kicked it aside. A huge Texas tree roach skittered behind a potted azalea. No time to fix his clock; I'd spray in the morning. I slid onto dew-wet grass, then glanced back for Trucker...as he hiked his leg against the azalea!

"Get your butt out in the yard and do your business!" I hissed. He tossed me that innocent look he's perfected, but dropped his leg.

A hint of solid white above the fog-line disappeared behind a cedar near the back hedge. The ghost was moving further and further away, towards the woods. Maybe I wouldn't have to confront it. Maybe it would go play with the bears and panthers in the East Texas Piney Woods.

No such luck. It stayed behind the cedar.

"Okey-dokey! You and I are gonna have this out here and now!" I haven't really been afraid of ghosts for a long while, but it pays to be cautious. I couldn't tell much about the apparition—male or female—old or young. Ghosts play by their rules, too. Nothing forces them to materialize into firmer, more seeable shapes until they feel darned well good and ready.

Trucker padded to me and sat, waiting for my next move. I was waiting for that decision, too. *Breathe*, I reminded myself. To be safe—as safe as possible when confronting a strange ghost—I pulled down white light around Trucker and me from my realm of psychic powers. It only took a second. That important protective skill deserves timely practice, which I respect.

"Hey, ghost! You're not scaring me! Come out or get outta here!" I approached the cedar, the sea salt now clumpy pebbles in my sweaty hands. Still, the pebbles would pepper the ghost like gravel. Go straight through it, but remind the ghost of the salt's power.

Now what? I nudged Trucker with a clenched fist. "Sic 'em."

Trucker cocked his head.

"Sic!"

He sat.

"Not sit. Sic!"

Trucker looked at the cedar, then back. He whined and didn't budge.

"Shit," I gritted. I started around the tree. Stopped just as quickly as I'd made the decision—a foolish one perhaps, with the dog leery. Then a sound erupted in the eerie silence. A harrumph, as if someone had cleared his throat. The ghost, getting ready to speak?

Instead, it spit. And my temper flared over my cowardice. I marched around the cedar. "Don't spit on my—!" Twin screeches split the air—mine and the ghost's!

Trucker bounded up, butt wagging his stubby tail and barking enthusiastically. He circled, then took off across the yard, as eager for playmates as if it were morning. Granny Chisholm and I stared at each other, both with our hands on our hearts, me with the sea salt clenched in tight fists. We screamed again at the same instant.

"What the heck are you doing?"

"Alice, you tryin' to give me a heart a'tick?"

We burst out laughing, and Trucker galloped back, urging us to let him share our fun. Granny sniggered and slapped her knee, and I sat down with a whomp, legs giving out in relief.

"You thought I was a ghost!" Granny cackled through her snickers. My shoulders heaved and laughter tears brimmed as I opened my fists to show Granny the globs of sea salt.

"What was you gonna do?" she asked with a wrinkled smirk. "Brain me with it?" She wore a white flannel gown, the hem soaked with dew. Frizzy white hair haloed her head and dangled down her back, the gilded hairpins that normally held a large bun lost somewhere during her night rounds. She carried her pecan-picker-upper in one hand, a pair of scissors in the other.

"What on earth were you doing out here this time of night?" I asked.

"Hey." She cocked her head in imitation of Trucker. "Shush up, dog!" Trucker minded her. Now I knew why he wasn't afraid of the ghost in my back yard. Instead, he'd wondered why I ordered him to attack. He and Granny Chisholm were old friends.

"The pecans could have waited until daylight," I said.

"Wasn't looking for no pepper. Why'd you think I'd be lookin' for pepper out here in your yard this time a'night?"

I wiped my eyes with the backs of my hands and glanced at Granny's ears. Ah, there was the problem. No hearing aid. I stood and said close to her ear, "I said pecans, not pepper."

"You don't havta shout!" she shouted. "I just put in new batt'ries!"

I brushed the sea salt from my palms. Taking her hand and transferring the scissors to mine, I lifted her hand to her ear.

"Oh," she said. "Fergot the dad-blasted thing again, huh." She dug in the pocket of her gown and came up victorious. "Didn't neither!" With a toothless grin, she plopped the hearing aid in place. "Now, where was we? You got any coffee on?"

"I can make some."

"What? Gosh dang it, Alice, you don't bake coffee. No wonder you can't cook."

Well, she didn't have to be so blatant about my lack of cooking skills. I sighed and reached out to turn on the hearing aid. Granny winked, deepening her face wrinkles.

"Thank'ee. Now, where was we?"

"I was going to make coffee."

"Now that you mention it, it's a little late for coffee. How 'bout a drink instead?"

"That sounds even better. Let's hit the bar."

Granny followed me across the lawn, pecan-picker-upper for a cane. She won't admit it—will deny it to high heaven—but she needs a tad of support. One rainy day I took her arm, and had to dodge the beautiful walnut walking stick she carries at times. A gift from her long-departed husband, she keeps the walking stick close in remembrance. But it makes a wicked weapon if a neighborhood dog mistakes Granny for easy prey when she strolls down our private road in the mornings to check the shared mailbox post.

Flicking on a lamp in the study, I headed for the bar. Granny smacked her lips as I reached for the Crown Royal. Tonight's adventure called for strong stuff. Briefly I tuned into the atmosphere, but didn't detect an unwanted presence. Probably it was just a passing spirit.

Granny limped over to the loveseat, the clump of her pecan-picker-upper muffled on the braided rug. The picker-upper is an ingenious device, something I'm sure a lot of Texans wish they'd patented when they discovered it after seasons of aching backs. A lever on a long handle triggers a basket the right size to grasp a pecan. *Voila*, another nut.

I poured a double shot over ice in one glass, then added a tad of Diet Seven-up. Granny cleared her throat in warning when only one jigger landed in the second glass, so I dumped in another shot. If I had to help her home, maybe she'd be too mellow to care. As I handed Granny her drink and we settled in the loungers, Miss Molly padded back in. Granny sipped, smacked her lips again, and gazed sternly at the fireplace. After a gulp of my drink, I rose to add another log to the fire, then closed the fire screen securely.

When I was back in the chair, Miss Molly leapt onto my lap and snuggled in for a snooze. Trucker wiggled over to Granny and lay down, offering his broad belly for a scratch, and she complied. She has the hard, yellowed fingernails of the aged, which I periodically help her trim, as well as her toenails, one of the few favors she tolerates. Trucker loves those nails on his belly, and he whimpered with sensuous delight.

"Still can't believe you was stupid 'nuf to have this beautiful dog fixed," Granny grumbled in a long-standing bone of contention between us. Truth be known, probably between Trucker and me, too. Granny knows why I had Trucker neutered, but I reminded her anyway. Old people forget. Well, so do writers. I glanced around at the sticky notes peppering prominent spots as I responded for the dozenth time, "He has allergies. The vet recommended I not breed him."

Granny stared at the area of Trucker's missing parts, gave him a final scratch, and leaned back to slurp her drink. "They got med'cine for it, don't they? They damn sure got med'cine for every little twitch they find in me. You know how much those fool pharmacies charge me." She cackled conspiratorially. "But I just go visit Ole Maude iffen I run out a'fore my check comes in first of the month."

"What were you doing in my yard this time of night?" I asked Granny in gentle reminder.

"Couldn't sleep," she murmured, and I nodded. At times during deadline-hell episodes I'd see her lights on. "Was gonna get some of them pecans and bake us a pie. Leave your half on your front deck, 'long with some roses in a basket." She tossed me a stern glare. "An' I fergot the pecans out there by the cedar, what with you scarin' the crap outta me like that!"

"I'll get them as soon as I finish my drink," I assured her.

Satisfied, Granny sipped, mind wandering off as it sometimes did. The slight palsy in her hand stilled as the alcohol took effect, and her eyes drooped. Silently, I enjoyed my own drink, as well as the comfortable company of a woman who shared my views on ghosts. Then Granny slit her eyes and stared at me with a knowing gaze. "Have a visitor tonight?"

"Yeah," I admitted. "But I guess it's gone now."

"Mebbe not." She eyeballed the room. I scanned the ceiling and probed the corners for a flicker of dancing light or misty shape. Nothing except a few dusty spider webs.

"Feel anything?" I asked.

"Mebbe," she repeated.

The temperature dropped at least twenty degrees. Granny shivered and set her drink on the end table. Eyes widening, she reached back and pulled the afghan around her. Without a convenient afghan, a film of goosebumps spread across my neck, flurried down my spine and over my arms, where the hairs waved around like hundreds of tiny, headless snakes. Uh oh, definite signs the visitor hadn't gone. And the sea salt was still scattered over by the patio doors.

I rubbed my arms and hoped Howard would appear. This wasn't a ghost I'd met before. Nor was it a previous acquaintance or former resident, now a spirit, who had crossed over and dropped back by for a visit, as they can do for short periods. My psychic senses told me that, and I've learned to listen to that inner voice from experiences—both bad and good.

Trucker pricked his ears, and Miss Molly stirred in my lap. They stared at my desk. Alert, Granny shifted to follow their gazes. The silence in the room closed in like a weight, and I glanced at Casper: two a.m. plus thirty-three minutes.

Trucker growled, and Miss Molly spat that damned weird meow-ser. The phone rang, and Granny and I both jumped. Miss Molly leapt, claws digging into my thighs through the caftan. I yelped, but the cat and dog scrambled to my desk, into their get-ready positions. Trucker sat, ears perked and tongue lolling out. On the desk, Miss Molly patted a black paw against the receiver, a chastising glare for my slowness on her cream and black face. Rubbing my scratched thigh with one hand, I hobbled over and grabbed the phone in mid-ring with the other. Not bothering with caller ID—it had to be Katy—I muttered an irritated, "Hello."

For a few seconds, only choking, unrestrained sobs from a woman on the verge of emotional madness were audible. "Katy? Katy, for heaven's sake, what's wrong?"

She gasped—and sobbed hysterically again.

"Katy!" I demanded. "What's going on?"

She gurgled and hiccupped. "He's...he's dead!"

Relieved and amused, I soothed, "Sir Gary's been dead for a long, long while. He's a ghost, remember?"

"No!" she burst out. "Not Sir Gary! The man in my pool! He's dead! Oh, God, Alice. Please help me!"

CHAPTER 3

Sir Gary Gavin, late of the House of Spencer and later still of the Gavin Shipping Company of the New World, hovered behind Katy. She sobbed into the phone in Esprit d'Chene's Great Room, ignoring his attempts to reason with her and...well, preferring to pour out her distress to a living person. Wasn't this a bloody dickens of a mess!

He'd tried to protect her from the sight in the pool, but the yard lights spotlighted the pink-tinged water. Determined to take a swim, poor Katy nearly dove straight in before she spied the body bumping against the ladder. Her curdling scream still echoed in his mind. Bloody hell. She could wake a coffin-enclosed corpse! Using senses developed through time, he listened to both sides of the phone conversation.

"Ohmigod!" Alice screamed. "What are you talking about?"

Katy collapsed in the chair beside the antique rolltop desk. The phone clunked from her hand, and she buried her face in the crook of one arm. More sobs. Damn, he never knew how to deal with crying women. He much preferred a feisty argument between the two of them about who actually had prior claim on the house.

"Katy! Katy, pick up the phone!" Alice shrilled.

Sir Gary waved his finger and nudged the receiver closer to Katy's ear. After another frantic demand from the other end, Katy gulped and fumbled. The ghost manipulated the phone into her seeking fingers and sighed when she raised her head. Maybe Alice could shake Katy back to sensibility. Though a tiny thing, a blond, blue-eyed, perfectly mannered Southern Belle by birth and breeding, Sir Gary had experienced the core of Katy's strength more than once.

"Katy!" Alice demanded. "Call nine-one-one!"

"I—he's—oh, Alice! All the blood!" Katy moaned, a long, strangled sound that scurried up Sir Gary's spine like icy fingers. He hadn't been on the receiving end of a chill for decades. Instead, he'd chilled those still alive with just his presence.

"Listen," Alice said. "Are you sure you weren't sleepwalking? Like you did as a child?"

Sir Gary chuckled. The writer obviously hoped for a trick on Katy's end—an attempt to make Alice get a move on. But this was real, not a ghostly trick.

"It's no dream! Help me, Alice!"

"Katy, listen!" Alice demanded. "You have to call the police!"

"I—oh —" The phone dropped again, and Katy's sobs escalated into a keening wail.

"Katy! Katy, pick up the damn phone!" Alice screamed.

No help for it. Sir Gary levitated the receiver. "Alice?"

"Who...Sir Gary?" Alice asked. "What's going on? Is there really a body in the pool?"

"I'm afraid so," he answered. "A quite messy one."

"Katy needs to call the police. Is the person dead? Can you do anything to help?"

"I very much doubt it," Sir Gary replied. "He's well and truly dead." Violence and dead bodies didn't faze him. He'd seen dozens in his life and death, been the perpetrator of more than he cared to recall when pirates attacked one of his ships. For now he'd protect the ladies from the grisly manner of death. He doubted Katy had noticed anything beyond the body and blood.

Alice muttered, "My God. How...what...?"

"Katy and I argued after you and she hung up," the ghost explained. "Then she went off to bed in a snit, and I turned on the television in the Men's Parlor. Later, I heard her in the kitchen and went to see if she might be over her...um...what do you call it in these times? Her time of the month irritation? She said she'd decided to have a drink by the pool, perhaps take a swim. Unfortunately, the drink's shattered, and she could use it right now."

Alice gritted, "Katy doesn't suffer PMS. Tell her that I'm calling Jack."

Sir Gary stared at Katy's huddled figure. He doubted she'd hear him. "Alice is calling Jack," he said as Alice muttered, "Where the hell's my cell phone?"

A strange voice answered, "Ain't that it? Beneath that voodoo book?"

"Thanks, Granny." A pause, then "Shit! The battery's dead. Where's my charger?"

The Granny voice answered, "I ain't seen that. What's going on?"

"A dead body in the pool at Esprit d'Chene. Katy's an emotional wreck."

The ghost heard drawers open and close as Katy snuffled an unlady-like gargle and leaned back. Red-rimmed eyes searched the desk, and a wobbly hand tugged tissues from a box on the corner. Then she stared at Sir Gary. "Is Alice still on the phone?"

He nodded, repeating, "She's trying to call someone named Jack on her cell phone."

"Oh, God," Katy moaned. "Jack's her ex-husband. A cop."

Wasn't that the logical step? "She said we needed to call nine-one-one."

"I—I can't! Tell Alice to do it. Please."

Before he could relay the request, Alice said, "I've got my cell phone plugged in. Get Katy back on the line!"

He murmured that information, but Katy shook her head and crushed a wad of tissue to her face. "You really should do as she asks," Sir Gary insisted.

Reluctantly, Katy held out a hand. "Alice?" she gasped at the same time Sir Gary heard a faint, disgruntled "Hello," a man's voice, probably on that cell phone.

"Katy, stay on this line!" Alice demanded.

"This ain't Katy," the man mumbled. "Y'got the wrong number."

"Jack!" Alice shouted. "Jack, don't hang up! It's Alice!" Too late. The other phone emitted a dial tone in place of Jack's voice.

"Katy, listen to me," Alice enjoined. "Don't hang up. I'm getting Jack back on the line."

"I guess that's all right," Katy breathed more than spoke, then louder, "Tell him to hurry."

"I will—Jack? Jack, don't hang up. It's Alice."

"Alice?" Jack grumbled. "What time is it? If you're under one of your blasted deadlines and need a murder question answered, call me in the mornin'."

"Jack, wake up. Katy's on the other line. There's a dead body at Esprit d'Chene."

"What?" That woke him. Sir Gary heard sheets rustle. Alert now, Jack demanded, "Has she called the Jefferson cops?"

"No," Alice told him. "She's distraught. I'm trying to calm her down."

"You sure this isn't one of Katy's nightmares?" he asked suspiciously.

"It's real, Jack," Alice said firmly. "You've got to get over there."

"I'm on my way." He slammed down the phone and Alice continued, "Katy, sweetie, Jack's coming. Hang in there. Is there someone closer you can call to stay with you?"

"I...I...don't want anyone else here right now," Katy said. "Just you. Hurry."

"Do you have any idea who the person in the pool is?" Alice asked.

"No. Maybe, but...no. I—I didn't look that close. He's...it's horrible! Please stay on the phone with me until Jack gets here."

Miffed, Sir Gary glided out of the Great Room. Katy obviously preferred comfort from a distant, living voice.

* * *

"I'll stay on the phone," I promised Katy as my gaze met Granny's in a sharing of misery.

"It's true, huh?" she whispered. "Somebody dead?"

I nodded, and she motioned with her drink hand. "Go get packed."

Carrying the portable phone receiver, I hurried down the hallway to my bedroom, explaining to Katy that I needed to pack some things. "Will you be all right if I lay the phone down for a few minutes? I won't hang up, I promise."

"Just don't leave me."

"Is Sir Gary still there?"

"Uh-huh. He's—oh, thank you." Through the phone, ice tinkled in a glass, and Katy said, "He fixed me another drink. That was nice of him, don't you think?"

The vagueness in Katy's tone foretold shock, but I couldn't do a thing about that. Hopefully the alcohol would stave it off until Jack arrived.

"Drink your drink." I bent to retrieve my suitcase from under the bed. "I'm laying the phone down." I tossed it on the bedspread and crawled beneath the bed for the recalcitrant suitcase, which had worked itself nearly to the middle of the king-sized frame. I snared the handle and yanked the suitcase to freedom, hefted it toward the mattress—and nearly threw it straight at Howard, who sat on the bed. It wouldn't do any good, except to express my irritation. The suitcase would pass right through Howard and mar the cherrywood headboard.

"Damn it, Howard!" I tossed the suitcase on the bed for good measure. "You could at least knock. And I don't have time to chat with you right now."

Howard just shrugged as I grabbed the phone receiver again. "Katy?"

"I—I'm here," she replied. "Go ahead and pack."

Satisfied, I dropped the phone and hurried over to the dresser, yanking out drawers as I tossed over my shoulder at Howard, "There's been a murder at Esprit d'Chene."

His reflection in the mirror nodded, and I whirled. "If you've been listening in, why the hell didn't you do something about that damned ghost in my study tonight?"

"Whoever it was didn't ask for my approval first," Howard grumped. Well, mentally grumped, since our relationship has evolved to the point where telepathy works. Evidently my visitor's powers exceeded Howard's. "And ladies don't swear."

"Ladies in your time," I reminded him as I snatched a handful of panties. If ghosts could blush, Howard would have. Ladies in his time—the mid-1800s—didn't scandalize men with a rainbow handful of Victoria's Secrets, even in front of a doctor like Howard. His misty aura turned pinkish.

"Think I'll go visit Wilma," he muttered.

"Wait a minute." I grabbed bras from the next drawer, hiding them in my caftan skirt in deference to Howard until I slipped them in the suitcase and closed the lid. "Do you know who was here?" Despite the urgent need to get to Esprit d'Chene, I felt extremely uneasy about leaving my home with a strange ghost prowling. Who better to question about a ghost than another ghost?

"Nope." Just "nope," and still grumpy.

"Did you see the message?"

"Yep." Just "yep." Howard's a ghost of few words.

"Well?" I prodded.

Howard shrugged. I sighed. "Do I need to perform some chants and put out sea salt?"

Howard considered that. "Don't think so," he mused. "She's already gone."

"She?"

"Ah ha!" Howard chortled. He loves to catch me in a psychic deduction mistake.

"Did you get a name?" I demanded.

"Nope."

"A first initial?" Sometimes ghosts let that much through.

"Yep."

"Well, damn it—"

"Ladies—"

"—don't swear," I finished with him. "I've told you more than once that I'm not the lady in this family. Katy is."

"Wasn't tonight, even on the first call."

"No," I agreed. "But I've had more experience with ghosts. And look how you drive me to swearing."

"Isn't me. You swear when I'm not even in the house."

Wow! A near two-way conversation with Howard.

"For Pete's sake, tell me what you picked up. Without me having to drag it out of you! I can't think straight right now, and—"

"Letter A."

"Last name or first?"

Shrug. Then, "Wilma liked her. That's about it."

The toilet flushed in the master bath. Wilma loved playing in that darn water. She only had an outhouse on the Kansas farm a hundred years ago.

"Wilma!" I called. "Don't run up my water bill! And come in here and tell me if you noticed anything about your new friend this evening."

Howard replied instead, "She doesn't know any more than me."

Evidently Wilma decided to continue letting Howard do the talking, because she didn't show up, no doubt peeved at my order. Remembering Katy, I grabbed the phone. "Katy?"

She responded with a tad of irritation, "Just get here!"

I tossed the phone down and stared around the room, trying to figure out what I'd forgotten. Oh, yeah—jeans and T-shirts.

"How long will you be gone?" Howard demanded, meaning, "How long will I have to ride herd on the kids?" Rick and Shannon, four and five when they died of yellow fever, hang around despite Howard's insistence they should cross through the light to their mom and dad. Howard values his peace and quiet while he browses the Zane Grey paperbacks in my library, but he doesn't push the kids. He often reads to them in the library, one curled on each side.

"I have no idea," I told Howard. "There's a dead body in Katy's pool."

Howard eyed me steadily. "You said it was a murder. Katy didn't say that."

I froze, T-shirts drifting into the suitcase in a tangled mess. "I did." Had I picked that up with psychic senses?

"Could be," Howard mused when he read my unspoken thought.

I grabbed a stack of jeans and jammed them in with the T-shirts. "I've got a book due next week," I reminded both Howard and myself as I stuffed the small traveling case stocked with personal items in and zipped the suitcase. "I can't ask my editor for an extension. Can't you just hear her if I say, 'By the way, I need more time. My cousin has a ghost problem. Oh, and there's been a murder.'"

Howard nodded and dissolved. I grabbed the phone again. "Katy?"

"Jack drove up the back lane a minute ago, Alice," she said in an unemotional voice, indicating her shock was escalating despite the alcohol. "Oh, here he is."

Jack's grim voice came on before my demand that Katy give him the phone left my brain. "I'm here now, *Chère*."

"The...pool?"

"Yeah," he confirmed. "Sheriff's on his way. I'll take care of Katy. Drive careful."

"I'll be there as soon as I can," I promised, then hung up. At least a live person was there for Katy. Of course, Jack wouldn't even realize Sir Gary shared the space. Katy wouldn't let on, since she knew Jack's views on ghosts. Still, I couldn't help but wonder what would happen if Sir Gary had any information about the corpse, especially with my inkling about murder. Jack sure as hell wouldn't question a ghost—or even believe Sir Gary might be any help. Jack would deny Sir Gary's presence to all and sundry. He didn't believe in ghosts.

CHAPTER 4

Keeping a wary eye out for the intruder, I reentered the study for my laptop and disks. Granny greeted me, a foil-wrapped pie pan in her hand. Trucker and Miss Molly sat on their haunches in front of the fireplace.

"Been to my house and found this pecan pie in the freezer." Granny set the pan on my desk. "Death means you oughtta take some food with you." I decided not to mention this wasn't a death calling for family-support offerings as she went on, "Guess I'm gonna be cat sittin'?"

Grabbing my laptop from the closet, I laid it on the desk and sat down to back up my novel. "I'd appreciate it." I'd take Trucker and Miss Molly with me, but Fluffy, Sherbet, Braveheart, Squeaky, and Nutmeg would need care.

Granny scrutinized me. "I got a feelin' 'bout this, Alice. You best take one of my assafi'ty bags."

Before I could catch myself, I grimaced, and Granny's frown pulled her wrinkles into a road map of intersecting byways and highways it would take a seasoned traveler to negotiate. She yanked one of those blasted asafetida bags from the pocket of her voluminous gown and held it out. She wrapped the brown kernels of asafetida in flowered handkerchiefs, snugged around the top with purple ribbon—purple for protection and spiritual attunement. She claimed asafetida helped her arthritis, as well as protected her when she wandered around my haunted house. Thankfully, a plastic zippered sandwich bag sealed off this one's vile, spoiled garlic smell. But gnarled fingers fumbled the bag open and removed the hanky and its malodorous contents. When she held the ribbon toward me, Trucker whined and laid down, paws over nose.

"Granny, I don't have time —" Stretching, she hung the bag around my head and patted it. The smell curdled the Royal Crown in my belly.

"Oh," I suddenly recalled. "Your pecans." Maybe I could accidentally-on-purpose lose the asafetida outside in the ground fog—

"Trucker already fetched 'em." Granny motioned at the basket on the end table, then limped over to pick up it, her pecan-picker-upper, and a fresh drink she must have fixed. "Left the roses. He'd've chomped them stems. I'll get 'em in the mornin'. I can see myself out."

"I can't let you do that," I murmured. Her hands were filled with her treasures—drink, basket, and picker-upper—and that front door stuck. Catching up to Granny as she toddled determinedly down the hallway, I opened the door to the front deck with the necessary jerk.

"Call me from Katy's and let me know what's goin' on," she ordered. "And 'specially iffen you need some help, hear? I'll put out 'nuf food for a couple days for them cats and be there quick as a bunny. My old jitney still runs fine, you know."

"I'll do that, Granny," I lied as she carefully made her way down the steps. But I'll be darned if I ask you to drive up to Katy's by yourself in that jalopy, I thought. It wasn't that the cherry 1950 Oldsmobile convertible secured in her garage wouldn't make the trip. Bubba Joe Haggerty changes the oil and tunes it up. Her eyesight is still keen, unlike her hearing. But Granny props herself up on three pillows to see over the steering wheel, and when she rolls majestically down the country roads at a stately twenty-five miles per hour on her weekly trips to the grocery store, she expects everyone else to concede to her pace. I couldn't begin to imagine her on the two-hour drive on the interstate between here and Esprit d'Chene.

A fish slapped the water on the lake, breaking into my thoughts. I tried to imagine how it would feel to stumble across a dead body on the shoreline and shivered in the night breeze. Smelled like dead fish on the shore. Oh, the asafetida bag. I yanked it off and started back to the study, then hesitated. I detoured to the kitchen, where I found another zipper sandwich bag in an unorganized cupboard and secured the asafetida in it like Granny had done. Back in the study, I shoved the sandwich bag and pie in my briefcase, along with my disks, then laid a couple manila files I might need on top.

The temperature had warmed, and things seemed to be normal—as normal as they get in a haunted house. No unusual movements. No books wandered across the room without any visible presence carrying them. No misty shapes feathered around. No green phosphorescence gleamed. But the subdued glow of the computer monitor caught my eye. Damn it, the intruder was back and had manipulated it even in dead mode! Propping my hands on my hips, I directed my stress outward. "You listen here, you sixth-dimension interloper! Another rule is you never mess with my computer! Hie yourself outta here, or I'll get out the chant book!"

Instead, words spread across the monitor. *Hurry. You will be needed.* Then the glow died and the screen blackened. Since time has no meaning in the spirit world, "hurry" could mean my presence would be needed tomorrow or next year. Who knew? I unplugged the computer, even though that wouldn't stop a persistent ghost.

CHAPTER 5

Sir Gary leaned against the weeping willow while a half-dozen bobbies scuttled about. Not one of them tried to drag the corpse out of normally crystal clear water. Something about some medical examiner having to declare the body dead first. As if the fact the corpse was missing its head didn't prove it couldn't revive and swim out on its own. He crossed his arms. Jack, the one who arrived first, had turned on the underground pool lights. A little later, Jack met the sheriff out front and the two of them had, as they called it, secured the crime scene.

The bobbies had no idea who the corpse was—wouldn't have until they found the missing head or figured out some other way to identify him. Had they asked, the ghost could have told them a little, although not a name. The corpse was dressed identically to the man who skulked around Esprit d'Chene the other night—same bib overalls, hole in the right knee. He'd slinked off about the time the ghost decided to get...ghostly with him.

A clean swipe of a sharp scimitar obviously did the deed. Sir Gary had always been good with a sword, and he'd committed a similar act once on a pirate captain who tried to board a Gavin Shipping Company ship.

Bloody hell. Why did that trespasser have to get killed at Esprit d'Chene? The ghost's plans were set, Alice agreeing to help him—with a nudge—and now this. Alice was on her way, but not to assist him. With a murder investigation in the works, all sorts of delays could interfere in his carefully orchestrated scheme. And damn, he was tired of this half-life, half-death. Ever since he'd read how Alice helped another wandering soul transcend the veil, he'd known only she could help him move forward on his journey. Her books were very enlightening; she knew her ghost business. He'd tried to use them on his own to overcome whatever blocked his path, but nothing worked. He knew he was dead, unlike some of the poor souls she wrote about. He didn't think his problem was someone across the veil he didn't want to meet up with. He'd never lacked courage to face his enemies.

No, he concluded from his reading that something tied him to this realm. Perhaps it centered on the mystery of his death, a memory blocked completely, like the selective amnesia portrayed on that television movie. Alice could get to the bottom of it, if she had sense enough to let the bobbies to do their job and not allow a deterrent like a new murder keep her from concentrating on him. He'd worked hard, and by gad, he had first claim on Alice's time.

Jack ended a conference with the sheriff over by the far side of the pool. The sheriff walked toward the front of the house where several police cars were parked, while Jack strolled over to where four other bobbies waited for instructions, near where Sir Gary stood. The ghost stifled a chuckle at their ignorance of his perusal. It was a perfectly spooky night, excellent circumstances for one of his ghostly witticisms. Hell, he had to have some fun once in a while. He could imagine their fright if he let out a moan, since the body floated within a few feet of them. They'd scatter, thinking the corpse revived, even without its head.

Or maybe he would yell, "Over there!" Probably all six bobbies would yank their pistols free and splat belly-down on the concrete, eyes searching for the killer. A brief snicker escaped at that perfectly stupendous vision. Only Jack grabbed at his pistol, hidden on his back beneath the orange vest. The detective stared at the willow, tempting Sir Gary to reveal himself, but discretion won. Jack relaxed his hold on the pistol. Interesting, though, that only Jack reacted.

"Franklin," Jack said to a thirtyish, balding bobby with a protruding stomach, "take your patrol car out the back lane and around to the main gate. Stop anyone from driving in here until we search the grounds more thoroughly."

Franklin hurried off. Next Jack directed two bobbies to scour the grounds near the pool with the high-power-beamed flashlights they carried. "Go slow," he warned. "And keep your eyes open. I doubt the perp's still around, but stay together."

Jack left the bobby by the pool to keep an eye on the corpse, then headed into the manor house. Sir Gary glided along behind him. Obviously, Jack couldn't see him, but the detective certainly heard the snicker, and that intrigued the ghost. Sir Gary had gleaned from Katy that Jack and Alice had been married, and it seemed strange that a ghosthunter would hook up with a non-believer. However, he'd only recently delved into the complexities of this ghost business himself, so maybe there was a method to the madness of that failed state of bliss. His own marriage hadn't been any bed of roses, but back then, divorce wasn't an option. Not for him, anyway, since his wife needed extensive care. He remembered all of his life up until the last hour or so, but no matter how hard he focused, the only hint he recalled of his death was that it wasn't supposed to happen that way.

In the kitchen, Katy paced and sipped her second drink—the weak one Jack had made. Sir Gary didn't much care for the way Jack mixed bourbon and soda. Everyone knew bourbon should be poured in last, allowed to steep through the soda, and Jack had mixed it backwards. At least the tears on Katy's pretty face had dried. Her blond hair remained tousled, somewhat charmingly, were the cause the result of a enjoyable situation. A tumble with a lover perhaps.

Pleasantly surprised to see Katy move in after he ran that other old fart off, Sir Gary studied her for a few weeks before he revealed himself. A woman of Katy's breeding and appearance would have set the entire Ton on its ear back in the days when he squired his share of eligible women around the London ballrooms. Truth be known, a few ineligible ones also succumbed to him. The first time he materialized to Katy, he'd thought her another easy conquest, but she soon overcame her initial awe at his illustrious presence. Over time, he'd realized Katy's relationship with Alice explained her fascination and lack of fear.

"I have no idea who he is, either," Katy was saying when he tuned into their conversation rather than his admiration of his house partner.

"He?" Jack queried.

When he pounced on that one word, Katy frowned. "I did see what he...it...whoever...was wearing," she said testily. "The body looked male. Haven't you at least confirmed that?"

"No," Jack said. "But you're probably right."

Katy emptied her drink tumbler. "I wish Alice would get here."

"It'll take her two, three hours," Jack said. "Can I call someone closer?"

"No! Good lord, word will get out soon enough. Every gossip in the county's going to be gibbering about me."

"I'd think that your reputation would be the least of your worries," Jack mused. "There's a murdered man in your pool. Someone's lost their life."

Katy's peaches and cream complexion blanched a pallid, curdled-milk color with spots of sickly flush on her cheekbones. "M—murder?"

"I thought you'd figured that out." The cop's eyes bored into Katy.

"I...I hoped...maybe he'd just drowned. All the blood, I know, but maybe he'd...injured himself when he slipped and fell."

Jack didn't bring up the fact of the missing head just then. Sir Gary gave him credit for that. As he suspected, Katy hadn't noticed.

* * *

A pink-tinged dawn lightened the eastern sky as I barreled east on I-20 in the Jeep I'd bought when I traded in my Buick, the hatchback loaded and Trucker and Miss Molly in the back seat. Traffic was mostly semis, a few cars mixed in. I couldn't do a darn thing for Katy until I got there, and I wasn't getting anywhere trying to make sense of the little I knew. A dead body in the pool. Blood. Murder or an accident? And a ghost in residence, a ghost whose talks with Katy indicated might not be the most controllable paranormal I'd ever dealt with.

Still, ghosts didn't kill people, despite mistaken common lore. Common lore at times was total bunk. Common lore said ghosts were tied to their place of death, but some of my residents were from different states. Common lore said ghosts had abilities they didn't, probably supposed facts fostered by fear and lack of knowledge. Ghosts manipulated objects and materialized in various shades of visibility. Others sent messages. But besides a sad tale or two I'd run across of someone suffering heart failure when confronted by an unexpected ghost, every ghosthunter I knew believed ghosts lacked the power to actually kill a living person.

Accident or murder? Damn, I wished Katy lived closer!

My cell phone perched on the console, but I knew my ex-husband wouldn't be patient with that sort of disruption. Besides, the monster eighteen-wheelers in the traffic meant I didn't need that distraction. I hadn't gotten around to buying a headset for the phone yet. Then the phone rang and I grabbed it, glancing at the caller ID. Jack.

"How's Katy?" I asked without a hello.

"How close are you?"

"Twenty minutes."

"I'll let her know."

"Jack!" I yelled, anticipating a disconnection.

"I know you're worried, *Chère*," he said, "but I can't talk about this over the air."

"I don't give a whit about your damned investigation. Just tell me how Katy is besides 'all right!' For God's sake, step out of your cop mode. Katy and I are like sisters!"

He hesitated, then said, "Emotionally, she's pretty whacked out. Seems she's worried about what the neighbors are gonna say."

Stunned at Jack's words and hard tone, I couldn't think of anything to reply. When we'd socialized with Katy, Jack had appeared to like her.

What changed his attitude? "I imagine she's worried about more than the neighbors," I finally managed. "Someone died in her pool."

"Yeah," Jack responded.

"Well, an accident like that happening on my property would—"

"It was no accident, Alice," Jack cut in. "And that's all I'm going to say."

He hung up, and I tossed the phone on the passenger seat. Not an accident? That left murder. My psychic senses were right. Thank goodness the turnoff to Jefferson loomed ahead. I switched on my blinker. Concentrating on the twists and turns, I made it to Esprit d'Chene's beautiful stone gate in ten minutes flat. But as I swerved in to barrel down the long, live-oak-lined driveway, a cop car blocked my path. The Jeep's tires flung crushed white oyster shells as I skidded to a halt a bare inch from the side door. That didn't endear me one iota to the balding, uniformed policeman standing there with his hand on his gun butt.

The cop unsnapped his holster strap and walked over to my window. While I sat there, heart pounding at the near miss, he wiggled his finger in a roll-it-down motion at the tinted window. I complied. "Officer, I—"

"Alice Carpenter?" he interrupted with a sniff and a hitch of his gun belt.

"I'm her. My cousin Katy lives here. Jack—Detective Roucheau—he's expecting me."

He held up a hand to halt my babbling and sniffed again. "Detective said to keep an eye out." All at once he noticed Trucker. Jabbing his hand on his pistol butt, he stepped away.

"He won't hurt you," I protested. "Can I please go on up to the house?"

He dropped his hand, but didn't re-snap the holster strap. "Detective said it'd be all right. But —" He eyed me suspiciously. "You got any ID?"

Gritting my teeth, I reached for my purse, then remembered it was stowed in the hatchback. Amidst the usual mess in my car, one of my books lay in a stack of papers on the front floorboard. I grabbed it, turned it over to the publicity photo on the back jacket, and handed it to him. "That's me."

That didn't soothe his suspicions. He studied the photo, then my face. "I clean up well," I fumed. "Look, keep the book. I need to go."

"Maybe my mama would read it." He thrust it back. "Can you write your name for her?"

I grabbed a pen from the console and opened the book. "What is her name?"

"Celia."

"S-E—"

"Naw," he interrupted. "C-E-L-I-A."

After a hurried scribble, I handed the book back and reached for the gearshift.

"You gotta walk," he said. "And stay on the grass. We got crime folks lookin' at tire tracks in the driveway."

"Haven't other cars gone up this way?"

"Detective Roucheau came in the other gate. Ordered the rest to do that, too."

There was another gate across what Katy referred to as the back lane. The locals knew about it, as did Jack from a couple of family visits, and it would've been closer for him from the cottage he rented. But driving around would take just as much time on the winding farm-to-market roads as walking from here. I opened the door, then glanced at my pets, doubtful about leaving Trucker here with Mr. Quick-to-Grab-His-Gun.

"You'll have to leave 'em here," Mr. Quick confirmed grudgingly. "Leave your a.c. on, and I'll keep an eye on 'em."

I set the parking brake and flicked the air conditioning on high. With an apologetic glance at the dog and cat, I pushed the button to roll the window nearly up, more to keep Mr. Quick away from Trucker than anything else, then scrambled out. On second thought, I tossed Miss Molly a stern look. "Your litter box is in the hatchback."

The cop overheard. "I ain't a cat person. Can't expect me to do nothin' if I catch her squattin' where she's not supposed to."

"The dog's name is Trucker." Frustrated and worried, I glared at the officer. "He wouldn't take it kindly if you messed with the cat." With a last stern look at him and my pets, I hurried up the drive. Mr. Quick's sniff hung in the air behind me.

Any other time I would have enjoyed the quarter-mile walk. Gigantic, evenly-spaced live oaks lined it, branches intermingled from either side to spread coolness even in summer. Wispy gray nests of Spanish moss floated in the higher branches. Dawn had given away to early morning light, and birds twittered in the trees or swooped from branches to a white board fence. I jogged too close to a peacock strutting from behind a live oak, and his raucous screech startled me as much as I startled him. I grabbed my chest and barely checked a kick. He flipped his head and sauntered away, fanning that multi-eyed tail as though brushing away a pesky fly. What Katy saw in those blasted birds was beyond me. Their eerie cries at inopportune moments can scare a person a heck of a lot worse than a ghost!

Around the curve in the driveway, I moved further into the grass to avoid two crime techs squatting inside yellow crime tape. They glanced up briefly, then went back to work with their cameras and tire casting gunk.

Ahead the Esprit d'Chene manor house rose into view. No one would dare call it a mere house. Three stories, with spindle-set balustrades circling both the first- and second-floor verandas, Esprit d'Chene sprawled majestically amidst well-tended gardens, shrubbery, flowerbeds, and red-brick footpaths. Despite my worry, awe at her beauty filled me. She always reminded me of a grand lady overseeing a flock of minions barely beneath her notice. Jean Leveau, my many-times Great-Grandpere Jean, spared no expense when he built Esprit d'Chene for the lady of his choice, my petite, flaxen-haired Great-Grandmere Alicia. Counted among the founding families of Jefferson, they moved here from New Orleans back when Jefferson's economy boomed, since the town grew on Big Cypress Bayou. At one time the bayou was northern Texas's only link to the waterways, and magnificent steamboats ferried passengers, lumber, and cotton up Big Cypress to Caddo Lake to bring the luxuries genteel ladies needed to furnish their homes in splendor. Until the dastardly Corps of Engineers blew up the Red River logjam and dropped the bayou water too low for the steamboats to turn around.

Murder shouldn't happen in this exquisite setting, but a slew of police and state troopers marred Esprit d'Chene grounds, originally designed for dainty ladies in pastel organza to wander with men who cherished them. Various breeds of cop cars parked helter-skelter along the driveway from the back lane—Jefferson and Longview police sedans, county sheriff and state patrol cars, and a couple unmarked vehicles. And lord, there was the medical examiner's hearse.

As though he'd been watching for me, Jack Roucheau hurried down the veranda steps to meet me. During the past two years, we'd maintained contact, and even had lunch a few times when I needed crime research for a book. He'd contacted me first when someone—Twila, I always suspected—told him that I was moving from New Orleans. I'd have had to call him anyway, since I'd discovered a few of his left-behind possessions.

He's a good-looking guy, six-foot, a well-toned but rangy body. A little gray has crept into the temples of his coal-black, silky hair over the past couple years. Deep brown eyes in a rugged face are a legacy from his Cajun ancestors, and tiny sun-wrinkles crease each side. Like me, he prefers jeans for daytime wear, but he's one of the few men who also enjoys evening dress—and looks damned good in it. He still turned my knees to jelly and curled my toes, but the papers in my file cabinet meant we'd already tried that road—and failed to navigate it.

Today he wore jeans and a knit shirt with the Longview Police Department insignia over the left breast pocket and western boots. A neon orange police vest, required attire during an investigation, overlaid the shirt. I'd once asked Jack why they wore the vests, and he'd explained that if they were chasing a perp, or jumped one hiding near the crime scene, they didn't want to take a chance on shooting one of their own.

"How's Katy?" I demanded.

"*Bon jour* to you, too, *Chère*," he said, a guarded look in his eyes. "Katy will be fine, now that you're here."

"The body." I wet my dry lips, a motion Jack didn't miss. "Who—?"

He laid a comforting hand on my arm. "We're not sure. Go to Katy."

It must be bad, I mused, hurrying up the veranda steps. I reached for the antique glass doorknob, then turned to see Jack staring after me, the stone face he normally wore during an investigation creased with worry. But a brown-uniformed state trooper approached, and he shifted his attention. Not before, however, he gave me a nod and motioned me through the door.

I entered the cool foyer and headed straight for the kitchen. The tall ceilings were painted white, as were the walls above the four-foot, walnut wainscoting. A border of red-berry holly vines twined adjacent to the ceiling. I nearly slammed into the wall where the door used to be before I realized Katy had moved it. Darn her and her continual remodeling! I detoured through the new doorway. Katy stood at the counter, kneading a ball of dough. She always bakes or cooks to calm herself. My turbulent thoughts still tumbled inside my mind—and belly—from strain and lack of sleep.

Katy heard my footsteps, turned, and raced across the room to fling her arms around my neck. A glob of dough landed in my hair as I hugged her tight.

"Oh, Alice." She pulled back, tears gleaming. "Sir Gary's done it now. How are we going to explain that my ghost committed murder?"

I swiped a thumb across the tear tracks on her cheeks. "Oh, Sugar, what makes you think Sir Gary killed him?" Goosebumps crawled up my spine and over my neck. I whirled, but didn't see Katy's resident ghost anywhere in the kitchen.

"He's here," she confirmed. "He's not going to show himself with all these policemen around. He says they remind him of the London Tower guards." She sniffed and daintily picked up a puffy tissue from the box on the table with a manicured finger- and thumb-nail. She patted beneath her eyes, careful not to smudge what must have been waterproof mascara, since I knew darn well her eyelashes weren't any longer than my stubby ones without help.

"Did I tell you that Sir Gary had been imprisoned in the Tower of London once?" she asked, then glanced around to make sure no one could observe her lack of etiquette except me and gave her nose a go-to-hell blow.

"I'm not interested in Sir Gary at the moment." I pushed her into a chair by the table and dragged another one around to face her. "What happened? What makes you think Sir Gary's involved? Who's in your pool?"

"I'm not sure." She ignored my flurry of other questions as she swiped her red nose and mumbled into the tissue, "I think...maybe..."

"I didn't hear that."

Katy slid another cautious look around the kitchen, then leaned closer. "It might be Senator Wilson-Jones's son."

"What?" I screeched, continuing despite Katy's frantic shushing motions, "Bucky? Good God Gertie, Katy! You promised you'd never let that asshole back on your property!"

"Alice, please," she whispered in the face of my rant. "I didn't let him...if that's who it is. And I most assuredly didn't check out who it was when Sir Gary and I found the body." She grabbed a whole handful of tissues and swabbed new tears, but I wasn't about to offer any sympathy. Bucky! Nasty, slimy Bucky Wilson-Jones. Probably not even Bucky's father would shed any more tears over his son's death than necessary to keep his public persona intact.

"What was Bucky doing here?" I hissed in a quieter, but just as deadly, voice.

"I didn't say it was Bucky, Alice. I said it *might* be."

"You sure as hell have some reason for thinking that. Spill it!"

"Ummm...well..."

Footsteps strode down the hallway. I knew those footsteps. I'd lived with them—and the rest of the body—for three years. He wouldn't appreciate me questioning a witness. Katy wrung her hands—only Katy can pull off that old-fashioned gesture with aplomb—and shot me a pleading glance. I didn't have time to ask what she meant.

CHAPTER 6

"We need to search the grounds more thoroughly, Katy," Jack said sternly, although I caught the touch of compassion in his eyes. "For clues and the victim's head."

Katy wailed and scrambled up. She raced to the counter to furiously knead bread dough.

"His head!" I gasped. "The murderer cut off his head?"

"Yeah," Jack replied. "The head was missin' when she found the body, though Katy claims she didn't know that until I told her a while ago."

"How...what...." A headless corpse floating in the pool surrounded by the beautiful lagoon area Katy had designed? The scenario sounded like it belonged in one of my books.

Jack glanced at Katy and kept his voice low. "Your great-granddaddy's sword."

"Ohmigod." I clamped my mouth shut. Maybe the ghost's interest in Grandpere Jean's sword last night *was* connected to the death, but Jack Roucheau would be the last man on earth to believe a ghost was involved in murder.

"What, *Chère*?" Jack prodded. "If you know anything, you need to tell me."

"I didn't even know it was murder until you hinted at it on the cell phone," I reminded Jack, hedging the best way I could, by distracting him from his question. But Jack's investigative mind didn't distract easily.

"You and Katy were always close. Talked all the time." He glanced at Katy as though concentrating elsewhere, but past experience told me that he remained aware of every nuance in a person's body language. The things a person recalls from living closely with someone, even for a brief period out of the short span of our lives.

"We still talk frequently," I admitted. "But that doesn't mean I know anything about this murder. Or that Katy does. I haven't had time to visit Esprit d'Chene for months." I continued trying to sidetrack Jack, "Where did you find the sword?"

"Somewhere not that well hidden." His frown shifted to Katy once more, then back to me. Obviously he wasn't going to reveal that fact, because the silence lingered.

"Your crime techs were examining some tire tracks," I said after a moment. "Katy told me she hasn't had any visitors for a couple weeks."

"That's what folks around here have been sayin'," Jack agreed. "That's not like Katy."

You wouldn't want to broadcast the fact that you've got a ghost who embarrasses you in your house, either, I thought. I could just imagine Jack's face if I voiced that, though. Instead, I said, "Everybody needs a break from the social whirl now and then."

"Not Katy," Jack said. "Not since I've known her. And *somebody* was here last night."

Ha! If he only knew. The white magnolia blossoms floating in the crystal bowl on the table suddenly appeared extremely fascinating. "Where'd you get magnolias now, Sugar?" I called across the kitchen.

Katy shaped a bread loaf and dropped it into a waiting pan beside some others already rising. "A friend in New Orleans. Orchids, too. Did you see them in the foyer?"

"I was too busy looking for the new kitchen door."

Katy tossed me a sad smile, but at least it was a smile. "I told you I was remodeling."

"You always are. Did you finish the Men's and Ladies' Parlors?"

Katy popped two bread pans in the oven. "Oh, yes. Would you like to see them?"

Jack huffed a frustrated breath. "We've got a crime investigation here, and you girls want to look at the redecorating?"

"We *women* aren't cops," I snarled, and continued in a mocking Cajun drawl, "We shouldn't have to worry our purty l'il heads 'bout no nasty murder. That be a man's job." With a haughty toss of my head, I swept past him out of the kitchen, Katy following.

"I need permission to search the grounds beyond the pool," Jack reminded Katy.

"Do whatever you need," she replied with a wave.

Instead of following me to the twin parlors, Katy halted in the hallway and furtively motioned me into the Great Room. Sure enough, Grandpere Jean's sword was missing from over the fireplace. Evidently the crime techs had already scoured this room, since fingerprint dust marred the mantle, furniture, and windowsills.

Katy grimaced at the mess. "Do ghosts leave fingerprints?" she whispered.

"Ummm...well, yes. There's that railroad crossing down in San Antonio, where people dust their bumpers and trunks with powder or flour. The kid ghosts push their cars across the track to safety, even with their motors turned off, and leave prints."

"Oh, no!"

"Sugar, I very much doubt Sir Gary's prints are on file, even if they are in your house. There will probably be a lot of other unidentifiable prints, too, since you have so many visitors. Used to have. You know, I've been meaning to get down to San Antone—"

"Alice!"

"Sorry. Somebody must have broken in. I've told you to get an alarm system."

"I don't want those nasty stickers and signs all over my windows and yard. Besides, I live out here around people I know and trust."

"People like Bucky Wilson-Jones?" I reminded her. "But should we be in this room? The cops might need to gather more evidence."

"They didn't put yellow tape across the door, like they did at the pool house," Katy said. "Look at this mess. Sue Ann will have to call her daughters-in-law to help clean."

I glanced at Grandmere Alicia's portrait. It hung in place, but Katy had tied the gold cord in an unattractive knot for now.

"I got out the sewing kit to fix the cord last night," Katy said when she noticed what I was looking at. "I re-braided it and started to sew it, but I pricked my finger because I was so agitated, and left it for this morning. But...well, things happened."

"What makes you think Sir Gary had anything to do with Bucky's death?"

"We don't know it's Bucky yet," she insisted.

"No doubt it is," a sexy English voice intruded. I whirled to get my first look at Sir Gary Gavin, the resident ghost of Esprit d'Chene.

"Holy shit," I whispered. He was everything Katy had said: tall, handsome as all get-out. Masculine from the tip of his head, covered in slightly wavy black hair meant for a woman to run her fingers through, all the way down his form-fitting trousers to the tips of his black leather boots. He stood by the fireplace, as solid as though he could walk across the room and spin one of us into a waltz.

"I thought you weren't going to appear with all the cops around," I said. "And what makes you sure it's Bucky?"

"The bloody bastard has met his proper comeuppance." Sir Gary leaned against the fireplace and hooked his thumbs in his belt, long, tapered fingers against a flat stomach.

"From what I hear, it definitely was bloody," I replied. And wished my words back immediately when Katy clapped her hands over her mouth to stifle her anguished cry.

"Sorry, Sugar," I said. "I'll try to watch my mouth." I turned back to Sir Gary. "Did you have anything to do with his death?"

He laughed, a deep, sexy rumble. "No."

I wasn't sure I believed him, despite my own knowledge of ghost lore, but Katy breathed a sigh of relief as he continued, "I probably should have, if he's the man I saw skulking around here last week. Someone else took care of that chore for me."

"I've never heard of ghosts actually being able to kill a living person," I insisted in order to gauge his reaction. "Despite what the movies try to make people believe, ghosts don't have that sort of physical power."

Sir Gary shrugged. "There are ways."

"Yeah," I mused, frowning an evil glare. "I suppose you could have manipulated Grandpere's sword through the air and sliced off —" Oops. I clamped my mouth shut and whirled to look at Katy, but she was digging in the needlepoint patterned sewing box. Her movements were so jerky, I thought about cautioning her to leave the repair for me so she wouldn't accidentally re-stab herself. But maybe it would be good for her to stay busy.

Taking advantage of Katy's distraction, I moved closer to Sir Gary. "I suppose you expect me to take your word that you didn't have anything to do with the murder?"

"I did not specifically say that I didn't have anything to do with it. I merely said that I did not commit the deed."

"Don't nit-pick my words! You sound like Jack!"

Sir Gary grinned, and I saw what Katy meant about that dimple in his cheek. But I had several more years experience combating masculine charm than Katy. "So who killed him?"

"I haven't the foggiest. But whoever it was did a jolly good job. I plan to make it a point to shake his hand if they catch him."

Frustrated, I rolled my eyes. "Let's start over. Did you see who was in the car in the driveway last night?"

"It didn't come close enough to get my attention. As I told you on the phone, I was watching television a while, a spooky movie from a book by this Stephen King fellow. You might like him yourself, given the vein of your writing. Or perhaps Koontz."

"I've read all of King's work, and Koontz's, too," I said inattentively as I thought back to my trip up the driveway and realized he was right. The crime techs had been at work where the driveway curved just before it made the circular loop in front of the manor house. A hundred and fifty years ago, horse-drawn buggies arrived at Esprit d'Chene via the drive, deposited their bejeweled and evening-attired ladies and gentlemen at the door, then circled out of the way to wait to drive the guests home. There was a good bit of driveway not visible from the house.

"Katy has a King book on her computer, but she won't let me read it," Sir Gary grumbled.

"Smart," I said. "Ghosts have no business messing with computer equipment. What else do you know about the murder?"

He heaved an irritated sigh. "Let the bobbies do their job. I asked you here for another purpose."

"Asked." I scowled. "You demanded that I come. And I don't appreciate it. I have a book due, and I don't have time for your foolishness. There's no reason you couldn't have waited another week. You've been waiting for centuries!"

Sir Gary quirked an eyebrow, and I caught his drift. I had to come because of the murder. So, had he been the one messing with my computer? He couldn't have been, since Howard insisted it was a woman, and I'd never found Howard to be wrong. Maybe some dearly-departed lady friend of Sir Gary's? Possible.

Something else niggled, though. The sword had been in the Great Room when Katy called me the first time, then been found somewhere else. How long had it been between Katy's two phone calls? A half-hour? No, less than that.

"There," Katy said over by the portrait. She'd re-braided the cord and sewn it together. Grandmere Alicia's portrait hung back in its proper place. Drawn by the gaze on Grandmere's face—a mixture of mischief and command—I slowly walked over.

Grandmere Alicia was even more petite than Katy; women in her era were smaller than today. Even into the late 1800's, the average height of women was barely over four foot, and their clothing bore that out. Twila and I were both Southern mansion tour addicts. We discovered lots of ghosts in those old houses. But according to family history, despite her small stature Grandmere had ruled Esprit d'Chene with no more effort than voicing her desires or needs.

"Remember how we found the portrait?" I asked Katy.

She giggled, and I glanced at Sir Gary to see a tad of interest on his face.

"The Hollow Room," Katy recalled. "We found the room in the attic —well, after we got locked in the passageway and couldn't find our way out."

"During the War Between the States," I explained to Sir Gary, "Southerners built secret rooms and passageways in their homes. They wanted somewhere to hide their treasures from the Damn Yankees. Also, few people realize that a portion of the Underground Railroad ran through Texas. Our Grandpere Jean and Grandmere Alicia were also involved in that."

Sir Gary shivered, and Katy whispered, "He's claustrophobic. It comes from his time in The Tower. He'd never enter the passageways in Esprit d'Chene."

I chuckled and studied the fine specimen of masculinity. Claustrophobic? A ghost? But then, their personalities did go with them.

"Have you seen Uncle Clarence lately?" I asked.

Sir Gary harrumphed grumpily, and Katy shot him a stern glare. "I need to tell you—"

One second Sir Gary was there, the next gone, without even a lingering mist left. Of course, he'd had a couple hundred years to finesse his powers. I hadn't heard Jack approach, but his smooth, cat-like stride matched his lanky body, and Katy had carpet runners in the hallways.

"You aren't supposed to be in here," Jack said from the doorway.

"They didn't put any crime tape across the door," I parroted Katy.

"Should have," he said. "C'mon."

When we joined him in the hallway, he said, "I thought you were goin' to the parlor."

"Did you find the...uh...rest of the body?" I asked instead of answering what I took as an *investigative* question.

"No." He sidelonged a glance at Katy, his eyes telling me we'd talk about that later. But Katy had heard.

"When can I have the sword back?" she asked.

"It might be a while," Jack replied. "It's evidence."

Katy grimaced in disappointment as Jack ushered us back into the kitchen. She immediately headed to the oven to check her bread.

"I'll need to take a statement from you, Alice," Jack said.

"Me? Why? And can I be with Katy when you take hers?" I knew about interviewing techniques from my research, although I'd never been on the receiving end of one. I also knew Katy would be on the list of suspects, a fact I hoped my cousin hadn't perceived yet. But there was no choice, especially if the detectives found out about Katy and Bucky and translated that into a possible motive on Katy's part. That is, if the body turned out to be Bucky.

"—gotta talk to Katy alone," Jack was saying when I tuned back in. "We took a prelim when we first got here, but we'll need more."

"Why me?"

"You talked to her last night. We need to know about that—and why you were already plannin' to come here before the murder was discovered, like Katy told us."

Uh oh. Wasn't that going to be an interesting conversation?

"I'll take care of both your statements, *Chère*," Jack assured me. "Don't worry. No dark room with a light bulb blindin' you. No good cop/bad cop."

"Does Katy need a lawyer?" I whispered.

The timer dinged, and Katy bustled over with hot pads.

"I'll let you know," he said, and my stomach churned.

"Should you conduct this investigation? You used to be part of this family. And this is Jefferson's jurisdiction, isn't it? You're on the Longview force."

"Jefferson doesn't have a homicide detective. Not enough funds. And nobody else around here has my experience, so the sheriff asked me to help when he found me here." He sighed. "We don't get many headless corpse problems. Mostly, it's straightforward. *Fais do do* on Saturday night, little too much to drink. Some femme dances too close to a man not her own." He shook his head. "Those are the bad ones, because you get to know the people. Be friends with some of them."

He surprised me with that. Jack had never talked about his emotions during a case. He'd always said he had to keep his distance—guard himself, to study the clues and suspects with an open mind. But he never had an ex-wife and ex-cousin involved in New Orleans.

"Jack, I'll only be here a couple of days. I'm under deadline, and I need to get home. I'll take Katy with me, so she won't be here alone."

"Not until we're done," Jack ordered. "You're out of our jurisdiction, and—"

"Damn it, Jack! We'll only be two hours away!"

"You have a laptop, don't you?"

"How the heck can I concentrate in the middle of a murder investigation?" Jack completely lacked an understanding of my work, another one of our problems. Interrupted and drawn out of that creative sea, it could take me hours to refocus. Sometimes I'd lose a wonderful thread and never find it again. While we were married, I'd shut my door when working, with a caution not to bother me unless the house caught fire—and then, not until he'd at least called the fire department. All I wanted was enough time to get my backup disks out of the house. But on weekends, Jack would have something to talk about that, in his mind, just couldn't wait, or need something in my study. He'd creep in, but I'd sense his presence. Besides, he kept forgetting to spray WD-40 on the squeaky study door hinges.

"Call your editor and get an extension," Jack said, what he considered a reasonable request. "Katy's gonna need you for a while."

There was no sense arguing with him, but I did anyway. "I can't put my writing life on hold under deadline—not even for a murder investigation. The book's slotted and the publicity push is ready, with my backlist scheduled for re-release. I've accepted speaking engagements, and I'd also planned on taking a vacation before I settled in to start my next book."

Jack just gazed at me with that look he always gets when he can't understand how on earth I set my priorities. "If you didn't have the time," he repeated, "what were you doin' takin' time off to come visit Katy right now in the first place?"

CHAPTER 7

"I—uh—aren't you supposed to be out there helping your crime team?" I evaded.

"They know their jobs. They'll come tell me if they find anything important I should know about. Why were you on your way here?"

"Oh, crap. It's a long story. And not exactly all mine to tell. Katy's involved, and —" The cop I'd nearly run down at the gate came to the kitchen door, and I breathed in relief.

"Detective," he said. "The lady—" he nodded at me "—can bring her car on up to the house now. They're done with the driveway."

"Couldn't you have driven it up here, Franklin?" Jack asked.

"Uh...no...well, maybe. But I didn't want to take a chance."

"Trucker's in the Jeep," I explained.

Jack's gaze at his officer relaxed. He'd seen pictures of Trucker, and even met the dog and cat once when he stopped by my cabin to get me to sign a book for his boss's wife. "Well, give the lady a ride down to her car before that dog dies of heatstroke," he ordered.

"I left the a.c. on," I fumed. "I'm aware animals shouldn't be left in a closed-up car!"

"Animals?" he asked.

"I've got Miss Molly, too."

"Hmmm," he mused. "You meant to stay a few days. You'd never leave your head cat longer than a day."

I narrowed my eyes. "Just remember, Jack Roucheau. I'm working on my book, so you can just schedule any *statement* from me around my work time!"

I started to huff out of the kitchen, but Katy called, "Alice, you brought Trucker?"

"Don't worry, Sugar," I said, still irritated. "I've broken him from marking his territory on the furniture."

"God, I hope so," Katy said. "But there's a fence around one portion of the back yard—"

"Trucker stays with me. If he causes any damage, I'll take care of it."

"Um...have you had Miss Molly declawed yet?"

"Nope," I told her, a tad satisfied at the worry on her face. I don't like it one bit when people won't accept my animals. But I relented. Katy didn't need additional stress. "I brought Miss Molly's scratching post, Sugar. Her litter box, too. Don't worry. Cats sleep a lot."

I hurried out before I got roped into more defenses of my animals. Katy kept animals at Esprit d'Chene, but they were for show. A couple horses—thoroughbreds, of course—roamed her pasture, plus those blasted peacocks strutted freely wherever their hearts desired.

"The dog'll be protection, at least," Jack said behind me.

I didn't hear Katy's answer, because I strode down the hall to where Mr. Quick—Officer Franklin, I guess his real name was—waited. Jack was right. For the most part, Trucker was a mild-mannered Rottweiler, raised with love and discipline. However, the breed has an ingrained protective trait, and woe the person who attacks a member of its circle of love. One night a half-drunk cowboy got lost and found his way to my place just about the time the driveshaft fell out of his rusty old pickup. When I incautiously walked outside to find the source of the noise, he tried to push his way in and use the phone himself, rather than let me call someone for him. Trucker changed the cowboy's mind real fast when he heard his threatening voice. A hundred and fifty pounds of angry

Rottweiler lunged straight through the storm door and launched itself at the drunk with a roar that even gave me the willies.

Lucky for the cowboy, I caught Trucker in mid-lunge. I still chuckle, though, when I recall the urine stain that spread down the front of those ragged jeans. Maybe from embarrassment, maybe from fear, he politely gave me the phone number of his brother and waited in his pickup until help arrived.

Officer Franklin drove me down to my Jeep, and I took advantage of the time to see if I could find out if they really thought it might be Bucky in the pool. There was a slew of representatives from various investigative branches of Texas law enforcement here, which meant they had reason to believe this might be a high-profile case. Of course, it was an especially grisly one, but someone—probably Jack—had called in reinforcements. Even his better-staffed Longview police force wouldn't have done that for a simple murder without just cause.

"Lots of investigators here," I mused to Franklin. "You'd think there was a mass murderer loose, not a lone body."

He glanced over. "Now, don't you worry your head none, ma'am." I hate it when somebody not *that* much younger calls me ma'am. "We've got it under control. And we'll keep an officer 'round here 'til we catch the perp."

"How will you even begin to investigate until you identify the corpse?" I asked. "And how can you identify him without a head?"

"Fingerprints, probably," he said as we neared my car and he eyed Trucker's nose sticking out the partially-down window.

"What if his prints aren't on file?"

He cast me a frown that I took to mean he wondered why this little woman was so interested in such a grisly matter. "I'm a mystery writer," I explained. "Remember the book? I know a little about crime investigations."

"Oh." He nodded seriously. "Like that Jessica Fletcher woman on TV." I wanted to harrumph and remind him that writers wrote those television stories, but he went on, "You sold any of your books besides that one you gave me?"

I gritted a tight smile. I never could decide which was worse: people who gush over me in false pretense while they try to finagle the secret of getting their own books published, or people who've never heard of my books. "A few," I said abruptly.

He pulled up beside my Jeep, a cautious distance away from Trucker's nose. "I'll ask Mama what she thinks after she reads hers. She don't get out much these days, what with her arthritis, so she'll probably get to it soon."

"Don't you read, Officer Qui—Franklin?"

"Sure. Got subscriptions to all the huntin' and fishin' magazines. Couple car magazines."

I got out of the patrol car, trying to think of another way to dig information from him, although Jack would give me what-for if he caught me sticking my nose in. Maybe Jack would forget his promise about no spotlight or good cop/bad cop. But as long as I had this niggling notion about Katy being a suspect, I felt obligated to ferret out all the information I could.

Both Trucker and Miss Molly waited for a chance to escape as I opened my Jeep door. I shooed them back. If either one of them caught sight of a blasted peacock, it would take forever to catch them.

"You know." I turned to Officer Franklin with what I hoped was an innocent expression. "I've got a similar situation coming up in a future book. An unidentifiable corpse." *Well, I might have; it sounds like a great storyline.* "What other ways are there to identify someone?"

A self-important look crossed his face, so I realized I'd hit on the right approach. "Oh, there's tattoos, birthmarks, stuff like that. Things a family might know about."

"I guess you can't check dental records unless you find the head. What about medical records, blood type, and DNA?"

"We gotta send DNA to one of the labs in Tyler or Garland. We don't have equipment like that here."

Just then the medical examiner's hearse came into view, rolling seriously down the driveway from the manor house with its important cargo. And my Jeep was blocking its path.

"You sound like you know a lot about crime investigation. Maybe I could talk to you, if I run into any problems on my book."

"Jack'd be better. I've only been on the force a year. Best move your vehicle, ma'am."

I tossed him what I hoped was my publicity smile, so he would get the connection between my professional photo and me dressed in jeans and T-shirt. Then I slid into my Jeep and snapped my fingers to order Trucker into the back seat. I didn't miss the fact that Officer Quick had forgotten to thank me for the book.

Trucker slobbered a kiss on my cheek, whined, and wiggled, telling me he needed a doggie potty break. Miss Molly snubbed me and curled on the front passenger seat to bathe, irritated at being cooped up. I sniffed as I dropped the Jeep in gear, but evidently she'd heeded my reminder about her litter box.

"You'll have to wait just another minute," I told Trucker. He settled down, but panted and stared longingly out the side window at the lovely, fire-hydrant trees. The hearse rolled by, and I noted both the driver's and passenger's faces. The passenger was probably the medical examiner. Surprisingly, she was a woman. That was normally a male province in the smaller East Texas towns. This woman looked to be in her mid-forties, a grandmotherly type, and I had trouble picturing her examining a headless corpse, let alone wielding the necessary autopsy tools. But come to think of it, I supposed any autopsy would be performed at a better-equipped facility than the locals had available.

I've never watched an actual autopsy, though. Research from books and interviews works just fine.

CHAPTER 8

S ir Gary hovered on the other side of visible until Jack and most of the other bobbies departed in early afternoon. They left yellow crime tapes across the Great Room door, around the pool area, and down by the curve in the live-oak-lined drive. One bobby stayed behind to patrol the grounds, and Jack promised they'd remove the crime tape as soon as possible, but it irritated Katy to no end.

They'd found no signs of forced entry on any of the doors or windows, no footprints, no fresh-turned earth where someone might have buried something, no clues at all beyond the unexplained tire tracks and the sword. The bobbies who examined the tracks said they were common tires from a pickup truck or SUV. Half the visitors to the plantation drove pickups or SUVs, so Sir Gary didn't see where that information would do them a damn bit of good.

They hadn't found the corpse's head.

Sir Gary listened to the final conversation between Jack and the sheriff.

"No doubt about it," the sheriff said. "That dagger-pierced rose on his arm."

"Yeah," Jack responded. "We picked him up once in Longview, so we got his sheet."

"All hell's gonna break lose when the media gets hold of this."

"Let alone the row we'll hear from the senator."

The two men shook hands and got into their vehicles. The sheriff drove off first, and Sir Gary started to visualize and head back into the house as Jack followed. Whoops. Jack must have been looking in his rearview mirror. He slammed on the brakes, and Sir Gary popped back into the other dimension. Jack lunged out of the car and crouched, pistol drawn. He scanned the area, arcing the pistol and following it with his eyes. Finally he stood, focused on a twin-trunked live oak, then holstered the pistol and rubbed his eyes, before he got back in the car and drove slowly away.

In the kitchen, Sir Gary found Katy insisting to Alice that they needed lunch, which she would prepare while Alice settled in one of the bedrooms. Deciding to stay invisible—still a little miffed at Katy's attitude toward him—he pondered the situation while Katy silently fixed a seafood salad from that pasta he couldn't imagine would taste like anything other than cardboard. Katy added some spices and cold, boiled shrimp, and it looked more appetizing. Not that in his state he ate anything, but he had memories. Normally Katy bustled around the kitchen whenever Sue Ann, her housekeeper, wasn't around, enjoying her meal preparations. Today her morose demeanor tugged at Sir Gary. Even though they'd had their differences lately, he hated to see Katy so downcast. He would miss her when he crossed over, but from what he'd read in Alice's books, coming back as a spirit to visit wasn't impossible. First, though, he had to find a way out of this half-existence.

He hadn't counted on that blasted murder. Even though the bobbies had combed the grounds thoroughly—he had to admit Jack knew his business—the ghost figured they might have missed something. Leaving Katy to her cooking, he glided through the Garden Room beside the kitchen, where Katy would serve the meal, on through the wall onto the grounds.

Concentrating, he moved to the pool area where Jack had found the Confederate sword tossed beneath a bank of ferns. He'd picked it up in a surgical-gloved hand and placed it in a large, plastic bag from a stock one of those bobby crime technicians transported in a suitcase. No doubt about it being the murder weapon. Blood tinged its blade, and Sir Gary knew the tempered metal had retained its sharpness. He'd admired that weapon more than once. Besides, when that matronly medical examiner gave permission and the bobbies removed the corpse, the ghost agreed with the assessment that the sword matched the wound—not vocally, of course.

Sir Gary stood beside the pool, trying to recreate how things happened. Someone obviously crept into the Great Room and snatched the sword after he and Katy went their separate ways. Bucky had been sneaking toward the manor house, in similar fashion to what Sir Gary had seen last week. That night the renegade had prowled clear around the house, then halted at the Garden Room door. Bucky gave up and left just about the time Sir Gary decided to run him off, probably because nothing other than a single light over the stove in the kitchen glowed anywhere, indicating Katy had long gone to bed.

Given the climate here, mist rose from the pool water at night, especially with the heater Katy had installed. Mist mingled with ground fog, thick dark gray at times. Quite good cover for a prowler—for human eyes, anyway. Last night's roiling mist had been especially thick. An appropriate atmosphere for a dastardly deed such as murder, he mused, even though stuff like that had been overdone in horror movies.

He tried to see the pool area with fresh eyes, even though he'd been at the plantation for years now. Plenty of hiding places; plants and trees grew thick and lush, excellent hiding spots for someone bent on murder. Why, once a thistle grew three feet tall almost overnight, and Katy inadvertently backed into it after a swim in that teensy bikini she started wearing after he visualized. The first month or so...but he needed to pay attention here.

Someone hid amidst the shrubbery—swooped out with the sword poised for attack—lopped the head off with scarcely a jolt against the well-honed blade. But why weren't there any tracks? And why dispose of the head, yet leave the corpse floating in the pool, easily discoverable? Why scrub blood from the edge of the pool?

Sir Gary glided over to the spot where Jack had squatted after one of the evidence-gathering bobbies sprayed some sort of stuff on the concrete and photographed it. Something they said would illuminate any blood spatters, even if they'd been scrubbed clean. Amazing Sir Gary, the telltale splatters appeared, their trajectory confirming Jack's notion of how the crime unfolded. Probably Bucky didn't even realize he'd been assassinated at first. Maybe he still didn't, but though Sir Gary had kept an eagle eye out, he hadn't sensed another presence.

He wandered behind the manor house, then decided to check out the tire tracks. He didn't have to worry about disturbing the crime scene; he wouldn't leave any passing signs of his presence. Inside the yellow tape, he crouched and studied the area. Small patches of white plaster dotted around, left behind from the tire casts. He'd have to take the bobbies' word about the vehicle. He didn't see much difference in this tire track and one from the Jeep Alice drove.

Small white rocks mixed in with the crushed oyster shells, a few disturbed, evident by the freshly-turned earth and small holes left in their former resting places. They almost looked like globs of that plaster, but the undersides were stained darker with earth.

One of the horses whinnied and trotted over, ears pricked. He'd always had an eye for a beautiful horse, as his wife had, and animals always seemed to see him. He glided through the crime tape and murmured to the animal before he headed back, not any more enlightened about who had killed Bucky than before. And just as frustrated at this interference with his plans.

* * *

Katy called, and I hurried into the Garden Room where she had laid out our meal on a small tea table beside the back wall. Windows took up that entire area, with a view of the yard and pool, and fans swirled lazily. None of Katy's plants drooped, nor did spider webs dust the ceiling corners. The windowpanes sparkled, a testament to Sue Ann's diligence.

Katy murmured something about getting her fresh bread, and I gazed out the windows. The yard covered nearly three acres, magnolia and pecan trees interspersed, cedar at the back edge. She'd landscaped with monkey-grass-bordered brick paths, beds of fiddle ferns, and red and white roses. A lot of Katy's roses were scores old, planted by the various women over the generations, the plants an intriguing mixture. Some spread and wandered up trellises; others her gardener kept trimmed and low-growing around marble statues of children or angels.

We couldn't see the gazebo, the guesthouse, or the half-acre maze from here. The gazebo was gorgeous, white gingerbread-trimmed, a place where family gathered for meals on cool days. Katy installed electricity and a fan. The guesthouse had formerly been the *garconniére*, a separate house from the manor house. Plantation sons moved into it in their teens, their own bachelor quarters away from their parents' alert eyes.

We'd only been treated with occasional visits to Esprit d'Chene over the years. Miss Emmajean, already elderly, didn't entertain much. But every two or three years, the clan gathered and spent a weekend helping Miss Emmajean paint or take care of some work she didn't trust to local contractors. While the adults worked and chatted, the children were left pretty much to their own devices, which included playing in the maze.

Nasty little brats we were at times, too. The older ones, who had learned the intricacies, led the younger ones in. Then we zipped down a path too quickly for them to keep up—hid in the maze and giggled until their curiosity turned to fear and shrieks. In between, we forgot about the willow switches our parents cut. Back then, our parents believed more in willow switches than time-outs.

Katy had grudgingly allowed Trucker and Miss Molly free run, and I'd set the litter box in the Peach Room, the bedroom I'd be using, their food and water bowls in the Garden Room. They'd both eaten sparingly, interested in re-exploring the house. They'd been at Esprit d'Chene twice before, just after Katy moved in, so Katy had been right to caution me about their habits. But I was determined to keep a close eye on them. Now they lay in the doorway, alert for a rare tossed tidbit of table scraps as Katy returned with a basket of bread and a bowl of *fleur de lis* butter patties in ice. I pigged out until I noticed Katy toying with her salad.

"Sugar, you need to eat. Bet you didn't have breakfast, either."

"No." She leaned back to gaze toward the pool area. She needed time to regroup emotionally from the invasion of a headless corpse and teams of investigators before we got deeper into the subject of Bucky Wilson-Jones, but she couldn't seem to get it out of her mind.

"Do you have any mint julep syrup?" I asked.

She gazed at the clock. Cocktail hour in her world didn't start until at least six p.m., and it was only two. "The syrup's in the refrigerator. I'll get some fresh mint."

Katy wandered out of the Garden Room door to the window box herbs while I stepped over Trucker and Miss Molly. I could see Katy's downcast expression as she snipped mint while I set the syrup on the table and removed frosty highball glasses from the freezer. Did her distress come from the fact that a murder had been committed on Esprit d'Chene property, or the possible identity of the corpse?

Katy kept most of her booze at the library bar, but a bottle of bourbon resided in a kitchen cabinet. Jack Daniels Black, nothing else would do for mint juleps. I set the bottle by the glasses and turned, expecting to see Katy with the mint. Instead, she trudged down a brick path to a rose bed, where someone had trampled one of the red roses. She leaned down and gently removed the huge bloom and stem, then laid her nose in the blossom as she gazed toward the other end of the landscaped area, which contained the maze. She dropped onto a concrete bench and buried her face in her hands, shoulders shaking.

I'm not good with crying people. Most of my tears are angry ones after loss of my too-close-to-the-surface temper. I hurried out and sat beside her, slipping an arm around her waist. "Katy, Sugar—"

Katy leaped from the bench and sniffed back her sobs. "I'm fine. Let's get our juleps."

See? I'm just no good with crying people at all.

In the kitchen Katy mixed the juleps. She added far more than a double shot of bourbon to both the glasses, dropped in sprigs of mint and handed me one drink. I started back to our lunch table, but when I sat down, I saw Katy still in the kitchen, half of her julep already gone. Sighing, I took a sip of my drink and grimaced. Now, I love Jack Daniels, but straight, I'd rather have it over ice alone. I added unrefined sugar from the antique container on the table.

Katy finally wandered in and sat across from me. She juggled three glasses and handed me another drink. Her first glass was nearly empty, and she'd fixed two more. She had admitted she hadn't eaten breakfast and barely touched her lunch. Even I knew better than to drink that much bourbon on an empty stomach, and Katy had always been an easy drunk. Still, I was reluctant to chastise. Her emotional trauma buried her bubbly personality, the strain visible on her face. Maybe the drinks would loosen her up. We had things to talk about, the two of us.

"Are you ready to talk?" I asked softly.

"Not yet. Not yet, Alice. We do need to talk, but...not yet." She finished her first drink and immediately started on the second.

"Would you rather talk about Sir Gary?"

"That man!" she fretted, as though he were alive. She took another deep swallow of julep. "I can't decide if I want you to completely banish him or just get him back in line!" Another swallow, and she stared across the table, eyes wide and troubled. "What on earth will we do if he's involved in this murder?"

A tingle of goosebumps crawled over me, and I gazed around. "It's extremely rude to eavesdrop," I said to the room at large.

Katy caught my drift. "Show yourself or have the decency to stay out of a private conversation!"

Sir Gary materialized by a huge potted fern. Face properly subdued, he walked over to stand by Katy. Trucker and Miss Molly eyed him warily, and Trucker growled low. He considered Katy a member of his circle of love, despite her irritation at him at times, and the dog expected mortals or ghosts to pay heed.

"Quite some animal." Sir Gary eyed the dog but didn't mention Miss Molly.

"You need to acknowledge him," I said. "His name is Trucker."

"Ummm? Good dog, Trucker, boy."

Satisfied, Trucker laid his head down, but kept a watchful eye on the ghost.

"The cat's Miss Molly," I said.

"Ah, the Egyptian breed, I see. She has a queenly air."

Miss Molly padded across the room. Traitorously, since she hardly ever tolerates anyone else, she curled around—well, through—Sir Gary's legs and purred. The ghost reached down to stroke her. His hand didn't stir a hair on her back, but Miss Molly accepted the caress and padded back to Trucker.

"I took it upon myself to also search the grounds," Sir Gary said.

"Did you find anything the police missed?" I prodded

He shook his head.

"I thought you weren't interested in this crime investigation, just your own problems," I reminded him.

He shrugged inside his silky shirt. "I assumed you'd be distracted from your true purpose here until we got this bloody mess out of the way."

Katy cringed...and swallowed more bourbon.

"Bloody's just an English expression, Sugar." I glared at Sir Gary. "A curse word."

"I apologize," he said with a slight bow. "But cursing is a male trait. Although I know it offends ladies, who don't share that vice. Or shouldn't."

He and Howard would get along just fine.

He motioned at the chair, which moved back so he could sit. "The tire tracks the bobbies were so interested in look like others I've watched Katy's gardener repair. Sometimes her guests leave rather tipsily—run off the driveway." Sir Gary stared at our drinks and glanced at the clock. At least he could tell time. "I presume you ladies are having some of that somewhat less than delightful *iced* tea?"

"As a matter of fact, it's bourbon." Katy took another defiant swallow.

"Sugar, why don't you rest up? I'll clean up."

Katy hiccupped and didn't bother to excuse herself. "I can't let you do that, Alish. You're my guesht."

Uh oh. "I'm family and friend, also, Sugar. And you've had a horrible day. Let me help you out for once."

She glared at Sir Gary and swallowed more bourbon. "I've had a horrible few weeksh. All my friendsh have 'bandoned me, 'cause of a ghosht who won't behave himshelf! And now somebody killed a man in my home!"

I didn't bother to correct her that the body had been found outside as I walked around to her chair. Taking the wobbling bourbon glass before she dropped it, I rubbed her shoulder gently and urged her to her feet. "Come lie down for a while."

Arm around her waist, I led her out of the Garden Room. Sir Gary watched us leave rather than following, a prudent move on his part, given Katy's and my irritation. Katy didn't need to negotiate the stairwell in her condition, so I led her into the Ladies' Parlor and settled her on a green fainting couch. Covered with an afghan, she stared up teary-eyed, probably from a combination of the bourbon and her emotions.

"Thank you, dear Alish," she said. "Thansh for being here." She snoozed off within the blink of an eye.

I smoothed her hair and started back to the Garden Room. As I left, I heard a hearty snore behind me and smiled. Katy would never admit that she snored—it wasn't lady-like. But I'd spent many nights with her and knew differently. "Snore away, darling," I whispered. "I'm afraid you're going to need it, because the next few days aren't going to be at all pleasant."

CHAPTER 9

Sir Gary stared at Alice's untouched drink. The cat curled on Katy's vacated chair, the dog on his haunches a few feet away. Alice returned but pushed the drink glasses aside and leaned on the table. Sir Gary fought a smile. Katy wasn't here to remind her that elbows on the table were a *faux pas*.

"Do you think they serve highballs on the other side of the light?" he asked. "I do miss a relaxing drink now and then."

"I don't know," Alice replied. "I never asked about beyond the light. I figure I'll know all about it some day. You're ready to make that trip, then?"

"That's why you're here. I have tried, but something blocks the portal."

"Not being able to cross over happens sometimes if you don't take advantage of your first opportunity. Would you care to enlighten me as to your death?"

He ran a finger through the moisture on the untouched drink glass. His finger just passed through. "I really cannot remember the actual happening. I recall the passageway, and knowing I had a choice whether to go or stay. However, I was extremely angry about something left unfinished. I wanted that done and over with before I continued." He leaned back and shook his head. "You cannot possibly know how many times I have regretted that decision."

He watched Alice closely to see if his story stirred sympathy. Most women—men, too—ran to beat the blue blazes when he visualized. Only Katy had been different. Had he been mortal, he and Katy would be a good match. She attracted him from his first glimpse. All that femininity packed into a petite, lush body. Perky breasts, long, slim legs, and buttocks the right size for a man's hands...

Alice broke into his musings. "Do you remember who you were with prior to dying?"

He drummed his fingers silently on the table. "Yes. Earlier that day. My lover."

"As opposed to your wife?" She flashed him a disgusted look.

He shifted and recrossed his legs. "You see, my wife and I didn't get along at all, and—"

"Don't give me that bullshit! That excuse is older than you are, and I'm not interested in justifications for adultery!" He tried to appear suitably chastised as she blew out a breath and continued, "You said it was murder, but undeliberate murder."

"Somehow I know that, but not the actual circumstances."

"I'll have to learn more about your life to see if we can figure it out. Especially the last few months. What you were doing. Where you were. Who your friends were." Reconsidering, she added, "Probably about your marriage, also, much as I hate to have to sit through that. But there's an excellent possibility your wife found out about your...shall we say, *indiscretions*?"

"My wife could not have been involved," he said softly. "She was injured in a riding accident shortly after we were married. It left her unable to walk."

"Oh." She studied his face, obviously searching for the possibility he was lying. He wasn't. He met her gaze direct, not caring if she discerned the lingering, shadowed pain he felt. The dog whined and moved closer, and Sir Gary stroked his head. Alice nodded, so maybe she filed that part of his story under truth in her mind.

"Well, then..."

"The accident was my fault."

He wanted to unload further, but Alice fidgeted. Possibly, like him, she didn't know what to say in situations where someone revealed abiding guilt. His wife still lived in his mind, although logically she followed him into death long ago. But his guilt was as fresh as his pain.

"I'm sorry," Alice interrupted when he started to speak again. "I can't spend all my time with you. We'll have to set aside a time to talk when I'm not busy with Katy or my writing."

Irritated, he stifled the urge to glare down his nose, not used to being delegated second place. But she might re-file the story about his wife under "consider," thinking him a good actor.

She shoved her chair back and rose before he could wheedle her into changing her mind. "I'll give you an hour this evening in the library. Say after dinner, around eight o'clock. I don't want Katy involved. Talk of mysterious death isn't something she needs to hear right now."

She swept toward the door with a haughty look that would have done the Queen proud, then paused. His loneliness abated and he eagerly leaned forward, waiting for her to return. But she only frowned and said, "Gary seems a strange name for a former English aristocrat."

He dropped his eyes. As they said in this time, he didn't want to go there.

"Well?" she prodded.

"I was the second son," he explained, hoping to leave it at that.

"So?"

"My older brother received our father's first name. James." He glanced up to see her staring unwaveringly at him and sighed. "From what I understand, my mother demanded the right to name me. Unfortunately, her father's name was Garfield."

Alice giggled, and he straightened in his chair. "I emigrated to the New World after my time in The Tower, and lived near Boston with that blasted name all my life. As you're well aware, from what I read in your books, some of us in this state can travel around until we find an abode we enjoy. I eventually found my way here to Esprit d'Chene via a convoluted trip through New Orleans. I never visualized to your dear Aunt Emmajean during my tenure, but I watched that television late at night when she slept. Once I saw this wonderful movie called *High Noon*, with this marvelous Gary Cooper in the starring role."

Alice studied him for a second longer. "So you changed your name," she mused. "Garfield, Gary." Then she nodded and conceded, "You do look more like Gary than Garfield." Her giggles lingered as she continued through the kitchen. The dog and cat paraded after her.

Humph. She could have left one of them behind for company. His lips thinned. Obviously, Alice had her priorities mixed. Too bad he'd overcome the urge to run that dastardly Bucky off the first time he laid eyes on him. Then the bloody fool wouldn't have been murdered here, glitching his well-laid plans!

No help for it. This damn murder had to be put to rest.

My luggage was already in the Peach Room, the loveliest room next to the Master and Mistress Suites. Those two, as the names suggest, were for the lord and lady of the manor house. Married couples back when the plantations were built seldom shared a bedroom. They each had their own domain, meeting in bed only to procure the all-important heirs. Society considered ladies too genteel to have their rest disturbed when husbands had to work late. Personally, I'd decided this was a male dictum, a need for privacy and chance for indiscretions. But our family lore indicated Grandmere Alicia shared the Master Suite with Grandpere Jean out of love, not duty. In her day, the Mistress Suite became a nursery, her children close instead of on the third floor, which held rooms for the servants and a nursery/school room. Other married couples over the years, though, took advantage of the separate accommodations.

A double set of cushion-lined bay windows allowed a view into the back yard. Satin peach drapes framed the windows, hems pooled four inches on the glossy hardwood floor. The overlong drape length was one of those understatements of plantation wealth—a visible announcement of financial security by a disregard for the cost of the material.

Miss Molly jumped onto a bay window seat, and Trucker settled just below her. I stroked the cat and reacquainted myself with the view. You could see the maze, and this was how our parents learned of our mischievous treks into that convolution. Whoever stayed in the Peach Room during a visit had a bird's eye view of our antics, and some parents delighted in tattling on the unruly behavior of children not their own.

The décor in this room soothed the soul. A gilded coal bucket of magnolia branches set in the gray marble fireplace until weather chilled enough to justify a fire. A muted blue and peach tone Persian rug covered the floor to within a foot of either wall, and a lady's boudoir desk with a delicate chair set between the bay windows. My favorite piece, a cherry-wood sleigh bed, set against the far wall, white crocheted bedspread and pillow shams highlighted by peach and blue throw pillows. You had to climb onto the high mattress with the help of a needlepoint-covered stool and scoot into position. I sometimes sprawled and wiggled my way into a comfortable position on the firm mattress, heedless of the old-fashioned, squawking springs.

With a final stroke to Miss Molly, I smoothed Trucker's head and rose to unpack. Clothing went in cedar-lined wardrobe, another piece of furniture handed down over the years, underwear in the gigantic bureau. Then I grabbed my laptop and the briefcase of files and disks. No time like the present to set up in the library. I was too wound up to nap, and besides, experience with my sleeping habits told me sleep now would interfere with tonight's rest.

Instead, I laid the laptop and briefcase on the bed and curled up beside Miss Molly, gazing past the maze at the huge live oaks bordering the landscaped Esprit d'Chene property. Sir Gary's mysterious, undeliberate murder wasn't the only foul play on my mind. Beyond the live oaks lay acres of fallow fields and woods. Had Jack and his crew combed them for clues? It would be fairly easy for someone well acquainted with Esprit d'Chene to slip up by this route. Duck through the maze, hidden from view since the Peach Room was empty.

Did that mean the murderer was someone Katy knew? Or who also knew which rooms were occupied at any given time? Heavens, surely not a family member! No one stepped forward to claim Esprit d'Chene except Katy after Uncle Clarence put it up for grabs. They all had their own lives, far removed from the isolated Piney Woods, no matter how lovely it was.

Could the murder have been an attempt to make Katy leave? Approaching and leaving by the maze didn't explain the tire tracks, though. And we still had no confirmation of the identity of the corpse. But if it was Bucky Wilson-Jones, I'd have to give the idea careful consideration. That might mean someone else had found out Katy's secret, and I'd been extremely certain only she and I shared that knowledge. Well, Katy, me, and the newly-deceased Bucky.

CHAPTER 10

I entered the library determined to put both mysterious deaths out of my mind and work. A huge room with two walls of bookcases stuffed with everything from priceless first editions and family diaries to modern fiction, I could lose myself in here for hours. And had at times. Another marble fireplace took up one wall and ten-foot-tall windows the other, with a view into the front yard and down the winding driveway. Live oak leaves trembled gently in a soft afternoon breeze, and the sky had clouded over. The horses in the east pasture frolicked in the coolness, and a pair of those dastardly peacocks strutted along the fence.

Miss Molly and Trucker chose to stay behind. They probably noticed my laptop and knew I wouldn't pay any attention to them while buried in writing. They'd sneak out and explore, but Trucker might need out. If nothing else, he'd follow my scent to the library.

I set the laptop up and opened my briefcase just far enough to retrieve the backup disk case. The desk was huge and beautiful. Grandpere Jean had ordered it from a master craftsman in Kentucky. It had been shipped down the Mississippi River to New Orleans, then up through the various rivers and bayous to Jefferson. In the Men's Parlor, he also had a bar from the same craftsman, a beautiful mahogany piece with carved horses' heads so lifelike you would swear they could neigh. Family lore said he'd actually removed the doorway and rebuilt it to get the bar in.

Pushing everything aside, within a few minutes I was re-reading the last few pages of my novel. Ah, now I remembered where I was going.

Barely two paragraphs later, I stared at the screen, the keyboard silent. Shit! Was Katy capable of killing someone? We never know another person completely. I'd read enough true crime novels to realize that. Ann Rule's meticulous, detailed books kept me both enthralled and shaking my head in sadness and horror at the perpetrators and victims of real-life crimes. Standard motives ran through my head: greed, revenge, power, hatred. Greed shouldn't fit Katy, but I didn't know the details of her finances, except that she always appeared to have plenty of money. Her ex-husband, Brian, supposedly left her well-off, in addition to her various trust funds. Not intentionally on Brian's part. Katy hired a cut-throat female lawyer, who grabbed Brian by the balls and didn't let go until the lawyer had what she considered Katy's due.

It was a rocky marriage. An only child and an orphan for several years by the time she met Brian at twenty-five, Katy was smart enough to know that some men weren't completely charmed by her beauty alone; they also peered inside her purse. Brian came from old money, though, a descendant of the carpetbaggers who infiltrated the South after the War Between the States—Southerners *never* call it the Civil War—and whose family later found they owned oil-soaked land. Katy fell head over heels, but at the behest of family members checked into Brian's finances. I was a bridesmaid at her wedding.

Brian showed his true colors all too soon. He reneged on his assurance that he wanted children, which Katy desired with every fiber of her being. However, Brian wanted Katy for a showcase wife and hostess, not mistress of a family, at least for more years than Katy cared to contemplate. A lawyer, he traveled a lot on business—so he said. As far as I knew, real estate lawyers don't travel much. But then, I don't know that many lawyers, except the one I used when I bought my cabin, and the entertainment attorney my agent consults. Jack's and my divorce attorney was a mutual acquaintance. Scratch greed. Katy couldn't possibly profit financially from Bucky's death. Could she?

Revenge? Katy had reason to desire revenge on Bucky. But would she kill him over that? Not likely, since she and I had taken care of that matter discreetly on our own. Power? I actually laughed. Katy had more power in her little finger than most women in their entire beings. Darn, I'd read too many of my own books! I snapped my mind back to work.

I finished a chapter and got half-way through the next. At first, I'd had my doubts; real-life worries overrode my fictional world. But I'd always also written for escape, and years of discipline worked today, at least for a couple of hours. Then I rose to check on Katy. On the way to the parlor, I wondered why the phone hadn't been ringing off the hook. Murder at Esprit d'Chene had surely made the rumor rounds by now. Small-town gossip spread like wildfire. One of the officers would tell his sweetheart or wife and swear her to secrecy. Sweetheart would just have to tell her best friend, also sworn to secrecy. And so it would go. I detoured to the Great Room and peered across the crime tape, noticing the phone was unplugged. I'd unplugged the library phone when I set up the laptop, so it wouldn't disturb my concentration.

In the parlor, Katy was stirring and moaning, hand across her forehead. She had another phone in the Master Suite, her bedroom, with a separate number she gave only to close confidants. Protective instincts aroused, I hurried up the stairwell to check the messages. Katy's friends could be both catty and insistent, and right now I didn't consider it as a violation of privacy.

On the bedside table set an outdated answering machine beside the phone. Perhaps some former family member had left it behind and Katy hadn't updated. It also had a rather old-fashioned look to it, so maybe Katy kept it for décor purposes. The light blinked the number three, and I pushed the button, keeping an ear out for Katy.

"Katy, child." Uncle Clarence, who owned Esprit d'Chene prior to Katy. "Ah just heard. If you want me to come, call. Ah'll be home 'til 'bout six." *Beep.*

"Katy! Katy, are you there? Oh, darling, I just heard! You must be devastated! Something like this happening on your own dear plantation! Call me, Katy! If I don't hear from you, I'll drop by this evening! I can't let you be alone at a time like this!" I didn't recognize the voice, but I recognized the intrusive, eager attitude of someone who wanted all the juicy details.

Beep. At first, I thought the caller had hung up without leaving a message, and I started to reset the machine. But...I listened more carefully. Someone was breathing, and in the background glasses tinkled. Another sound I couldn't quite make out, then the caller hung up. I hit replay, not making any more sense out of the second sound—a slight click preceding a noise suspiciously like one of Katy's peacocks gearing up for a raucous cry.

Katy's hesitant footsteps ascended the stairs. I had to let her hear the messages, so when she walked in, rubbing her head and face paler than usual, I stayed by the phone.

"Messages, Alice?" she asked. "Oh, my head aches. I need some aspirin. Will you play back the messages while I take some?"

"Sure, Sugar," I said. "There's just a couple."

Katy wandered into the master bath, converted from a former dressing room and now a delightful area with two sinks, a separate shower, and a gigantic whirlpool tub. I rewound the tape to the first message.

"Oh, Uncle Clarence." Katy rummaged around in the medicine chest. "He's probably at the ice house by now, and I'm not about to have him drive over here after he's been drinking." During the second, Katy said, "Irene." I pushed the button before the last message as she confirmed, "She wants all the juicy details. If she comes by, will you say I'm not receiving?"

"Sure." I opened the answering machine and removed the tape. "Katy, the tape's tangled. Do you have another one?"

She walked out of the bathroom, tossing aspirin in her mouth and following with a huge gulp of water. "Drawer beneath the phone. They already have my message on them." She finished the entire glass of water as I replaced the tape. "Heavens, I'm thirsty."

I couldn't resist. "Overindulging dehydrates you."

"I didn't—!" Then she giggled. "Maybe a little."

"Who's Irene?"

She fluttered her hand. "This year's chairlady of the Daughters of the South. I swear, I can't stand that woman."

"Then why's she got your private number?"

"She found out about it and couldn't understand why she didn't have it. Irene's one of those people you'd rather have on your side than against you. Know the type?"

"Definitely." While Katy returned her glass to the bathroom, I slipped the tape into my jeans pocket to give to Jack at the first opportunity. Maybe he could make something out. It could possibly just be a wrong number, but with what had happened, I didn't want to be accused of withholding evidence. It might not be a smart idea anyway.

The phone rang, and I glanced at Katy. She shook her head and indicated for me to answer. "Hello."

"I've been trying to reach you." Jack's voice. "Did you turn all the phones off to write?"

Guiltily, I snapped, "I didn't unplug the one in the Great Room. Someone else did. And Katy's been napping."

"I found this number on Katy's statement from this morning. I need to know when you and Katy can come in."

"Can we do it in the morning? Neither of us really feels like driving to Longview now."

"I'm working out of the Jefferson office for a while," Jack explained. "But morning will do. Uh...you may want to lock the plantation gates tonight, though."

"Don't tell me the media's already on our tail!"

"Yeah," Jack confirmed. "The senator flew into Shreveport, and we're expecting him here any minute."

I gulped. "Then...you've identified the body?"

"Yeah," he repeated.

"Bucky," I barely breathed.

Another "Yeah," and he added, "I'll tell you more tomorrow."

Call-waiting beeped, but I ignored it. "I'll lock the main gate, but there's no gate on the back lane."

"There is now." Sue Ann Purdy stood at the bedroom door, hands on slender hips of a six-foot body and a protective glare on her chocolate face. "Gabe's with me and I had him lock one of his log chains 'crost it. And I already locked the front gate."

"Alice?" Jack said.

"Sue Ann's here, Jack, and she's taken care of both gates. We'll see you in the morning around nine or so."

"Call my cell phone if anything at all bothers you tonight," Jack ordered. "I'll be sendin' Officer Franklin to relieve O'Neil around ten, so you'll have to open the gate for him. But no one else. And turn your phones back on!"

"Gotcha," I agreed. "'Bye."

"Alice?"

"Yes?"

"I don't want to scare you, but keep in mind that there's still a killer on the loose. I'd come over and stay, but there's stuff I need to take care of."

"You mean, in case I decide to leave the phones off and go off into my own world and work on my book?" I gritted. "There's a cop on the grounds, and I imagine Sue Ann will keep Gabe here. Plus we've got Trucker. How much more protection do we need?" I didn't think it prudent to mention that Sir Gary would also be prowling the grounds, and he'd probably be as much protection as the entire rest of the crew.

"If I knew who we were lookin' for," Jack said seriously, "I might be able to answer that. Y'all just take care, hear?"

"I will," I relented.

He hung up, and I looked around for Katy. She was enclosed in Sue Ann's comforting embrace, and a strong desire to race across the room and ask the tall black lady to hold me, also, consumed me. But I stiff-upper-lipped.

"Me'n Gabe are both stayin'," Sue Ann corroborated. "Long's we're needed."

"Thank you," Katy whispered.

"Me, too—" I began, then stared past them in horror. Lucky for Katy's and Sue Ann's sanity, they headed for the bathroom, Sue Ann murmuring for Katy to take a bubble bath.

"I'll bring you up some supper on a tray, Miss Katy," the housekeeper said.

And I raced out of the bedroom, into the hallway.

Nothing. Maybe I'd imagined it. God, I hoped so. But it made sense that a second ghost now prowled Esprit d'Chene.

CHAPTER II

Hightailing it down the stairwell, I sharply scrutinized every nook and cranny and tuned into my psychic senses. No other-dimensional entity made contact, not even Sir Gary. In the library, I caught my breath and tried to think. I'd never dealt with a *recent* ghost; they'd all been dead for years. Some of my ghosthunting friends had handled frantic calls from residents of a scene where a recent death had occurred, but I'd never been that lucky—or unlucky, considering the tales I'd heard about dealing with a confused newly-departed. Newly-dead ghosts were unsure of themselves, befuddled—and dangerous. Some didn't even know whether they were dead or alive—or half of each, which made sense to a ghosthunter but not to the deceased.

Inexperience demanded I call in a heavy-hitter; someone trustworthy, who'd been at this ghost business a lot longer. Once she'd been called to a friend's residence. While the friend was on vacation, a prisoner escaped and holed up in the house. Police officers shot and killed the escapee when he came out, the deer rifle from the well-stocked gun case inside blazing. Seemed he would rather die immediately than return for trial and a possible seat on death row.

But when the owner returned, the prisoner's ghost stirred up havoc before he even got in the door. Ongoing havoc: books, lamps, a chair, and even kitchen knives thrown at him. He got a glimpse of his shotgun lifting off the gun case rack just before he withdrew with all due haste and called for help from the one person he knew who had a chance against the entity.

Aunt Twila reasoned with the unhappy ghost for several hours. The key came when the ghost insisted he'd been wrongfully charged with murder and found a receptive ear. Twila convinced him that he was prolonging his punishment by staying on this side of the veil, and that since he was innocent, he'd be much happier enjoying his after-life on the other side of the light.

I punched in all eleven numbers on the phone before realizing there was no dial tone. "Crap!" I grabbed my cell phone from the briefcase instead of reconnecting Katy's phone. Agitation made it impossible to stick that little plastic do-hickey into the hole with the phone jack down on the floor baseboard. Besides, crouching down would leave my back-side unprotected, and the glimpse I'd had in the hallway lingered. I sure as hell didn't want that evil-looking entity materializing anywhere near me without my knowledge.

"Hello, Alice." Caller ID, not Twila's psychic abilities.

"I need you! Urgently."

"At Esprit d'Chene," she said. Now *that* was her psychic ability work-ing, since she certainly couldn't identify where I was calling from by my cell phone number. "But why me?"

"Early this morning, Katy found a corpse in her pool," I whispered. "Someone cut off the man's head with Grandpere Jean's sword." Sue Anne's footsteps—heavier than Katy's dainty ones—sounded on the stairwell, and I glanced over my shoulder. "The murdered man's ghost is roaming around. And...he's headless."

"Hmmm," Twila mused as Sue Ann passed by the library door toward the kitchen. "Looking for his head, I suppose. He could be dangerous in that mode."

"What should I do until you get here?"

"Keep away from him!" she stated emphatically.

"Oh, sure. How the hell can I hide from a ghost? Or keep him away from the other people here? Katy's out of sea salt, and I only brought one canister. This house is huge!"

"Good point," she reflected. "Use white light, the sea salt you do have, and...uh...do you by any chance have any asafetida?"

My nose wrinkled. "As a matter of fact, Granny gave me a kernel before I left."

"Break it into enough pieces for everyone. That should work until I arrive."

"For Sue Ann and Gabe. But can you see Katy walking around smelling like asafetida?"

"She *has* to do it," Twila insisted. "I'll bring some quince seed and soap, since I don't imagine you have any of that."

"No," I confirmed. "And..." I bit my lip, debating whether or not to discuss my other worry. But she'd pick up on it anyway, so I went on, "Katy could be a suspect in this murder."

"True," Twila agreed. "So you'll need to make sure the police do a proper investigation, not just blame their first suspect and go on to some other crime."

"Jack's in charge."

"Good—my God, what's happening?" Her voice dropped, hushed and apprehensive.

"Nothing." But before my frantic gaze could search the room, the commotion broke loose. Darn, Twila was so much more experienced!

Something crashed, then Sue Ann screamed, "God damn you, dog!"

A second later, preceded by frenzied howls and growls, Trucker raced into the library. Miss Molly right behind him. Scattering the throw rugs in his path, Trucker skidded across the hardwood floor and bumped into the desk, his weight trembling even that staid old piece of furniture. Miss Molly whirled at the doorway, arched her back, and hissed.

"It's Bucky," I whimpered to Twila.

"Yes, I'm getting that name," she reflected—all too damned calm, cool, and collected on her end of the phone, a thousand miles away from the disturbance. "I suggest you dig out everything you can think of in the

86

protective vein, including several layers of white light. The soonest I can get there will be tomorrow. I'll have to check the flights."

I calmed down a little, knowing professional help was on the way. "Jack's ordered me to stay here and be available for the murder investigation," I explained as I stroked Trucker's head but roved my gaze around, watching, seeking. "But I don't care whether you can get here faster by coming to Shreveport or Dallas. Let me know which. If I don't answer, leave a message on my cell phone voice mail. I'll meet your plane wherever."

"Will do. I should know something in fifteen minutes or so."

She hung up, and I replaced the cell phone in the briefcase before inching across the library floor. Miss Molly still sat at the door, but at least she'd stopped hissing. As I approached, she padded past me and sat by Trucker, who leaned against the desk as though drawing comfort from the wood after I abandoned him. I peered left down the hallway. Then right—and screeched and clutched the doorjamb. Sue Ann blinked deep brown eyes and shook her head. My cheeks flushed when I realized she held a broom, not a sword.

"What's the matter you?" she asked. "I was comin' to tell you that dog of yours broke Miss Katy's crystal bowl when he bumped his big hind end into the kitchen table. I'm gonna clean it up, but I'm fixin' to keep the kitchen door shut. Don't like no animals in my kitchen."

"I'm sorry," I said, relief overcoming hysteria. "But you can't shut the door. Trucker needs free rein. We're depending on him as a watch dog until they catch the killer."

"Oh." Sue Anne stared at my trembling watchdog. "If you say so, guess I can tolerate him. He eat scraps? Mebbe he wouldn't be so hyper, he had a full belly."

"I give him scraps now and then," I said inattentively as my eyes roamed and probed for a trace of the headless ghost—who was no doubt the reason for Miss Molly's and Trucker's agitation. "But strictly limited. His bowels get runny if I don't regiment his diet."

Her nose wrinkled as though she'd caught a whiff of the asafetida in my briefcase.

"Sue Ann? Do you believe in ghosts?"

Her hand flew to a leather thong on her throat. "H-haints? You betcha." She tugged on the thong, and a flowered hanky emerged from her bodice. "Me an' Gabe always keep the *gris-gris* bags we got from Gabe's gramma with us— 'specially when we're workin' in one of these old houses. Lots of folks done come through here. And some ain't in no hurry to move on."

"Let me give you some asafetida to add to your *gris-gris* bag."

She shook her head. "Gabe's gramma told us not to mix our charms."

"All right," I conceded, knowing the power of *gris-gris* from research. "But promise me that if your *gris-gris* bags don't keep all of the...departed entities away—"

"They will," she said with a grim nod.

"Well, if they don't, will you let me know?"

"I can do that. Miss Katy tells me that you're one of them folks like Gabe's gramma. Them who can talk to those that's gone on. You seen any ghosts around here?"

"Maybe," I hedged. "But just let me know if *you* do."

Sue Ann headed back toward the kitchen. Indecisive, I wondered whether to pursue finding Bucky or try to contact Sir Gary and see if he'd run across his companion yet. Bucky Wilson-Jones, Senator John Wilson-Jones's second son, was now a disembodied, confused ghost, an entity in need of control. On top of that, when the police released information as to his identity, even more hell would break loose in both the media and among the locals.

I'd met John Wilson-Jones a few times, at parties among our relatives in New Orleans and once at Esprit d'Chene, since he traveled the same social circles as Katy. A stereotypical politician, always "on," always on the lookout for someone whom he could glad-hand favors with. Not that he hadn't done a lot for Texas, but ever alert for whatever faction of his political supporters could benefit his career in return. Bucky had been the one fly in the ointment of the senator's career, but he handled that by not hiding the fact he had a black-sheep son. Rather, he acknowledged Bucky as a blight and concentrated on his older son Jeremiah's accomplishments, which gained him sympathy and many of his constituents' votes. Rather like President Carter and his brother Billy. Personally, both Katy and I sympathized with John's plight.

Trucker yipped. Well, one decision made. Sir Gary stood beside the desk, stroking Trucker's head. "It's nearly eight," he reminded me.

"It's only seven," I corrected. "You must still be on Boston time."

He frowned, pulled out a shiny gold pocket watch from his trouser pocket, and clicked the boar's head cover open. Amazed that his watch still kept time, I explained, "There are different time zones in the U.S. these days. Boston's an hour ahead of Texas."

"How can that be? Why would people want the time to be different?"

"It's a long story. And I hate to have to do this to you, but I really don't think I'm going to have time to talk to you tonight. At least, not about—"

"We have an appointment," Sir Gary snapped. "I honored your wish to work on your novel. Now it is your turn to keep your part of our bargain and—"

"We don't have a bargain! I came here for Katy, not you! Given your shenanigans, I was afraid she'd do something foolish and try to run you off on her own. And let me tell you something, *Sir* Garfield/Gary Gavin! It might take me a while, but I can force you out of Esprit d'Chene and keep you away for good if I want. You can wander around all by your lonesome until you find someone else to bug. How do you like them apples?"

Them apples were something he evidently thought he should gnaw on, because he evaded my glower and stared out the window into the front yard. "I see. If you do, how will I ever find my way on my own?"

I waved a nonchalant hand, although that stab of sympathy for him jabbed me. "You'll probably run across some other ghosthunter somewhere. There are quite a few of us around."

"I don't want someone else, I want you." He gazed at me, this time sincerely. "I've read enough to know that you are very knowledgeable in your field."

Flatterers can be like cats—

"There's people better. My Aunt Twila, for instance. She'll be here tomorrow, and she'll have more time for you than I do. Katy and my book have to come first right now."

"Ah, I see." He stuck his thumbs in his belt and rocked back on his heels. "You are all talk, but no show."

—*they lick just a'fore they scratch!*

I closed my eyes to count to ten, but only made it to two. Then I slipped my hand in my briefcase, pulled Granny's asafetida bag out, and removed it from the sandwich bag. Dangled it on the end of the thong and thrust it out as I stomped toward him. Trucker and Miss Molly scrambled to the far side of the desk to escape the smell. Sir Gary threw up his hands in horror and backed towards the window.

"All right, all right!" he shouted. "We'll do this your way! Please, put that away! What the bloody hell is it, anyway?"

Relenting, I dropped my arm and stared at the asafetida, bemused. I hadn't used it before, but Granny—and Twila—evidently knew its force. Much stronger than sea salt!

"What it is, is something you don't want to experience again," I said. "So you better mind me! Besides, Bucky's roaming around here now, too. Go scout him out."

When I looked back at the window, Sir Gary was nowhere in sight. But he thrust one last message into my mind. *I will keep my place, and see what I can find out about this Bucky person. But do not forget that I need your help, too!*

I'll remember, I mentally telegraphed.

And I just might have an idea that can help clear up this bloody murder, he thrust. *If you see fit to honor our next appointment!*

Intrigued, I briefly contemplated allowing him back. But the ghost had tried to manipulate me too often. His supposed idea was quite possibly just another ploy for attention.

"We'll talk tomorrow," I said aloud, and an exasperated "harrumph" answered. Anger fading, I replaced the asafetida in the bag, sat in the desk chair, elbows propped, face buried in cupped hands. Trucker whined and nudged my thigh, and Miss Molly scattered disks and strew papers when she leaped on the desk.

"What on earth are we into?" I stroked them both. Neither answered. "A murder, a demanding, claustrophobic ghost, and a headless ghost. Not to mention that it's looking more and more like I'll have to ask for an extension on my novel." Overwhelmed with worry, including whether or not to contact a friend to recommend a good attorney for Katy instead of waiting on Jack's advice, my eyes clouded. Furiously, I wiped the tears away. Nope, Alice Carpenter didn't go down that road. Not at all.

But— "Oh, Twila, hurry up."

As though in answer, my cell phone rang. I grabbed it. "Twila?"

"I'll be in Dallas tomorrow afternoon at four. American 2011."

"I'll be there."

"If Jack insists you hang around, I'll rent a car."

"I'll be there," I repeated. "If it turns out you need a car while you're here, Katy has at least three in her garage."

"Fine. Glad the asafetida worked."

She hung up, me in awe of her power. She'd zoned into the situation here, a thousand miles away, to keep an eye on it. We'd always had that link between us—known when some disaster or heartrending circumstance called for a phone call or visit. Never was that link between us more important and welcome than right now.

Mindful of Jack's orders, and asafetida sandwich bag in hand, I crouched to plug in the phone. Then I opened the bag again and broke the asafetida in two.

* * *

Hands deep in trouser pockets and head bowed, Sir Gary slouched down the second floor hallway. Alice couldn't really mean what she'd said to that aunt of hers, could she? Why would anyone think Katy a suspect? Not his Katy, the first friend he'd found since his death. The person who'd led him to Alice—even though Alice wasn't fulfilling her responsibilities!

Petite, tiny Katy couldn't kill someone, especially in such a dastardly manner. Not that women weren't capable of violence; he'd seen a few murderesses over time. Should Katy ever explode to the brink of blood-shed, however, he would imagine her performing the deed in a less violent and messy manner—perhaps a knitting needle in the eye or a shove down a steep stairwell. Anything that would keep her always-proper attire spotless.

But...Katy had been on her own for quite some time while he watched television. She knew as much as he did about the sword—fine-honed blade, balanced precision. She'd been dressed differently in the kitchen—a cover-up outfit over her bikini. Had she changed to swim, or donned the cover-up due to blood spatters?

There was no way to tell how long Bucky had been dead, given the water he floated in, filled with blood from his severed vessels. Perhaps that medical examiner would know more later. And the head...he couldn't picture Katy picking up that gruesome object to hide. No! He would *not* believe that of his Katy. Still, some buried memory tried to surface...some other woman...something similarly unbelievable...

The memory floated away, and he shook his head. The bobbies weren't getting anywhere. True, they'd finally identified the body, but it didn't appear they were any closer to unmasking the perpetrator nearly eighteen hours after the body was discovered. And Alice had evidently seen Bucky, sensed him at least. So the man...ghost...shared Sir Gary's dimension. He had to question him. How? Could he speak with a head-less entity?

That idea he'd been prepared to tell Alice, had she not been so snotty, had merit. Who but someone like him, with experience in this business of being a ghost, would come up with the perfect inspiration? With a jaunty stride, Sir Gary dissolved through the Peach Room door.

CHAPTER 12

T ime to talk to Katy, ready or not. I'd barely started up the stairwell before the faint sound of a blaring horn floated in. *Must be somebody down by the gate.* Well, they could blow their horn elsewhere. I wasn't driving down there. The policeman on guard would investigate.

Katy lay in bed, staring in the open drawer of her nightstand. She shushed me with a finger, reached in the drawer, and pulled out what at first I took to be a cell phone. The horn sound blared clearer when she handed it to me. "The intercom to the front gate," she whispered. "You answer it. Please."

"I didn't even know you'd installed an intercom," I muttered. The button labeled "Transmit" gave under my thumb and I spoke into the tiny, round speaker. "Yes? Who's there?"

"Katy!" a vaguely familiar voice called through static, but at least the horn quit blowing. "Katy, it's Irene! I've come to help!"

"Irene, this is Alice, Katy's cousin. I'm sorry, but she's not receiving this evening."

"You let me talk to Katy! She'll see me!"

I took great satisfaction in retorting, "Katy's not receiving *anyone.*

And there's a police officer on the grounds. I'd suggest you leave before he investigates the ruckus!"

"I know every policeman in this county!" she spat. Damn, she was persistent. "Now, put Katy on right now!"

Katy sighed and reached out, but I shook my head. "I hear you." *Bitch*. "My answer's the same. Katy's not up to visitors."

Irene muttered a disgruntled curse but said, "Will you at least tell her I was here?"

"Yes. And since you're a friend, you can pass the word along that Katy will let people know when she feels like receiving again."

"Anything!" Irene shrilled. "I'll help out any way! Katy has my four phone numbers!"

"Good night, Irene." I clicked off the intercom in the middle of her "Gh—" and laid it back in the drawer, then thought better of it and stuck it in the back pocket of my jeans. "I'll take care of this, Katy. You rest. I promised Jack we'd be at the station tomorrow morning at nine."

"You're a dear, Alice. But first..." She fiddled with the answering machine.

A new message played back. "Payback's hell, bitch." Click.

Damn. The call that I'd ignored while talking to Jack. "Do you know who that was?"

"No. It sounds like someone I've spoken to before, but I can't put a face or name to her." Given the nature of the message, Katy's intonation was far too calm. She yawned. "I'm sorry, Alice. Sue Ann gave me a tranquilizer, and I can hardly keep my eyes open."

"You need to eat," I reminded her. "And from now on, let's leave this answering machine off." I turned off the offending machine, then removed the tape. Drat, at this rate, Wal-Mart for more tapes loomed—if even that everything-in-one-stop store carried outdated technology supplies. "I'll give this tape to Jack. And I'm turning off the ringer on your phone. I'll keep an eye on the Great Room phone answering machine."

I flipped the ringer to "off," then punched star-sixty-nine on the off-chance the caller hadn't blocked the source. The nasal recorded message informed me that I couldn't reach the previous caller that way. Katy's eyes drifted closed, and I touched her arm to get her attention. "Don't you have call filtering on your phone?"

"Ummm, guess not. No caller ID on this one, either. Just on the Great Room phone. People who have this number are supposed to have it."

She started to snooze off, but I shook her shoulder, making a quick decision not to tell her about Bucky...yet. "I talked to Twila a while ago. She's coming in tomorrow to help out with Sir Gary. Until then, she wants us to keep some protection near."

"Whatever," Katy murmured. "I trust Twila." Her eyes snapped open, however, when I pulled the asafetida from my pocket, even though I'd also halved the plastic and wrapped the pieces in it. "Oh, no! I'm not wearing smelly garlic. Sir Gary's a ghost, not a vampire."

"It's not garlic, it's asafetida. Please, Katy."

Stealing myself to expose the fact that Bucky's ghost was roaming the manor house, no matter how that would scare Katy, I sighed in relief when she asked, "Twila said we had to?"

"Yes."

"Would you get my locket out of my jewelry box? The one Uncle Clarence gave me."

I rummaged around in the jewelry box until I found the one she was talking about, shoved the piece of asafetida not on the thong in it, then gave it to Katy. She held her breath and secured the chain around her neck, but the locket contained the smell. Wishing I had a similar one, I patted her arm.

Sue Ann came in without knocking, carrying a tray wafting smells in a wonderful contrast to the asafetida. "Your supper's in the kitchen, Miss Alice," she said, "if you don't mind eating with Gabe. Otherwise, I'll bring you a tray after Miss Katy eats."

The implied caution puzzled me. "I have no problem eating with Gabe, Sue Ann. What would make you think that?"

She just smiled and settled on the bed, placing the tray across Katy's stomach. My stomach grumbled and I left, detouring to the Peach Room to wash my face. I'd never met Sue Ann's husband, Gabe, I realized, descending the stairwell a moment later. Well, I'm as friendly a person as the next outside the isolated writer's life.

Gabe Purdy might just be the one person impervious to friendly chatter. He was six inches shorter than Sue Ann, but as slim and wiry. He wore bib overalls and a neat plaid shirt, but a stubble of graying beard covered his craggy face. He didn't look up as I entered—only shrugged and continued eating after I said hello. I shrugged, too, which he didn't see, then headed for the bowls and dishes on the counter. Yum. Gumbo, rice, and fried green tomatoes. A bowl of bread pudding with what smelled like lemon sauce, my absolutely favorite dessert. I dished up gumbo over rice and laid a few of the crusty tomatoes on a plate. Food on the table, I opened the refrigerator, found a pitcher of iced tea, and poured a glass.

"I'm Alice Carpenter." I sat and extended my free hand to Gabe. "Katy's cousin."

Gabe grunted, ignored my hand, and popped the last bite of a sandwich into his mouth. I grimaced. He'd layered his fried green tomatoes between bread. What a waste of delicious delicacies, I mused as he finished off his bread pudding in three bites, then picked up his bowl and silverware. Wandering unhurriedly over to the sink, he clattered them in before he fixed another bowl of bread pudding and carried it through the Garden Room, on out the door.

"Nice evening," I said to the empty chair. "How was your day? Yes, that was a horrible story on the news. Do you think we should vacation in Cancun or the mountains?" Shaking my head at my silliness, I called, "Trucker! Miss Molly?"

They both bounded into the kitchen, evidently over their anxiety about the new ghost prowling the manor house. Maybe Bucky had found his own way into the light, without any help. I sure as hell hoped so, but honestly doubted it. Pets on guard, I spooned up a heap of spicy gumbo and rice, sniffing the welcoming odor, tongue and stomach eagerly anticipating.

The spoon stalled as questions in that ever-questing brain of mine overrode the hunger growls rumbling in my stomach. Why the heck hadn't the cop on the grounds investigated the ruckus at the gate? Maybe he had, but only after I finished talking to Goodnight Irene. Esprit d'Chene grounds were expansive. Still, I would have thought Officer O'Neil would stick close to the house. I'd heard the horn all the way from the gate, so where was he?

It was full dark now, although every security light blazed bright enough to make me wonder how we would sleep. Still, I didn't want to roam around looking for Officer O'Neil while keeping an eye over my shoulder for Bucky. Damn, why hadn't I asked Gabe to check on the cop? The smart thing would be to call Jack and see if the officer had reported in. I pushed the gumbo back and stared at the bread pudding. Reluctantly, I rose and started out through the Garden Room. Trucker whined and shot ahead of me, blocking the door when I reached for it.

"Do you want out?" I opened the door wide enough for him, but he didn't budge—only stared outside and growled low in his throat. I looked past him. Saw nothing unusual. The pool, pool house, yellow crime tape flittering in the night breeze. I'd avoided that area like the plague. The vibes there would curdle my stomach and leave me shaking with the willies, even if I protected myself with white light.

No Officer O'Neil there. No Gabe. Then...in the back yard a crumpled figure lay beside the concrete bench where Katy had cried that afternoon. Overalls and plaid shirt. Gabe! The bowl of bread pudding shattered on the walkway. Someone had attacked him!

I started out the door. Trucker grabbed my jeans-clad leg and hung on. Frantic, I yanked against him before it dawned that he was protecting me. The dog didn't want me out there right now for what he considered a very important reason. Suddenly Trucker let loose of my jeans and pricked his ears toward the kitchen. Faster than he'd ever moved except when he attacked that drunk cowboy, he raced away. Miss Molly stood on my chair, nose reaching for the bread pudding, tongue flicking out.

Trucker hit that chair with a whomp! Miss Molly screeched and sprawled on the floor. The chair clattered over with a crash. And I crashed over the chair to the brick floor, since I was right behind Trucker, my mind racing with implications. No one had attacked Gabe—except maybe some tainted food. Trucker's dash to prevent the cat from tasting my dessert could mean nothing else. Tainted, spoiled...or poisoned! Something was horribly wrong with the food.

There wasn't time to worry about the pain in my hands or the bruises that would show up on my legs tomorrow. I lunged upright and grabbed the bowl of bread pudding. Then dumped it and the pan containing the rest in the sink and covered it securely with a plastic dishpan.

The gumbo! Maybe it, too—ignoring shooting knee pain, I ran back across the kitchen and grabbed that bowl. Slammed it into the sink along with the pudding and checked the crock pot to make sure the lid was secure. Then, screeching louder than Miss Molly, I half-galloped, half-limped out of the kitchen. "Sue Ann! Katy! Don't eat the bread pudding!" Leaning on the welcome assistance of the handrail, I rushed up the stairwell, two steps at a time. "Sue Ann! Damn it, Sue Ann! Answer me! Don't let Katy touch that bread pudding—"

Two pair of confused eyes met mine as I dashed into the bedroom. Sue Ann gaped at me, and Katy groggily held a spoonful of bread pudding a few inches from her mouth.

"Dooon't!" I screamed. "Poison!"

Katy blinked sleepily. Sue Ann gasped. I rushed the frozen pair and slapped the spoon away from Katy's mouth, slung the tray to the floor.

"What in the name of heaven?" Sue Ann asked, stark alarm registering.

"I think someone poisoned the bread pudding," I gasped.

"Where's Gabe?"

"In the Rose Garden. On the ground. Go, while I call Jack." She sped out of the bedroom, and I hollered after her, "Take Trucker outside with you!"

Katy appeared more alert as I grabbed the phone. She stared at the mess on the floor and shook her head. "Gumbo roux will never clean out of my carpet."

Jack answered in mid-ring. "What's wrong?"

"Poison!" I gasped. "Someone poisoned the bread pudding!"

"Where's O'Neil?" he barked.

"I don't know. Gabe's lying on the ground in the Rose Garden. We'll need an ambulance! Hurry, Jack!"

"I'll send the ambulance from here. Stay inside!"

"Don't worry." But I spoke to a dead phone.

Katy scooted up in bed, rubbing her face. "Someone tried to poison us?"

"Get up!" Sheets flung back, I urged her to her feet. "Come wait in the kitchen. I want all of us together."

Katy balked at the foot of the bed to pick up her robe and slide into her slippers. Far be it for Katy Guyedan to leave her room without a robe, even if someone *had* just tried to poison her. I closed the door firmly, not taking a chance that Miss Molly would slip off and find another bowl of pudding before we cleaned that mess up. By the time we got to the kitchen, Katy was even more alert. She headed for the coffee grinder and dumped in some beans.

"Better not," I cautioned. "We need to check all the food."

Katy whirled, dread dawning. "Someone's been in here? In the kitchen?"

"We can't take any chances."

In the Rose Garden, Sue Ann had Gabe on his feet. "Thank God," I murmured as they stumbled up the path. Trucker plodded behind them, protectively on guard, ears up and head swiveling side to side as he sniffed the air. They came into the Garden Room, and I helped Sue Ann sit Gabe on a chair beside the tea table. He leaned forward, clutching his stomach, groans nearly drowning out the ring of the phone in the kitchen.

"I made him vomit," Sue Ann said. "But he needs a doctor fast."

"Jack's got medical help on the way." I started back into the kitchen, then halted and asked Sue Ann, "Did you give Officer O'Neil any food?"

"Yeah," she said. "A few minutes before I fixed Miss Katy's tray. He had some sandwiches with him, and only wanted puddin'."

"God," I murmured.

In the kitchen, Katy hung up the wall phone. "Jack," she said.

"Reminding us that we need to open the gate. Darn, I wish I had some coffee."

"You're doing fine, Sugar." Duly impressed at how she'd overcome her semi-drugged stupor and seemed to be coping—actually helping—I groped in my jeans pocket for the gate opener. But only the answering machine tapes met my seeking fingers. Exasperated, I recalled leaving the gate intercom/opener on the bathroom sink while I washed my face.

"I left the damn gate transmitter in my room," I told Katy. "Oh, no! Where's Miss Molly?"

In a panic, Katy and I searched the kitchen until we found my cat cowering in the pantry. Katy picked her up, and Miss Molly cuddled in her arms, eyeballing Trucker apprehensively. Her huge buddy had never done anything like that before.

"I'm going after the gate opener," I said.

"Take the dog," Katy insisted.

At my finger click, Trucker padded along behind. I stared up that long, winding stairwell. Even with the lights gleaming brightly, I hated to climb it. Even with Trucker. But we needed that gate opener.

Trucker nudged past me. Following in his wake, I kept a cautious eye out, but nothing bothered us. It dawned on me to try to contact Sir Gary, but my psychic powers were in shambles right then. I had a real-dimension problem to handle, and contacting the other side would have to wait. And no matter how I tried to stifle that questing mind, the possibility that the new entity haunting Esprit d'Chene had just tried to poison us wouldn't extinguish. As Sir Gary had reminded me, there were ways...

I inched past Katy's bedroom door, down the hall to the Peach Room. Carefully, I peered inside. Trucker tried to edge past me, but I laid a hand on his neck and ordered, "Stay." He sat, vigilant, a whine in his throat. I hurried across the room, into the bathroom, and grabbed the gate opener from the sink. Back in the bedroom, Sir Gary stood beside Trucker, stroking his head.

"What's going on?" the ghost asked.

"Someone put something in the bread pudding to make us sick. Where've you been?"

He tossed me an irritated look. "Surely you don't think I—?"

"No, damn it. But we can't find Officer O'Neil. I thought you might know where he is."

"A while ago, the housekeeper gave him a bowl of something at the Garden Room door."

"Will you please go look for him? He could be dying."

With a grim nod, Sir Gary dissolved.

CHAPTER 13

Trucker by my side, I handed the gate opener to Katy in the kitchen. When she started to push a button, I shook my head. "Wait until we hear someone at the gate."

"Oh." She laid the transmitter on the table.

I sniffed and smelled coffee. New alarm spread through me and I glared at Katy.

"It was a sealed pack I found in the pantry," she defended herself. "Unopened. I checked the package, and it hadn't been tampered with."

"What about the coffeepot?"

Katy stared across the kitchen, then rushed over and unplugged the coffeepot. Reaching beneath the sink, she pulled out a jug of bleach. I didn't caution her about destroying evidence. By then, I longed for a caffeine jolt myself.

In the Garden Room, Sue Ann knelt in front of Gabe, and I went in to check on him. "How is he, Sue Ann?"

Gabe puked all down the front of Sue Ann's dress. Grimacing, she jerked her apron off and mopped at the mess. "Guess he didn't get it all out in the garden. Where's the ambulance?"

"On the way." I steadied Gabe when he wobbled. "Let's lay him down."

Gabe gagged again as Sue Ann and I scooted him onto the floor and gazed up with bleary eyes. "Thankee."

"So you can talk?" I offered on a half-humorous note.

"When I need to," he agreed.

"Did you see Officer O'Neil anywhere?"

"Didn't have time to look."

"We need to find him and get him pukin' pretty quick, too," Sue Ann put in. "Ain't no tellin' what this stuff is."

Sir Gary blinked into the room, stared at Sue Ann and Gabe, and blinked out. He reappeared out in the Rose Garden, motioning frantically at me.

"Alice, I'm opening the gate," Katy called. "Jack's here."

"Tell him I'm in the Rose Garden!"

"No!" she yelled.

But I was already out the door, Trucker by my side. We hurried to Sir Gary, and the ghost motioned us toward the maze. "Not that I care that much about bobbies," he said as he floated ahead of me, "but he's in fairly bad shape."

"He's in the maze?"

"Perhaps he stumbled in there unaware where he was going. Confused by the poison in his system."

Sir Gary led us in, then left and right through several more turns until I figured I'd need Trucker or him to lead me back out. It had been years since I'd been in the maze, and I doubted very much that I could recall its intricacies. Someone groaned ahead of us, near what I thought was the center of the hedges. I rounded a corner and a blue-uniformed officer lay on the ground. As I raced to his side, he curled into a fetal ball, clutching his stomach.

"Officer O'Neil?" I asked stupidly. Names didn't matter right now.

"Hurts," he gasped. "What's wrong?"

"Have you vomited?" He groaned, and I shook his shoulder and repeated the question.

"No," he finally answered.

"Do it!" I demanded. "Don't hold back. There was something in the pudding."

O'Neil heaved upright. He only made it to his hands and knees, and I steadied him by his shoulders as he weaved back and forth. "Vomit!" I ordered.

He gagged, but nothing came up. He clutched his stomach with one hand and I shook him more violently. "You have to get that stuff out of your stomach!"

O'Neil went limp and fell to the ground again. His eyes fluttered, and I grabbed him by the shirt front. "Up! You have to get that stuff out of your stomach!"

He made it to his hands and knees again, head hanging between his elbows. Nothing else for it. I stuck my finger in his mouth, down his throat. Pulled my hand back an instant before his stomach contents erupted. I held him while he gagged and shook and shuddered. Beside us, Trucker whined, and I glanced over to see him gazing down the path we'd just come up. And heard the shout at the same moment. "Alice! Damn it, where are you?"

"Go get Jack," I ordered Trucker, and he took off. I looked around for Sir Gary, but O'Neil shuddered and collapsed again. He was a big man, but I managed to drag him aside, away from the pool of vomit. Then I saw Sir Gary a few feet away, a sickly look on his face.

"Are you all right?" I asked, half-listening to the voice still calling and Trucker yapping.

"I...ah...don't handle sickness very well," Sir Gary replied. "I'm going now. The other bobbies are here." He disappeared, and sure enough, Trucker led Jack and a paramedic up. The paramedic knelt by O'Neil, and I stumbled into Jack's arms. Damn, they felt good just then.

He held me close, then pushed me away to look at me. "Are you all right, *Chére*?"

Given a sympathetic ear, all my aches and pains hit me at once. Tears clouded, and no matter how hard I tried to hold them back, a couple spilled down my cheeks. My hands burned from sliding on the brick floor. My knee and thigh hurt from falling over the kitchen chair. And tension knotted my back muscles so tightly my lower back ached. I nodded, though I could tell Jack didn't believe me. He pulled me back into his arms, and I snuggled willingly while he talked to the paramedic.

"How's O'Neil?"

"Sick," the paramedic answered. "I can't do much until we know what he ingested."

"I better go get someone with a stretcher," Jack said.

The paramedic glanced up. "Yeah, and a guide to get us out of here."

"I'll come back with the dog," Jack told him. His arm comfortingly around me, Jack started down the path, then halted and turned to the medic. "I don't like leaving you alone."

"Leave Trucker," I said. "I think I can remember how to get out of here."

Jack nodded, and I clicked my fingers to get Trucker's attention. "Stay, boy." He marched over and sat down by the medic. From the medic's face, I wondered if he wasn't more uneasy about the huge dog than he would have been alone.

Despite my insistence that I could find my way, I hesitated at one intersection. Noticing my confusion, Jack pulled a flashlight from the holder on his gunbelt and shone it on the ground. "That way," he said, pointing to some trampled grass. A few seconds later, we emerged.

"I'm all right now, Jack," I said. "Go get your stretcher."

"Not 'til I get you in the house," he said grimly.

Obediently, I walked beside him, my arm securely around his waist as I darted my gaze around. At the Garden Room door, Jack gently shoved me inside. Before he left, he said, "Have Katy look at your hands and put some salve on them."

I only then realized I'd been cradling my right hand against my stomach, curled inward to protect the deep scratches. Both hands had skin seared off on the palms, more deeply on my right, which took the brunt of my weight.

"One, two, three," I heard behind me. Another medic and Sue Ann lifted Gabe onto a stretcher, and the medic rolled Gabe out, Sue Ann behind them. In the kitchen, Katy held a cup of coffee out to me.

"Do you have a first-aid kit first?" I asked, extending my palms.

"Good heavens, Alice," she said. "What happened?"

She thrust the coffee cup onto the counter and opened a cupboard door as I answered, "I fell over the chair. Trying to keep Miss Molly out of the bread pudding. But Trucker got there first. Where is Miss Molly?"

Katy pulled a first-aid kit from a cupboard. "Curled in a basket of towels in the laundry room." She urged me into a chair at the table. "I remembered that you said she always loved to curl in your laundry baskets at home."

"Thanks for taking care of her."

"She's a beautiful cat. Even if she isn't declawed." She opened the first-aid kit and continued as she tended my palms, "I'm going to call a friend in New Orleans and ask him to recommend a guard company."

"Probably a good idea," I agreed. Much as I hated the thought of living in an armed camp, the fact that someone had slipped in here and poisoned the food gave me chills. And I couldn't seem to keep my blasted mind from wandering into areas that should be off-limits except when working on a book. "Katy, how long has Sue Ann been with you?"

Katy's stared at my face. "Why, you know. I hired her when I first moved in. You met her on one of your visits."

"Didn't you have another housekeeper at some point?"

"About six months ago. Sue Ann said she needed some time off. I held her job, and she sent a relative to help out until she came back." Katy gripped my hand so tightly, I pulled it free in pain. "You don't think—?"

"Oh, probably not," I said dismissively. "Surely she wouldn't have served the pudding to her own husband."

"Well..." Katy mused. "The other day they had a huge argument in the Rose Garden. I asked Sue Ann about it, and she said Gabe wanted to dig up the rhododendron bushes in the back corner. That they were too much trouble to take care of in this climate."

"Sounds like a silly thing to fight over."

"Yeah," Jack said from the Garden Room doorway. "To me, too." He strode over, Trucker padding behind him, and glanced at the pink-tinged water on the table. "You in pain?"

"Not that much," I denied, lying to him and me.

Katy squeezed a glob of salve onto her finger. As she rubbed the soothing ointment over my right hand, she said, "Rhododendrons are a branch of the oleander family. Toxic."

Jack jerked his cell phone out and dialed. "When the ambulance gets to the hospital with Gabe Purdy and O'Neil, there'll be some bagged samples with them. Have the lab check for toxicity similar to oleander."

After he disconnected, I said, "I can't believe Sue Ann would do this. I really don't know her, and never met Gabe until tonight. But she was horribly concerned about Gabe. I don't think it was all an act."

"Maybe not," he agreed. "But someone's running around out there, and he...or maybe she, killed Bucky. And made an attempt on the rest of you."

Hands still on mine, Katy caught her breath. "You've identified the body?"

"The senator identified a couple scars. Appendix operation, bite mark from a 'gator."

"An alligator bit him?" I asked.

"He's been known to do some poaching," Katy said as she tidied up the first-aid kit.

I frowned, but didn't ask Katy how many of Bucky's activities she'd kept apprised of. Not with Jack standing there. Jack hadn't missed the comment, though. I caught his body language. But, surprising me, he didn't mention that.

"I heard you say you were gonna check on a security company," he said to Katy. "I've got a friend in New Orleans who runs a top-notch one. I'll have him get some men out here first thing in the mornin'."

Again I stifled my tongue. We'd mentioned that guard company a few moments before I'd realized Jack was at the doorway. He'd obviously been listening a while before he made his presence known. Trying to see if Katy and I would let something slip pertaining to the murder?

The thought reinforced my need to get Katy alone...and find her an attorney.

"Thanks, Jack," Katy said, unaware of Jack's investigative interest. "Tell him price is no object. I want professionals."

"That they'll be. 'Til then, I'm staying here tonight."

My stomach growled, relieved somewhat of its stress and reminding me that it hadn't had anything to eat since lunch. Well, a late lunch, but my belly was already grumpy again. "I don't suppose there's a pizza delivery service anywhere near?"

Jack replied, "Closest thing open this time of night 'round here is a gas station on the freeway."

My stomach growled more insistently, disappointed in that news. Then I remembered Granny's pie. "I'll be right back." I walked out of the kitchen, Jack right behind me. Katy, too. In the hallway, I quirked a questioning eyebrow.

"I don't want you roamin' 'round alone," Jack explained.

"And I'm not staying alone, either," Katy put in.

The three of us continued into the library, where I flung my briefcase open. Then I tossed aside the manila folders in a *voila* motion. There in what I knew was all its sugary glory beneath the aluminum foil was Granny's pecan pie, which I'd stuck in there and forgotten about. Triumphantly, I lifted it out, mouth already watering.

"You didn't have that briefcase locked," Jack said. "Somebody could've gotten to that pie. Tampered with it."

Frustration seized me—and didn't do a damn thing to quell the rumbles in my belly. "No one else knew the pie was there."

"You sure enough about that to risk eatin' it?" Jack asked.

I pulled back the foil and stared at the pie—each individual pecan half-submerged in the rich, luscious filling. Flaky crust, browned just right. All Granny's crusts were made from scratch, and she brushed egg whites around the edges to turn them so crisply brown.

I thrust the pie at Jack. "I'm hungry," I said somewhat petulantly. Well, pretty damned petulantly. "Katy at least got some gumbo this evening. That should mean it's safe. Gabe ate some of that, too. It was the pudding that was tampered with."

"I've got some things in the freezer," Katy offered.

"No," Jack said firmly. "I don't want anybody eatin' anything in this house. Soon as my men get through combin' the grounds, I'll drive you both down to the gas station, and you can pick up enough stuff to get you by 'til tomorrow. I'll want the men to check here in the house, also, so we can leave while they do that."

"Well, we can at least have some coffee." Katy led the way back to the kitchen. "I cleaned the pot with bleach, and besides, I've already had a cup."

"Could've been some evidence in that coffeepot," Jack said under his breath. I tossed him a grim look, though, and he shrugged. "Guess I could use a cup, too."

He laid the pie on the counter as Katy got another coffee cup from the cupboard. She dumped some bleach into it and rinsed it out before she poured Jack a cup. Then dumped the cold cup she'd offered me down the drain and poured each of us a fresh one. I hate black coffee, but I sipped this. I wasn't about to use any of the cream in the refrigerator. I caught Jack staring at me. "What?"

"You were in the maze when I got here."

"So?" I asked, although I knew immediately where he was going.

"How'd you know my officer was in there—clear in the middle of that place?"

I swallowed more coffee, a ploy for time that Jack recognized. For a slim second, I considered telling him the truth—Sir Gary had found the sick officer. At some point, we had to discuss the ghosts, but I preferred to get Jack alone first. His reaction wasn't going to be kind to either Katy or me. Better yet, having Twila here would be the best bet.

"Trucker," I murmured, letting Jack make his own call, assume the dog had led me.

CHAPTER 14

Jack set up shop at the tea table in the Garden Room. For nearly an hour, and two more cups of coffee, his officers periodically reported to him as they canvassed Esprit d'Chene grounds for the second time that day. Just like before, they could find no evidence of a prowler or anything else suspicious. Jack assured Katy they would go over the same area in daylight, but I was skeptical they'd have any better luck then.

And with Jack and his officers so close, Katy and I couldn't discuss anything more important than whether we thought it might rain the next day. In the back of my mind, however, I listened to every word the officers told Jack. Nothing gave any clues as to who the poisoner might be, and Jack grew more and more uneasy. At one point I wondered whether maybe there were actually some similarities between Jack's investigative mind and my creative one after all. We both niggled a problem to death when the solution eluded us.

The logical person to have administered the poison was Sue Ann, of course. Still, with everyone in and out of Esprit d'Chene today, it could have been anyone. I recalled Sue Ann's face when I raced into the bedroom shouting. She'd stared at me as though I'd materialized out of thin air, even though I'd been shouting at the top of my lungs all the way up the stairwell. She hadn't questioned me after I slapped the spoon away from Katy and slung the food tray to the floor. Wouldn't somebody be a little bit confused at first when a person showed up screaming like that and about the food she'd prepared herself? She was either a damned good actress or had instinctively run to her husband, not questioning me. To protect herself from exposure?

I hated being suspicious of each and every person...living or deceased. But I could have ended up writhing on the floor and puking my guts out, too, as well as Miss Molly. She was so small, despite her chubbiness, that she might not have survived even a tiny lick of the pudding. *Curiosity killed the cat.* I spilled coffee as I slammed the cup down and leaped from my chair.

"What's wrong?" Katy asked, a frightened look on her face.

"I want Miss Molly out here with us." I hurried into the laundry room, adjacent to the pantry. Trucker sat guard at the door, and I realized I hadn't been paying any attention to where either one of my pets were for the last hour. Damn it, if I had to, I'd put them on leashes!

The laundry room was dark, and I clicked the light switch. The bulb flashed and burned out. "Katy," I called. "Do you have another light bulb? Or a flashlight?"

Jack appeared at the door beside me and handed me his flashlight, the beam already shining. "What's wrong?"

"Katy left Miss Molly in here, and I don't see her." I panned the flashlight beam around the room. No cat in the laundry basket. No cat on the dryer. Shelves full of cleaning supplies, securely capped, so even if Miss Molly did prowl the shelves and knock one off, she wouldn't end up tasting a pool of toxicity. On one end of the room set an ironing board and iron. Did people actually iron these days? More shelves containing neatly stacked bed linens and blankets securely sealed in plastic, zippered bags. Where was my cat? It would take forever to search.

"Trucker," I called, but Jack pushed on by me and pulled the half-shut dryer door open. He reached in and lifted Miss Molly out, and she yawned and cuddled against his chest.

"Probably gonna have to re-wash the towels in the dryer," Jack said. "Cat hairs."

I reached for my cat, and she settled in my arms. "I should have realized," I murmured. "She always lays on the laundry at home."

As I carried her back to the table, I considered putting at least Miss Molly on her harness and leash. But that was in the Peach Room, and I didn't really want to ask for an escort. Instead, I settled her on my lap and scratched her under the chin to keep her happy. She loves that. Soon her purrs trailed off and she went back to sleep. Katy had already cleaned up the spilled coffee and refilled my cup. My hand shook slightly, sort of like Granny's palsy, as I picked the cup up.

Finally Jack set two of his officers to searching the manor house and gathering up the food—both prepared and frozen—then ushered Katy and me out to his unmarked Longview Police cruiser. Trucker trotted along beside me, and Katy carried Miss Molly. No way would I leave my pets behind, with a poisoner loose and a newly-dead ghost roaming around. I made a mental note, also, to see if the all-night station had any dog and cat food. My pets weren't going to eat anything that came into the manor house with me that morning either!

"Jack," I said as soon as we settled in the car, Katy in front with Miss Molly and me in back with Trucker. "Aunt Twila's arriving in Dallas tomorrow at four p.m. And I don't want any guff out of you when I tell you I'm driving in to pick her up."

Jack glanced in the rearview mirror as he drove down the driveway. I couldn't read much in his face in the dark car, but to my relief, he nodded. "Get right back. And keep your cell phone on."

"I'd planned to check on Granny and my cats, but I can call instead," I compromised.

"It'll be dark by the time y'all get back," Jack reminded me. "I'll have the guards Katy wants in place by then, and probably come by, too, if I can get away."

We didn't talk much more on the way to the gas station, except at one point Katy asked Jack to call the hospital and check on Gabe. He dialed his cell phone, then handed it to her, so he could concentrate on the road.

"Hello," Katy said. "This is Katy Gueydan. I'm calling to check on Gabe Purdy. And the police officer."

Katy listened for a moment, and I stroked Trucker in the back seat. Too bad there wasn't a burger stand open. I'd buy Trucker one of those juicy double-meats he loved. He deserved that and more for all he'd done this night.

Wrong mind trail. My mouth salivated again. I made a mental note to get some hamburger and maybe even a few steaks tomorrow, one for the dog. We'd have to buy out a grocery store somewhere to replenish Katy's kitchen, after we finished our statements in Jefferson and before I headed for Dallas.

Jack was a careful driver, and he knew these country roads, since he'd been traveling them the past two years. He sped along fast enough that anything beyond the edge of the road blurred. Mind stress-tired, I laid my head against the back seat and let it wander away from the day's grisly happenings. The car stopped abruptly and I jerked, realizing I'd been asleep. I glanced through the windshield, where an armadillo ambled across the road. Once it safely reached the other side, Jack drove on.

Stifling a yawn, I said, "Uh...I fell asleep, Katy. How are things at the hospital?"

"Both Gabe and Officer O'Neil are going to be all right. They pumped their stomachs and gave them an antidote. They're keeping them overnight."

"Any lab results back yet?" I asked.

"I didn't think to ask. Should I call back?"

"No," Jack said as he drove into the gas station and pulled up to the pumps. "I'll check later. Might as well fill up while I'm here. You two go on in. I'll keep an eye on the animals."

When we hit the gas station door, I said, "I've got to pee." The coffee was clamoring for release. Someone once said you didn't buy coffee, you just rented it. Come to think of it, they say that about beer, too.

I emerged from the restroom to find that Katy had piled the counter full of various items. The night clerk stared in awe, and at first I thought he was excited about the great sales tally. But he said, "You're Miss Katy, ain't you?"

Katy nodded. The gas station/convenience store was only about ten miles from Esprit d'Chene, and it didn't surprise me that the clerk knew Katy. Everyone in the county probably either knew or had heard of Katy Gueydan, even though she'd only been living there a little more than a year. Katy's the type of person people notice, and who enjoys the notoriety. On the other hand, I enjoy my seclusion. Hmmm. Wonder why Katy and I remained so close, despite our differences, yet that same rift of attitudes helped destroy mine and Jack's marriage? Probably because Katy and I never tried to live together.

Losing interest in what I assumed would be a gushing oratory from the clerk at meeting a local celebrity, I grabbed a bag of dog food and cans of cat food. Miss Molly might turn her nose up at that brand, but she'd eat if she got hungry enough. Trucker would eat just about anything I put in front of him. When I approached the counter, Katy was saying. "Do you remember who it was?"

"Nah, didn't know her," the clerk said. "It was rainin' here yesterday evenin', and she just stuck her head in the door. Had a raincoat on, black one, I think. Could've been blue, wet like that. Kept her umbrella nearly over her face."

"What are you talking about?" I asked.

"Some woman was here yesterday asking how to get to Esprit d'Chene," Katy told me.

I plopped the dog and cat food on the counter. "I'm getting Jack." But I didn't have far to go. I nearly bumped into Jack when he came in the door.

"Jack! Someone was here asking how to get to Katy's yesterday evening. Oh, and I forgot about these." I pulled the tapes out of my jeans pocket and handed them to him—too harried to recall that Katy only knew about one tape.

"You're giving him two tapes, Alice?" Katy asked. I turned to see her staring at me with a quickly-masked glare. "I thought the first tape was just tangled."

"The call I kept from you was probably just a prank," I assured her. "You were pretty shaky. I didn't want to bother you with it, what with your hangov—uh...all the stress you'd had."

"I want to hear that other tape. After all, it came from my answering machine."

"We'll listen to them when we get back," Jack put in. "What's this about someone looking for Katy?"

"She didn't actually ask for Miss Katy," the clerk said. "Just directions to the plantation."

"You got video surveillance?" Jack asked.

"Sometimes." The clerk glanced at a camera mounted on the wall. "If the manager don't forget to change the tapes. The one I changed when I came on this evenin' was from a couple of days ago."

"What was she drivin'?" Jack questioned.

"Donno. She parked over on the side of the buildin', so I didn't see her car."

"Sounds like she was trying to keep anyone from identifying her," I said thoughtfully.

"I'll be back to talk to you tomorrow," Jack told the clerk. "In the meantime..." He pulled a business card from his wallet and a pen from his shirt pocket and wrote a number on the card. "My cell phone number. Call if you remember anything else about the woman."

"Okey-dokey." The clerk stuck the card in his shirt pocket.

Jack took a credit card from his wallet. "Put all this on here. I paid for my gas at the pump."

"No," I said, when Katy just stood there accepting Jack's offer to pay for the groceries. "I'll get the groceries."

"Alice..." Jack began, then shrugged in resignation. "Do it her way."

As the clerk rang up the groceries, Katy wandered away. Trying not to be noticeable, I watched as she went to the candy aisle and picked up a couple off-name-brand bags of candy, a bag of chips, and beef jerky, and some of those two-for-a-buck, usually stale, bags of peanuts. She was so inattentive, she almost appeared to be walking in her sleep. When she returned to the counter and laid the items down, she seemed to wake up, staring at them in confusion.

"When did you start eating junk food?" I asked.

"I...don't. Uh...I'll put this stuff back."

As Katy returned the junk, I dug out a credit card of my own, since I hadn't brought that much cash with me. I'd have to hit an ATM tomorrow.

"Sorry," the clerk said. "We don't take American Express."

"Look," Jack said. "Let me—"

"Do you take debit cards?" I interrupted.

"Yeah, if we can reach your bank this time of night."

I handed him my debit card, and he ran it through the machine. Evidently, the phone lines between Jefferson and Six Gun were working, because after I punched in my code, it came back approved. The clerk bagged the groceries, and I looked at what Katy had bought.

Ugh. Some microwave sandwiches and pizzas. A half-dozen frozen dinners that looked like they were probably freezer-burned. A few cans of stew, the cans so dusty I could see her fingerprints on the tops. At least she'd found some soup, but two of the cans were so dented they looked as though they belonged in a grocery surplus warehouse. The cat food cans looked fresher. Maybe I'd share Miss Molly's food.

The clerk had the groceries bagged before it hit me that Katy hadn't bought any milk or eggs. I'd seen those in a cooler near the cat food. "Katy, you and Jack take these things on out. I'm going to get a—"

"She's already in the car," Jack said. Sure enough, there Katy sat in the front seat of Jack's sedan. Miss Molly peered out the window while Katy stroked her.

"Well, I like that," I muttered. "We're not her servants."

"I don't think she was thinkin' at all," Jack reflected.

"Yeah," the clerk agreed. "It's like she's in some other world. Not what I expected when I got to meet Miss Katy from the manor house."

Jack gathered the groceries, but I stayed behind to pick up some fresher items: the eggs, some bacon—damn the cholesterol—milk, biscuits, cold cuts, and bread. I added a few apples, oranges, and bananas from a basket on the counter. All the while I planned how to jail Katy in her bedroom when we got home to find out what the hell was going on inside her mind.

* * *

I kept my silence on the drive back to Esprit d'Chene, using the time to reexamine my suspicions and get my ducks in a row. Katy had to understand that she couldn't hold back information. I'd have to tell her that she was on the list of suspects.

But Katy escaped me. As soon as we arrived, she jumped out of the car and hurried ahead of us into the manor house with Miss Molly—once again leaving the groceries to Jack and me. By the time we got everything in the kitchen, she wasn't anywhere around. Only Miss Molly sat there, tongue smoothing her ruffled fur. And Mr. Quick, sipping a cup of coffee. He set the cup down with a clatter when Jack walked in.

"Everythin' in the house is clear, Detective. I just made another round."

"Thanks, Franklin. I'll handle the house patrol for the rest of the night."

"Yessir!" He grabbed his coffee cup and carried it through the Garden Room, on outside.

"I've got some calls to make," Jack said.

"I'm in the Peach Room, but you can use any of the other bedrooms, I'm sure. Even if Katy's not around to tell you which ones are made up. There are sheets in the laundry room."

"I'll be staying down here tonight. Franklin's gonna patrol the grounds, and I kept another officer here, too."

"There's nothing really suitable downstairs to sleep on, Jack."

"I won't be sleepin'."

"Well, at least let me fix you some bacon and eggs."

"How 'bout I fix the bacon and eggs, while you get ready for bed?"

"Humph! It's microwave bacon, directions right here on the package. And anyone can scramble eggs."

Jack shook his head and took the package of bacon from me. "Like I said, I'll fix us somethin' to eat. I can make my calls just as well while I'm cookin'."

"You still haven't forgotten those damned scorched breakfast tacos, have you?"

"Seems to me those were microwave tacos, too."

"Well, hell, nobody told me that different microwaves have different settings!"

"It's marked right on the dial. See?" He laid a finger on Katy's fancy microwave. "Defrost. Medium. Reheat. Hi—"

"I'm going to get a shower! I'll be down in a while. Watch Miss Molly for me." I stomped out, glancing around for Trucker. He'd come in with us, but I'd lost him somewhere between there and the kitchen. I peeked in the library—and fear turned me into a statue. I tried to scream, but my vocal cords might as well have been encased in marble, also.

CHAPTER 15

Bucky stumbled around the library in all his undead glory, waving his arms, shirt and bib overalls soaked with blood. He couldn't see where he was going, of course. Being headless will do that to a person. He staggered against a bookshelf, and it surprised me when a few volumes thumped to the floor. He shouldn't have been solid enough to do that, but perhaps the books were ready to fall anyway. I suppose he didn't hear the noise, with no ears, since he ignored it and rambled over to the desk.

Another sound penetrated my senses, although I still couldn't move. It was the pitter-patter of bare feet racing down the stairwell. Katy dashed up beside me in her nightgown. "Sir Gary said—ohmigod!"

I broke my frozen state to clap a hand over her mouth, but she jerked away. "Sir Gary said there was another ghost down here and it might hurt you! I'll get Jack."

She started to rush away, and I grabbed her, nearly tearing her gown off her shoulders. "No," I whispered furiously. "You know Jack doesn't believe in ghosts."

Bucky ambled through the desk, straight at us, and I changed my mind. Especially when Katy shrieked and tore out of my grasp. She raced toward the kitchen, shouting Jack's name. I dodged the ghost and frantically pawed through my pockets until I found the asafetida and removed the plastic. Now what? I wasn't about to approach that thing as close as I did Sir Gary.

Bucky stopped at the doorway, then turned and stumbled toward me. Once again my feet failed me. But not my arm. I screamed and threw the asafetida at him. It went through his chest. He didn't make even a slight noise. Hell, he didn't have a mouth to say anything with. He just cringed and shuddered—at least that's the impression I got from his headless body. Then he flew out through the front windows just as Jack raced into the room, gun drawn.

"What the hell's going on, Alice?"

Katy peeked out from behind Jack's broad shoulders. "I told you, Jack. It was a ghost! The headless man from the pool! Bucky!"

Jack stared around the now-empty room before he reholstered his gun and turned to Katy. He left me standing there shaking, which I sure as hell didn't appreciate.

"Now, look, Katy." He clasped Katy's arms gently. "A lot's happened here today. Why don't you have Alice take you on up and tuck you in bed?"

Katy knocked Jack's hands away and screamed, "It was a ghost! I saw the damn thing, damn it!"

"Katy—"

"Oh, hell. Let Alice explain it to you." She whirled and pitter-patted back up the stairwell, her filmy negligee flying behind her like a bride's veil.

"You still messin' with that blasted ghosthunting?" Jack snarled. "Look what you've got Katy believin' now."

"For your information—" I snarled straight back. Then shut my mouth and stalked across the room to grab the asafetida bag. Then back to the desk, where I gathered my files, disks, and cell phone and jammed them in my briefcase.

"Talk to me, Alice," Jack demanded.

Ignoring him, I unplugged the laptop and left the power cord dangling. I picked up the laptop and briefcase, and silently walked out of the library, toward the stairwell.

"You coming back?" Jack asked in an exasperated voice. "I've got eggs frying."

"Smells to me like they're burning," I tossed over my shoulder. And it did. The smell wafted out of the kitchen door.

Jack raced down the hallway, and I continued on up the stairwell. At Katy's bedroom door, I hesitated and shifted my load to try the doorknob. As I expected, she'd locked the door. The hell with it. Let Sir Gary protect her!

In the Peach Room, just Trucker's butt stuck out from under the bed. I shoved the briefcase and laptop into the wardrobe, then squatted beside him.

"Come on out, boy. I ran Bucky off."

Trucker whined and scooted deeper under the bed. "Shit."

I wanted my cat up here, too, and I'd left her in the kitchen. I tied the asafetida bag on a belt loop, thinking I'd pin it on my nightgown next and sleep with it there. Then changed my mind as I walked back into the hallway amidst the smell. Maybe I'd just hang it from the bedpost and put a pillow over my head. At the top of the stairwell, I smelled air freshener mixed with burned eggs, even over the spoiled garlic odor filtering from my chest. Satisfaction stabbed me at the burned-egg aroma.

"Kitty, kitty! Here, Miss Molly!" Within seconds, she bounded up the stairwell, and I reached for her when she skidded to a stop by my feet. Her claws came out, and she hissed. I hoped it was just at the asafetida, not me—or someone unseen. She raced past me, down the hallway, into the Peach Room. I carefully scanned the shadowy hallway. For damned sure, tomorrow I'd bring my own flashlight in out of my Jeep. I followed Miss Molly, hand securely on the asafetida bag. Bucky could be anywhere by now.

In my bedroom, I slid the bolt on the door in place, not that that would keep Bucky out. But at least it would secure Trucker and Miss Molly in here. I didn't see the cat, and assumed she was under the bed with Trucker. Yep. I could see them when I crouched down. Then I glanced at the clock on the nightstand.

Three a.m. Damn, it felt like a week had passed since this morning, rather than less than a day. Well, it was yesterday morning now. My eyes were grainy from lack of sleep, my stomach grumbling in disgruntled annoyance. But I could stand to lose a few pounds. Lack of sleep, though, would catch up to me sooner or later. I sometimes slept on and off for two days once I finished a deadline hell marathon and Fed Ex picked up my manuscript, only waking long enough to feed and water the animals and let them in or out of the house.

I didn't need to be groggy and inattentive right now. A few hours of sleep were a dire necessity to have the stamina to start what could be a new round of bizarre activities again in the morning, if things kept on like they were. I had no doubt they would. Damn, I wished Twila were already here.

The Peach Room had its own bathroom. Nothing nearly as fancy as the one off the Master Suite, but it was well stocked with fluffy towels, scented soaps, and shampoos. I noticed a white candle on the sink and murmured in a semi-chant, "White candles are for protection against evil spirits," as I searched for matches and found them in a vanity drawer. Candle lit, a pleasant magnolia smell filled the bathroom, nearly, but not quite, overpowering the asafetida.

I hung the asafetida on a shower curtain clasp and stripped. Longing for a soothing bubble bath, I settled for a brief shower, the asafetida bag protecting me from any prying eyes. I did wash my hair, since it tends to hang in oily lanks if I miss that chore more than every other day. After toweling, combing my hair out, and leaving it to dry naturally, I wrapped in another fluffy towel as I went into the bedroom.

The silence in the room was more eerie than soothing tonight. As I took a nightgown out of a drawer—nothing filmy like Katy's, just practical cotton—Trucker and Miss Molly inched out from under the bed. I dropped the towel and slithered into the gown before I stood silently and took a deep breath, held it, and released it, blowing through my mouth.

Continued the stress-relieving action several more times. Tension eased, maybe I could sleep.

I had thought I was too tense to close my eyes, but that was an automatic response to the exercise to relax both my mind and muscles. When I opened my eyes, Miss Molly was curled on the bed, Trucker lying quietly at my feet. I squatted and stroked him. Even scratched his belly when he rolled over and offered it. Probably not as good as Granny, but Trucker enjoyed it.

I tossed the throw pillows to one side and pulled back the bedspread and sheets. A faint floral scent of a sachet Sue Ann must have used in the linen closet greeted me. Crisp, ironed sheets, also. Obviously, Sue Ann put the ironing board in the laundry room to use. The sheets beckoned, and I stepped onto the stool. Then someone—or something—knocked, and a roar erupted from Trucker. He lunged across the room, growling and snarling, and hit the door with enough force to shake it on its hinges. My foot slid from the stool, and I grabbed for the mattress. But bedspread and sheet slid smoothly off, floating and tangling around me as my ass hit the floor.

CHAPTER 16

Miss Molly meowed and clawed her way out of the tangled bedspread and sheets, digging her claws into my legs as she leaped free. I batted the linens off my face, then froze. The damn asafetida bag still hung on the shower hook!

Jack's voice penetrated over Trucker's ferocious clamor. "Shut up, Trucker! It's me! Alice, open up!"

Trucker whined, staring at the door. It took me a few seconds, but I untangled myself and limped across the room, rubbing my aching tailbone. Started to slide the bolt back. Then stopped. I'd known a ghost or two to be a fairly good mimic. "Jack?" I called.

"Yes, Alice," he said in a frustrated voice. "I brought you something to eat."

My stomach rejoiced, but my mind still balked. "What did you bring?"

"Alice, what the hell's wrong with you? Open this door!"

I reached for the bolt again, but my fingers listened more to my mind than my stomach. I couldn't force them to slide the bolt back. "What did you bring?" I repeated.

Despite the heavy oak door between us, I thought I heard his teeth grind. Or maybe that was my psychic senses at work.

"I brought you a bacon sandwich," he gritted.

"What did you put the bacon on?" I asked.

"Bread, damn it! Now open this door, or I'll feed it to Franklin!"

"What sort of bread?" I asked.

"Toast!" he shouted. "You don't like bacon on soft bread!"

Okay. It was Jack. Probably, anyway. Whenever we'd had BLTs for lunch, I always toasted my bread, but he fixed his on bread straight from the loaf. My fingers—and mind—agreed this was proof enough, and I opened the door.

Jack stood there, jaw clenched and exasperation on his face. "What the hell's wrong with you?" he repeated. "You, me, and Katy are the only ones in this house."

I grabbed the two paper-towel-wrapped sandwiches from him before I said, "No. We're just the only three *living* people!" And I slammed the door and secured the bolt again.

For a long, silent period, I stood at the door. It was nearly a minute later before Jack decided whether to pound on the door or leave. He clumped down the hall, footsteps mirroring his anger, audible despite the carpet runner. Since I hadn't heard him approach, his mood was obviously darker than when he arrived with the sandwich peace offering.

Sighing, I limped back to the bed and boosted myself onto the mattress. Re-making the bed could wait until my belly felt like it. I tore one sandwich in fourths, gave Trucker three of them and called Molly onto the mattress to feed her the other fourth on the paper towel. I gobbled the other sandwich, then wished I had something to drink.

I settled for water from the bathroom, carrying the asafetida bag back when I returned and hanging it on the bedpost. Draining the crystal glass, I set it on the nightstand. Only Katy would keep crystal glasses in her bathrooms rather than plastic. Plastic glasses were plebeian. Fighting exhaustion, I picked up my cell phone and dialed Katy's private number.

The beep-beep-beep startled me. Who the heck was Katy talking to this time of night? Would she even tell me? What secret was my cousin keeping?

Katy definitely wasn't herself lately. Initially I'd blamed that on Sir Gary, then the murder, and the murdered man's headless ghost, which she experienced herself this evening. Here I was lurking alone in my room, but at least I had the power of my abilities for protection, as well as my pets for company and added security. Katy was alone, obviously not feeling the need for any protection from the horrible apparition beyond the asafetida in her locket.

Or did her need for privacy for her phone conversation overwhelm her fear?

I slid from the bed and picked up the water glass. Padded barefoot to the door and slid the bolt back. Trucker and Miss Molly wandered over, but I shook my head. "Stay here," I ordered. I glanced back at the bed as they went over to the window seat, obeying me. Uh oh. Hurriedly, I strode over, grabbed the asafetida bag, and hung it around my neck. This time, I opened the door and inched into the hallway.

Nothing either dead or alive waited out there. I closed the door and fumbled for the hallway light switch, wondering why this span of lights, out of all the others at Esprit d'Chene tonight, weren't blazing brightly. The switch clicked, but nothing happened. My own home had dozens of light bulbs that needed periodic changing—lamps, ceiling fan lights, other bulbs overhead and in the appliances, such as my refrigerator and stove hood. Probably Katy just hadn't had Gabe get around to that maintenance lately. I hoped so, anyway.

Still, I called down a triple layer of white light, and on second thought, added the same measure to the pets I'd left behind. Then inched on down the hallway, wishing once again I had my damned flashlight. Nothing bothered me, though, either because nothing was around or due to the protection of the white light and asafetida.

At Katy's bedroom, I laid the glass against the door. I'd read once that sound transmitted through glass. Indeed it did, but not well enough for me to make out the words, only a mumble of agitation in Katy's voice inside the room. The sound moved closer. Evidently she was pacing the room, portable phone in hand. "No," I heard her say. "We can't. Not yet." Then she walked away from the door, and her voice returned to mumble mode.

There are four areas of psychic senses: feeling, intuition, hearing, and vision. All psychics are stronger in one or two of these areas, weaker in the others. My strengths lay in vision and feeling, not hearing or intuition. Thus my ability to see into the other dimension—the ability to see ghosts—but I couldn't necessarily tune into a low-beat conversation. Nor did I experience precognition, as Twila did, which was fine with me. I had no desire to handle that sort of pain. Also, I sometimes ignored my "gut feeling" ability, much to my later sorrow.

Katy possessed a measure of psychic vision ability herself, although as far as I knew she'd never bothered to develop it. She could see Sir Gary, and definitely had seen Bucky earlier. A suspicion that I'd been ignoring one of my "gut" feelings gnawed at me. Now that I'd been slapped in the face with Katy's deceit, I needed to find out what was going on. Especially if it meant protecting my cousin from her own folly.

There are also some ethics involved in psychic powers, and one that Twila and I believed in strongly was that we didn't tune into other people's private thoughts. Read minds, as it were. Besides, as I said, I'd never had much success with the psychic hearing ability feature. Still, I set the glass down, closed my eyes, and touched both index fingers to the clairaudience area just above my ears. Grimly, I focused on the conversation in the room.

Too late. Katy said "goodbye" and hung up the phone.

I grabbed the glass and hurried back toward my room. I doubted Katy would let me in if I knocked, given her penchant for privacy right now. I'd call her again. At my door, I stubbed my toe on something. Reaching for the wall to keep from falling, my hand landed on the light switch. The hallway bloomed with light!

"Damn ghosts," I muttered. They did stuff like that at my house, also, so I didn't think much of it. I was more interested in what I'd tripped over.

Eyes stared back at me. Ohmigod! The head!

But before the shriek left my throat, sense returned. Instead of Bucky's missing head, a doll baby's head lay on the floor. No body, just the head on the edge of the carpet runner. Surely it hadn't been there when Jack came up with the sandwiches. I tried to recall if the hall lights had been on when I opened the door. Yes, I thought they had been, although I'd only had a sneak peak out the door and was more interested in the food. The lights had been off when I came out five minutes ago and hadn't responded to the switch. Now, they did. Maybe to illuminate the doll head for me to find?

Or maybe it was a wig stand? If so, the wig needed drastic attention.

Gingerly, I bent down and touched the head. Rubber. And it looked old, fairly large, not like one of the porcelain-headed dolls people collect. More like something a past-babyhood toddler would drag around. But how had it gotten there? Was someone else, or some*thing* else, leaving clues about the murder?

I picked it up and studied it in the light now chasing away the shadows in the hallway. Wisps of blond hair straggled here and there on the skull, and the eyelids opened and closed as I rocked it back and forth. Blue eyes, and pink-dusted cheeks. A rosebud-pink mouth. Below the chin, a round opening to insert the head onto the body.

I really should take it down to Jack, but I could imagine his reaction. *What the hell's an old baby doll face got to do with this murder? You're trying to make me believe a ghost left a clue.*

A huge yawn stretched through me. I needed some sleep! Opening the door, I carried the head in and propped it on the lady's boudoir desk. I'd give it to Jack in the morning, and let him say what he would, when I had more strength to contradict him.

Re-making the bed took the last bit of my store of strength, and I forwent calling Katy until I could think straighter. Snuggled between the sheets, I whistled and "kitty-kittied" my pets onto the bed. It was only a double-mattress, but I made room for Trucker's bulk. Miss Molly curled in her favorite spot behind my legs.

CHAPTER 17

Jack wasn't anywhere around by the time I stumbled into the
kitchen the next morning around seven a.m., Trucker and Miss
Molly padding behind me. An officer I hadn't met sat at the table,
sipping a cup of coffee. I garbled a greeting in return to his "good morning," and headed straight for the coffeepot. I am *not* a morning person—
not until after my second cup of caffeine. And especially after a lack of
sleep.

"Good dog," the officer said tentatively. I turned from the inviting
coffee aroma. Trucker sat at the kitchen door, ears alert, but he wasn't
growling.

"Sorry, officer. Trucker, it's all right. This is a policeman. Uh...sorry. I
didn't get your name." My hand wandered toward the coffeepot. He was
young, probably mid-twenties, with an open, honest face.

"Sergeant Smith," he answered. "Detective Roucheau left me in
charge when he left for Jefferson about fifteen minutes ago."

"Ouch!"

"You all right, ma'am?"

"Fine, *sir*," I semi-snarled. "I touched the coffeepot, and it's hot."

"I just made it, ma'am," he said reasonably.

I poured coffee into one of the foam cups on the counter, wondering where they'd come from but not caring right then. Flavored creamer was stacked in a bowl of ice beside the pot. I dumped in three containers of chocolate amaretto.

"Look, Smith," I said after a sip of coffee. "I'll make you a deal. I won't call you Smitty if you don't call me ma'am."

"My friends call me Smitty. But point taken about the ma'am. Don't tell my mama, though. She raised me to call all women ma'am."

"It makes me feel old," I said between slurps.

"Can't see why," he mused. "You can't be more than a couple years older than me. And I'm twenty-five."

His compliment jolted me better than the coffee. I actually smiled at him and said, "Thank you," not bothering to mention the huge discrepancy in his guess. "And me without even my hair combed yet."

He grinned back at me, then picked up a book I hadn't noticed until then on the table. "Hope you don't mind, but I was passing time in between rounds and noticed your books in the Great Room. Been reading this one. Doubt anyone could miss who you were, ma'—Miz Carpenter, with this picture on the back."

Nobody but Officer Quick, I thought, but wandered over to sit down with him. "You have good taste in reading material," I purred.

"Yeah. Well, I'm still learning about investigative techniques. I plan to take the detective exam some day. And mysteries and true crime novels have a lot of information in them. You writers must do a lot of research."

"We do," I agreed. "And we get lots of information from policemen. By the way—"

Trucker nudged me, and I nearly spilled my precious coffee. I knew what he wanted. Out. That meant I had to go with him, especially with other officers on the grounds whom he hadn't met. There would also be the guards Katy was hiring to introduce him to later on. Sighing, I carried my coffee towards the Garden Room. "Come on, Trucker."

He bounded after me. I nearly closed the door on Miss Molly, but she slipped through. They both headed off into the dew-wet grass, and I strolled down a path to sit on one of the concrete benches. Forgot it, too, was dew-soaked and stood up immediately, the seat of both my gown and robe wet. Shoot, that spot of the bench was dry now, so I sat back down.

Morning mist shrouded the rose bushes, trellises, and tree trunks. It lingered later and heavier in the shorter, cooler autumn days. Overhead, though, the puffy-cloud, blue sky gave promise of a beautiful day. Football weather, East Texans like to call it. I enjoyed the game on TV once in a while, though I have no desire to wade through crowds to watch it live in a packed stadium. Maybe it was the uniforms. You saw them—and the cute butts—better on TV.

The first view I'd had of Jack was his jeans-clad, firm buttocks as he bent over a bare-breasted blonde who'd tripped over her own feet on Bourbon Street one Mardi Gras evening. I think what impressed me the most was that Jack only lifted Blondie up and wandered off, not paying that much attention to the firm 38Cs peeping out from a slew of beads. Well, not *that* much attention, anyway. After all, he is a man.

I didn't know he was a cop. But my friend Leslie called his name, and he strolled over to us. Seems Les knew Jack from one of her frequent book signings in the area, where he bought her books as presents for his mother, who passed on a year after we met.

The three of us spent the evening together, drinking hurricanes and beer and gazing at the outlandish sights on Bourbon Street. Laughing at them, too, rather than sneering, like some of the out-of-town tourist trade. Despite the rumors of sordidness and crime mixed in with the gaiety of Carnival, I've always enjoyed it. Mainly the drunks are happy drunks, and I relished an opportunity to let my hair down along with them after periodic bouts of solitude while I wrote.

Jack and I got to know each other over the course of our fun. When he asked me for my phone number as we searched for a cab to head home, I gave it willingly. I'd rented an apartment for a few months on St. Charles Avenue, since I was working on a book set in my favorite city then, too, and hadn't quite made up my mind where I'd light next. I loved the freedom my writing gave me, and hadn't bothered to buy an actual home for myself until the one I had now.

By the time my book was finished, Jack and I weren't. That took another three years.

Trucker completed his business, and I called to Miss Molly, who was pawing around beneath a rose bush, probably covering up her droppings. She was neater than Trucker. I reminded myself to come back out and scoop up Trucker's mess before Katy found it. I also needed to get Katy out of bed so we could get to Jefferson for our statements. And groceries. And I had to drive into Dallas, an eight-hour round trip, to meet Twila. I'd have to leave by noon at least, and hope I didn't run into any construction traffic jams.

When the three of us reentered the kitchen, Officer Smith was waiting for me.

"Someone's at the gate," he said, indicating the transmitter in his hand. "Do you know a Clarence Devereaux?"

"He's our uncle," I confirmed. "Both Katy's and mine. Please. Tell the officer down there to let him come on to the house."

"He's cleared," Smith said into the transmitter. "Let him in."

I replenished my coffee and wandered down the hall to open the front door before Uncle Clarence arrived. He drove a black pickup so new he hadn't removed the sticker from the window. I admired the truck as I sipped coffee and he pulled to a halt in the circular drive.

Uncle Clarence slid out and came around the truck. He hadn't noticed me in the doorway yet. A dapper old Southern gentleman— that's the way I always think of him—even this early in the morning, he wore a starched, snow-white shirt and string tie. His lush, white hair had been dark at one time, and only whitened, never fallen out to leave him bald. A white, brushy mustache filled the space beneath his nose and down the sides of his mouth.

He stood for a moment at the front of his pickup, studying the grounds. He was a sturdy-bodied man, just under six foot, one of those men who could eat half a barbecued brisket and drink a case of beer yet never gain weight. Today he carried a walking stick and leaned on it while he gazed around. I frowned. He appeared to be catching his breath, although he'd only walked a few steps.

One of those damned peacocks strutted out from behind an ornamental shrub, and Uncle Clarence watched it as it wandered toward him. Head bobbing and tail trailing on the ground, it stopped by his feet. He reached in his trouser pocket and scattered something on the ground. Corn, it looked like. The peacock gobbled the offering, and three more birds rushed from the shrubbery. Uncle Clarence's hand returned to his pocket, and he scattered some more food.

He left the birds eating and slowly strolled toward the veranda, pausing now and then to look around. As he got closer, I noticed that he'd lost weight. His leather belt was notched a couple holes past its normal closure, the faded, lighter tan streak testifying where he'd belted it in years gone by. He climbed the steps, still swiveling his head. I took a swallow of coffee, and he caught the movement. He smiled, a huge, Southern smile, and leaned on his stick.

"Alice, mah dear child," he said in that wondrously smooth, Southern drawl. "Ah'm so glad you came to be with Katy."

He held out his arms to pull me into a tight hug. I could feel his ribs as I clasped him.

"Uncle Clarence." I kissed his dear, wrinkled cheek, then stared into his bright blue eyes. Despite my worry over his physical condition, his eyes gleamed merrily back at me. "How have you been?"

"So-so," he replied. "I woke up this morning, so that's always a good day."

I chuckled at the standard reply I'd heard for more years than I liked to think about. His mustache lifted with the corners of his mouth.

"You got a new truck, I see."

"And she's a sweetheart." He gestured his walking stick at the truck, an arm around my shoulders. Maybe to steady himself? "Ah been meanin' to get me one of those beauties for a couple years. Ordered one a while back, so's Ah could get all them bells and whistles Ah wanted. Bubba Joe just got it in yesterday mornin'. Got one of those Bose stereo systems in it, too, and Ah got all the Old Hank songs on them new CDs. You want to take a little spin with me? Ah'll even let you drive."

"Maybe later. Katy and I have a pretty full day scheduled."

"How is my dear Katy this mornin'?" he asked in a concerned voice.

"I haven't seen her yet."

"She needs her rest, Ah'm sure."

I opened the door to allow Uncle Clarence to go in first, but he'd have nothing to do with that. Ladies preceded Southern gentlemen, no ifs, ands, or buts. We slowly made our way down the hall, Uncle studying the walls and ceiling. Or appearing to. I had a feeling his intent examination was a ploy for him to stroll slowly and not let me know his physical capabilities were somewhat wane. What else could it be? He appeared to scan every inch of the hallway.

"Wonderful job dear Katy's doin' with the house," he murmured as he headed toward the kitchen. "Ah haven't been inside since Ah moved out."

I took his arm and steered him away from where the kitchen door used to be, assuming he would make the same mistake I did. "Katy moved the door," I explained.

"Ah see. Yes, yes, this is a good place for it."

In the kitchen, I steered him to the table. Trucker and Miss Molly strolled over as he sat in a chair. It didn't surprise me that both of my pets gravitated to this wonderful old man without a hint of suspicion. Animals and children loved Uncle Clarence. We all did. I introduced Sergeant Smith and Uncle Clarence, then left them making inane conversation while I fetched Uncle a cup of coffee. He allowed that simple courtesy, since women in the South waiting on men in that capacity was totally acceptable.

"I'm sorry we don't have anything to offer you to eat right now," I said as I set the coffee and bowl of creamer on the table and moved the sugar bowl closer to him. "Unless you want a banana or orange. Maybe toast? We're rather afraid to eat anything around here except for the stuff we bought at the gas station last night."

Uncle Clarence added sugar and creamer to his coffee. "Ah've already eaten. Ah understand that someone tried to poison y'all yesterday evenin'." At my amazed look, he continued, "Word's already spreadin'. Y'all know what small-town gossip's like."

True, I mused, recalling Katy's late-night phone call. I'd bet she was talking to Uncle. But before I could ask him, Katy wandered in, already dressed for the day in a lime-green dress and low-heeled pumps. She'd pulled her hair into a chignon, a few curls brushing her cheeks and nape of her neck. Carefully applied, nearly invisible makeup didn't completely cover the dark circles beneath her eyes. She raced over to throw her arms around Uncle Clarence.

"Oh," she said after the required kisses and hugs. "You didn't have to come."

Uncle Clarence patted her shoulder. "Now, let's not have any of that, dear Katy. When have Ah not been there for my favorite niece when she needs me?"

"Never," Katy admitted, tears in her eyes. "But actually coming to Esprit d'Chene—"

Uncle Clarence tenderly placed a finger on her lips to shush Katy. "Ah see you've kept the peacocks fat and sassy," he said. "They look wonderful."

"I order that special corn mix from Ray Bob that you told me to feed them. They'll always have a home at Esprit d'Chene."

"There's coffee," I told Katy. "I need to get dressed, so we can leave by eight-thirty."

Katy barely glanced at me. "Whenever you're ready. I'm going to call the hospital."

I thought I'd have to call Trucker with me, since he remained rapt at Uncle Clarence's side, but the instant I moved toward the doorway, he rose. He accompanied me to my room, and when we got inside, he cocked his head and whined. Sir Gary stood by the window seat. Trucker padded over, but I propped my hands on my hips.

"I don't tolerate ghosts in my bedroom." For good measure, I glanced at the asafetida bag I'd left on the bedpost once again instead of remembering to carry it with me.

"I apologize," he said. "However, I was wondering what time you wished to appoint for our chat today. And don't worry. I'm not about to come any closer with that blasted bag of...whatever it is, hanging on your bed."

"It's —" I changed my mind about identifying my protective charm. He might do some research and find some way to counteract it. "Never mind. And I told you last night that you'd have to wait for Twila. I've got my hands full with Katy right now."

"I wasn't exactly demanding that we chat about your true purpose for being summoned here." He ignored my semi-snarl and continued, "I believe we have a new problem here, and your powers don't seem strong enough to master it."

"Bucky," I agreed.

"I do not believe he realizes that we can see him."

"He sure doesn't seem to see us," I mused. "Not without his eyes in his head."

Suddenly I remembered the doll's head, and stared at the lady's boudoir desk. It was gone! "Oh, no!" I gasped. "I—you didn't take the head, did you?"

He grimaced in distaste. "I have no use for another soul's head. I have my own."

"No! No," I said. "A doll's head. I stumbled over it in the hallway last night, and it nearly scared the crap out of me. I put it right there on the desk."

"It wasn't here when I came in," Sir Gary said with a nonchalant shrug. "Perhaps you misplaced it."

"It was right there!" I pointed at the desk to reinforce my words. Then rubbed my index fingers in a circular motion at my temples. Damn, I was getting a headache. "Tell me something. How long did it take after you...died...to be able to manipulate objects?"

"I honestly cannot recall. One day I was just aware that I could do it."

"Can you do anything about Bucky?" I demanded.

"Like what? I cannot communicate with him. He has no auditory abilities. I cannot scare him away. He has no—"

"—eyes to see with," I finished with him. "Can you at least keep track of him? Let us know if he's doing something dangerous to us?"

He shook his head. "He appears to...well, *appear* with no warning. And disappear the same way. Believe me, after last night, I've been trying to contact him. But I've had no luck."

I stomped over and opened the wardrobe. Grabbed my briefcase and slung it on the bed. I removed my cell phone and dialed Twila. Her answering machine picked up, and I disconnected. She hadn't told me what time her flight left, but I knew she had at least an hour's trip to the nearest airport. Still, it was fairly early for her to have already left the house.

Closing my eyes, I took a deep breath, blew it out. I grounded myself with a few more breaths, then—my cell phone rang in answer to my mental call for help.

"What's going on?" Twila asked.

"Where are you?"

"On a payphone at the drug store." Twila didn't own a cell phone. Or a computer, for that matter. "I have to get Jess and Caroline's prescriptions before I leave town."

Jess and Caroline were her husband and mother, and both of them depended on her for so many things. Neither drove, and she probably had a half-dozen errands to run before she left. She cared deeply for both of them and wouldn't want to worry while she was gone.

"I just wanted to know if you have any more advice about how to handle Bucky until you get here," I said. "I'm really concerned about the havoc he can cause, and I'll be gone from the manor house quite a bit today."

"Bathe the manor house and all the occupants in white light before you leave," Twila said. "That should help. And I'm bringing a kit of stuff for us to use."

"Twila —" I hesitated, but then went on, "Could a headless ghost use a substitute head?"

"Hmmm," she mused. "I've never heard of that. But I suppose it could be possible."

"Mrs. Brown?" I heard someone say in the background. "Your prescriptions are ready."

"I need to go, Alice."

"All right. I'll see you at the airport."

"One thing you need to do is think positive," she reminded me before she hung up.

"Think positive," I said to the dead phone. "Sure. That's easy as hell."

She was right, though. She'd told me that over and over when we started out on a ghosthunt. Our mental attitude had as much to do with protecting us as the various wares we carry to keep the ghosts in line. I didn't have a very positive attitude about Bucky, though. I was only positive that I hoped I never laid eyes on him again until Twila was here with me.

CHAPTER 18

I lugged the litter box out before we left, and Trucker and Miss Molly rode in the back seat of my Jeep. Uncle Clarence drove sedately down Esprit d'Chene's driveway ahead of us. He turned right at the gate, me left. I waited until we were half-way between Esprit d'Chene and Jefferson before I confronted Katy. When I whipped into a small dirt road and slammed on my brakes, I caught her off guard. Jamming the Jeep into park, I twisted on the seat.

Panic flashed across her face, and a stab of guilt shuddered through me. It wouldn't have surprised me if she'd opened the door and fled. She looked so small and vulnerable inside the wide seatbelt harness, the lamb's wool padding I'd wrapped around the shoulder belt for comfort snugged against her elfin face. All the years of love and friendship we'd shared surged against my anger at her deceit.

Then she crossed her arms and glared out the windshield. "We need to get to the station, Alice," she reminded me.

Forgetting my injured hand, I clenched a fist and batted the steering wheel. My fingernails bit into my palm, and the horn blared, pain mixing with the startling blast of sound. Katy jumped as, instinctively, I cradled my hand against my chest, heart pounding in frustration. "We'll get to the station," I muttered. "But first, what the hell are you hiding from me?"

"I can't tell you," Katy replied in a shaky voice. "Believe me, if I could, I would."

I brushed a strand of hair from her face. "Katy, do you realize that part of the reason you're giving this statement this morning is because you're a suspect?"

She finally looked at me, eyes wide in shock. "A suspect in what?"

"Bucky's death."

"I had nothing to do with that! You know I didn't! I couldn't have!"

"It's SOP," I said quietly, my need to make her realize the trouble she could be in warring with my love. "Standard operating procedure. The investigators look at people connected with the murdered person first. Family. Friends. Former acquaintances."

"You're giving a statement, too!"

"As a witness," I explained. "I have an iron-clad alibi."

She bit her lip. "Jack would never make me a suspect."

"Jack's a homicide detective first, Sugar. Above all else, he has an obligation to uncover the killer's identity. Over and above any obligations he feels toward people he cares about."

"But I didn't have anything to do with Bucky's death!" Katy cried again.

"I don't believe Sir Gary did, either," I told her honestly. I didn't, either. The ghost still intrigued me, and I didn't totally trust him yet. However, he'd made quite a few points with me by warning Katy that I was in danger when I confronted Bucky in the library. Well, confronted wasn't the right word, I guess, since Bucky's ghost probably had no idea who or what was in the vicinity, without a head to see his surroundings.

I sighed. "You and Sir Gary were the only ones at Esprit d'Chene the night before last. Except for whoever came up the driveway."

"Then that's who the police need to concentrate on. Not me!"

I draped my wrist over the steering wheel. My stinging palms reminded me how close we'd all come to eating the bread pudding. "What's it going to take to make you understand, Katy? You're not just in danger of being charged with murder. Someone's trying to kill someone else at the plantation."

Katy clenched her hands in her lap and stared out the windshield, her obstinacy unbreakable. Maybe because someone had always come to Katy's rescue, she couldn't imagine that her security could be threatened. Hell, I had my suspicions, also. Who could help it, with the way she'd been acting? Had Katy counted on the fact that Jack had once been family to steer the investigation away from her? If so, she didn't know my ex-husband as well as I did.

"I thought we were friends, not just relatives," I reminded her.

She glanced at her wristwatch. "We're going to be late."

Stubbornly, I tried to wait her out. That had worked when we were kids. I'd want Katy to follow me on some misadventure that would get us both grounded for a week if we got caught. Like borrowing a relative's car on the pretense of going to a movie or shopping but instead sneaking off to a bar known not to check IDs that closely. Shoot, Katy had learned to boot-scoot right along with me by the time we were both sixteen. Now, however, we were women. And we'd shared much more important confidences than which cowboy was the best kisser.

I shifted into reverse, but didn't back up. "I want you to know, Katy, that I'm here for you. But I can't help you if you aren't honest with me. This is serious, not a silly lark like sneaking down to Bourbon Street to drink hurricanes."

"I know, Alice," she replied. I passed my glance over her face as I checked the county road behind us and backed up, noting her relief. "You always have been. I know how important your writing is to you, but look how you came when I had trouble with Sir Gary."

"Good thing, too," I said.

"Yes," she agreed. I waited, hoping she'd keep the communication channels between us open, but she only went on, "How are your hands this morning? I can drive, if you want."

"I'm fine. But thanks for the offer."

"Alice, there is something I should tell you."

"Please," I said with a quick glance. "You have to understand, Katy, that a murder investigation isn't something to mess around with."

She waved a negligent hand. "It's not about the investigation. It's Uncle Clarence."

Sadness filled me. I'd already suspected something was wrong with the dear old man. "He's ill," I guessed.

She sniffed and reached for one of the tissues on the console. "He won't be with us much longer. I've been taking him to Tyler for treatment, but there's not much they can do."

"Cancer?" I asked, but Katy shook her head.

"It's some sort of blood disease that affects older people. Nothing that radiation or even any of the new, experimental treatments can help."

I reached for a tissue myself to wipe my eyes so I could see the road. Dear Uncle Clarence. He'd bounced us on his knee, pretending to be a pony. He'd taught us how to fish, with cane poles and minnows in the spring when the white perch spawned and night crawlers at night for catfish. Before he'd retired and moved to the Jefferson area ten years or so ago, he'd lived on Lake Ponchetrain in New Orleans. His home now was a smaller manor house than Esprit d'Chene, but just as elegant.

Uncle Clarence had never married. Katy and I weren't supposed to know it, but family rumor said a bad case of the mumps when he was a teenager had left him sterile. Maybe knowing he couldn't leave behind an heir had destroyed his desire for a wife and family. Maybe he just never found the right woman.

Uncle Clarence had looked for a woman, though, by gosh. I'd never seen him at any of the parties or balls in New Orleans without some ravishing beauty on his arm, usually someone from the *right* side of the social sphere. But Katy and I had run across him once or twice in our teenage rounds of trouble, and the women around him then were blue-jeaned and teased hair. Fact is, we liked the ones we met on our boot-scooting forays better than his Chanel-spritzed, evening-gowned socialites.

"Remember Cat Dancer?" I asked, still sniffing back tears.

"She died a few years ago. Uncle Clarence and I went to her funeral."

"You didn't mention that."

"It was while you and Jack were having problems. We didn't want to bother you."

"He was seeing her all those years?"

"I asked him once why they didn't marry, but he just shook his head and changed the subject. I really liked Cat. She read the Tarot cards for me once in a while. In fact, she tried to warn me about Brian, but I didn't listen. Not all of her card readings were totally accurate."

"No psychic claims to be one hundred percent." I had my own idea about why Uncle Clarence and Cat never married. I remembered Cat's beautiful, lush body and her silky black hair curling down her back. Her high cheekbones and brown eyes. Her full lips. Today hardly anyone cared whether or not the person they fell in love with came from a mixed-blood background. But Uncle Clarence was a born and raised Southerner, and family meant everything to him. Some of our Southern relatives would have ostracized him, had he had the audacity to actually marry Cat and make her mistress of his home.

Cat could trace her roots clear back to Marie Leveau, the voodoo queen of New Orleans. She'd run a bed and breakfast in the French Quarter for years, with a steady, income-producing clientele that ranged from her psychic friends to the just-curious. Twila and I had spent a night with Cat once, and experienced one of the most awesome séances of our lives. Neither of us doubted Cat's powers.

Jefferson came into view ahead, and the chance of prodding Katy diminished with each turn of the Jeep's wheels. My darned suspicious mind couldn't help wondering why Katy had chosen this exact moment to tell me about Uncle Clarence. In order to sidetrack my questions? I couldn't actually believe that of my cousin. But then, I couldn't quell the thought, either.

I pulled into the parking lot across from the county jail and courthouse. I drove through, looking for Jack's Longview cruiser, frowning when I didn't see it.

"Jack said he was working out of Jefferson," I mused.

"Maybe he's at the city jail," Katy put in.

The city jail was on the next block, and when I stopped at the red light at the intersection of Austin and Polk Streets, I saw Jack's cruiser parked between two city police cars. A small, blue sports convertible took up the remaining space in the tiny parking area. I scanned the street for another spot, but that side of the street was full. On the other side, in front of The General Store, an old building full of tourist regalia and an old-fashioned ice cream fountain that served delicious sundaes, I spotted a place. U-turning at the end of the block, I grabbed it.

Mindful of my pets, I left the engine running and took the extra set of keys from the console, so I could lock up and still get back in. Katy waited for me on the sidewalk. Fear marred her fragile features as she gazed at the front of the jail.

"Hey," I said to try to put her at ease. "You'll get early wrinkles if you frown like that." She shrugged, then took a deep breath and marched toward the jail.

I'd never been inside this building, and when we entered, I stared around in confusion. How on earth did they get any work done in this crowded space? Files covered both desks, and four uniformed cops conferred over a spread of papers on the far desk. The uniform stripes identified three as two patrol officers and a sergeant. Behind the desk sat the police chief. Their discussion must have been consuming, because none of them so much as glanced at us. Their conversation did, however, cut off abruptly. Papers shuffled, then the chief nodded at his men and they turned to leave, striding past us out the door with a bare tilt of their heads in greeting.

"Can I help you ladies?" the chief said. "Oh, hello, Katy."

"Hello, Chief," Katy replied. "We're here to see Jack Roucheau."

"He's in the other building." The chief grabbed his hat from the edge of his desk and jammed it on his head. "You must be Miz Carpenter," he said, extending his hand as he approached us. He had a firm grip, and a kind, pleasant face.

"Yes. We're here to give Jack our statements."

"This way." He motioned us back out the door, then led us down a path between the concrete jail building and the City Office Building, which fronted Polk Street. Behind the building we'd just left was another building. The path led past the door and on into the alley between the jail and The General Store. The chief opened the door and motioned us to precede him. Feminine laughter floated out, but Katy distracted me when she gripped my hand so tightly the injured palm shouted pain. I gasped, and Katy dropped my hand.

"I'm sorry, Alice. I forgot."

I slipped an arm around her waist. The chief was waiting for us, but I squeezed Katy in comfort. "It's going to be fine."

A mini-skirted redhead sat on one of the desks, legs crossed and thighs exposed. Jack sat behind the desk, and I bit back my query as to whether the redhead wore any underwear. Jack had the perfect view to answer that, but I thought better of it even as the question formed. Redhead swung around, and her blue eyes widened. Not at Katy and me, though. At the chief. She scooted off the desk, scattering files on the floor, then bent down to retrieve them. Yep, she did have on underwear. Blue bikinis.

The chief and Jack exchanged a purely masculine look. Then the chief said, "If you've found the Singleterry file, Carol, please put it on my desk."

The redhead straightened and held the file to her full breasts. "Yes, sir. It's right here. I'll get it back in order."

"Do that at your own desk, please," the chief said, and she skittered out the door as the chief glanced at Katy and me. "She truly is a good secretary and dispatcher."

"Brightens up your office, too, I imagine," I mused.

Jack laughed and rose from his chair. "Did either of you manage to get any sleep?"

"No," Katy said, at the same moment I said, "A little bit."

"I'll leave you to business," the chief said, and followed the redhead.

The office was a small, windowless area. A door in the middle of the back wall evidently led to yet another part of the building. Thick steel, it was firmly closed.

"The cells are back there," Jack explained, although I hadn't asked. My eyes had landed on a steel cabinet beside the door. The door hadn't been fully closed, and I could see the hilt of Grandpere Jean's sword on a shelf. A clear, plastic evidence bag covered it, a red tag wrapped around the hilt.

"Chain of evidence?" I asked with a lifted eyebrow, nodding at the sword and open cabinet door.

Katy followed my gaze, and blanched. I steadied her and pushed a chair over to her to sit in. Jack rose and shut the cabinet. "I was checking evidence against the officers' reports, so the evidence chain's intact, Alice. Do you have somethin' you can do for a while?"

Katy grabbed for my hand again. "Can't she stay?"

I jerked the hand back, mindful of the pain, and Katy's wide-eyed, fearful gaze tore at my heart. "I'll go do some grocery shopping. Anything special you'd like me to pick up?"

She only shook her head, eyes pleading with me. I left her there to Jack. Maybe he could get further with her. Something had to make Katy understand her secure world was on the verge of collapse. This situation was a hell of a lot more serious than her divorce. All our huge family had supported her through that, but family support wouldn't help her now. If it came to that, her best bet would be a hard-nosed lawyer.

Trucker and Miss Molly greeted me in their usual fashion, Trucker with a slurp on my face, Miss Molly curling up in indignation on the passenger seat. I turned right at the stoplight, driving through town toward where I remembered a fairly decent-sized grocery store on the other end of the tourist section. Jefferson is filled with beautiful, restored buildings containing antiques, both real and trendy replicas, as well as bed and breakfasts and bargain stores with cut-rate necessities. I let my mind wander and scanned the sides of the street to see if any new, interesting place had opened since I'd last visited rather than focus on my forthcoming statement. Anyway, I didn't think that would take long. Given that I was still half-pissed over Jack's continued insistence that anyone who believed in ghosts had a hallucinogenic problem, I figured I'd throw his just-the-facts crap in his face. But this time, the facts would be my facts—true, whether he believed or not. Let him make what he would of them. With a little sleep behind me, I felt better able to confront Jack without Twila's support.

At a Y intersection, I turned left and pulled in at the grocery store. As I reached for my purse, I noticed Katy's and my wrinkled tissues on the floor and picked up my cell phone instead to dial Uncle Clarence's number. He answered on the second ring.

"Uncle Clarence." I had no idea at all what to say. If I could have written him a letter, I'd have been able to fill it with everything inside me. I just wasn't that good with actual, hands-on sympathy. "Um...how are you feeling?"

"Katy told you, Ah assume," he replied.

"Uncle Clarence. I just—I don't—I love you," I finally sputtered.

"And Ah love you, child," he said softly. "Don't worry about me. Ah've missed my Cat quite desperately since she left me."

I glanced at Miss Molly with a frown, before it dawned on me that he was talking about Cat Dancer. "She was a lovely lady. I wish Twila and I had known about her passing."

"She's not that far," Uncle Clarence said in a whisper. "If you get a chance, come by the house. She's waiting for me to cross over with her."

I could believe that. After all, I believed in ghosts. "Tell her I said hello."

"Ah will. And don't you worry none about me, child. Ah've lived a full life. Maybe not exactly what Ah would have chosen, had Ah had a say in it. But a full one. You take care of our Katy when Ah'm gone."

"I will," I promised.

"You always did, Alice, my sweet. Now, how about you and Katy coming over this weekend and Ah'll make us some jambalaya and crawfish gumbo? Ah've got some mudbugs in the freezer, and you remember how you like my jalapeno cornbread."

"I'd love that. If we can find the time. But I can help cook—"

"Ummm...no, that's all right." Uncle Clarence chuckled. "But you can ask Katy to whip up one of her red forest cakes, if you want."

"I'll do that." I didn't even have the heart to tease him back about my lack of cooking skills. "I'll call you within the next day or so and let you know if we can make it."

"Wonderful. I need to check my trotline. Maybe we'll have some fresh catfish, too."

"Goodbye, Uncle," I said. "I love you."

"Love you, Alice. Bye."

I stared at the phone. Maybe Uncle shouldn't be out on the bayou running his trotline in his condition, but Katy and I had both been raised to respect our elders. I wasn't about to try to dictate anything to Uncle Clarence at this late stage in the game. Sighing, I left my pets once again in the car, Miss Molly curled in feigned disregard, Trucker accepting of the imprisonment he couldn't change.

In the grocery store, I filled a cart to the point where I was afraid the latch on the front of the conveyance might spring open if I placed one more box or jar in it. After I checked out, and as I pushed the cart full of bags toward the doors, a woman rushed in. She halted when she saw me, and a familiar voice shrilled, "You must be Alice, Katy's cousin! I recognize you from your picture on the back of your books! I'm Irene!"

She rushed me, hand extended. Pudgy, her boutique-style dress strained at the waist and hips. Ferret-like brown eyes peered out from a plump face, topped by obviously-dyed black hair, a white skunk-streak down the right side. If she was trying for fashion, I hoped that style never caught on. She pumped my hand vigorously before I could jerk it free.

"Ouch!" I snarled. Goodnight Irene didn't notice.

"Can you believe this mess our dear Katy has found herself in?" she cooed as best she could in that piercing voice. "Why, I'd be in the hospital under sedation! Where is dear Katy?" She dug in her purse and pulled out a cell phone. "At home in bed? I better call!"

"Katy's not home," I gritted.

She batted long, had-to-be-false eyelashes. "Then she must feel better! I'll drive by!"

"No. You won't." I didn't feel a bit embarrassed at my lack of diplomacy. "The plantation's under guard, and *no* one's allowed in!"

"We'll see about that! I'll have you know, I'm Katy's best friend!"

I stifled the urge to twist that bodice even tighter around her chubby neck. Katy had to live with these people after I left. Somehow, I reached into my realm of good manners and changed my tactics.

"Irene," I said in a smarmy, just-the-two-of-us tone, "Katy's told me what she thinks of you. And I know you're the type who'll be staunchly at Katy's side." If nothing else, to be the primary purveyor of choice gossip tidbits, I mused as Goodnight Irene nodded eagerly. "The best help you can give Katy right now is to keep doing exactly what you have been—protecting her so she can have the solitude she needs. Katy's genteel sensibilities have never had to deal with anything like this before."

"I understand completely!" Irene shrilled conspiratorially. "Ladies like Katy and I weren't raised to be the center of such rife gossip and speculation!"

"Um..." I stalled, slipping a glance at my wristwatch. Sometimes gossip and speculation include interesting elements, drawn from a molecule of truth. After all, where there's smoke—

Irene appeared to take my reluctance to part with her a shared sisterhood, lending itself to confidences of like-minded society matrons. She leaned closer, eyes darting around to make sure no one could overhear us. "I've been telling everyone who repeats that one nasty bit of fanciful rumor that it has to be untrue!" she whispered, the shrillness in her voice even at that level. "Someone who looks like Katy! She just wouldn't do that!"

"I totally agree," I whispered back, no idea what she was talking about. "You know how easy it is to fool some people."

"Yes!" She nodded her head emphatically, her mouth a tight line. And didn't say another word. What now?

"Uh..." My gaze landed on a rack of paperbacks. "Why, I use that mistaken identity ploy in my books all the time. It's easy to confuse an eyewitness. Even easier to confuse more than one of them. They all see something different. Especially in a place like...you know."

"A smoky bar late at night!" Irene rang forth in her normal shrillness, falling straight into my trap. "Exactly! Katy Gueydan wouldn't be caught dead in a place like the Holey Bucket! Let alone with a slimy swamp rat like Bucky Wilson-Jones! Why, even his father disowned that boy!"

"Exactly," I parroted. Where the hell was the Holey Bucket? I'd bet my pack of T-bones that Uncle Clarence knew where. Well, all the T-bones except for Trucker's.

"I do have to go, Irene," I said, thinking I should leave her some tidbit to pass along to her greedy friends. A payoff, as well as a sacrifice to the society gods to keep Goodnight Irene a happy informant in case I needed her again. "Katy's giving Detective Roucheau her statement as we speak. I'm sure by the time she's done with that horrible chore, she'll feel much better emotionally. I'll tell her that you asked about her and wish her the best."

"A statement?" Irene pulled back in horror. "Don't they only ask suspects to do that?"

"No!" I said. Civilians! They just didn't understand, like those of us who study interesting things like murder investigations. "No, no, no. Don't you watch TV? They have to talk to everyone. I have to give a statement, and I didn't even arrive until after they found the body."

"You?" Uh oh. The grimace of distaste indicated I'd shoveled dirt into my communication channel with Goodnight Irene. "Uh...nice talking to you. Do give Katy my regards." She shuffled determinedly away from me, clutching her oversize purse to her strained bodice. "And do tell Katy that we'll all understand perfectly if she has to miss the Daughters of the South meeting tomorrow evening."

"Wait. I—"

But Irene whirled and escaped. I hesitated and saw her wave frantically at another fake matron heading down a store aisle. My last glimpse of them before I angrily pushed my cart on was a set of spray-starched hairdos bent together so close it looked like they were kissing.

I shoved the shopping cart toward the hatchback, in between the Jeep and a black Cadillac parked four inches over the yellow line. Fuming at Irene's stupidity—and mine for attempting to manipulate her—I inadvertently nicked the Cadillac's rear fender with the cart. I pushed the cart on around to the back of the Jeep and returned to see what damage I'd caused.

Not much. Shoot, the paint was barely scratched. Noticeable, but a good bottle of black fingernail polish would take care of it. With Halloween this close, there was plenty of black nail polish available. Besides, it probably was either Irene's car or belonged to her small-town society friend inside. Everything else in the lot was either pickups or elderly, family-type sedans, except for a red Mercedes.

Groceries in the Jeep, hatchback slammed, I marched the cart to the space provided and shoved its nose safely into the butt of another one. I got as far as my driver's door before Irene burst out, carrying a small, plastic grocery sack that looked as though it only held a loaf of bread. She headed straight for the Cadillac, squeezing between my Jeep and her door, jerked the Cadillac door open, and it slammed against the Jeep's passenger door. Irene didn't stop to assess the damage. She thrust her pudgy body through the too-small opening, fired up the Cadillac's engine, and zoomed out of the parking place.

I mentally noted her license plate number and stormed around the Jeep, expecting to find a huge dent in the door. There was only a smudge in the dirt. Evidently, the Cadillac had those rubber protective strips on the door. Probably Goodnight Irene needed them! I sighed and someone called, "Ma'am?"

A tall, handsome man stood in the store entrance, a frown on his face. I quickly rearranged my irritation at the "ma'am" into my publicity smile. When he caught my eye, he strolled toward me. He wore faded jeans and a knit shirt with the store logo over the pocket. As he drew close, I could read the nametag pinned under the logo. *Cory Stevens, Store Manager.*

"I'm Cory Stevens," he confirmed, holding out his hand, which I accepted. "I saw Irene hit your door and wanted to make sure she hadn't damaged it." His grasp was firm, and he held my hand a little too long, which a stab of pain from my injured palm told me. I must have reflexively stiffened, though, because he turned my hand over and gazed at my palm. "You've injured yourself."

"It's nothing," I assured him. "And the car's not hurt. Just some dirt knocked off, and you won't even be able to tell that after I get it to the car wash."

He studied my face and stuck his fingertips in the back pockets of his jeans. "Well, I wanted to make sure. I...uh...haven't seen you shopping here before."

"I'm Alice Carpenter. Katy Gueydan's cousin."

"Katy," he replied with a grim nod. "Will you tell her that if there's anything at all I can do, to please call me?" Unlike Irene, his offer sounded sincere.

"You know her, then."

"Yes, of course. She's my cousin, too. Come to think of it, just like you are."

My interest waned. Related. Huh. The first interesting man I'd laid eyes on in Jefferson, and he was a cousin.

"Uh...Katy and I are cousins by marriage," Cory put in, maybe noticing my face.

I brightened. "Oh, then that makes us cousins by marriage, too," I purred. "Distantly."

He considered me for a moment. His eyes were brown, a lighter shade than Jack's, his chestnut hair full, styled more than just cut. "Very distant," he mused. "But not too distant for me to buy you lunch, I hope."

"Oh. Darn it, I can't. Today, I mean."

"Tomorrow?" he asked in what I hoped was a...well, hopeful voice.

"You can call me at Esprit d'Chene." I dug in my purse and pulled out a business card. I always keep them handy, but they're convenient for pleasure, also. "My cell phone number's on the card, and it has voice mail."

He gazed at the card for a second, then tucked it in his jeans pocket. "You can bet on it." He turned to re-enter the store, saying over his shoulder, "Now, don't you believe a word Katy tells you about me. That hayride last summer was just an accident waiting to happen." He winked just before the door closed. But my mood was already dimming once again. Obviously, he and Katy had dated. I'd never much cared for the thought of her castoffs.

It doesn't matter, I thought to myself as I drove back to the jail. *I'm not in the market for a man anyway.* I giggled and stroked Trucker's muzzle when he nuzzled my ear. "Even a man who runs a market that sells T-bones, huh, Trucker?"

* * *

Jack and Katy were chatting over foam cups of coffee, a tape recorder open on the desk between them. They both smiled, Katy's face serene. Evidently the statement had gone well.

"Hello, *Chére*," Jack said. "Carol's typing up Katy's statement, and we can do yours now."

I handed Katy the keys to my Jeep. "I've got the groceries."

"Wonderful," Katy said as she stood. "I think I'll wait at the soda counter in The General Store. Will Trucker and Miss Molly be all right?"

"They'll be fine. I'll see you in a few minutes."

With her back to Jack, Katy tossed me a grimace and a slight shake of her head. She tapped a manicured thumb on a fingertip. Jack must have taken her fingerprints. Then she hurried out the door. I sat in her chair, crossed my legs, and waited while Jack put in a new tape. He closed the lid, locking the tape in place, leaned back, and crossed his arms as he studied me.

CHAPTER 19

We played the game of who's going to break eye contact first for at least fifteen seconds. Jack broke first. "I think maybe we should stay off the record for a minute." He cupped his strong chin in a palm. "I don't want you repeatin' any of your ghost foolishness on this tape. Katy doesn't need to have people around here talkin' about her like that, and we won't be the only ones listenin' to this."

"Whether you believe it or not, the reason I was on my way to Katy's was because she called me to come before she found the body. Called because of a ghost named Sir Gary Gavin, who died two hundred years ago! And if you want the truth on that tape—" I nodded at the recorder "—you'll have to take what you can get!"

"*Chére...*" Jack shook his head.

"Remember who came screaming into the kitchen after you last night?" I said. "Katy. And she told you she'd seen Bucky. Bucky, who had been dead for several hours by then."

"According to the prelim we got out of the Dallas M.E., since about two or three a.m.," Jack said with a sigh. "But the M.E. said the heated water made it hard to give a definite time."

"Unlike if you'd had a body lying on the ground and some lividity to go by," I said.

"Yeah."

I frowned. "Why is the Dallas medical examiner doing the autopsy? I saw the hearse and Jefferson's M.E. at the plantation."

"Jefferson doesn't have an M.E. That was one of their JPs, Maxine Campton. Her husband was drivin' the hearse. Campton's Funeral Home, edge of town."

"Oh." I'd forgotten that piece of investigative research. Small towns use a local Justice of the Peace to declare a body dead. Even a body with a missing head couldn't be moved until the JP actually declared it unrevivable. And without a trained medical examiner in the county, the body would be shipped to a larger district.

"How's the senator taking all this?" I asked.

Jack shrugged. "He really didn't hang around long enough for me to ask. Sort of cold about it, you ask me. The kid was his son."

"A son who gave him nothing but embarrassment. You don't suppose—no, that's outlandish."

"Your tryin' to tell me the senator might've decided to get rid of his own son? For political reasons?"

"Katy mentioned a while back that the senator was thinking of running for President," I recalled. "But I doubt he'd need Bucky out of the way if he did that. He's never hidden the fact he has a son who didn't live up to expectations."

Jack made a note on a pad by his elbow. I could see what he wrote.

"Check the Shreveport passenger list? You think the senator lied about when he arrived? Maybe he was already here?"

"I need to take your statement. Without you sayin' anything about a ghost."

"Not if you want the truth."

"Hell," Jack muttered. "Guess I can use my laptop and type up your statement myself."

"Whatever."

Jack glared at me briefly and pushed the "on" button of the recorder.

The statement didn't take long. In fact, the narration portion of it took about the same amount of time as my giving my name and address, after Jack noted the date, time, and location. I told him that Katy had called me around two a.m., so upset about her resident ghost, Sir Gary Gavin, that I feared she might take matters into her own hands and try to drive him off herself. I mentioned that Granny had been with me when the second call came in—Katy hysterical about a dead body in the pool—but not that Sir Gary had been with Katy. I'd only push Jack's belief system so far. After that, I told him I packed and left for Esprit d'Chene. He knew the arrival time, but I repeated it anyway for the tape.

Jack concluded the statement with a glance at a wall clock and the time, then started to turn off the recorder. I stayed his hand.

"There's one other thing you need to know."

He quirked a questioning eyebrow.

"Sir Gary was messing with Grandpere Jean's sword that night."

"Oh, for God's sake, *Chére*—"

I glared grimly. "During the first call from Katy, he levitated the sword and cut the bolster holding Grandmere Alicia's portrait. Surely you noticed that Katy had the bolster tied in a knot when you checked the Great Room yesterday morning."

"Yeah, but —" Jack clicked off the recorder. "We need to get your fingerprints."

"You want me to get Sir Gary's for you, too?" I asked in a sweet voice.

"I'll let you know," he said, avoiding my gaze.

As soon as we finished with the distasteful fingerprinting, I stormed out of the office without a goodbye and headed for The General Store. Damn it, I'd always thought Jack at least had an open mind when it came to investigating a murder. Obviously, he closed the trap door when it veered toward a paranormal channel. Not that I really believed Sir Gary had anything to do with Bucky's death, but he certainly could have useful information. I'd have to be the one to follow that line.

The General Store was a huge old building with wooden floors. A tourist attraction, it sold everything from stuffed armadillos to raunchy T-shirts and local delicacies. Tempting arrays of samples were everywhere: muscadine and jalapeno jellies, marmalades, canned cobblers, pickled okra, apple butter, along with crackers and plastic spoons. A Zydeco song rocked from the hidden speakers, all fiddles, guitars, and steel washboard, a foot-tapping piece meant for clogging. The soda fountain lined the right-hand wall, past the glass-top counter filled with racks of tapes and CDs, the lower case with trays of chocolate fudge and coconut bonbons.

Katy's slender body was slumped dejectedly on a plastic-seated stool, a melting chocolate soda in front of her. The waitress at the far end of the counter pretended to clean an already gleaming spot and eyed Katy fearfully.

Katy jumped when I touched her shoulder and caught my gaze in the mirror behind the fountain. "Oh," she said, rising. "Are we ready to go?"

"Yes. Jack will call us when we need to come back and sign our statements."

"You..." Katy glanced at the waitress, who jerked her eyes away and scrubbed at the counter. "You told Jack about Sir Gary, didn't you?" Katy whispered.

I nodded and took her arm to lead her out of the store. At the curb, I dug for my keys in my jeans pocket before I remembered Katy had them. She was staring at the jail, and I had to nudge her to get her attention. "You've got the keys."

She reached in her purse and handed them to me. After I opened the passenger door, Katy lifted Miss Molly and curled the cat to her chest as she scooted into the seat. By the time I was in the driver's seat, she had her seatbelt snapped.

We made a fairly silent trip back to the plantation. At one point I asked Katy how her statement had gone, but she only said, "Fine, I guess. I told Jack that I'd found the body around two thirty a.m., and he knew most of the rest. He's staying over at The Meadows, you know. It's not that far from there to Esprit d'Chene. Miss Alexandria has that lovely carriage house she rents out."

"Did you tell Jack how you came to go out to the pool that time of morning?"

"No." Katy shook her head forlornly. "But I'm glad you mentioned the ghost. I didn't think he'd believe that Sir Gary accompanied me out there."

"Probably not. But you should mention that end of the story to him now." If nothing else, to hit Jack between the eyes with both of us mentioning the ghost.

"I'll call him when we get home."

We fell out of conversation again. Katy stroked Miss Molly's back, and a faint purr of contentment rumbled in the air. Trucker stretched out on the back seat, snoring softly. I thought once about telling Katy that I'd met Cory, but the time didn't seem right. Besides, he might not even call me. Men are like that. Out of sight, out of mind.

"I just remembered," Katy said when we pulled to a stop at the manor house. "Jack said the guard company would have its men here by early afternoon."

"I thought maybe you'd want to ride to Dallas with me."

"I probably should be here when the guards arrive."

"I suppose. Maybe Sue Ann will be back soon."

"I called the hospital on your cell phone. They're keeping Gabe and the officer another day, so Sue Ann's coming back here. Oh, and there was a voice mail on your phone."

She slid out, Miss Molly in her arms, and I popped the hatchback from inside so we could unload the groceries. For once, Katy did her share. She grabbed a plastic bag of groceries, while I dialed my voice mail. The message was from my editor, not Twila or Granny. I called and assured her the manuscript was nearly ready, mentally calculating whether I was lying. We chatted about her pregnancy, and I managed to finagle the information out of her that the only thing her arsenal of baby items lacked at this point was a beautiful carousal mobile she'd seen at Sachs. I hung up and redialed.

Within half an hour, I was ready to hit the road again. With Katy's heartfelt consent, I'd decided to leave Trucker and Miss Molly behind. Before I left, I bathed the manor house and all its occupants in white light and reminded Katy to keep the asafetida locket with her.

"I will," she promised fervidly. "Please, hurry back."

"Are you sure you don't want to go along?"

She appeared on the verge of agreement, but then slowly shook her head. "I better not."

"I'll stay with her," a voice said from behind us. Sir Gary stood over by the potted fern. "As long as she keeps that blasted locket sealed."

"Have you seen Bucky?" I asked.

"No. And believe me, I'm hunting him."

My wristwatch indicated I'd have to hurry if I wanted to meet the plane on time. With a last glance at Katy and Sir Gary, as well as my pets, I walked through the manor house. I tuned into the atmosphere as I strode down the hallways, but nothing appeared to be disturbing it.

* * *

An hour and a half later, I reached for my cell phone as I passed the turnoff to Six Gun. Granny didn't answer, and she didn't own an answering machine. Said she'd lived this long without missing any important phone calls, so why ask for that type of intrusion. I glanced at the dashboard clock, wondering if I could push the speed limit any further. Then my cell phone rang.

"Hello?"

"Alice, it's Twila. There were a couple seats on an earlier flight, and I rented a car. I'm just outside of Dallas, at a pay phone on I-20. Where can we meet for a late lunch?"

"Wonderful," I said. "I wasn't looking forward to getting back to Esprit d'Chene after dark. There's a Cracker Barrel just off the Tyler exit on I-20. Probably take you about an hour."

"Sounds good. See you there."

Twila hung up, and I breathed a sigh of relief. Despite the protection of white light, security guards, Sir Gary, and Trucker, the farther I'd driven from Esprit d'Chene, the more worry consumed me. I'd niggled the worry to death, but I couldn't decide if it came from Katy's deceit and my suspicions, or whether my cousin might be in danger.

I arrived at the Cracker Barrel and made a round through the restaurant, just in case Twila had gotten there ahead of me, but I didn't see her. Normally I'd have browsed the old-time memorabilia—after all, it was nearly time to start Christmas shopping, a chore I loathed—but I forwent that pleasure today. Instead, I returned to the front porch and sat in one of the dozen rocking chairs. Cell phone in hand, I called the plantation house.

Katy answered before the first ring faded. "How is everything?" I asked.

"The guards arrived, and I introduced them to Trucker. Jack came by, too, with the statements. I told him about Sir Gary, but he just said he was glad I hadn't put that on tape."

Katy fell silent for a second, then said, "I called Uncle Clarence and asked him to have this attorney friend of his contact me. Mr. Jeeves is retired, but he was a criminal attorney down in Houston for years. I almost wish I hadn't done that, though. Uncle was so upset—completely undone about me being under suspicion. I do so worry about his health."

"You did the right thing. If nothing else, you'll have legal counsel on notice. If Mr. Jeeves can't help you, he'll know someone who can. It's asinine to think you'd have to do that, but I'd do the same thing if I were in your shoes."

"I know. I've seen it in your books. Even the innocent suspects hightail it for a lawyer when they're involved in a murder investigation. You've told me fiction is written the best when it's based on facts."

Relieved, I took advantage of the distance and non-confrontational face-to-face factor. "Is there anything else you think I should know, Sugar?"

Katy hesitated until I was afraid maybe the cell phone had disconnected. As I got ready to pull it from my ear and check the menu, she said, "When you get back, Alice. You and Twila both. We all need to talk."

"I'm very glad you're ready to do that."

"It's time. Don't worry. I'm a grown woman. I can handle things until you get back."

"Just don't forget to hang onto the asafetida. Twila's bringing more protective stuff."

"Roger, dodger," Katy said with a slight laugh. I giggled at the old childhood saying we'd used in days gone by. "I'll see you when you get here. Tell Twila I'll have the Blue Room ready. She'll like that one."

"Roger, dodger," I said. "I think that's her in the car pulling in now. 'Bye, Sugar." I shoved the cell phone in my purse as the bright red T-bird pulled into a nearby space, Twila's red hair shining even through the tinted windows. She met me halfway across the parking lot, her brown eyes filled with concern.

"I'm starved," she said by way of greeting. "Let's talk over something to eat." But we hugged each other tightly first.

The lunch hour was over, but there were still a lot of full tables. Plenty of empty ones, though, and we didn't have to wait. The hostess led us past several elderly couples and even a young couple who stared into each other's eyes, completely unaware that they weren't the only two people in the room.

"Honeymooners," Twila said after the hostess seated us and took our drink orders—iced tea for Twila and a mug of apple cider for me. "I think they're in for the long haul."

"One of the lucky fifty percent. How are Jess and Caroline?"

She gave me a run-down of our various, shared relatives, as well as the antics of Ghost, her huge, white cat, in between studying the menu and ordering our meals. We both had healthy appetites and waited until the food arrived and hunger pangs died before we entered the difficult part of our discussion. Twila started with a teasing gibe. "I saw bread pudding on the menu."

"Yuk." I grimaced. "You'd think the damn poisoner could've picked something else to poison," I said with a huge sigh. "I'll probably never be able to eat bread pudding again."

"Too, too bad." She slipped me a sly grin. "I can't imagine not having to sit across from you on the verge of gagging while you scarf down that disgusting mess."

"Harrumph! But, given that the poison could have been a form of oleander, it probably had a fairly bitter taste. I bet it was in the lemon sauce, not the bread pudding."

"You talk to Jack about that?"

"Not yet. It's too soon for the toxicological tests to be back. They probably had to send the samples out to a lab. Besides..."

"Besides," she finished for me, "Jack's not communicating real well with you ever since you tried to make him believe there were ghosts involved in this situation."

"Speaking of which," I said, pushing my chair back, "I don't like leaving Katy there alone too long."

"I'm not finished eating." Twila grabbed a French-fried sweet potato and dipped it into her bowl of white gravy. "You can't let this ghost jerk you around and be at his beck and call. Either one of them."

She popped the potato in her mouth and serenely reached for another as I leaned across the table, whispering frantically, "You haven't seen this other monstrosity, Twila. And you didn't know Bucky when he was alive. He was a slimy, self-centered SOB. One of those nasty redneck types, who think women are put on earth to bring them a beer with the top already popped!"

"The apple doesn't fall far from the tree," she mused.

"You mean, maybe the senator's that way, too? But his other son didn't turn out like that."

"We need to understand this ghost, Alice, before we can control it. You spent quite a length of time discussing Sir Gary with Katy before you finally met him at Esprit d'Chene. That gave you an edge over him. What was Bucky's mother like?"

I sat back, stunned, mind racing. Twila might have hit on exactly the problem. How the hell did she do that, without having met anyone connected to Bucky? And I hadn't even told her, my closest confidant, about Katy and Bucky.

"That's something we'll have talk to Katy about as soon as we get to the plantation," I said. "You see, Bucky blackmailed Katy a long time ago. But I swore I'd never reveal those circumstances to anyone. Katy will have to tell you about it. It involves Bucky's mother." She didn't probe. Sworn confidences are sacred.

"What about this head thing?" I continued. "The spirit's not part of the physical body. But Bucky gives signs of not being able to see, hear, or think without his physical head. How can we reason with something like that? Even Sir Gary says he can't make contact with Bucky."

"Confusion," Twila said. She stirred her iced tea and took a sip. "The spirit's confused as to whether it's in physical form...or spiritual form."

"So," I deduced, "physically or spiritually, it thinks it can't...*think* without its head."

"The news reports are making a big deal about all this," Twila said, changing the subject. "Your local authorities have a leak somewhere. The media knows Bucky's head's missing."

"I doubt it's the authorities leaking info. It's the small-town rumor mill."

"Could be," she agreed. "What's the media situation like in the area?"

I frowned. "Now that I think about it, we haven't experienced the hordes of reporters you'd think would be crowding into the county with a high-profile case like this."

"It's been less than twenty-four hours since word got out."

"It feels like twenty-four days! But you're right. Maybe the senator has enough influence to keep the media from crowding us."

She shook her head. "Initially, perhaps. He can't control it for long. And it's extremely hard to conduct a paranormal investigation in the midst of a feeding frenzy of media sharks."

"They won't get into Esprit d'Chene past Katy's security company."

"We'll need that privacy to deal with Bucky. Now, give me a brief rundown on exactly what's happened—from the moment you got the first phone call from Katy."

I did. She laughed so hard when I described how I chased poor Granny Chisholm through my back yard with handfuls of sea salt, I thought she'd choke on her French-fried sweet potatoes. By now, I could reflect back on the experience and enjoy the hilarity myself. Had we been in a less public place, we'd have given in to one of those rip-snorting spasms of jocularity that befall us at times. Like the time at Eagle Nest, New Mexico, when we got to discussing the attributes of the red-hot candy fireballs she carries in her purse and I nearly drove the car into a flag-lined construction hole due to the laughter tears in my eyes.

"You should've listened to Trucker," she said through her snickers.

"Oh, yeah? Like you *didn't* listen that time Trucker wouldn't go into the old Dawson graveyard we found way back in the hills? And you ended up huddled behind a tombstone while that sheriff and outlaw shot it out?"

We whooped with laughter again, and the diners around us glanced at us uneasily. She lowered her voice. "Don't remind me. You had to take me back to the hotel to change underwear after that one!"

"Hell, my panties were just as bad off as yours. And I had to throw that wonderful T-shirt from Angel Fire away. It had engine grease all over the back of it from hiding under the car with Trucker and Miss Molly."

We grew serious once again, however, as I described the rest of the hours that had passed since then. We had time to share a piece of strawberry-banana pie, which she ordered when the waitress came by to refill our drinks. Even her psychic senses, though, couldn't draw out any more information from the other dimension than Howard and Wilma had as to who the being in my study could have been. And the more I told her about how Katy had been acting, the more worry shadowed her brown eyes. I also told her about Uncle Clarence's terminal illness, as well as Cat's death. We grew quiet, hands clasped on the table to comfort each other.

"Another thing is something even Katy doesn't know that I know," I said finally. "The rumor mill in Jefferson is saying that a woman meeting Katy's description was seen in a local hangout called the Holey Bucket. With Bucky."

"Katy?" She shook her head in disbelief. "That place sounds like one of those honky-tonks you and I used to sneak off to. Our walks on the wild side, with those biker bad boys."

"The guys we played around with at least had a reason for their reputations. And some of them turned out pretty good. Bucky didn't come from a white-trash home. He turned his back on all his advantages and gloried in being the bad seed."

"You never know what goes on inside a person's family life," Twila reminded me. "He could have had his reasons. But we need to confront Katy with this."

"Definitely. And we *have* to find Bucky's head. They've combed the grounds twice now. Maybe the murderer took it with him."

"Or maybe it's hidden inside the house."

"It can't be!" I insisted. "Jack's men searched the manor house also."

"Other than those tire tracks and Grandpere Jean's sword, Jack doesn't appear to have any evidence at all," Twila mused. "Why not look where the evidence doesn't point?"

I solemnly considered that as the waitress slid our check on the table. Twila grabbed it a half-second before my fingers. "You can get the next one," she said, our usual way of splitting meal tickets. Conceding, I dug out the tip and left it on the table.

Before we stood, I said, "I need your help with Sir Gary more than Katy."

"We'll take care of both, don't worry."

In the parking lot, Twila said, "You lead, and I'll follow in my car. But keep your foot out of the carburetor."

CHAPTER 20

I kept a cautious eye on the rearview mirror for the red T-bird. If it dropped back too far, I slowed down. Finally I set the cruise control on sixty-five, even though that meant every other car on the interstate, as well as the huge semis, zipped past us in the fast lane. We'd still get to the plantation well before dark. Or so I thought.

A traffic jam appeared over a rise in the roadway. I bumped the brake to disconnect the cruise and slowed, joining the crawl of vehicles, Twila's rented T-bird right behind me.

"Must be a wreck ahead," I said. Then I realized neither of my companions were riding with me and felt silly. It had to be a wreck, though. I hadn't seen any construction signs since we left Tyler. A slight fender-bender can account for a huge backup on a Texas highway, with a gaggle of rubberneckers heading the opposite direction.

I turned the radio down. Why do we do that when we find ourselves lost or in heavy traffic? Instinct, maybe, so we can concentrate? I'd noticed Jack and other men perform the same operation, so it wasn't just a woman thing. I spontaneously stretched my neck, like the drivers beside and ahead of me, as though we could see around the traffic. Not only were the lanes of traffic bumper to bumper, several semis pulling high trailers blocked the view.

Fingers tapping on the steering wheel, I tried to decide between the right or left lane. Didn't matter. Neither lane seemed to be making much progress. We spent fifteen minutes in the tie-up before hitting a fairly flat stretch of highway. The sun was setting by now, but the Jefferson turnoff wasn't that much farther. And I could see far enough to realize where the holdup was. Cars and semis were playing "you're-next" at a blockade point, each occupant of the fast lane politely allowing a right-lane car or truck to edge over in front of it. Sometimes Texas drivers actually can be polite. Past that point, traffic sped off in a fast flow.

Ahead of me was a pickup, then a semi in front of it. To my left was a black SUV, ahead of it another SUV, pulling a trailer. I waited patiently for my turn at you're-next as the SUV/trailer courteously allowed the semi in my lane to proceed. The SUV/trailer sped on, and I craned my neck again to see around the pickup in front of me.

OH! MY! GOD!

The SUV beside me allowed the pickup to go. Now nothing inhibited my view of Granny's red and white Olds, stately motoring down the interstate, her hand flicking out the window to wave gaily at the people who blasted horns as they passed. I could see through the rear window of the Olds. Granny had her white hair pinned up in a bun, her jaunty red and white yachting cap perched on her head. No doubt she wore her red and white peony-flowered pantsuit, which she called her Sunday-go-to-meetin' outfit, even though she religiously wore it to the grocery store each week.

A horn blared beside me, and the driver of a yellow Corvette angrily waved me to take my turn at passing. I shook my head and motioned him onward. I expected a one-finger salute in return, and he didn't disappoint me. Behind me, a police siren blared. The driver behind the Corvette slowed his pickup, and I stuck my arm out the window to motion him onward. The raggedy Chevy next in line didn't even bother to slow. It sped on with a roar of bad mufflers, and the car behind it followed.

Now a flurry of horns from behind Twila's T-bird joined the noise of the siren. Probably pissed as hell that we'd disturbed the flow of traffic past the impediment to their destinations. I glanced in my rearview mirror to see Twila with her arm out the window, imitating my go-around wave, and decided to ignore the disgruntled drivers in our lane. A good half of them were probably on their way to the gambling boats in Shreveport, and it wouldn't hurt them at all to keep their rent money in their pockets an extra half an hour. Still, a strong urge to follow them and lose myself in the sound of clanging bells and screaming whistles in my favorite casino jabbed me. I could be there within an hour—

The siren closed in, the cruiser speeding cautiously up the highway shoulder. It slowed when it got to Twila, even more when it came up beside me, the astonished face of a state trooper peering over. He pulled up beside the Olds. The siren died, and Granny motored onward. He gave the siren a couple more experimental blasts, and she turned her head and finger-waved at the trooper.

The trooper indicated for me to let him in the lane. I did. He turned the siren on full bore again, but rather than pull over, Granny stately drove on down the road to the next exit, thankfully, the Jefferson one. Olds, cruiser, Jeep, and T-bird paraded off the highway, and at last Granny pulled to the side of the road. Cruiser, Jeep, and T-bird pulled in behind her and the siren warbled into silence.

I jammed the Jeep in park, leaned on the steering wheel, and rubbed my face. When I looked through my windshield again, nothing had changed. Granny still sat behind the wheel of her Olds, the trooper in his cruiser. Behind me, Twila sat in her T-bird, shoulders shaking with laughter as she wiped at her cheeks.

I suppose the trooper was checking out Granny's license plate number before he approached the Olds, and I slid out of the Jeep to...well, I wasn't exactly sure what the hell I was going to do, but I had to be there for Granny. I had better sense, though, than to stalk right up to an armed policeman. He had his window down, so I called, "Officer. Officer?"

For a second, he didn't respond. Then he opened his door and stood, six-plus feet in a starched, brown uniform and gleaming black boots. Even this late in the evening, he wore his wraparound sunshades, and a tan Stetson perched on his head. He slowly turned to face me.

"Sir, I...she's...she does have a driver's license, sir." I couldn't think of a damned thing else to say.

The trooper stared at me. Turned and looked at the Olds. Then snickered. I swear I heard it, even though he was several feet away. And he confirmed it when he followed the snicker with a roar of laughter.

Another deluge of choking laughter assaulted my ears from behind. Twila walked towards me, sopping at her streaming eyes with a wad of tissue.

"This isn't funny," I said in a harsh whisper. "That's Granny."

"I know!" she screamed gleefully. "I know Granny's car!" She grabbed her stomach and bent over. Straightening, she choked, "Isn't it hilarious? I hope I'm just like her at eighty!"

I bit my lip and whirled to check on Granny again. She sat serenely in the driver's seat, her purse propped on the steering wheel as she dug into it.

"Hush," I ordered Twila. Not that it did a damn bit of good, especially when the trooper lost it completely and sat down with a plop on his driver's seat, burying his face in his hands and bending over his knees. His hat tumbled from his head, but he ignored it. Twila, however, walked on around me and picked it up for him.

Still snickering, she nudged his shoulder with the hat, and he looked at her. He took the Stetson and tossed it in the car, accepting a wad of tissues she held out to mop his eyes. "Thanks," he finally said. "I assume you ladies are with the Olds?"

"We are indeed," Twila told him. "Now, anyway. We don't have that much farther to go, Officer. Only —" She turned toward me. "How much further is Esprit d'Chene, Alice?"

"About ten miles."

The officer stood, shaking his head. "I'll get out of y'all's way if you promise me that one of you will lead, the other one follow the Olds. But first I better go pay my respects to Miz Chisholm. Mama'd have my hide if I didn't do that."

"You know Granny?" I asked, finally with courage enough to approach the cruiser.

"Everybody knows Miz Chisholm," he said. "But did I hear right? You ladies are headed to Esprit d'Chene?"

"It's all right, sir," I assured him. "I'm Katy Gueydan's cousin, and this is my aunt, Twila Brown. We're expected."

"You might wanna sneak in the back gate," he told us. "Last I heard on my radio, there's a flock of media nuts at the front."

"Shit," I muttered before I could stop myself.

"Yeah," he agreed. "That's what this is turning into. You ladies drive careful, hear?" He strolled over to the Olds, and we followed.

Granny stuck her arm out the window, a handful of papers in her hand. "I'm not sure what all you want, Officer. Got my driver's license, insurance, and reg'stration here."

"That's not necessary, Miz Chisholm," he said.

Her face creased in a foreboding frown. "Then why'd ya pull me over?"

"Uh...I...well, ma'am—"

Granny's frown turned into a mischievous, toothless grin. "Why, Chuckie Dawson. How's your mama's coon dogs doin'?"

"Just fine, Miz Chisholm," he said. "Fact is, we was talkin' about you last week. Mama said next time I go huntin', I should get an extra coon. Skin it and drop it by your place."

"I'd sure 'preciate that, Chuckie. Been a while since I had baked coon with apple'n bell pepper stuffin'. Now, you be sure'n get all them glands outta it, iffen it be a boar."

"Yes, ma'am," Trooper Chuckie assured her. "Uh...these ladies seem to know you, Miz Chisholm."

Granny appeared to notice us for the first time. "Why, hello, Alice. Twila. What were you two doin' to break the law and make Chuckie pull you over?"

I rubbed my hands down my face and let Twila handle that one. She'd quit laughing.

"Nothing, Granny," Twila told her. "We recognized your car and assumed you were probably heading to Katy's, too. We can all drive along together."

"That'd be nice," Granny said. "You want me to go first?"

"I better go first, Granny," I managed. "Chuckie...uh...the officer says news media's staked out at the front gate, and we'll go in the rear. Katy's housekeeper had that gate secured with a log chain, but I can call ahead on my cell phone and have it unlocked."

Granny nodded agreeably, and Trooper Chuckie said his goodbyes in a respectful voice as Twila and I returned to our vehicles. "Now, don't you forget that coon," Granny called.

"I won't, Miz Chisholm."

He pulled out around the Olds, giving Granny a wave. I followed slowly, allowing Granny plenty of time to pull in behind me ahead of Twila. At the stop sign at the intersection, Trooper Chuckie sat in a vacant lot on the other side of the road. I don't think he was watching us. He was too busy leaning on his steering wheel, laughing.

CHAPTER 21

It was completely dark by the time my Jeep edged into the dirt drive and the headlights illuminated the log chain lying on the ground. I drove on across and stopped far enough down the drive for Granny and Twila to get their cars in. It was quiet—quiet and dark. No security lights. Private meant private. This end of the plantation marked the edge of deeded land. In years gone by, horse- and mule-drawn wagons traveled this way, hauling crops to market in Jefferson. The East Texas Piney Woods is sometimes referred to as The Thicket, and anyone who's driven the county roads can see why. Without continued maintenance, briars, ferns, and yupon bushes with thorns and prickly leaves took over any open space. Around us, an impenetrable mass of underbrush was dotted with pines and trash trees. The waning moon highlighted the darkness beyond our headlights, and idling engines overrode night noises.

"We'll go on as soon as I re-lock the chain," I told Granny as I passed her Olds.

The T-bird's headlights blinded me for a second, and I stumbled on a root protruding into the roadway, catching myself on the fender. Twila turned her lights off, and I trailed my hand on her car as I walked past, eyes adjusting to the dimness. The rattle of the chain caught me off guard. And the figure rattling it drew a shriek from my throat.

Twila swung her door open, and it scraped my hip. I grabbed at the pain with a different cry as she jumped out of the T-bird. The Olds's door opened, also, and Granny tottered to her feet, armed and ready with her walking stick.

"What is it?" Twila whispered in a frantic voice, clutching my arm and trying to pull me into the car. Granny toddled toward us, echoing Twila but in a much louder voice. "I'll bash your brains out!"

"Whassa matter?" the figure asked. I recognized Gabe's voice and nearly collapsed in relief. "I'm just re-lockin' the chain."

"Oh, God," I breathed. "I didn't see you there, Gabe. How are you feeling?"

"Who's Gabe?" Granny asked.

"Sue Ann's husband. I thought he was still in the hospital."

Granny lowered her walking stick. "Huh. He's gonna end up back there, he don't quit skulking 'round in the dark."

"Huh," Gabe said right back as he re-snapped the chain lock. "They said my belly needed a rest after that poison. Told 'em my belly needed something 'sides runny hog slop." He reached behind a tree and came out with a double-barreled shotgun. "An' I ketch anybody who ain't supposed to be here 'round here, they best be able to outrun double ought buck."

Granny contemplated her walking stick, then tottered past me before I realized her intent. "That there looks like a mighty fine piece of fire power. Brownin'?"

"Yep. My daddy give it to me when I was five." In the age-old gesture of a man proudly showing off his weapon, Gabe flicked the barrel open and removed the two shotgun shells. He handed Granny the shotgun— she handed him her walking stick to hold.

"Turn your lights back on, Twila," Granny ordered.

Twila agreeably complied. Gabe and Granny bent over in the red tail-light gleam to examine the shotgun, murmuring as Gabe pointed out attributes. Twila and I waited. And waited. Finally Granny closed the barrel and hefted the gun to her shoulder. Even though I knew the shotgun was empty, I ducked. Twila stifled a chuckle as Granny's tiny figure aimed the massive gun at a fence post and snuggled her wrinkled cheek against the stock. Satisfied, she handed the shotgun back to Gabe and retrieved her walking stick.

"Do you want a ride back?" I asked Gabe.

"Nah. I'll walk."

"The security guards—"

"We done got to know each other. Y'all go on. Sue Ann's got fried chicken for supper."

"Hope she don't fry it in that there veg'table oil," Granny said. "Takes peanut oil to keep chicken from dryin' out when you fry it."

Oh, lord, I mused as Twila got back in the T-bird and I edged Granny into the Olds. Sue Ann and Granny both in the same kitchen. Wasn't that going to be a lot of fun.

The Jeep led the parade, the sandy soil well-packed from recent vehicle traffic. We drove past the pool area, and I parked beside a THIBEDEAUX SECURITY van. On the other side of it was a beautiful Harley Davidson motorcycle. Granny and Twila pulled in beside me, and Granny toddled out with her walking stick and thump-limped over to the bike.

"Hmmm," she said. "I'd sure like to get me a ride on this here purty hog."

"We might be able to handle that," Jack drawled from the front of the van. He strolled out wearing jeans and a faded black T-shirt with a skeleton grinning from the back of a speeding motorcycle, the words LIVE FREE OR DIE encapsulating the picture.

"Jack, Granny. Granny, Jack," I introduced, since he already knew Twila.

"Howdy, Jack," Granny said. "You best be serious about me gettin' a ride. I'm gonna remember your promise."

"Howdy, Granny," Jack replied. "I won't forget."

"That's your bike?" I asked. Jack had always been more of a Jaguar or Ferrari man.

"My second childhood. I was lookin' for a birthday present for a friend one day at the Harley shop in Longview. Next thing I knew, I was test drivin' that bike." He grinned and hugged Twila. "So, how's everybody in Yankee land?"

"Fine, Jack. Jess and I've been talking about coming down for Mardi Gras this spring."

"I'd like to see that old reprobate."

"We'll see what we can do. He finds out you've got your own hog, though, we'll have to tow a trailer with his Indian on it."

"I've got room in my garage," Jack said with a chuckle. "Tell him to bring it on."

Granny had wandered back to the bike, and I called, "Can I get your bags, Granny?"

"Iffen you would, I'd 'preciate it. And don't worry none 'bout your cats," she went on as I opened the rear door on the Olds and pulled out a suitcase. "Maud's gonna drop by."

I carried the suitcase over beside her and said, "What on earth made you decide to drive to Esprit d'Chene?"

She grew serious and stared at me solemnly, her blue eyes filled with worry. "I got a TV, you know." She lowered her voice conspiratorially. "You seen another ghost here yet?"

I said softly, "That's why I called Twila."

Twila joined us and reached for Granny's suitcase. "I'll take this on in. Jack says he needs to talk to you for a minute, Alice."

Jack was leaning against the back of the van, thumbs hooked in his belt and a boot heel propped on the bumper. He straightened and motioned for me to follow him toward the pool area. He halted at the edge of the deep end, and I resolutely kept my eyes on him.

"Katy asked if she could drain the pool, and I told her to go ahead," Jack said, correctly interpreting my reluctance to look at the scene where the body had been found.

I glanced beyond him, but the empty, blue-painted space wasn't any more reassuring than a pond of pink-tinged water would have been. I shivered involuntarily.

"He wasn't killed in the pool," Jack said. "It happened over there, near the shallow end. Someone came out of those ferns there. Probably surprised him, accordin' to how we interpret it. He fell in the pool afterwards."

"His body, not his head."

"If the head went in, someone pulled it out."

"Do you have any suspects yet?"

Jack studied the toes of his western boots. "We got prelim blood types back from the samples on the sword. Most of it's Bucky's."

"Most?"

"There's a small spot of a different type blood on the handle. Could be, the killer nicked his hand when he was handlin' the sword."

The atmosphere around the pool was dark and threatening, despite the security lights gleaming. Clamminess weighted me at times when I hunted ghosts in places where someone had died violently. My psychic senses even experienced the same pain and emotions the person went through at the time of his or her death. That's one reason I'd stayed away from the pool since I arrived. I didn't feel like experiencing Bucky's death, even in a second-hand way. My hand was at my neck, rubbing it gently, and I jerked it away. "I need to get out of here."

He started to say something else, but I whirled and hurried back to the parking area. I leaned against the Jeep's front fender, breathing in deeply and blowing out through my mouth. The stress-relieving technique didn't help. Dark atmosphere pushed on my shoulders like an unwanted lover.

Jack was still back at the pool. He walked to the shallow end and studied the massive bank of ferns. Finally he jammed his hands into his jeans pockets and strolled towards me. "Katy told me a while ago that she'd talked to Tyler Jeeves," he said, carefully studying me.

"I know," I replied. "Well, not that she'd already talked to him, but I know she asked Uncle Clarence to have Mr. Jeeves contact her."

"You heard of a place 'round here called the Holey Bucket?"

"I—not until this morning," I answered honestly. "Do you know where it's at?"

"Down a dirt road out near Caddo Lake. The sheriff tells me it's a swamp rat and biker hangout."

Dejected but not surprised that Jack had learned about Katy's assignation with Bucky, I stared at the manor house, the grounds, the meticulously cared-for flowerbeds, footpaths, and neatly-trimmed hedges. Katy loved the plantation and the life she was building here. What would she do if it all collapsed around her?

"I know my cousin," I said firmly. "There's no way in hell Katy could kill someone. If she had a problem with Bucky, she'd come to me."

He jammed his hands deeper into his pockets and kicked a large piece of oyster shell beside his boot. "Those answering machine tapes had several messages on them that hadn't been erased. And we checked with the doctor Katy's been using since she moved here. Her blood type's the same as that stray spot we found on the sword. DNA'll take a while."

My mind skittered frantically down one path, doubled back, and headed down another, like a frightened mouse trying to outsmart a determined cat in a warren of false trails and dead ends. I wished like hell I'd gone on in to talk to Katy. Then I realized the foolishness of my thoughts and faced Jack without evasion. A murder investigation wasn't a situation in which to be hiding information from a homicide detective.

"Katy didn't kill Bucky! I don't care what evidence you have. I know Katy as well as Twila. Like a sister. Katy pricked her finger trying to sew the cord on Grandmere Alicia's portrait back together. Probably before she put Grandpere Jean's sword back over the mantle."

"After a ghost took it down and cut the cord."

"Yes! Damn it, Jack—"

"You think a grand jury's gonna believe a ghost killed Bucky Wilson-Jones?"

I gaped at him. "A grand jury?"

"There'll be one. If nothing else, to review the autopsy findings and confirm the cause of death. Decide whether to issue a warrant for a John Doe murderer."

"Can't you—?" I bit back the rest of the words before they could tumble past my barely-formed thoughts. No, Jack couldn't—wouldn't—shouldn't even suffer me asking him to sidetrack suspicion from Katy.

"I couldn't," Jack agreed, even though I hadn't asked the question. He kicked the oyster shell into the shrubbery and stared after it. "You got any worn-out jeans with you?"

"Of course!" I said, understanding dawning. "What time do you want me to be ready?"

"Thought you had a book to write."

"Are you rescinding the invitation?"

He chuckled. "Guess that's what comes of knowing a person as well as we do each other. Besides, it'll make me less conspicuous if I walk in with my own babe on my arm."

"We'll look just like an old set of used-to-be's revisiting our days gone by."

As we walked toward the manor house, I slipped my arm through Jack's, just like in our days gone by, but clung tightly. "Jack," I said as we climbed the steps, "nothing will ever make me believe Katy killed Bucky."

"Not even if what you and Katy aren't tellin' me comes to light?"

I paused and looked into his face. "I want some time to talk to Katy alone before we leave. Okay?" He nodded and reached for the doorknob, but I pulled his hand back as I recalled what he'd said a minute ago. "What was on the answering machine tapes?"

He gently disengaged my grasp and reached for the door again. "We'll talk about that later, too, *Chére*. Be ready to go about nine."

CHAPTER 22

I found Katy, Granny, and Twila in the Master Suite, Granny in a rocking chair, Miss Molly curled on her lap and Trucker by her feet. Twila and Katy were on the floor on either side of Trucker, both stroking the dog. They were all silent, glum-faced, staring into space.

"The jury's convened?" I teased.

Katy's frantic gaze flew to my face. "Tyler Jeeves says that I should just keep my mouth shut and not say anything, Alice. But he's never been a suspect in a murder case!"

"They found your blood on the sword, Sugar. I tried to tell Jack what happened, but you don't have a witness."

"Of course she does." Sir Gary materialized by the fireplace. "I saw her prick her finger." Twila studied the ghost with interest, and he bowed his head in acknowledgment. "I am available at your convenience."

"Definitely at my convenience," she murmured, setting the ground rules. Her lips quirked in a mischievous smile, and she continued, "It might be an extremely interesting adventure, a ghost testifying in court."

"Shit, Twila," I burst out. "That's not going to happen."

Granny scooted Miss Molly off her lap and creaked to her feet. Head

179

cocked, she approached Sir Gary, a grin a mile wide on her wrinkled face. "My, my, my. If you was a few years younger, you an' me might just make a fancy couple." She slapped her knee and cackled in glee. "Always wanted to say that to a man!"

"Madame," Sir Gary said with a regal bow. "We would have made a fine couple."

"Ain't you the cat's meow?" Granny beamed. "Twila, you need some help sortin' this handsome rascal's story out, count me in."

Twila rose and took Granny's arm. "Good idea. Why don't the three of us adjourn to the Blue Room? I believe Katy and Alice have things to talk about."

"I'll meet you there," Sir Gary said.

He dissolved in a blink, and Granny picked up her walking stick, which was propped on the back of the rocking chair. At the door, Twila allowed Granny to precede her, then turned to Katy and me. "I have some things for you both. I'll let Granny entertain Sir Gary for a few minutes and be right back."

She closed the door, and I chuckled. "Maybe we can hold a soiree and Granny and Sir Gary can come."

Katy didn't laugh. She scooted onto the bed, glaring at me. "I didn't kill Bucky!"

I sighed, then joined her. We sat cross-legged, as we had as kids, facing each other. But this time we had something a lot more serious to discuss than whether we should "Do It."

"What else was on those answering machine tapes?" I asked.

"You gave those damn tapes to Jack!" she fumed. "You should have asked me first!"

"We're not going to get you out of this mess by hiding evidence. What was on them?"

She buried her face in her hands, shoulders shaking. When she looked up, her face had changed from anger to worry. "I didn't want you involved this time, Alice. I know what bad publicity can do to your writing career."

Stunned, I could only stare. "What's my writing got to do —" Then it dawned on me. Old illicit acts coming home to roost. "The blackmail ten years ago. That's involved in this?"

"He called me a couple weeks ago."

"Bucky?"

"Yes, Bucky, damn it! Who are we talking about? Don't ask me how he got my private number, but it was probably easy, given this blasted small town. I hung up on him the first time. Let the answering machine pick up when he called back." She curled her arms across her stomach. "He said he'd lied when he told us he hadn't kept a copy of that VCR tape. And I better talk to him if I knew what was good for me."

"So you talked? And he said...?"

With a preliminary knock on the door, Twila walked in. I wasn't ready yet to involve my aunt when it looked like maybe now Katy and I were both on the wrong side of the law. *I'm protecting Twila the same way Katy was protecting me*, I thought as Twila dropped some items on the bed.

"There's quince bath soap here." She picked up two bars of plastic-wrapped soap. "Both of you bathe in it immediately, and also add sea salt to your water." She handed us each a small circle of brown seeds. "Quince seeds. Wear these bracelets at all times, even in the bath. They're coated and won't soften."

"Have you sensed anything?" I asked.

"Yes." I waited for her to elaborate, and a strange look crossed her face. "There's the violence, of course, but a lot of confusion, also. It's probably due to Bucky's newly-dead, bewildered state. But there's something more here that I'm going to need to delve into deeper."

"You haven't seen him?" Katy asked as she clasped the bracelet on her slender wrist.

"No, but he's here. No doubt about that."

I shivered, recalling the stumbling monstrosity in the library. "Don't worry. We both know he's here. Are you absolutely sure quince works?"

"It works even better than asafetida," she reassured me, "without the smell. I've also brought some candles, blessed with chants. I want them burning in our bedrooms constantly."

"Why not the whole house?" Katy asked.

I picked up Katy's hand. "Sugar, we don't want him completely banished. At some point, we need to confront him."

"A ghost is timeless," Twila elaborated. "He can outwait us, and the moment we have a lapse in our protection, he'll slip right in. The best thing is to face him, and either insist he cross over or behave himself. Make him realize we have power over him. But first we have to pin him down long enough to exercise the power."

"It's not a complete power," I explained when Katy continued to look confused, reminding me of all the questions I'd had a few years back when I started trying to understand the world across the veil. "After all, he's in another dimension now."

"And he's still trying to get a handle on things himself," Twila went on. "He's not only dangerous, he's extremely unstable, considering the personality he crossed over with."

Katy squeezed my hand, then dropped it, and I grimaced. Noticing my pain, Twila handed me a small glass jar. "I want you to use this, also, Alice."

"Not Katy?"

She chuckled. "It's some aloe ointment for your hands. It'll help your cuticles, too."

That was something I could use. She picked up the tall fluted vase with a white candle in it, set it on the mantle, then pulled a packet of matches from her pocket and lit it. "I've already told Sir Gary that I'll deal with him after I get all the protection in place." She turned and studied Trucker and Miss Molly. "Which bathroom can I use to give the animals a bath?"

"In quince soap?" I asked.

"Of course. They're involved in this ghosthunt, too."

"Granny's in the Green Room," Katy said. "But the White Room's free."

"I'd rather use a laundry tub," Twila said.

"The laundry room's off the kitchen," I told her. "You won't have any trouble with Trucker. He loves a bath. But you better let me help you with Miss Molly."

"You don't have time." Twila gathered up Miss Molly and snapped her fingers for Trucker to follow her. "You have things to do." The dog padding obediently after her, she closed the door behind her, and I shook my head for the thousandth time over her honed abilities. She probably knew even more about what I had to do than I did. And right now, what I had to do was take advantage of this privacy with Katy to drag some more information out of her.

"What did Bucky say when he called you?" I demanded.

She fiddled with the quince seed bracelet and ducked her head. I none-too-gently tipped her chin up to face me. "Don't hide anything from me, Katy! This is serious business!"

The heartbreak in her eyes floored me. She'd never looked so fragile, so ready to fall to pieces, even back when we were dealing with Bucky the first time. But then, we were older now, more mature. Knew the consequences of actions we'd gone into hell-bent and take-no-prisoners in our younger days.

"He wanted to reform," she said. "He'd seen his father here at Esprit d'Chene and wanted me to act as a go-between."

Puzzled, I frowned. "That doesn't sound so bad."

"I thought so, too. That's why I agreed to meet him and talk about it."

"At the Holey Bucket?"

Katy's eyes widened. "Someone saw us!"

"Jack knows, too. As well as half the county, if your friend Irene has as big a mouth as I think she does."

She grabbed my arms. "He wrote a book, Alice. He said that if he didn't get back into his father's good graces, he was going to send copies of it to all sorts of people. He said he was tired of living like a swamp rat when his father and brother were living rich."

"My God," I breathed. "What if someone else has that manuscript now? With all this uproar over Bucky's death, hell, it would be a best-seller before it hit the shelves."

Sue Ann tapped on the door, then opened it and stuck her head in. "Supper's ready."

"We'll be down in a few minutes," I said.

She slammed the door, and Katy said, "She doesn't like people late for meals."

"We're not going anywhere until we both take our baths." I scooted off the bed and picked up my bar of soap. Hesitating, I said softly, "You know we're going to have to tell Jack some of this."

Tears clouding her eyes, she nodded. "I know. I know. Soon. But please, let's wait a while. Maybe the investigation will turn up something. But feel free to tell Twila all you need to. Bucky's scaring me more dead than alive."

"Have you thought any more about who that other voice on the answering machine was, Sugar? The one who threatened you with payback?"

"It's one of those voices I know I've heard before, but recognition hangs just out of reach. You know?"

"Yeah. Let me know the moment you think you recognize it."

CHAPTER 23

In the laundry room Twila hummed one of those oldies songs she loved amidst splashing sounds. Jack's gunbelt and pistol hung on a peg with some multi-colored aprons over by the door. I stuck my head in the laundry room door. Trucker sat quiescent on the floor, draped in one of Katy's fluffy bath towels. Twila rubbed another towel over Miss Molly and, much to my surprise, the cat didn't struggle like she did when I infrequently bathed and flea-dipped her. Twila had a way with cats, though, even those not her own.

"I'll be in the dining room in just a second," she told me. She'd already changed into a long, straight skirt and a soft, hip-length sweater. Uh oh. We were eating in the dining room?

I felt out of place in my worn jeans and T-shirt when I walked into the formal dining room. Sue Ann had set the table with china, candles, and a fall foliage centerpiece. Golden fried chicken heaped on a silver platter, with mashed potatoes and various other vegetables mounded in crystal bowls. A crisp salad set in front of the two unused place settings. At the head of the table, Katy wore a flowing blue pantsuit, Granny on her right in a high-necked silk dress, clasped with a cameo broach. I'd never seen her look so spiffy. Even Jack, on Katy's left, had come up with

185

a jacket somewhere, and the black T-shirt beneath it gave him a rakish, stylish air.

I sat beside Jack. "I didn't know we were dressing for dinner."

"We normally do," Katy answered.

"I'll remember." I reached for a silver pitcher of salad dressing. Yum, blue cheese, my favorite, despite the cholesterol. "Everything looks wonderful."

"Chicken's a little dry," Granny said, but she had a bare leg bone on her plate and was working on a breast.

I buttered a still-warm yeast roll, and managed to eat every bit of half of it and a few bites of salad before all hell broke loose. Miss Molly's yowl signaled the beginning of the riot. Everyone froze, forks poised with chunks of food. For a split second, I thought Twila had finally found a cat she couldn't charm, but knew instantly that was a lie. Trucker let loose next, a series of howls and growls. The hair on the back of my neck crawled as though hundreds of fleas were scurrying through it.

"Alice!" Twila screamed, but I was already out of my chair, Jack right behind me.

The cat met me at the dining room door, the towel-caped dog behind like a four-legged super hero. Miss Molly crawled up my leg, claws digging in, and I yowled in pain. Her claws sank through my T-shirt, and I jerked her loose as she went for my shoulder just as Trucker hit my legs. The dog knocked me into Jack, who reacted—but not quickly enough. We fell into the table, and Miss Molly sailed out of my grasp, splattering straight into the mashed potatoes.

She's not a potato cat. She yowled and leaped free, scattering china, dishes, and centerpiece in her bid for a hiding spot. She scrambled off the far side, claws tangled in the snowy white linen and lace.

"Oh, no!" Katy grabbed for the tablecloth, but the cat's weight pulled it out of her hands. Precious china and crystal were now history—as was our meal.

Jack set me on my feet, and I glanced around for Trucker. He was halfway curled onto Granny's tiny lap, his head on her shoulder, trembling and whining. I grabbed his collar and pulled him to the floor, and Granny heaved a sigh of relief.

By then, Jack was out the door, and I raced after him. In the hallway, I stuck my head back in. "Stay in here!" I ordered Katy and Granny.

"Bet your boots," Granny said. Katy only sat there, stunned, staring at the mess.

Jack stood in the kitchen, gunbelt hanging from his wrist and pistol drawn. After the cacophony in the dining room, the eerie silence here gave me the creeps. "I don't think that gun will do you any good," I whispered. Then tiptoed to the laundry room door, motioning Jack to stay back when he tried to grab my arm.

He grabbed again, and dragged me to a halt. "I'll go first."

"Damn it, no!" I jerked free. "You're out of your depth here, Jack. And Twila's in danger!" I edged to the door, Jack close behind. With a breath of courage, I eased into the room.

Twila was at the laundry tub, the bar of soap in her hand held out protectively. Bucky stood over in a corner, the doll's head from my room perched on his neck.

"My God," I breathed.

The doll's head swiveled to stare at me. The mouth opened, and I half expected to hear a "mama" bleat, but no sound emerged. Bucky evidently hadn't learned to manipulate the vocal cord part of his new appendage.

"What do you want me to do?" I whispered to Twila.

"About what?" Jack asked. I whipped a quick glance at him. His puzzled face stared around the room, pistol lax in his hand. Damn, he couldn't see Bucky.

But Bucky saw him. Or maybe it was me he was after. The ghost lumbered forward, then stopped and lifted one hand to his nose. The head swiveled toward Twila, and she jabbed with the quince soap. Bucky took a step backward.

"He smells the soap," Twila whispered.

"Who?" Jack asked.

"Get over here with me, Twila," I said quietly.

She slowly slid one foot, then another in a sideways motion, the quince soap extended. Bucky watched her...me...continuing to rub the back of his hand across the doll nose.

"Will one of you tell me what the hell's going on here?" Jack demanded.

Twila slid a little closer.

"If you know what's good for you, Jack, stay behind me—watch out, Twila!"

With Jack distracting me, I yelled too late. She stepped in a smear of soap bubbles on the floor, and her evening sandaled-foot slid from under her. Instinctively, I rushed forward, but my rubber-soled tennis shoes didn't have any more purchase than her sandals. We whomped together, tangled our arms around each other, and stayed on our feet somehow. I hit the laundry tub and swore viciously as tears of pain clouded my eyes. Damn, I was going to end up with a mess of bruises and scratches on my body before this was all over with.

"Don't, Jack!" Twila screamed.

I disentangled myself and batted at my pain-teary eyes—in time to see Jack totally ignore the warning. He headed straight for Bucky, whose doll head now focused on the new antagonist. And Jack wasn't protected by quince soap.

"Jack, get the hell out of here," I warned. He ignored me and walked another couple steps, a grim but confused look on his face as he stared around the small room. His hand hung by his leg, the pistol dangling.

"There's nobody else in this room," he muttered.

"There is!" I contradicted. "You just can't see him!"

He rolled his eyes. "A ghost, huh?"

"Yes!"

He started to re-holster his pistol. "My jurisdiction doesn't cover that end of the county."

And that's when Bucky lunged.

"Watch out!" Twila and I both screamed.

Bucky swiped the pistol out of Jack's hand. Jack's mouth gaped, and he froze as the pistol thudded on the top of the industrial-size washing machine, skidded across, and bounced against the control panel. Twila and I were already on the move. I lunged for Jack, placing myself and my protection between him and the ghost. Twila went after the pistol. Bucky beat her to it. He grabbed the gun, holding it threateningly. I glanced at Jack, imagining what he saw: pistol wavering in the air, pointed straight at him.

Twila threw the quince soap. It hit Bucky's gun arm, and he howled. I guess his vocal cord was working with his new head. Or perhaps the surprise and pain reestablished his vocal ability. He dropped the gun and grabbed his arm.

Two things happened. Twila dove for the pistol and hit the floor in a flurry of skirts and body-thud. She pulled the gun against her body. Sir Gary materialized behind Bucky and slapped that silly doll's head off his shoulders. It rolled toward Twila and she froze in fear.

I went for Twila. Grabbed her by the sweater and hauled. The sweater ripped, but I dragged her several feet, Jack just standing there, shaking his head.

"Damn it, help me, Jack!" I screamed.

He lunged forward, but didn't help me get Twila to her feet. Instead, he took the pistol from her fingers and aimed it at Sir Gary. "Who the hell are you?" he demanded.

Shit. At least he saw *that* ghost.

Sir Gary stared haughtily at Jack. "I, sir, am Sir Gary Gavin, Earl of the House of Spencer. And you?"

Flustered, Jack replied, "Jack Roucheau. Homicide." Then his mouth dropped as though he couldn't believe he'd actually spoken.

I couldn't help it. I laughed. And Jack glared at me.

The confrontation between the two of them distracted Twila's and my attention from Bucky. I heard a thud on the washer as the head bounced there. Bucky had somehow found it on the floor. He fumbled again and victoriously grasped it, plopping it back on his shoulders. Then he leaped straight through the laundry room wall and disappeared.

"How the hell does he manage to take that head with him through a wall?" Twila mused. "It's real, not an other-dimensional object."

"If you'll tell that bobby to point his bloody gun elsewhere, maybe I can answer that," Sir Gary said.

I stifled a stab of satisfaction at Jack's white face. Still, he held the pistol in a ready-to-shoot grasp, both arms extended, the barrel steady, pointed at Sir Gary.

"Jack, he's a ghost." I chuckled with both relief at Bucky's absence and amusement. "If you shoot, you'll just put a hole in Katy's dryer."

Jack took his eyes off Sir Gary. Stared at me. Stared at Twila. Then he slammed the pistol into his holster. I reached out to touch his arm, but met his back. He stormed out of the laundry room and slammed the door behind him with a resounding thud.

"Well," Twila said. "Looks like Jack's finally met his first ghost."

"And a perfectly fine meeting it was," I said with a nod. "I wonder why, though, he could see Sir Gary but not Bucky."

"Because Sir Gary's a much more developed ghost," she explained as though chastising a small child. Which she was in effect doing, given her weighty experience against my fairly fledgling status. "He's been a ghost a lot longer than Bucky. But did you notice? I do believe Jack saw the doll's head, once it was off Bucky's shoulders."

I quirked an eyebrow at Sir Gary, silently asking for the explanation he'd promised. He shrugged nonchalantly. "I assume it becomes part of this Bucky person when he attaches it, thus, invisible to those who cannot see us." He grimaced at the door. "Especially a bobby who thinks with his brains rather than senses."

"Jack's a disbeliever," I said, "but make no mistake about it. He's not a bumbling cop."

"No?" Sir Gary said. "Not like that Columbo detective I see on Katy's TV, huh?"

I bristled in defense of my ex-husband. "If you've got anything to do with Bucky's death, Jack will ferret it out. He *will* crack this case." My anger died as I remembered just which way the investigation was leading. "No matter who the killer is."

"Well." Twila stared around the floor and crouched to dig her bar of quince soap from a stack of plastic laundry baskets. "I, for one, would like to have something to eat."

Sir Gary stepped away from us, and his back half disappeared into the wall behind him. "Uh...you aren't going to bring that stuff with you during our discussions, are you?"

"No," Twila reassured him. "I'll do a white-light procedure when we talk. Even though I've bathed with it, it won't bother you then...unless you give me a problem of some sort."

Sir Gary sniffed in disdain. "I have an important quest. I have no time for foolishness."

"You really helped us with Bucky," I told him. For once I felt quite happy with Sir Gary. "We both thank you for that. But you might not be around the next time. Do you have any idea where Bucky's hiding out?"

"None at all."

"Jack says that one thing that helps him in an investigation is to put himself inside the mind of the killer," I pondered. "Maybe the same thing would work for us—trying to figure out what Bucky's thinking. I suppose he *can* think now, with the he—"

Twila and I both stared at each other at the same time, mouths agape in understanding. Then we looked over at Sir Gary, who gave a regal nod. "His real head," we all whispered.

"Yes," Twila confirmed. "And since he's hanging around Esprit d'Chene, he obviously believes the head is hidden here somewhere."

"They've searched the manor house," I told her. "And the grounds. Sir Gary's searched, too. Maybe we're wrong, and the killer did take the head."

"I don't think so." Twila placed a finger on her cheek. "If he...or she...had taken the head, I believe Bucky would be off there looking for it, rather than here. Now, maybe I better go change again before I go into the dining room. This sweater seems to be a tad ragged."

"Uh...there's nothing left to eat. Miss Molly made a mess of the table. But Katy's probably whipping up a replacement meal."

The laundry room door opened, and Katy peered in. "Everything all right? Hello, Sir Gary. Jack's waiting outside for you, Alice, and there's another platter of chicken in the oven, Twila."

Mouth watering, I headed for the oven. Let Jack stew a few more minutes. After all, he had at least part of a meal under his belt. I didn't have to worry that he'd head off to the Holey Bucket alone. He had way too many ghost questions.

CHAPTER 24

Irritated to no end, Sir Gary searched for the elusive new ghost again. Things had worked out as he planned—up to a point. Bucky had found the doll's head, which Sir Gary retrieved from the closet in the Peach Room. As intended, the second ghost...connected with the head. Too well, it appeared. Sir Gary had thought the new head would make Bucky both communicative and visible. By all rights, they should have been able to follow the bobbing doll's head while Bucky tried to hide. Instead, the head became a part of Bucky—except when disconnected. It hadn't dawned on him why, until Alice questioned the phenomena.

Sir Gary admitted that trying to keep his Katy from being arrested had overcome his quest. When he heard her on the phone to her uncle, that dastardly old fool, admitting she needed an attorney, the uneasiness erupted. How could he leave Katy in this mess?

Try to put yourself in the mind of the killer. Alice's advice ran through his mind. Where would the killer hide the head? Wouldn't he be in a hurry to leave? Why even bother to hide it?

He glided into the *garconniére* for the fifth or sixth time. The new ghost was obviously keeping on the move. Why? Was it, as Alice indicated, confusion? Or was he deliberately binding himself here for some reason and until he fulfilled his own quest? Maybe if Sir Gary could remember why he hadn't passed through the light himself when he had the opportunity, he could understand Bucky's plight. Not that he had any desire to understand him over and above making sure his Katy was safe from the authorities after he left. Too bad that hound of Alice's wasn't a bloodhound. Maybe the two of them could track down that blasted head.

The *garconniére* was dark, but that didn't bother him. The three rooms weren't large—a small parlor and two bedrooms. Dusty, as he'd noticed before, except where the bobbies had disturbed things in their searches. Sue Ann didn't bother to clean in here unless Katy informed her someone would be using it. He couldn't imagine that either he or the multitude of bobbies had overlooked a clue, but nothing was too much effort to protect Katy.

Jack was undertaking his investigation the same way the cops on TV did: following the victim's trail during the hours leading up to the crime. The same way Alice had informed him that she would undertake to uncover the mystery of his death. But so what if Katy had been seen at some dive called the Holey Bucket? He'd known plenty of Ton women who walked on the wild side. Something told Sir Gary that what they needed was right under their noses...somewhere.

Evidently not in the *garconniére*, though. Ah, well, he might as well enjoy a movie while he waited for Twila to summon him. There might not be movies once he crossed. A TV with an out-of-date VCR set in a corner of the parlor. Katy had long ago gone to DVDs, but a selection of VCR tapes on the shelf looked promising. He liked the older movies, anyway. He wagged his finger and turned on the TV, then levitated *High Noon* from the shelf.

The tape hovered on the verge of inserting. Someone had left a movie in the machine, probably whoever last used the guest house. It was playing, sound muted. A home movie? Hmmm. Could be interesting. He discarded *High Noon* on an end table. Where was the remote to turn on the sound?

A roar of rage split the room. Bucky stood in the open door of the *garconniére*, fists upraised in a fighter's stance.

"Well, well, well," Sir Gary mused. "I prefer swords to fisticuffs, but we can have a go at that, if you wish."

Bucky charged. Sir Gary easily evaded him, cocked his fists, and danced around on his tiptoes the way he'd seen that pugilist Ali do on TV. Bucky whirled to confront him again.

"You know," Sir Gary said, ducking a wild swing, "we could talk about this. I have no idea if we can actually engage in a brawl in our states. And you must feel the need to understand the state you're in. I've got the experience to pass on to you."

Bucky paused. "You're dead, too?" he said, his voice unused and rusty.

"For a lot longer than you." Sir Gary made the mistake of lowering his fists. Bucky connected with an uppercut that rocked his head back.

"You son of a bitch!" Sir Gary snarled. Bucky swung again, and Sir Gary dissolved. He materialized behind Bucky as the other ghost peered around the room and tapped Bucky on the shoulder. Bucky never made his turnaround. Sir Gary slapped the head off, and it bounced on the back of a settee, on behind it.

Headless, Bucky dove through the settee. When he emerged, with the doll's head firmly in place, he headed for the door.

"Wait just a blasted minute!" Sir Gary zipped after Bucky and chased him across the Rose Garden, well behind him. Damn, that bloody fool could move! He lost him in the maze, despite knowing the intricacies of it. Obviously, Bucky knew the secret to the puzzle also.

Giving up, Sir Gary glided back to the *garconniére*. But the tape was gone.

* * *

Jack didn't ask me any questions right away. He silently handed me a helmet and forked the Harley. He wore a beautiful black leather jacket now over his T-shirt. The engine rumbled to life, and he revved the engine in a series of sharp thrusts. I took my time adjusting my helmet before I slipped on and settled my feet on the passenger foot pegs. Then grabbed Jack around the waist as he popped the clutch and roared down the driveway, scattering oyster shells and a pair of peacocks.

I chuckled, unnoticed by Jack, since the deep-throated engine roar covered the sound. Jack might be trying to pull off the strong, in-charge façade, letting me know the ghosts hadn't bothered him one damn bit, but the direction he took told me his mind wasn't exactly up to par.

The gate loomed ahead—across the driveway and locked. Jack braked a bare foot from the iron bars. Feigning nonchalance, I watched one of the horses at the fence. The Harley's engine idled, Jack's legs straddled on either side of the bike to hold it upright.

"You gonna get off and call the house to have them open the gate?"

"You gonna admit you saw Sir Gary?" I threw back.

His body stiffened. He dropped the kickstand and started to swing off.

"Just a second," I told him. "I asked Katy to let us out when she figured we'd had enough time to reach the gate. By the way, what happened to all the media?"

"I ordered them away. Threatened them with a gag order from the District Judge if they didn't respect Katy's privacy. How long did you tell Katy to wait before she opened the gate?"

In response, the gate slid sideways. I decided not to prod Jack any further right then. After all, he was the one in charge of navigation, and I wasn't too sure how this motorcycle riding worked. I'd only ridden a couple times before, and on much smaller bikes. He might find a way to scare the bejesus out of me.

Jack roared out of the gate into a sharp left turn. I grabbed him around the waist and dug my nails into his stomach, but it was as flat as a Zydeco band washboard. I ended up with more T-shirt than skin. I'd grabbed a light jacket, since I knew I'd be open to the elements on this blasted motorcycle, but the cold wind penetrated the quilted flannel. I closed my eyes and lay my head against Jack's back, but that only made me seasick. Or motorcycle-sick, whichever. I opened my eyes, and the roadside whirred past in indistinguishable blackness.

Finally I'd had enough and raised my head to shout. Jack hit the brakes about then, and we skidded to a stop, sideways in the road. I peered over his shoulder in time to see a deer in the roadside under-brush, wide-eyed in a caught-in-the-headlight stance. Another deer bounded across in front of us. The movement broke the first deer's trance, and it followed, flipping its white-flag tail.

Jack sat motionless after the deer disappeared. I waited him out, my fingers never once relaxing their grip. At last he heaved a sigh. "Sorry," he apologized. "I'll take it easier."

"I read somewhere that this county has the highest deer population in Texas. And even as small as they are, I understand they can damage a car real bad, let alone a bike. Plus there's dogs running loose all along this road."

He muttered a grunt, shifted the bike, and eased the throttle. Instead of proceeding down the country road, he pulled into an intersecting dirt road, where he cut the engine and dropped the kickstand. Disentangling my fingers, he slid off the bike, lifted his helmet visor up, and jammed his thumbs into his back pockets.

I flipped my visor up, also. "Beautiful night. A little chilly, though, don't you think?"

"You're telling me," he growled, "that that...*thing* in the laundry room was a ghost."

"Both of them," I replied.

"I only saw one."

"At least you admit that part of it. Tell me what you saw."

"Look, Alice —" He heaved a sigh of resignation. "A man. Dressed in clothes probably from the nineteenth century."

"Eighteenth," I corrected.

"He had a British accent."

"I noticed you could hear Sir Gary, too. That's good. You'll turn into a ghosthunter yet."

His mouth thinned to where I was afraid the next sound would be his teeth grinding. "I have no damn desire to hunt ghosts. I don't want to see ghosts. I don't want to hear ghosts. I don't believe in ghosts."

"Then maybe you have an explanation for what you saw?" He didn't, but he wasn't about to admit it. "I told you, Sir Gary's the reason I was already planning to come to Esprit d'Chene the other morning. He wants me to investigate his death."

"A couple of hundred years ago."

"Yes. But now Twila has to take on that. I'm too busy elsewhere."

He bent his head and stared at the dirt road. Leaned down and picked up a small rock, tossed it back and forth between his palms. "No damn ghost killed Bucky."

"No," I agreed. "Sir Gary denies it, and I believe him. However, if I'd ever get some time to talk to him myself, instead of worrying about Katy, maybe Sir Gary would remember something that might help us figure out who actually did."

"You want me to interview a ghost in a crime investigation? I might as well hand in my badge! I'd be laughed off the force!"

I shrugged. "I didn't say you had to do it. Or, even if you did, you wouldn't have to write up a report, would you?"

"Hell, yes! Especially if I got any useful information —" Jack glared at me for another few seconds before he threw the rock into the woods. It hit a tree trunk and bounced off. "I don't believe this! I'm standing here talking about...about talking to a ghost!"

"We don't have to decide anything right now, sweetie," I soothed. "You can think about it. Or I'll talk to Sir Gary for you. But I'll need to know more about the investigation."

"I can't discuss that with a civilian."

"Then how will I know what to ask Sir Gary? Or Bucky, for that matter. If we can ever pin him down long enough to get him to talk through that doll's head."

"The doll's head? That head rolling around the laundry room?"

"I stumbled over it in the hallway the first night, and put it in my room. But when I came back after breakfast the next morning, it was gone." I shivered at the thought of Bucky prowling my room. "Bucky's using it now."

"A headless ghost is using a doll's head in place of his own head."

"Uh-huh," was all I said.

"What a piece of bullshit!" Jack spat.

I hummed a few bars from the *Twilight Zone* theme song. Off-key, but Jack grasped the idea. His fists clenched at his sides, maybe to keep from throttling me. I glanced around casually, as though perfectly at ease out here in the dark night, on a lonely country road miles from help with a man trained in dangerous arts. A man totally infuriated with me.

I put on a pretty good act, if I do say so, but inside my stomach was tight and I had trouble swallowing. So much depended on Jack's acceptance of the fact that, not only were there ghosts at Esprit d'Chene, but there was a good possibility they had information for us. Especially Bucky. I should have been there right now, trying to contact Bucky, trying to prove that Katy hadn't killed him, instead of heading for a rundown honky-tonk for a beer. But I also needed desperately to find out where the investigation was leading, and Jack was my best source.

Hell, and I needed to get some writing done. Other than the little I'd managed after I arrived, my laptop had sat dead and silent. Maybe dead wasn't the right word to use just now, I mused when an owl hooted somewhere nearby. The spooky sound sent a shiver up my spine before I distinguished between that sort of chill and the chill that precedes a ghost's appearance. Wouldn't it be a trip if some long-dead soul wandering the woods decided to make contact now?

I wondered if I could ride a motorcycle on my own. Probably not. And, thankfully, I didn't have to find out. Jack flipped his visor down and slid back in front of me. After he heel-kicked the kickstand up, I laid a hand on his arm.

"What?" he snarled.

"Are you going to let me help?"

He ignored me for a full thirty seconds. Rustles sounded in the underbrush. An armadillo wandered out, armor pale gray against the red dirt. It shuffled across the road, then rooted at a rotting log in the ditch in search of grubs. I envied that small refugee from the dinosaur age. Its tiny brain left no room beyond the instinct for food, survival, and procreation. Protected by its shell, it had a total unconcern for the ineffective dangers in its habitat. Its major problem came from speeding cars, whenever it decided to cross a busy highway, and I doubted any gleam of fear had time to penetrate when it met such a swift, sure death.

Jack started the bike.

"Okay," I said. "Twila and I will work on our own."

"I'll tell you what I can," he finally said. "We'll talk at the bar."

CHAPTER 25

J ack drove cautiously now, and I relaxed, actually enjoying the huge machine. There was something about being out in the openness, part of wind and nature. No cushioned steel doors and soft leather bucket seats, no roof overhead. Just me, Jack, the bike, a pleasant rumble between my legs, and the wilderness. I sort of missed my radio, though, which would have kept my mind off the trail of wondering whether Jack and I would still be together if we'd discovered the closeness of motorcycle riding earlier. My toes curled, and I sat back, away from Jack.

I would have overlooked the turnoff—probably more than once. A small steel rod with a red reflector light marked the drive. Jack edged in confidently. The underbrush grew thick on each side of the small, dirt path. Once the headlight shone briefly on a dingy gray bra dangling from a yupon limb. We bounced through puddles that splashed our jeans legs, and the bike slid on a downgrade. I grabbed Jack, but he kept the bike upright and eased the throttle higher to climb a small bank.

I couldn't imagine bringing my Jeep through here. The holly, yupon, and briars would make short work of its paint job. A couple of times a branch reached out and snagged my jacket. We crossed a wooden bridge, planks rumbling, and I inched my head high enough to see over Jack's shoulder just as the honky-tonk came into view.

A rickety wooden shack sprawled low to the ground beyond a sparsely-graveled parking lot. A half-dozen bikes plus three rusty pickups parked helter-skelter. A neon-orange bucket, tipped sideways, leaked a stream of neon drops from the bottom beside the purple letters: OLEY UCKET. Strains of an old Hank Williams tune filtered out. The door was propped halfway open, and I wrinkled my nose in anticipation of the noxious atmosphere inside as wisps of cigarette smoke drifted out.

Jack eased between a pickup and another bike, and cut the engine. He dropped the kickstand and slid off. I followed more clumsily, legs unsteady from being cocked at an angle on the footpegs. Jack slipped an arm around me until I got my balance, then stepped away, probably still pissed. Well, let him be. That was another major difference between us. Though a trifle scared when I faced my first ghost, the excitement of the moment still lingered. Jack's just-the-facts brain was having trouble grasping something he considered nonfactual.

He snapped his helmet strap around the handlebar, and reached for mine, which he secured on the other side.

"Nobody will steal our helmets?" I asked.

"Bikers don't mess with other bikers' machines or equipment," he muttered. "But you might want to hang onto your pocketbook."

"I didn't bring one. This is your treat."

Ignoring the attempt to lighten the mood, he steered me toward the door with a hand on my back. No one paid much attention to us. The bartender, a gray-bearded guy of at least three hundred pounds, did glance up and nod. Tables scattered on the open floor, empty, and a row of booths lined the far wall. Everyone else was seated in the booths or gathered around the pool table, sipping longnecks. And every one of them had a cigarette either sticking between their index and middle finger or thumb and index finger. A leather-clad man at the pool table bent over his cue stick, cigarette dangling between his lips, ash threatening to drop on the green velvet. He eyed his next shot through a smoke-squinted gaze.

Our feet crunched on empty peanut shells flung amid scatters of sawdust on the warped board floor. I scooted onto a dirty, black-and-white cowhide upholstered stool, identifiable only because the dark gray areas were a tad lighter than the black. Jack leaned against the bar and propped one booted foot on a steel pipe running the length of it a foot from the floor. The bartender swished a beer mug in a sink of nasty-looking water and clunked it on the counter with a couple dozen other mugs as he quirked an eyebrow at Jack.

"Two Buds," Jack answered the unspoken query.

"Make one a Bud Lite," I said.

"Longneck or draft?" the bartender asked, already setting Jack's bottle in front of him.

"Longneck, please," I replied. The bottles had been through the bottling process and were cleaner than the mugs.

He grabbed my light beer from the cooler and set it in front of me. Then he added a smaller glass from his stock behind the bar, tipping it over the bottle neck. Red lipstick smeared the glass rim, and I clunked the glass back on the bar as Jack handed over some money.

Tiny pieces of ice slid down the bottle to melt on the bar. One thing Texas beer drinkers insist on is icy cold beer, summer or winter. I picked up the bottle and took a long swallow. Ah, it tasted good, especially in this smoke-filled, stifling bar. The bartender noticed my beer drinking skill and winked approval as he laid Jack's change in front of him. Jack left the money on the bar, the age-old indication we'd be drinking more. He pulled out a half-empty pack of Marlboros from his jacket pocket, shook one partway out, and offered it to me.

"We don't smo—" I began, before I caught the warning glint in his eyes. Okey dokey. When in Rome...or a Texas bar...and all that stuff. I rolled the cigarette around in my fingers. It wasn't that I hadn't once been a smoker—a two-pack a day, hard core, gotta have my cigs with my morning coffee smoker. I justified the heavy habit by telling myself that I probably burned up at least half of each cigarette in the ashtray as I worked at my computer, forgetting I'd lit it. But I knew better. And when it got to the point where the morning coughing and hacking made me sick at my stomach, I quit. Cold turkey, too, and I was damned proud of myself.

I'd never quit wanting one, though. I stared at the Marlboro as Jack held out a disposable lighter, flame burning. I hesitated, then told myself I wouldn't inhale and bent forward. Damn, that smoke felt good in my lungs, even though it did make me slightly light-headed. Uh-oh. I wasn't going to inhale. I laid the cigarette in an already overflowing ashtray— there was one in front of each bar stool—and picked up my beer.

"Ain't seen you folks in here before," Bartender said.

I stayed quiet—like a good little biker babe—and let Jack handle the conversation.

"Heard about it a while back," Jack said. "Decided to have a look."

"It don't get goin' for another hour or two," Bartender said. "And we gotta couple rules. Any fights go outside. And...you carryin'? Smoke or hidden?" I knew the language. He was asking Jack if he had drugs or a weapon.

"Nope," Jack said.

"Take your word for it, but I find out different, you won't be back." He came up with a short-barreled shotgun from under the bar, held it in sight for a second, then slipped it back.

A commotion erupted over by the pool table, and I swung around. The stool squawked, and I vowed once again to lose that extra ten pounds. Two burly men pounded leather-clad on the shoulders. I'd played a few games of pool in the past, and I scanned the table. He'd cleaned off all the solid balls, and the eight-ball was missing. Several striped balls still scattered on the green velvet, so he'd won the game.

"Hey, tarbender," one of the congratulators called. "Put Bubba's beer on my tab!"

"You ain't got a tab," the bartender called back. "It's bucks up front."

The man pulled a ragged billfold attached to a chain on his belt out of his pocket and strolled to the bar. "Howdy," he said to Jack as he handed the bartender a twenty, then stuck out his hand. "Rick."

"Jack," Jack replied as they shook hands.

The bartender stuck a hand across the bar, too. "Max."

Jack shook. He didn't bother to introduce me. This was a man's world, although a couple other hard-looking women nursed their drinks in the shadowed booth in the farthest corner.

"You ride?" Rick asked.

"Harley," Jack said.

Rick and Max grinned with approval. "Buy you a beer?" Rick asked.

Jack held up his still-full bottle. "Maybe later."

The bartender slapped some bills and change on the bar, and followed it with three longnecks from the cooler. Rick stuffed the change in his pocket and grabbed the beers. "Later," he said to Jack, and strolled back over to his buddies.

"What next?" I asked Jack quietly.

He picked up two ones from his pile of change and handed them to me. "Jukebox," he said, slanting his head at the elderly machine over by the pool table.

Ah, man, just what I wanted to do. Sidle through that mass of half-drunk testosterone to play some songs for their enjoyment. But I slid off my barstool. In bars like this, women did grunt work like playing the jukebox.

I carried my beer with me to signal that I already had a date, in case someone hadn't noticed me come in with Jack. As I approached the pool table, leather-clad emitted a low wolf whistle, which in another life might have given me a feminine flutter. His only made me wish I hadn't removed my jacket and left it on the barstool. My black T-shirt was a flea-market special: cheap. I bought it for the saying, not quality, and it shrank the first wash. I lingered long enough for leather-clad to read the saying: I'VE GOT PMS AND A HANDGUN. ANY QUESTIONS?

Rick said something in an undertone to leather-clad, and he glanced at Jack and stepped back to give me room to pass. I slid the first dollar into the opening, and the jukebox slurped it up. It spit the second one back. Damn. I ran my fingernails along the edge of the bill to straighten it out. No go. The machine still didn't like it.

"Here, honey." Rick held out a crisper dollar bill.

"Thanks," I said, handing him the worn one.

Rick shook his head and strolled off. "Just play something slow and easy," he said over his shoulder. "It's early yet."

Rick's dollar found a home, so I browsed the selections. There wasn't a song newer than five years old, although I did see a couple of Garth Brooks. Mainly, though, considering where I was, I punched buttons for some early Grand Old Opry type numbers. The first, a Loretta Lynn number, gained grunts of approval from the pool players, so I finished out the selections that way. With one remaining, I rebelled and chose a rock song—Credence Clearwater.

Duty done and pretending I didn't want to interrupt the pool game, I strolled to the far side of the bar on my way back to Jack. The two women bent close, in low-voiced conversation. One was a dyed-blonde; the other had black hair from a bottle she should have diluted first. Evidently, I wasn't not-obvious enough. The blonde jerked her head up and glared.

"You got a nose problem?"

I gave her back glare for glare. Women in places like these had a set of go-by rules, too, and backing down wouldn't gain me any status. I swigged my beer, then said, "Just checking out the competition." I nodded at the bar. "That one's mine."

Dark-hair checked Jack out. "Lucky bitch."

"Yeah," I acknowledged. And strolled on over to Jack, slipping onto the barstool, knowing without looking that there were two pairs of female eyes on me. Looping my index finger in the back of Jack's belt, I leaned close. He chuckled, gaze on the mirror behind the bar, the women in the corner reflected in it. His mouth quirked into that devilish grin that had drawn me to him so many years ago.

"I've been staked out as private property, huh?"

"They'll come around to get to know me. See what there is about me that attracts such a handsome hunk." Jack laughed and swigged his beer, then played his part by draping an arm across my shoulders so I could cuddle even closer. The gesture brought back some memories I didn't need, and I stiffened momentarily, then relaxed. It was only a game.

Max said, to me this time, "I wouldn't get too chummy with those two. Tildy—the blonde—she's on the tequila tonight. Drownin' her sorrow over Bucky."

We hid our start of interest. Jack tipped his beer up again, and I started to take a swallow of mine before I noticed the bottle was already empty.

"Bucky," I said thoughtfully. "Oh, that man they found murdered at the plantation near here? What's its name? Spirit something?"

"Esprit d'Chene," the bartender said in perfect Cajun French. "Means Spirit of the Oaks. And yeah, Tildy was once married to Bucky."

"Don't know them," I lied. "Can I have another beer, honey?"

Jack frowned. "You already drank that one? I don't wanna have to tie you on the bike to get you home."

I batted my eyes. "I only had a few before we came here."

"You finished off that six pack," Jack growled. "Oh, hell." He nodded at Max, who pulled out another Bud Lite and slapped it in front of me.

"You ain't heard about the murder?" Max asked Jack.

Jack grinned down at me. "I been sorta...busy lately. Her old man's a trucker, and he's been off on a cross-country run the last three days."

I elbowed Jack—hard. That was going a little too far. "Shush, *honey*," I muttered.

Max winked at Jack. "Seems like they found Bucky in the swimmin' pool at that fancy plantation. Somebody lopped off his head." He shook *his* head sadly, the brushy beard sweeping across his wide chest. "Bucky was one of my best customers, but he left me high and dry with his monthly tab. Even for the drinks he and Katy downed here a couple weeks ago."

"Katy Gueydan?" I tried for confusion, but the mirror told me I looked more like a puppy eager for a kiss. "Doesn't she own the plantation?"

"Ladies," Max said with another blatant wink at Jack. "They do like the gossip, don't they?" To me, "I suppose you wonder what a lady like that was doing in this dive. Lemme tell you, it wasn't the first time. Usually she kicked up her heels a bit, but that night she and Bucky was more interested in talkin' over in that booth Tildy's usin'."

Jack emptied his bottle and handed it to Max, who affably set another in front of him and retrieved the price from the bills on the bar.

"You gotta admit," Jack mused, "women like that Katy's supposed to be aren't usually seen 'round our hangouts."

Max shrugged. "Maybe she's like the lady in that 'Tight Fittin' Jeans' song."

Someone came in the door, and my eyes widened. This could complicate our undercover operation. I slid off the stool. "Honey, I left my powder puff in the saddlebag. Be right back."

At the door, I eased over to Uncle Clarence, who was staring at Tildy in the corner booth. I didn't see Tildy's friend. Maybe she was on a potty break. Uncle Clarence was overdressed for the Holey Bucket, trousers and starched white shirt, black string tie with a turquoise-eyed cow skull clasp. Uncle Clarence dressed to his own tastes, not anyone else's idea of casual.

I feigned a misstep and brushed his shoulder. "Excuse me, Sugar," I simpered. "How could I miss a good looking man like you standing there?"

Uncle Clarence frowned, then glanced at the bar. He must have recognized Jack, because he said *sotto voce*, "Doin' a little investigatin', Alice?"

"Don't blow our cover," I whispered.

He smiled and leaned on his walking stick. "Why, little lady," he said louder. "Ah'm sure it was my fault. Can Ah buy you a drink to apologize?"

"I'd like that, Sugar, if my boyfriend—" I flicked my head toward Jack "—doesn't mind."

"Ah'll be sure to get his permission," Uncle Clarence said with a regal nod.

Breathing a sigh of relief, I hurried through the door.

CHAPTER 26

In case anyone watched from the shadows, I pawed through a collection of tools, greasy rags, and a couple biker scarves with *RIDE TO LIVE and LIVE TO RIDE* on them in both saddlebags. After the pretend, fruitless search, I wandered over to Uncle Clarence's new pickup, as though admiring it. The dim light from the neon bucket sign didn't reflect much, but the brushy trail to the bar had left a few scratches on the hood and passenger door. Why on earth would he drive his brand new truck down that trail? Uncle Clarence, who took pride in his possessions, be they clothes, vehicle, or woman. This was the type of place he liked to drink at, so he'd probably been here before. You'd think he'd realize what would happen to his paint job. I traced a finger down one of the deeper scratches. These wouldn't buff out even with a wax job.

Jack appeared at the door, swigging his beer, and I hurried over. "Thought you might've run into some trouble out here," he said, low-voiced. "A biker bar parking lot's not somewhere you should be wanderin' around in alone, *Chére*."

"Jack —" A giggle from the shadows drew our attention. Tildy's dark-haired friend with Rick. Rick had pushed her up against the wall, crotch to crotch, and she wasn't struggling.

"Honey," she gasped. "Oh, you do feel good. But I might have to drive Tildy home."

"Forget her, Rhonda, babe." Rick jammed his pelvis tighter and circled it against hers. "Max'll bed her down in back if he has to. Won't be the first time."

A pair of bikes growled up the trail and into the parking lot, headlights briefly illuminating the couple. Jack eased me inside as Rick pulled Rhonda-babe around the building.

"Your uncle's going to buy us a beer." Jack led me toward one of the tables. "What's he doing in a place like this?"

"Uncle Clarence lives and breathes places like these," I explained. Uncle Clarence sat at a table in the middle of the floor, where two fresh longnecks leaked ice chips into puddles. He held a highball glass filled with a smoky brown liquid.

"It's always nice to find new faces in a place," he said. "Makes the evening less borin'."

The newly-arrived bikers—two men and two women—walked in, but they headed for the bar. My uncle had probably chosen this table for its placement. The light fixture above illuminated it, and most patrons in a bar sought shadowed recesses, nursing their drinks and dates. Which meant we could talk without being overheard, at least until the place filled up.

Jack set his half-full warm beer aside and picked up the fresh longneck. I reached for mine, then recalled that I'd already had two beers and decided I'd better pass the rest of the evening sipping rather than guzzling. I played with the label with my fingernail.

Uncle Clarence focused on Jack. "Ah assume you two have heard that Katy was here at the Holey Bucket with Bucky. Ah hope you don't think that means she had anything to do with Bucky's death."

Jack took another swallow of beer.

"We heard that wasn't the first time Katy's been here," I blurted. I expected an under-the-table shut-up kick from Jack, but he only stared at the new pool game. Shouts of drunken laughter erupted as the shooter broke the triangle of balls with an explosive crack, scattering them in flashes of arcing color on green velvet. So I continued, "Shoot, Uncle Clarence, you taught us both to boot-scoot and Zydeco in Bourbon Street bars. But I thought we left those days behind us a long time ago."

"Katy still likes to dance," Uncle Clarence said with a shrug. "That bastard...excuse my French...she was married to had an image he wanted to project. Besides, he didn't know a two-step from a waltz. And when she moved to Esprit d'Chene...well, she got tired of Daughters of the South meetings and small town theaters once in a while. Got that from my genes, maybe."

"It doesn't look good, especially that rumor going around," I insisted.

"No," he agreed, lifting his drink. "It doesn't look good...sound good." He set his glass down.

I noticed a sheen of sweat on his brow. "Should you be drinking, on top of the medication you must be taking?"

He laughed and took another swallow, finishing off his drink and motioning with the glass to Max for a refill. "Ah appreciate your worrying 'bout me, sweetheart. But Ah have my own plans for the time Ah have left."

Sadness filled me. "Yes, sir," I murmured obediently.

Jack did nudge me under the table this time, a questioning frown on his face while Uncle Clarence exchanged his empty glass for the full one Max brought over. I mouthed, "Later."

Rhonda-babe slipped in a side door, a disgruntled Rick a few seconds behind her. Rhonda hurried to Tildy, Rick stalked to the bar. He slapped some money down and flicked his head toward the booth. A moment later, Max carried two drink glasses over to the women.

Rick pouted through half a beer before he picked up his bottle and wandered over to our table. "Howdy, Clarence," he said. "How's it hangin'?"

"Have a seat, Rick," Uncle Clarence said politely. "You meet my new friends here?"

"Yeah." Rick pulled out a chair and unsteadily found the seat. He propped his elbows on the table, beer dangling from one hand, cigarette from the other. "You talked to Tildy tonight?"

"No." Uncle Clarence glanced at the booth. "Doesn't look like she's in the mood for male companionship."

Rick growled, "Rhonda and I had a date. I don't like bein' stood up. Like she thinks she's the only fish in the sea." He sized Jack up over his bottle, and I cringed.

"Might do her good to realize she ain't," Rick said as a slow, moody song started on the jukebox. "You mind if I borrow your old lady for a dance?"

"Sure," Jack said without concern. "Just bring her back when you're done."

I accidentally-on-purpose stepped on Jack's foot as I pushed my chair back when Rick stood and held out his hand. My tennis-shoe-clad foot didn't do much damage through his cowboy boot, but hopefully I got my point across.

Rick dragged me all the way over by the jukebox, to a tiny dance floor that couldn't have held more than three or four couples at a time. That was the point, so the couples would cuddle close to make room for everyone else. He burped—at least he didn't fart—and pulled me close. I kept my arms between us to give myself distance from his beer- and smoke-laden breath, but he wrapped them around his neck. More to protect my sense of smell than in a spirit of cooperation, I tucked my head on his chest.

He settled his palms on my back, just above my hips, and slowly slid into the rhythm of the song. He was a good dancer, and after a few seconds, I relaxed and decided to enjoy the dance. I'd always liked dancing, and it didn't matter whether the music was pop, country, blues, or Zydeco. Rick turned me in a tight circle, so he could keep an eye on the booth and Rhonda's reaction. Evidently, he either got the reaction he wanted—or didn't—because soon he moved his palms down further and cupped my hips.

I pulled back and adjusted his grip upwards. "Uh-uh. I'll play along, but only so far."

He cocked his head and studied my face. "How tight are you and Jack?"

"Tight enough," I said. "I'm not on the prowl."

"'Cept from your husband, huh?"

Damn Jack, I thought, *and Max, too. And Max said women liked to gossip!* I forced a dreamy smile, glanced at Jack. "I'm asking for a divorce as soon as he gets back from this run," I lied, then quickly changed the subject. "How long have you and Rhonda been together?"

"Met her when I moved here couple months ago from Corpus. Got divorced myself down there and figured I'd start fresh somewhere. Found me a job over in Longview at a bike garage. You tell Jack he ever needs any work done on his hog, I'm his man."

"But why is Rhonda ignoring you tonight?"

"Her and Tildy's been best friends since grade school. Ronnie says she owes her some help gettin' through her grief."

"Grief? Max said Bucky was Tildy's ex. How much grief can you have over an ex?"

"That's what I been tellin' Ronnie," Rick said with a pout. He nodded at the door as another woman walked in, this one without an escort. Her red hair flowed down her back in a riot of curls, and she'd probably deliberately washed her pink T-shirt to get it to conform to her D-cup bust that tight. "Hell, Red's got a better right than Tildy to be sorry 'bout old Bucky. She was his main squeeze lately."

"Red?"

"Yeah. Her name's Carmine. Carmine Medina. You can see why we call her Red, tho'. Hey." Rick frowned. "Why you so interested in old Bucky and his girlfriends? It ain't healthy right now for nobody to let on they's interested in that murder." His frown deepened, and I followed his gaze to Jack. "An' ain't I seen your boyfriend somewheres? Maybe I've already worked on his Harley sometime or another."

"I doubt it," I put in quickly. "Jack's bike is new."

"Maybe that's where I seen him. The garage I work at's connected to the shop that sells new bikes. Probably saw him when he came in to pick out his bike."

Thankfully, the song ended, and I disentangled myself. "I better get back," I insisted as the next record—my Credence song—dropped into place and the fast-paced music blared into the smoky tranquility the slow number had fostered.

"Aw, let's do one more," Rick said, grabbing for my arm.

I dodged him and shook my head. "No, I—Jack can be the jealous type."

Someone shoved me none-too-politely aside with a hip, and I breathed a sigh of relief when Rhonda/Ronnie wiggled in between Rick and me. "I think this one's our dance, honey," she simpered, and Rick immediately lost any interest in me.

I passed Uncle Clarence and Red on their way to the dance floor and stifled the brief thought of whether it was good for Uncle Clarence's health to be dancing to that sort of music. He wouldn't appreciate my concern. At the table, I took a long swallow of cool beer before I noticed Tildy's gaze on my uncle and Red. It wasn't friendly, either, more of a glare of rage. I eased into my chair beside Jack and nudged him to draw his attention to the booth. He only nodded and said, "She hasn't taken her eyes off the redhead."

I quickly explained what I'd learned from Rick. "So we'd probably better get out of here before Rick remembers where he's seen you. I'll bet every biker around here knows that a cop bought his own bike."

"Damn," Jack muttered. He pulled his wallet out and dropped some bills on the table. Rising, he took my arm and nearly lifted me to my own feet, then steered me toward the door.

"Y'all come back, hear?" Max called, and Jack waved at him.

We nearly made it.

CHAPTER 27

At the door, I remembered my jacket and saw it still hanging on the barstool. "My coat."

Jack dropped my arm to go get it. Max stretched over the bar, grabbed it, and tossed it at Jack, who caught it and turned back toward me.

That's when Tildy screeched and lit out through the ashtray and bottle-covered tables toward the dance floor. Jack didn't see her at first, but he turned when Tildy screamed, "You bitch! Payback's hell!"

I gasped, recognizing that voice. But Tildy grabbed a beer bottle and broke it as she passed the next table top, leaving me no time say anything to Jack. Bar fights, especially women catfights, aren't my thing. I tugged Jack's arm and sidled toward the door. He muttered, "Shit," and took off my hold.

Tildy headed for Red and Uncle Clarence. One of the pool players swiped for her as she barreled past, snagging her shirt. Tildy swung around, dagger-sharp bottle raised, and he ducked. He warded her weapon off with one arm, hanging onto her shirt with his other hand.

Tildy didn't let that stop her. She half-dropped to the floor and skinned out of her shirt in two seconds flat, the broken bottle in her fist ripping through the fabric. Waist-up naked, she surged upright and dove for Red, who gaped around Uncle Clarence's protective stance.

"Stop it, Tildy!" my uncle commanded. He and Rick converged on Tildy, Rick reaching for the broken bottle, Clarence for Tildy's waist. Red screeched and unfortunately raced for the new protection of the pool players.

A bare instant before Rick grabbed the bottle, Tildy ducked and swiveled in a move an Olympic gymnast would have been proud of. Rick missed, but Uncle Clarence managed to clasp a breast—and drop it just as fast. He tottered, and Rick steadied him.

Red tried to hide behind the largest pool player, but he warded her off with his cue stick, laughing uproariously. "Uh-uh, sweetheart. Fight your own battles!" He and his partner backed over against the wall, as Red raced around the table, Tildy hot on her trail.

By then, Jack was across the room. He paused to check on Uncle Clarence. Even through the hanging clouds of cigarette smoke, I could see the white strain on my uncle's face. I broke out of my fascinated trance and hurried towards him as Jack shoved a nearby chair at Rick, indicating for him to get my uncle into it. And swiveled just in time to clutch Tildy by her jeans waist as she raced past after a screeching Red.

I have no idea where Tildy learned her moves. She didn't try to jerk away—instead, she dropped, a dead weight, but Jack hung on. On her way down she must have unsnapped her jeans, because she wiggled out of them like a slippery eel and rolled away from Jack like a fish in water through the sawdust and peanut shells. Jack stood, jeans dangling from his grip.

The pool players pounded their cue sticks on the floor and chanted, "Fight, fight!" Several other bikers picked up the call. Longnecks in hand, they wandered over to line the wall as Red circled the pool table, passing Jack, who crouched, arms spread to tag Tildy. But the bleached-blonde fooled him again. She tumbled onto the pool table, rolled once and surged to her feet. Naked except for a pair of booty-type white socks, sawdust particles, and a few red-hull peanut skins, she brandished the broken bottle, swiping at Jack when he reached for her. The chants and cue-stick thumps mingled with ear-splitting, thumb- and finger-in-the-mouth whistles and rebel yells of "Eee-haw!"

She wasn't a natural blonde. You could see that from the dark patch of hair at the apex of her legs. She had a fairly decent body, though, despite the white stretch marks testifying to child-bearing marring her poochy stomach.

Red headed for the door like her pants were on fire, shoving aside tables and chairs blocking the shortest path to her destination. I knelt by Uncle Clarence, and his white, strained face and shaky breathing over-shadowed any interest I had in a titty-bar show on the pool table. Someone thrust a glass of ice water into my hand, and I nodded grate-fully to Max, but he headed straight back to the bar.

Cupping my hands around Uncle Clarence's trembling ones, we lifted the glass to his mouth. To my left, Jack lunged again for Tildy—and jerked back barely in time to miss a jab at his face from her bottle-knife.

"My pills," Uncle Clarence gasped. He held a prescription bottle out. I opened it and shook out a pill, which he stuffed in his mouth and swal-lowed with a sip of water.

The crowed roared as Tildy tried to jump off the far side of the pool table and two men surged forward, blocking her. She sprang back, and one of the pool players hefted his stick—then swiped it in an arc, catching her behind the knees. She splatted down on the table amid hoots and cheers from the crowd, but kept a firm grasp on her beer-bottle weapon.

Jack leaped onto the table. Wild-eyed, breasts bouncing with her gasping anger, Tildy scrambled up to face him. He didn't try to approach. Instead, he aimed a kick at her hand. The beer bottle sailed off the tip of his cowboy boot at the same instant a shotgun blast split the air and bikers belly-dived, longnecks and cue sticks flying. Some woman screamed, but it wasn't Tildy. She ignored the shotgun and, shouting, "You sonuva bitch!" lunged for Jack.

He caught the spitting, snarling woman, spun her around and, with a deft move, swept one foot in front of her ankles and yanked backward. With a screech of rage, Tildy went down again. Jack didn't take any more chances. He went down right on top of her. Straddling her bare butt, he grabbed her arms and pulled them behind her.

Still, she bucked and snarled curses. He transferred both her wrists to one hand and tangled his fingers in her hair, pushing her head flat against the velvet. Here and there, a few bikers started to rise. The shotgun chambering another shell dropped them back to the floor.

Credence banged out one final salvo, and the song ended, leaving an eerie silence. Well, except for Tildy's muffled curses and Jack's heavy breathing. He glanced at me and flicked his head. "Get my belt off," he ordered.

I checked Uncle Clarence as I rose. Satisfaction gleamed on his face as he stared at the pool table, a wry grimace on his mouth. The pill must have worked, because his cheeks were flushed now, not white, his brow unbeaded.

I crawled onto that damn table—the utter last thing I wanted to do —and reached around Jack to unbuckle his belt. I had to straddle Tildy, too, and she kicked upward from the knees, knocking her heels into my butt. Jack muttered for me to tie the belt around Tildy's wrists, and I jerked it a little tighter than necessary before I scrambled off the table.

Max wandered over, shotgun propped negligently on his shoulder, and the bikers started once again to cautiously rise to their feet. He nodded and waved a consenting hand. "Rick, go set up a round for everyone at the bar." Then he studied Jack, still trying to quell a squirming Tildy on the pool table. "You got some good moves," he drawled with narrowed eyes. "Sure you ain't had some cop training?"

"I just keep in shape," Jack replied. "Hand me something to cover her with."

A couple of bikers laughed and hooted encouragement for Jack to leave Tildy naked, but Max's stare shut them up in mid-hoot. He swiped Tildy's T-shirt from the floor and tossed it to Jack, then handed his shotgun to me. I gingerly laid it on a table.

Max climbed onto the pool table and helped Jack pull the T-shirt over Tildy's head. They left her arms belted behind her, and the T-shirt didn't cover her tush. She was silent now, still, and tears trickled out from her tightly-squinched eyes. I searched the room for my jacket and saw it on the floor a few feet away. As I retrieved it to help cover Tildy, Jack asked Max if he'd called the cops yet.

"I don't need cops messin' in my business and threatenin' to shut me down again. She'll be okay when she sobers up. It's the tequila."

Jack wrapped my coat around Tildy, turning her over to secure the sleeves at her waist and buttoning a couple appropriate buttons. He left her to Max and jumped smoothly to the floor.

"We need to get Uncle Clarence ho —" Oops. I clamped my mouth shut, but the damage was done. I'd let slip that we hadn't just met my uncle tonight. Jack caught the slip and Max's interest and hustled me to Uncle Clarence. Thankfully, all the other patrons lined the bar, eagerly reaching for the free beers Rick dished out.

"Let's go," Jack said to my uncle. "Alice can drive you home."

I grabbed the walking stick from the floor and handed it to him as Uncle Clarence slowly rose to his feet. With Jack on one side, me on the other, we guided him out of the bar, into the starlit night. I told myself not to look back, but my darned writer's curiosity got the better of me. Max was off the pool table, Tildy cradled in his arms, unwavering frown fixed on our departure.

Uncle Clarence's pickup wasn't locked. We helped him into the passenger seat and I hurried around to the driver's door while Jack strode over to his bike. I'd have to lead—as far as I knew, Jack didn't know where my uncle lived now. The keys dangled from the switch, and as I started the engine, Uncle Clarence laid his head back and closed his eyes.

Oh, God. I reached for him, thinking maybe we needed to get him to the hospital. But a soft snore issued, and I settled for buckling the seatbelt around him.

Jack followed, the rumble of the bike's engine and the headlight in the rear window a comfort as I negotiated the rutty trail out to the county road and turned back toward Esprit d'Chene. Uncle Clarence lived near Katy, and I hoped I could remember the way. I'd only visited his new house once, my second trip to Katy's, when we'd had a crawfish boil.

Twenty minutes later, I turned into the driveway. Uncle Clarence's house wasn't nearly as large as the Esprit d'Chene manor house. A sprawling, two-story brick, with only six white pillars across the front and three elderly live oaks in the yard, a detached garage set off a few yards to the right beside a row of huge cedar. The pickup headlights illuminated the brick sidewalk and hedge across the smaller veranda, the hedge badly in need of a trim job. That wasn't like my uncle. He hired local help for any work he didn't feel like doing himself.

I parked in the drive rather than in front of the garage. Jack and I woke him up, and Uncle Clarence shook us off when we tried to assist him into the house.

"Ah can make it on my own," he grumbled. And he did, with me noticing that he hadn't locked his front door, either. He paused, not inviting us in, though I made my intention to accompany him inside clear.

"Ah'll be fine," he said. "You two go on now."

"Maybe I should come in and call your doctor—" I began.

"No," he cut me off. "All Ah need's some rest."

"Well...I'll check on you tomorrow morning."

"If you want." He shrugged and closed the door gently in our faces.

Jack stuck his fingertips in his back pockets and studied the door contemplatively. I studied Jack, wondering what was going through his mind. But...he didn't tell me, even after he glanced my way and had to have read the questions on my face.

"You need to get back?" he asked.

"Why?"

"You wanted to talk about the case. Thought maybe we'd drop by my office. Should be quiet there now. Private."

CHAPTER 28

The city jail was silent, dark, only a single light glowing. I didn't suppose they needed much security—the violent perps could be housed over at the newer county facility. The two major tourist attractions in Jefferson were the spring Mardi Gras Upriver Celebration and the Pilgrimage the first weekend in May. Mardi Gras Upriver weekend garners more than its share of arrests, with the people who can't afford the Louisiana celebration making do with a local event. And trying to out-do the N'awlins folks with their revelry and alcohol overindulgence. Even the historical old jail fills to overflowing.

Jack guided me down that dirt path and pulled out a set of keys. Door open, he flicked on the inside lights. As he walked over to one of the desks, I examined the surroundings closer than I'd had time to before. A photo of two officers showing off the results of a drug bust hung on the wall, bales of marijuana displayed in plastic-wrappings used in a misguided attempt to fool the trained drug dogs. Beside it was an artist's depiction of a drug raid, the agents protected by shields and helmets as they lined the front porch of a frame house and prepared to batter in the door. Maybe I was wrong about the need for security. Katy's guards sounded better all the time.

"You wouldn't think there'd be such a large drug problem in these small towns," I mused.

Jack glanced up from pulling files out of a drawer. "The dealers think the same thing. But we've got well-trained officers schooled at state and national law enforcement seminars. They work with the federal marshals and Texas Rangers." He sighed and continued, "A lot of marijuana busts come from vehicles with South Texas plates. Women drivers, who the dealers haven't figured out yet we'll bust just as soon as a man, if we've got a reason to be suspicious. But..." He flicked his head, indicating the artist's depiction. "The dealers who set up labs—coke and crack—figure they can hide the smell of their operation by using an isolated area. Mostly rental properties. Folks call the anonymous tip lines, though, neighbors, even folks just drivin' through, who see somethin' suspicious."

Jack motioned me to sit and took his seat in the bedraggled office chair behind the desk. He pushed a manila folder across, and I leafed through the photos. The first one was Katy's pool, water pink-tinged against the blue bottom. I held my breath as I set it aside, hoping the next one wouldn't show the body.

"I've got the gruesome ones in another file, *Chére*," Jack said softly. "But you wanted to know what was going on—what evidence we had."

I studied the next photo—the hilt of Grandpere Jean's sword. The photo after that was a blowup of an area with the spot of dried blood. Next came the tire track, half camouflaged by the oyster shells in the driveway, half-visible in the mud at the edge of the drive. I don't know that much about tires, but it was wide, the tread grooves deeply cut, not worn. My Jeep's tires were wider and higher than passenger car tires, and this looked more like them.

The next photo was taken further back and showed a four-foot area around the tire track, grass, and part of the oyster-shell drive. Then a picture of the track filled with casting plaster and another of the plaster after it had been removed. I picked up the one of the track and the area around it again. But it still looked the same—I didn't notice anything out of the ordinary, except that a couple of the larger oyster shells looked freshly disturbed. Dirt dulled the white from where they'd been turned out of their nests.

There were pictures of the pool area, some with a measuring tape laid out to indicate distances that meant something to the crime investigators. Next came the Great Room and the front and rear doors of the manor house. I assumed the door pictures were taken to show there wasn't any evidence of tampering.

"What about the windows?" I asked Jack.

"We've got photos of them, too. Nothing. No pry marks, no glass cracked."

I dug through the pictures to the one of Grandpere Jean's sword. "Fingerprints?"

"Only Katy's."

"Which is to be expected," I insisted.

"Not necessarily."

"You care to explain that?"

"Katy has a lot of visitors. Lots of interesting stuff in her house. Makes sense she'd let her guests look at or examine the sword. But everything was wiped off both the blade and handle."

"Except Katy's prints and blood."

"Yeah. We sprayed the blade with Luminol. The perp washed it in the pool, but the spray brought out blood traces."

"Katy handled the sword and pricked her finger *before* Bucky was killed. Whoever the real killer is probably wore gloves!"

"If you believe Katy's story," Jack agreed. "And there's the lack of footprints. It rained that night, but earlier. Whoever was in that truck would've left prints...unless he never got out."

I looked at the tire print photos. "I'm a writer, Jack. I fit the clues in around my murder while I write, not vice versa."

Jack pointed to the edge of the tire-cast plaster. "It's not noticeable to the untrained eye, but this track shows both the forward movement of the tire—when it stopped—and the backward movement—when it pulled out. A pickup tire. The truck backed up, but the wheel was turned just enough to tell us that the driver backed out onto the driveway, then on through the gate. Instead of going on up the driveway and turning around."

"He didn't want to be noticed. He parked far enough away from the house to stay hidden. Maybe it was someone just passing by. They took a wrong turn, realized it, so they backed out." I tossed the photo down, recalling the scene in the bar. "The answering machine tapes! Jack, that one voice is Tildy's!"

"How do you know?"

"Didn't you hear her when she screamed 'payback's hell?' It's the same voice, nearly the same words."

"Didn't dawn on me. I was too busy trying to keep someone from getting slashed. Why didn't you mention it then?"

"Would that have been enough for you to arrest her?"

"Probably not," he conceded. "But we need to check her out." He dialed the phone and informed whoever answered to send an officer to the Holey Bucket and pick up Tildy.

When he hung up, I said, "I talked to Katy. I know that Bucky was in contact with her again. And why."

"He wanted to reform." Jack snorted in disbelief. "It was on the tapes. Knowin' the swamp rat mentality, I'd be willin' to bet he had somethin' devious in mind to accomplish that, rather than just decidin' to become a johnny-be-good citizen and let time take its course."

"The tapes didn't tell you?" For some reason I shuffled through the photos until the tire track ones lay spread out in front of me.

Jack let the silence linger, but I stubbornly didn't offer anything further. Silences like that are a technique cops use. Suspects rush to fill the gap in conversation, sometimes babbling information they didn't intend to reveal. But I had a huge measure of guilt on my shoulders already for handing over the tapes, not realizing I was implicating Katy even further. I wanted some time to reflect on what I was learning before I opened my mouth again.

One reflection hit me just then. "Sue Ann!"

Jack raised one eyebrow in question.

"The fingerprints," I insisted. "I'm sure lots of people did handle that sword. Katy's extremely tidy and protective of her things, though. She wouldn't care if people admired the sword, but she'd want to protect it from harm. Sweat from people's hands. Either she'd clean it or have Sue Ann do it."

"That could explain it," he agreed. He retrieved another file and shuffled through the papers until he found the one he wanted. "Traces of cleaner were found on the sword."

"See?" And I couldn't help adding, "Men don't think of stuff like that. Women do." My eyes were irresistibly drawn to that file, even knowing it probably contained the more grisly crime scene photos. Pictures of the body—but the next report was labeled "Toxicology."

"Is that the report on the poison used in the bread pudding?" I asked.

"It was in the sugar canister. Y'all can have the rest of the groceries back, if you want."

I shuddered. "That won't be necessary. I suppose anyone could have done that."

Jack leaned back. "I can't keep them from arrestin' Katy much longer, *Chére.*"

"What?" I shoved my chair back, jumped to my feet and leaned across the desk. "She didn't do it, Jack! You're wrong! Wrong, wrong, wrong!"

"It's not totally for me to say, *Chére,*" Jack said softly. "I—"

"You're in charge of the investigation! You—"

"Katy had means...the sword. Opportunity...she admits she was home when he was killed. Motive...according to the tapes, Bucky held something over her head."

I could only stare at him, stunned. "But...but..." I spluttered, then plunged on, "she...we...didn't kill him when he blackmailed Katy before! Why would we this time?"

"We?" Jack quirked a questioning eyebrow.

Uh-oh. Damn, I wished I'd listened to those tapes entirely before I turned them over to Jack. Had Katy told me everything? But even if I'd heard something incriminating on the tapes, could I have withheld evidence like that?

"*Chére*," Jack prodded, "I need to know the whole story. The senator's demandin' an arrest, and every bit of evidence we've got points to Katy."

"There are plenty of other people around here who had reason to want Bucky dead," I said staunchly. "People who are the *type* to kill another human being! Katy's not!"

"I'm doin' the best I can to look at everybody. But I'm limited with the staff I have. And bein' out of my home territory. And, to put it bluntly, it doesn't look good...my connection to the family."

"They knew that when they asked you to take charge!"

"Not all of it," he denied. "I was convenient and had the best background and trainin'. But when you showed up on the scene, my ex, Katy's cousin..."

My heart plunged. I hadn't even considered that my involvement would actually be detrimental to Katy.

Jack rose and walked over to a coffeemaker in the far corner of the room. While I stood there biting my lip in frustration and anxiety, he filled the glass pot from a ten-gallon container of water, dumped it in the coffeemaker, and took a packet of pre-measured coffee from a cabinet. Within a few seconds, the inviting aroma of dripping coffee filled the small room.

Back to me, Jack watched the stream of coffee. I wanted desperately to see his face—to try to imagine what he was thinking. His stance reminded me of the night we'd had our final discussion about our marriage. The cold knot in my stomach grew as I realized Jack was steeling himself to give me some more bad news, just as he had that night, when he openly admitted his misgivings about us continuing to live together.

He didn't have to, though. The bad news walked in right then.

Smitty ushered a sobbing Katy through the door. She wore her gray all-weather coat, and rain misted it, which must have begun after Jack and I got to the jail. But it didn't take long to see the real reason she wore the concealing coat. Her wrists were handcuffed, her shoulders slumped so the sleeves would hide the embarrassment.

Smitty looked nearly as upset as Katy. His gaze shot to Jack. "I had orders. The chief and sheriff got a warrant from Judge Evans."

I started toward Katy, but Jack caught my arm. "Sorry, *Chére.* No contact right now."

"You think I'm gonna try to bust her out?" I snarled. He looked away, and I called to Katy, "Don't you say a word, Sugar. I'll call your lawyer!"

"She called Jeeves from home before we left," Smitty told me. "He's down in South Texas, dove hunting."

"I'll find someone else," I fumed. "You're not keeping Katy here in jail!"

Katy stared at the floor, tears running down her face. I could imagine what was going through her mind in addition to the dismay and terror of being charged with a crime as horrible as murder. Phones were probably already ringing across the county with the story.

"Book her," Jack said in a quiet voice.

Stunned, I watched Smitty lead Katy over to the other desk and remove a file of papers, then an ink pad and camera. He took a finger-print card from the file, removed the handcuffs, and gently rolled each one of Katy's fingers in the ink, pressed them to the paper. Katy shuddered inside her coat, eyes closed. He touched her shoulder and murmured, "Here, Miss Gueydon," and handed her some tissues for her fingers.

"They took our prints earlier," I reminded Jack, but the anger had faded from my voice.

"Have to repeat it," he answered.

Rummaging in the desk drawer again, Smitty came up with one of those numbered signs and, after checking a list on a clipboard, changed the numbers. He led Katy to a portion of the wall that was clear and hung the sign around her neck.

"Jack," I whimpered, but Katy stoically stood there as Smitty snapped one picture, then turned her sideways for another shot.

"She'll have to have a bail hearing," Jack said. "I'm sorry. There's nothin' any of us can do right now."

Smitty glanced at me sympathetically. "I'll finish the rest of this in the back."

He picked up the file and a pen from a holder on the desk, then urged Katy toward the huge steel door in the middle of the back wall and opened it. Katy shuffled on through, her sobs hanging in the air. I evaded Jack to see where Smitty was taking her and cringed in dismay. The space wasn't much larger than the office. Straight ahead was a rusty shower stall, a dingy plastic curtain hanging from the rod. Four solid steel doors with tiny, barred windows about a foot square in each lined the sides of the narrow room. Smitty opened the first steel door on the left. Four bunk beds hung on the walls, two on each side, each with a dark-green, plastic-covered mattress. No linens, no pillows. In the rear of the cell was a commode and sink.

"You can't put her in there!" I spat. "It's horrible! It doesn't even look clean!"

Jack tugged me out of the cell area, but I fought him hard enough to keep an eye on what was going on. Smitty helped Katy out of her coat. She wore a set of sweats—stylish, not like the well-washed ones I lounged around in. Smitty removed a couple rings and a diamond-studded wristwatch and said, "I need your shoes. I'll get you a pair of slippers."

Katy's tears had dried, but she still wouldn't look at me. She sat on the bottom bunk on her left and toed off her tennis shoes. By now her face was white with strain, her eyes dead, as though she might be going catatonic.

"Why does he want her shoes?" I snarled.

"The laces," he muttered. "It's standard procedure."

Smitty started to close the cell door, Katy's possessions in his hands. "Damn it," I called. "It's cold back there. At least give her her coat so she can stay warm!"

Smitty looked at Jack, and he nodded. "Just until you get her some blankets."

But first Smitty removed the belt from the coat before he tried to hand it to Katy. She just sat there. With a sigh, Smitty tossed it on the bed beside her and shut the door.

And locked it. The sound of the key turning sent more dread through me than the clunk of the cell door closing. My vivid writer's imagination conjured up the horrible experience of being confined in such a devastating place for who knows how long. Maybe hardened criminals were used to something like that, but it could well send Katy into an emotional jungle of terror that it would take years of counseling to overcome. Tears gathered in my eyes, and I blinked furiously to clear my vision.

"I'll go back in and finish the paperwork as soon as I secure her things," Smitty told Jack.

"I'll do that." Jack took Katy's belonging from Smitty, and asked in a low voice, "You search her yet?"

I clenched my fists, and actually lifted one half-way before I thought better of cold-cocking a cop. Lucky for Smitty—and my freedom—Smitty replied, "Did that before I put her in the patrol car."

My spasm of relief faded in a heartbeat when Jack reminded him, "Procedure says a second search at the jail."

Smitty hung his head, glancing in trepidation at the steel door, and Jack patted his shoulder as he nudged me aside and closed the door separating the cells from the office area.

"Damn it, someone's going to pay for doing this to Katy!" I threatened. "I want to talk to her, Jack! At least for a few minutes."

"You'll have to leave now," he said, stuffing Katy's belongings in another set of lockers beside the evidence cabinet. "We need to finish processing her."

I buried my face in my hands and let the tears flow. Jack guided me to the chair in front of the desk, then knelt in front of me and pulled my hands away. Clasping them in his, he stared at me. "You can't help Katy if you fall apart."

"Didn't you see her? My God, Jack! Treating her like...like a common criminal!"

"She's charged with murder, Alice. The best thing you can do is get her a lawyer. We'll let her attorney in to talk to her all he wants."

"And we better get him quick," a voice said from the corner of the room. "Some bloody bastard who's not afraid to tell these incompetent bobbies that they've made the biggest mistake of their careers!"

Jack's jaw dropped as he stared at Sir Gary over by the other desk, a glare of outrage on the ghost's face, hands propped on his hips. Jack slowly rose. I, on the other hand, surged across the room to take my stand with Sir Gary.

"What happened at Esprit d'Chene?" I asked, forgetting that he wasn't solid and reaching out to grab his arm. My hand went right through him, but I didn't step back at the stab of cold. "Was it horrible for Katy?"

"Bloody horrible," he agreed, gaze fastened on Jack. "Worse than when we found that bastard in her pool. The bastard that someone *else* killed!"

Jack's hands dangled at his side. His fingers twitched as though he were wishing for his gun, which he hadn't worn to the Holey Bucket. I smirked, noting his white face and trepidation.

Smitty came out of the cell area and tossed his file on the desk as he glanced at Jack. He frowned and looked at me, and I waited to see if he could see Sir Gary. Evidently not, since he turned to Jack without any sort of alarm on his face or mention of a fourth person in the office.

"Everything all right?" he asked.

Jack cleared his throat. "You gonna be stayin' here the rest of the night?"

"Yeah. Someone's gotta—"

"I don't suppose there's a taxi in town," I interrupted.

"I'll take you back." Jack shot Sir Gary another uneasy glance, then returned the photos on the desk to the file folder, the folder to a desk drawer. Lucky for his peace of mind, I suppose, my ride walked in the door just then.

Granny preceded Twila, but the fury on their faces matched my feelings as they clomped in. Smitty stepped back, probably hoping Jack would handle the angry women.

"I ain't never seen such a bunch of damned Keystone Cops in all my life!" Granny fumed, thumping her walking stick for emphasis. "You let

Katy out of here right now, or...or..." Sudden tears clouded her bright eyes, and she choked. She cast me a forlorn look, and Twila wrapped an arm around her tiny, shrunken figure and pulled her close.

"Is there anything we can do to correct this stupid mistake?" Twila directed her question at Jack, a grim look on her face.

"There has to be a hearing..." Jack began.

"You told me there had to be a grand jury hearing before you arrested anyone, Jack!" I exploded. "So why wasn't there?"

Jack dropped his gaze to the floor, avoiding all our angry eyes. "It's not always necessary," he evaded.

"Yeah," I snarled. "Especially when you've got someone like Senator Wilson-Jones harping on a bunch of small-town cops to make an arrest! Even if it's the wrong arrest!"

"Where is that piece of self-important garbage?" Granny said with another emphatic thump, wiping her other hand across her eyes. "I'm gonna go jerk him right outta his nice warm bed and tell him what I think of him!"

"He's at the Jefferson Hotel," Smitty said in awe, obviously believing Granny meant what she said. Jack shot him a warning glance, but he didn't notice as he stared at Granny.

"Let's go, Twila." Granny tottered for the door. "It's only a couple blocks."

"No," Jack said in a resigned voice. "If y'all try something like that..."

"We might end up sharing a cell with Katy, huh?" I finished when his words trailed off. "For disturbing the peace."

Granny, Twila, and I exchanged glances, and three heads bobbed in agreement. Sir Gary glided over to Twila and Granny, me following. We formed a rough and ready gang, and Smitty gazed in stunned amazement. Jack, however, quickly wiped a grin off his face.

"Y'all can't do Katy any good from inside the jail," he reminded us. "You better go on back to Esprit d'Chene."

"My car's on empty," Twila said. "We drove the last couple of miles with the low-fuel dinging. I don't suppose there's a gas station open?"

"Not this time of night," Smitty said. "Be one open around six in the morning."

"I'll take y'all home in Smitty's patrol car," Jack offered.

I quirked an eyebrow. "*All* of us?"

His gaze centered on Sir Gary. The ghost met Jack's look directly, and he mused, "I have never ridden in one of those conveyances. I might enjoy the experience."

Smitty frowned and said, "There's plenty of room for four people in the patrol car."

"I want to talk to Katy first," I insisted. "Damn it, what can it hurt for her to know we're going to be doing everything we can do to get her out of here as soon as possible. Don't even open that darn cell door. Just let me speak to her through that teensy window."

Granny leaned on her walking stick and Twila crossed her arms over her chest. Sir Gary chuckled.

"If he refuses your request," the ghost said, "I'll carry your messages." He glided across the floor, passing close to Smitty, who shivered and looked around as though checking for a draft. Half in, half out of the connecting door, Sir Gary fixed Jack with an amused look.

If it hadn't been so serious, I might have been amused, too. Jack swung his head back and forth from Gary to the rest of us, and Smitty followed Jack's motion as though watching ping-pong. With a resigned sigh, Jack strode over to the door. Smitty headed for a cup of coffee.

Jack drew his hand back instantly when Sir Gary stood firm instead of sliding on into the cell block. The two sized each other up like a pair of male dogs deciding if their territory was worth defending—and who had the upper hand...or paw.

Smitty grew more and more confused. "It's not locked, Detective."

Sir Gary flicked the index finger of his left hand and tumblers disengaged. Jack grabbed the handle just as the door creaked open. I'm not sure if Smitty realized it wasn't Jack opening the door or not. Didn't much care at that point. Sir Gary bowed and swept his arm wide, and Twila, Granny, and I marched through the door.

"The window's closed," I prodded Jack while Twila and Granny took up waiting stances in front of the first cell...mistakenly the one on the right. When Jack held out his palm to Smitty, the cop shrugged and walked over to hand him a set of keys, one dangling from his fingers. Jack opened the cell window, and Granny and Twila moved over to wait their turn in the correct line. Sir Gary glided straight through the door, Jack moving back hastily to allow him unrestricted passage.

I gazed inside. Katy was curled up on one of the hideous green-mattress bunks in a fetal position, coat bunched under her head for a pillow, blanket pulled up to her nose, eyes squinched closed. She shuddered miserably.

"Katy. Sugar," I called. "Jack's going to let us talk to you."

"Go away," she replied wretchedly. "I don't want anyone to see me like this."

"My Lady," Sir Gary said, and Katy opened her eyes. "Do not turn away from those who seek to help you. We won't let you down."

Jack peered through the window. There wasn't a lot of room for two heads, and his breath feathered in my hair. He stifled a grunt as Katy jumped up and rushed toward Sir Gary...but of course, went right through him when she reached out for him to hold her.

"I am sorry I am unable to comfort you," Sir Gary said. "Never have I wished to be able to hold a lady more than right now."

Granny sighed, so she must have had her hearing aid turned on. "Ain't no man never said nothin' so sweet to me."

Katy's lower lip pooched and she stared back and forth from Sir Gary to the window with abandoned puppy distress. Deep, dark circles curved under her eyes, not a whip stitch of makeup left, and she looked so beautiful and delicate that my heart went out to her even more. I uttered a nasty word that I normally thought hard about before even using it in one of my books.

"I am going to wake up every lawyer in the state of Texas until I find someone to come down here and get you out," I assured Katy.

She bit down on her lip. "Thank you. I didn't do this, Alice."

All my unspoken doubts vanished. At that moment, I believed her totally. I had no idea how the actual killer had deliberately left a trail of clues that pointed to Katy, but I damned sure was going to find out. One way or the other. Whether Jack liked it or not.

Twila gently nudged me aside—not so gently Jack—so she could peer in the window. "Our best recourse is to find out who actually committed the murder," she told Katy. "Is there anything you can think of that we should know?"

I held my breath, but Katy must have just shaken her head. Jack alertly kept an ear on every word, and Granny impatiently waited her turn. Twila sighed and said, "Well, know that we're doing our best, Katy. If you think of anything —" She inclined her head at Sir Gary, indicating the ghost could act as a messenger. I smirked at the understanding on Jack's face.

Twila moved back, and Granny thumped up. She had to stand on tiptoe to see inside; her eyes barely cleared the bottom of the window. "Don't you worry none. Well, not any more'n you have to, bein' inside that there nasty place." She swiveled her head toward Jack. "Looks like your cleanin' people are about the laziest bunch on God's green earth. Iffen you want, Katy, I'll bring me a bucket and bleach in the mornin' and give that place a good scrubbin'."

"Thank you, Granny," Katy replied. "But I'll manage. It helps more than you can realize just to know you're all working to get me out of here."

"We'll be back," Granny said with an emphatic nod. She stepped back, and Jack reached to close the window. But not before he glanced inside. He raised the keys toward the lock, but three huffs of in-drawn breath made him change his mind. He left the window partially open.

For a brief minute, none of us moved, as though we were taking a moment's silence to properly revere an absolutely horrible situation. We stared at the steel door, the tiny window. I think every one of us was imagining ourselves inside there—imagining the close confines, the concrete walls, no contact with anyone. The absolute aloneness.

Recalling Sir Gary's claustrophobia, I wondered for a second how the ghost was standing it. But at least he knew he could leave anytime he wanted to.

CHAPTER 29

After the ladies left, Sir Gary sat on the bunk beside Katy. Again, he yearned to hold her, comfort her, assure her that she wouldn't be here long. But his glib tongue, usually so easy with any and all nearby females, failed him.

"Your claustrophobia," Katy said anxiously. "This cell..."

Touched by her concern when she was the one locked in this dreary space, Sir Gary said, "I find I can somehow overcome that in order to be with you, My Lady."

"Alice may need your help," Katy said staunchly. "I'll be all right."

"I shall leave in a moment. First, there is something I haven't had time to tell Alice."

Hope flared in Katy's expression. "Something that might help me get out of here?"

"I am not sure. Do you know anything about a strange videotape that might have found its way into your guest house?"

"Ohmigod! Please tell me you've got that tape hidden somewhere. It'll really seal my fate if Jack finds it!"

"I believe that Bucky person has it secreted elsewhere," Sir Gary said. "He led me a merry chase when I discovered it, and somehow evaded me

235

long enough to beat me back to the guest house and remove it. What does it have to do with this situation?"

Katy sighed and shook her head. "That tape...did you watch it?"

"It wasn't my cup of tea, but I saw enough to know it was taken clandestinely as two people were...um...engaging in...um...but I didn't recognize the participants."

Katy pulled the blanket around her shoulders and hunched into it. "Alice and I thought we were doing such a good deed before. Bucky secretly filmed his mother during one of her...indiscretions. And...and her...well, paramour in your language...was my fiancé's father. Back then...even now...something like that could ruin a person's career, let alone someone like the senator. It would have been a scandal for my fiancé's family, too. Bucky decided that, since it was my fiancé's father, I'd be the most likely blackmail target. And he was right. I paid Bucky some money for the tape. Quite a bit, actually, but I could well afford it."

She bit her lip, and Sir Gary waited for...as they say on that radio show he enjoyed...the rest of the story. After a deep breath released on a sigh, Katy continued, "Now Bucky's threatening to expose everything. Well...I mean...he was...but...darn it! I suppose he still can, even being a ghost."

"The rest?" Sir Gary prodded.

"He's written a book about it. I told Alice that part of it, but not all. Not what all was in it. It'll ruin Alice's reputation, too, if it comes out that she was involved in a blackmail scheme. Covering it up rather than exposing it. She might even be arrested, too!"

"I very much doubt that," Sir Gary said. "Isn't there something about some statute of limitations rule under these laws your bobbies enforce with such...*discrimination*?"

"You don't understand. The publicity would hurt her."

"Or possibly make her more intriguing," Sir Gary argued.

"I didn't want to take that chance. Bucky promised he'd turn the manuscript over to me, along with the copy of the tape he kept, if I'd be the go-between with him and the senator. Help him become a respected citizen again. I...I told him I'd have to think about it, but he was killed before we came to any decision."

Sir Gary sneered. "And you believed he would keep his promise?"

"I didn't have a choice. Both the senator's wife and my ex-father-in-law are dead now. According to the senator, his wife died of complications from heart problems. But she had a severe alcohol problem, maybe was even into drugs. Bucky probably inherited that gene from her. My ex-father-in-law was killed in a car wreck. Still, exposing all this sleaziness would hurt people still alive."

Sir Gary pondered whether to bring up his next thought, but he imagined a woman as smart as Katy had already considered it. "And it would give the bobbies an even stronger motive to prove you killed Bucky. To protect Alice."

Katy nodded sadly. "Please don't scare Alice."

"She has a right to know," Sir Gary insisted.

"No!" Katy reached for him, but drew her hand back. "Let's just wait until I get a lawyer and see what my chances are."

"You're willing to stay here in this nasty cell to protect Alice?"

"This mess is my fault. Alice tried to talk me out of paying off Bucky the first time. I won't allow her name to be dragged through the mud, if I can help it."

Quirking an eyebrow, Sir Gary lifted a finger and pointed it at the door. The tumblers clicked. The door inched open.

Katy surged from the bunk and pulled the door closed, engaging the lock. "No!" She rounded on him. "Look, you can go your merry way whenever you want, hiding or visualizing at your choice. But Alice and I have lives to live! I'm sure as hell not going to live my life as a criminal on the run!"

Sir Gary studied her closely. She probably didn't mean her words to be so harsh, given his situation, but they stung anyway. He didn't have a life to live, however you looked at it. And his living death couldn't be reversed without some sort of help—help from either Alice or Twila. He supposed it might behoove him to...

Katy finished the thought for him, making him well aware that she was still thinking clearly. "You'll be wandering around for years, maybe even centuries, if Alice gets tied up even deeper in this mess. I'll make sure Twila has nothing to do with you, either."

Sir Gary smiled, and Katy's glare deepened. "I mean it! I—"

He held up a hand. "I understand. And I realize how selfish I've been. My existence...my *nonexistence* is important, but not as important as freeing you from this dreary cell. Thus, I shall do all I can to assist. Whatever the consequences."

"Right now, you need to find that tape. I'll bet the manuscript is with it. If Alice finds it first, she'll give it to Jack. I know she will, no matter what the outcome."

"Your wish is my command, My Lady." Sir Gary glided through the cell door. On the other side, he peered in the tiny window. Katy paced back and forth for a few seconds, then flung herself on that shabby bunk and beat her fists on the mattress.

"When will I ever grow up?" she cried.

* * *

None of us wanted to sit in front with Jack, so Granny, Twila, and I all piled into the back seat of Smitty's patrol car, Granny in the middle, her walking stick upright in front of her like a prophet's staff. Twila and I sat by windows made of some sort of hardened Plexiglas, cloudy rather than clear.

Jack adjusted the rearview mirror. "Home, ladies?" he asked.

We didn't give him the satisfaction of lightening the mood. Three sets of arms crossed over three chests, wordless. Logically I knew it wasn't Jack's fault, but he was the closest target for our anger and frustration. He sighed and started the car.

The rain heightened as we drove, and Jack turned on the wipers. I'd hated driving or even riding in a bad storm ever since one of my cars hydroplaned in a downpour and ended up two inches from a steep cliff edge. A crack of lightning followed by a roll of thunder descending into the distance didn't help my state of mind. Had I been driving, I'd have pulled into a side road to outwait the deluge. But Jack continued on, albeit at a slow, steady pace.

I should have been trying to figure out how to get Katy out of that blasted cell, but my mind refused to cooperate, not dredging up even one lawyer's name. When we got back to Esprit d'Chene, I could pour over my address books. Not that I'd have lawyers' names listed, but I could call everyone listed to get input—and home numbers to roust the attorneys out of bed.

The patrol car radio buzzed with unbroken static, the sound nearly drowned by the rain pounding on the roof. Granny broke the silence. "Don't sound like there's nothin' goin' on with the police t'night. Ain't no school zones for them to watch over this time a'night, I suppose."

Twila chuckled, and Jack shot Granny a half-grin through the rearview mirror. I was too tense from the storm and thoughts of Katy to respond. Another crack of lightning brightened the sky briefly, and Jack slammed on the brakes, skidding on the wet pavement. Sir Gary, in the passenger seat, tossed Jack a casual glance.

"Why have we stopped? Did this conveyance run out of the petrol it needs, like Twila's?"

"I wish the hell you wouldn't pop in and out like that with no warning!" Jack snarled.

Sir Gary shrugged. "It's the way I travel."

Jack's jaw clenched, and we chuckled. "How's Katy?" I asked the ghost as Jack eased the patrol car on down the road.

"How do you expect?" Sir Gary answered. "Feeling rotten and scared." He muttered something else under his breath, which I didn't catch, but Jack glared quickly at him before he turned his attention back to the road.

"We don't have any choice now," Twila said.

"No," I agreed.

Granny bobbed her head, and Sir Gary shifted around to look at us, then slowly nodded. "I have all the time in the world," he said. "Right now, Katy's more important."

"Any of y'all want to let me in on what you're plannin'?" Jack asked.

Silence answered him, so he drove on for a few more miles without another word. As we neared Esprit d'Chene, I relented, although I was pretty sure what his reaction would be.

"We need to find Bucky's head."

"What the hell good's that going to do?" Jack gritted. "And just how the hell do you plan on doin' that, when none of the investigators...*trained* investigators...have been able to?"

"Maybe they aren't trained in the proper investigative techniques," I threw back at him in answer to his second question first.

"Ghosthunting techniques, I suppose," Jack growled.

Sir Gary fixed him with a haughty glance. "And you have a problem with that type of investigation?" When Jack refused to answer, Sir Gary turned his attention to the burst of static that erupted from the radio, covering up some broken words.

"Damn storm." Jack reached for the radio knob with one hand and steered with the other.

"Maybe you should try that button." Sir Gary waggled a finger. The siren blasted through the night and red, green, and blue flashed, illuminating the downpour. Sir Gary cocked his head, eyes wide with delight.

"Keep your damn hands off the equipment!" Jack yelled. He pushed a couple buttons, twisted a knob or two, but the lights and siren continued unabated. The radio crackled again, and one word penetrated the racket: "Detective?"

Jack swerved into the plantation driveway and slammed on his brakes. "Turn those things off!" he snarled at Sir Gary. "Whatever you did, undo it!"

"Ooooaa, ooooaa, ooooaa," Granny joined in with a snicker.

"Why?" Sir Gary asked with a laugh. "It's a jolly good show. I might not get to ride in one of these carriages again. What is that button there?"

Jack jammed the gearshift into park and switched off the key, but the siren just kept blaring, the lights circling. Now the radio joined the cacophony of sound, but not with police transmissions. Instead, a Cajun band blared, a rocking song that set my toes tapping and Granny and Twila's shoulders bouncing.

"Damn it!" Jack yelled. "Someone from the station's trying to get through to me! Someone could need help, and you're all actin' like you're at a party!"

That drained our amusement, and Sir Gary quickly waggled his finger at the dashboard. The siren and lights died, the radio went dead. The frantic voice on the police radio burst into the quiet. "Detective? Oh, shit."

Jack grabbed for the microphone, but his cell phone rang. He jerked it out of his pocket and spat, "Yeah?"

Sir Gary evidently figured out how to open the radio communication, because Smitty's voice flowed out so we could hear the conversation. "What's wrong with your radio?"

"Never mind. What's wrong?" Jack responded to his cell phone...and through the radio.

"Some sort of trouble at Esprit d'Chene," Smitty said, and we gasped. "Sue Ann got cut off when she called. You want me to call in some backup?"

"I'll let you know. Stay by the phone." Jack threw his cell phone on the seat and started the engine. Unfortunately, the gate was closed, as it should have been.

Jack glared at Sir Gary. "You wanna use your finger for something useful?"

Sir Gary wiggled his finger and the gate swung open. Jack floored the gas pedal, none of us saying a word. When the car rounded the bend and we could see the manor house, I held my breath in horror. Every light was on, four of Katy's guards on the veranda, two with pistols drawn, backs against the wall on either side of the door. The other two held a battering ram.

The two with the battering ram paused as the car skidded to a halt. Jack, Twila, and I flung open doors and rushed into the pouring rain, Jack racing toward the veranda. Inside the house, Trucker's howls and growls were furious, along with Miss Molly's high-pitched screeches. A scream

—a woman—probably Sue Ann—from the Great Room, to the left of the door. Chills chased up my back, and I glanced across the car roof at Twila.

"Bucky," she confirmed.

Sir Gary was no longer in the front seat. I hoped he'd gone into the house.

A splintering crash sounded. The front door now lay in the foyer. But the guards didn't seem all that eager to push in. They gathered around the opening and peered inside.

Jack didn't take that sort of precaution. He grabbed a pistol from a guard and ran through the door, crouching slightly, pistol gripped in both hands, leading the way. Another scream, then a loud crash. The four guards trickled one by one into the house.

I dashed toward the veranda, onto the steps. And barely ducked the Queen Anne's chair that flew through a window. As it was, I felt a pain in my forearm and saw a sliver of window glass sticking out. I jerked it out and tossed it down.

Twila grabbed my uninjured arm as I started through the doorway. "Wait."

"Where's Granny?" I asked, worried that my elderly friend might have fallen.

"I told her to wait in the car. And we're not going in there without more protection."

We quickly joined hands, concentrating both our minds on pulling down white light. The noise inside distracted me—another crash, raised voices now—men's, confused—asking what the hell was going on. But we got a measure of protection around us before I broke Twila's hold.

Miss Molly screeched again, and I dashed into the foyer, Twila right behind me. I didn't have to decide which way to go. The noise continued to be centered in the Great Room.

The four guards stood outside the doorway, peering in, shaking their heads and fidgeting with their pistols, raising them, lowering them, glancing at each other. I pushed into the room. And ducked as a silver platter flew at me. Behind me, Twila oomphed. The platter clattered to the floor, and I whirled to check on her. She shook her head, rubbing her shoulder.

Sue Ann was crouched behind the settee, Gabe on his hands and knees peering around one end. Miss Molly stood on the back of it, back arched and every hair on end. She hissed and snarled, staring at the fireplace. At Bucky, whose doll head swiveled as he looked for another object to pitch.

Gun aimed, Jack examined the room. Trucker snarled and barked at his feet, then plunged toward the fireplace. Bucky leaped straight at him. Trucker skidded on a throw rug, all hundred and fifty pounds of him sliding on a collision course with the ghost.

Miss Molly flew through the air, claws extended. She and Trucker both hit Bucky at the same time, sailed through him. Miss Molly hit the floor, and she and Trucker whirled to confront Bucky side by side. The ghost just ambled on across the room, toward Jack.

"Move, Jack!" I shouted.

He had sense enough not to question me. He ducked over to join Twila and me, and Bucky swiveled his head to follow Jack's progress. And saw a new set of antagonists.

"Where the hell's Sir Gary?" I muttered as Bucky considered his next move.

I searched the room, a corner of my mind confirming that Katy would be devastated if we didn't get it cleaned up before she came home. An Oriental vase of fresh-cut flowers lay shattered, the table it had set on tipped. Water pooled on the polished floor, discoloring it. The phone was on the floor beside Katy's desk, the receiver emitting that weird off-the-hook sound. The figurines Katy kept on the mantle were scattered around, probably thrown by the angry ghost. Some had landed on the settee and fainting couch; others were splintered on the hearth.

"Wonder how Katy's going to explain this to her insurance company?" Twila mused.

Suddenly an eerie silence spread through the room, broken only by various panting breaths and a tinkle as a piece of window glass dropped from a pane. Even Trucker and Miss Molly fell silent, staring at the ghost, and Miss Molly inched beneath Trucker's broad belly. At the doorway, the guards stared in confusion, not seeing anything to...guard anyone from.

"What's happening?" Jack whispered.

"I have no idea," Twila said in a normal voice. "But I assume we're about to find out."

Sir Gary materialized by Grandmere Alicia's portrait. Bucky silently turned to him.

"I suggest you've done enough damage for the time being," Sir Gary said. "You're not getting what you want with these temper tantrums. Why don't we join forces and see if we can't make some distinctive progress, rather than defeating your purpose by acting like a buffoon."

"Who's the ghost talking to?" Jack asked.

"Hush. It's Bucky," I whispered. Jack briefly closed his eyes, shook his head, then glanced at the guards, who hadn't moved one inch from the doorway.

The mouth on the doll's head dropped open, exposing tiny, pearly white teeth. Then closed again. A noise like someone clearing his throat erupted, and the mouth opened again. A rusty, squeaky voice emerged. "How..." The mouth closed again, another throat clearing. "How long ya been like me?" Bucky asked Sir Gary.

"Eons, like I tried to tell you earlier," Sir Gary replied. "Watch." He wiggled a finger, and the set of fireplace tools on the hearth clanged together. Then the poker rose into the air.

The guards lifted their guns, but Jack waved at them to subside. The poker danced in the air, then slid smoothly back into place with the gold-crowned log hooks and hearth brooms.

"Purty good," Bucky said with a nod. "I ain't figgered out how ta make stuff go where I wanna aim it."

"Why don't we find a private place to chat?" Sir Gary said. "I'll teach you some things."

Bucky considered that, glanced at us, glared down at Trucker. Trucker growled low.

"Don't like dogs like that," Bucky said. "Ugly cat, too."

"Now you listen here…" I began, but Twila nudged me into silence.

"What the heck are you people looking at?" one of the guards asked.

"Hush," Twila and I said in unison.

Bucky swiveled his head toward the guards, then around the room before he cocked it and examined Sir Gary. "Got some fancy duds, doncha? I ain't real happy with the ones I got on. Any way to change 'em?"

"We might be able to manage that."

"Lead the way. We ain't got all night."

"Well, my friend." Sir Gary strolled over to Bucky. "There you may be wrong. I believe we have plenty of time."

"Katy doesn't," I reminded him, and Bucky stared at me.

"What's that s'posed to mean? Where'd she get off to? And what you doin' here? I tol' Katy to keep your interferrin' nose outta our bizness this time."

"What—" the same guard asked.

"Hush!" Jack growled.

Sir Gary heaved a sigh. "If you're coming with me, let's go." He glided toward the fireplace, Bucky following hesitantly. I really wanted to question Bucky, but when I opened my mouth, Sir Gary caught my eye and shook his head in warning. He glided on over to the wall, but Bucky stopped in front of the fireplace.

"Hey," he said. "You think we could make like Santy Claus?"

"Who?" Sir Gary asked with a frown.

"St. Nicholas," I explained.

"After you." Sir Gary waved at the chimney opening.

Bucky giggled and dove at the fireplace. He zipped straight up the chimney, and Sir Gary watched with an amused smile. Then he jerked his shirt cuffs, gave us a wink, and laid an index finger beside his nose. And zipped after Bucky.

Twila broke into gales of laughter, and I chuckled, sneaking a peek at Jack. He stared at the fireplace, me, Twila, and turned to Gabe and Sue Ann as they slowly stood up behind the settee. Trucker and Miss Molly paced to the settee. The cat leaped onto a cushion and snuggled down to bathe herself, the dog plopping down in front of her and laying his head on his paws.

Sue Ann held out a hand to me, *gris-gris* bag in her palm. "You told me to let you know iffen this thing didn't keep the haints away. Well, it ain't."

"Get back on the grounds," Jack ordered the guards. As they scattered, he turned back to Sue Ann. "You and Gabe saw what was goin' on in here?"

"Yeah," Sue Ann muttered. "Didn't you?"

"I saw Sir Gary," Jack admitted.

"T'other one was Bucky," Gabe put in. "Ain't no doubt. And he ain't a happy haint. Just look 'round."

"What...how did it start?" Jack asked.

"That there vase of flowers crashed over first," Gabe explained. "And when we came in to take a look, Sue Ann grabbed the phone. Called nine-one-one. But he chased her away from there in nothin' flat. Kept us from gettin' out the door, too."

"We heard the sirens comin', tho'," Sue Ann said. "But didn't seem like you was ever gonna get here. And Bucky must've done somethin' to the front door. Back one, too, 'cause the guards couldn't get them open. We heard them poundin'."

Suddenly a guard in the front yard shouted. We could hear him clearly through the broken window. The few remaining panes shattered in a rain of glass as something thunked solidly into the chimney bricks the same instant the retort of a rifle sounded. Jack was out the door in a flash.

Two more rapid shots followed, but I didn't hear them hit. All of us lunged for the floor, but something seemed to be helping my fall along. I hadn't figured out yet what. An instant later, a barrage of pistol gunfire erupted.

CHAPTER 30

I uncovered my head and opened my eyes. Gabe and Sue Ann were beside me, Gabe protectively covering his wife. Twila lay in front of the settee, Miss Molly cuddled close, Trucker standing over the two of them. A red-hot poker stab of pain made me gasp, and I stared at a wet spot on my T-shirt. I'd been drenched outside, but this looked different. It spread, and I inched my hand up, pulling it away smeared with red and stifling a groan. Twila's eyes flew to mine. Miss Molly wiggled out of her hold and raced over, sniffing at my hand, then trying to crawl closer.

"My God!" Twila gasped. "You've been shot!"

"I guess so." I fainted dead away.

I couldn't have been out very long. When I opened my eyes again, Gabe and Twila were dragging me behind the settee. Sue Ann had retrieved the phone and was punching in numbers.

"We need an ambulance at Esprit d'Chene. Now!" she shouted. "Someone's been shot!"

Twila and Gabe laid me down, and Twila grabbed a pillow from the settee, sliding it under my head. Fully conscious, I probed at my wound, but Twila slapped my hand away. "Let me see how bad it is!"

"I don't think it's that bad," I replied. "It hurts, but not that much."

"It's sure as hell bleeding like it's bad!" She grabbed my T-shirt collar and ripped the shirt down the front.

"Granny," I reminded Twila. "She's out there!" The gunfire had ceased, and I eased to a sitting position, despite Twila's restraining hands. "It's just a minor flesh wound. Granny's the one in danger now. The guards don't know she's in the car! Stray gunfire might hit her!"

Twila thinned her lips. "I can go. You stay here."

When I moved to disobey her, she glanced at Sue Ann. The housekeeper crawled away from the phone. "You go ahead. She tries to move, I'll whap her on the other arm."

Sighing, I leaned against the settee. Miss Molly whimpered a concerned cat sound and placed her front paws on my uninjured shoulder. She gazed at me with those blue eyes, and I gave in. "I'll stay quiet. I promise," I said, stroking the cat.

Twila started out of the room in a crouching crawl, but Granny appeared in the doorway. Her wrinkled face reflected her horror and concern when her gaze fell on me, and she hobbled toward me as fast as she could. Twila met her halfway and Granny took her arm as she crossed the remaining distance.

"We should stay down," I reminded everyone.

"Damn shooter's gone," Granny said in a tight voice. "Cops are chasin' him. But I heard a car peel off out on the road, so they ain't gonna catch him." She let go of Twila's arm and continued, "Get her up on the couch, so I can see better."

With their help, I stood and wobbled around to the front of the settee. "Someone shot me," I mused in an empty voice.

"Go get me some first aid stuff," Granny ordered Sue Ann, who hurried out of the room, Gabe on her heels. "An' bring her a shot of whiskey!"

That sounded like the best thing to me. "I hope she brings the bottle," I muttered.

Then I heard Jack's voice in the hallway, Sue Ann's in reply. Jack rushed in even before Sue Ann finished, face white with strain. He was at the settee in two strides. He didn't say a word, just sat down and gently brushed my hair back from my shoulder. Then he pulled a handkerchief from his jeans pocket and laid it over the wound.

"It's clean," he muttered distractedly, keeping a slight pressure on it. "How are you feeling? Sue Ann said the ambulance is on the way."

"Call them on the radio and tell them they aren't needed," I insisted. He glared that bull-headed look I'd seen dozens of times before, indicating that he'd do no such thing. "Look, it's nothing worse than a small cut. I don't need to go to the hospital."

He ignored me, and I glanced at Twila for support. She crossed her arms and tapped her foot, the mulish look on her face mirroring Jack's.

I hadn't really looked at the wound, so I steeled myself. I don't like blood, especially my own. I have trouble even writing about it. But I pushed Jack's hand away, lifted the handkerchief, and gazed at my shoulder. There was a small furrow, but the bullet hadn't penetrated too deeply. Surely not deeply enough to merit a trip to the hospital. Besides, there were things that needed to be done here. Now, not later.

"See?" I shot both of my jailers an exasperated look. "It's nothing that a Band-Aid and a little antibiotic salve won't take care of."

"The bastard who did this isn't gonna care how bad he hit you when I catch him," Jack snarled.

Though I appreciated his concern and had my own craving for retribution, I snapped back, "This should prove you've got the wrong person in jail! Someone's still out there!"

"It doesn't necessarily prove anything, *Chère*," he admonished. "But you let me worry about that. You need to—"

"*I* need to correct a mistake law enforcement's made!" I battled the weakness even the slight wound had fostered and tried to sit up. I didn't resist very hard when Jack gently pushed me back onto the settee.

Sue Ann hurried in with the first aid kit, and I was glad to see she hadn't forgotten the whiskey. It wasn't Crown Royal, but I didn't care. She opened the first aid kit beside me on the couch and as Granny pawed through it, Sue Ann said, "Gabe's getting some plywood outta the storage shed to cover the window."

"Go ahead and give her a drink." Granny picked up gauze and tape.

Then she laid that back down and lifted a bottle of alcohol. I stiffened, and she relented and exchanged it for some peroxide.

Sue Ann poured me a shot of whiskey in the glass she carried on the bottle neck and I drank it down in one fiery gulp before Granny uncapped the peroxide. Sirens sounded in the distance, and I shot Jack a pleading glance. He looked at Granny, though, as did Twila.

Granny confirmed, "I can handle this."

Reluctantly, Jack rose. "I'll send them back."

He left the room as Sue Ann handed Granny a spotless kitchen towel, and she held it in her gnarled fingers to catch the overflow as she poured the peroxide on my shoulder. It bubbled and foamed, easing the pain somewhat as it worked out any infectious residue from the gunpowder. When Granny was satisfied, she pulled out salve and smoothed it over the wound, then taped a soft piece of gauze in place.

Sue Ann gathered up the first aid kit and set the whiskey bottle on a side table. "I'm going out to see if I can do anything to help Gabe."

Granny sat back. "We gotta find that head."

"Yes," I agreed. "But first I need to make some phone calls. Try to get Katy a lawyer."

Jack came back in just then, his cell phone in his hand. "I called Smitty and he gave me a local lawyer's name. He's on his way to the jail. I figured that was the least I could do, given that you ladies seem determined to ignore my orders to keep out of this investigation. So tell me. What's so damned important about the head?"

We gaped at him, shaking our own heads. "We need to calm Bucky down so we can ask him who killed him," I explained in a reasonable tone. "Since the cops don't seem to be able to find out who the real killer is."

Jack snorted in disbelief. "You're going to ask the murder victim who committed the murder."

"Of course," Twila said. "Who better?"

I rose, wincing at the stab of pain, then headed for the door. "First I'm changing my shirt," I said as I passed Jack. Miss Molly stayed close to me, nearly under my feet, but I didn't chastise her. Granny grunted to her feet, and her step-thump followed me.

Trucker sat on his haunches in the hallway, and he whined when I appeared. He fell in on the opposite side from Miss Molly, alert, brown eyes gleaming. I started up the stairwell and glanced behind me. Twila and Granny were first, but Jack was right after them. "Can you make the stairs, Granny?" I asked in concern.

"You bet your booties," she said with an emphatic nod and grabbed the railing.

I waited for all of them at the top. It took Granny a few seconds longer, but she made it with the help of the railing and the walking stick. As soon as Jack and Twila hit the last step, I led the parade of animals and people down the hallway to the Peach Room.

Twila accompanied me into the bathroom. We threw my T-shirt in the trash and she unsnapped my bra. She ran some warm water into the basin and washed away the blood residue on my arm and chest—with quince soap.

"I'll get you another shirt," she murmured. "No sense bothering with a bra. The strap's too near your wound."

I stared at my ravaged face in the mirror. Shot. I'd actually been shot! Had the shooter been aiming directly at me? Or was it a scare-tactic attack? It damned sure wasn't a random assault—some poacher out night-hunting, not watching where he aimed. The second and third shots confirmed the Great Room was the shooter's target. But who was he shooting at?

Jack brought the T-shirt back, and I grabbed a towel to cover myself, frowning at him. He grinned, a quick twitch of his lips, but the amusement at my discomfort in his presence didn't reach his brown eyes. At least he didn't make any smart-ass remark about having seen me naked before. He just handed me the shirt, and I turned my back and dropped the towel.

When I tried to raise my right arm, though, I stifled a groan. Even the slight wound would give me trouble for a while. Jack reached in front of me and took the shirt, pulling it over my head and helping me get my arms through the sleeves.

I turned around, and Jack said, "I wanted a minute with you. This changes everything. I'm calling in some more guards, and I want one of them with you at all times."

"Jack, I appreciate your concern. But I'm not about to have some cowboy riding herd on me every minute. We don't know the person was aiming for me."

He gently placed a finger to my lips. "I'm not takin' any chances with your life. Or Twila's or Granny's. And when I phoned the jail, I had Smitty call in an extra officer, just in case someone's after Katy. Someone who didn't know she was already under arrest."

Renewed horror crawled through my mind. "Someone who figures if they kill Katy, at least that part of the investigation will grind to a halt. The cops will figure Bucky's killer's dead."

"If that's what's goin' through that sonuvabitch's mind, he's wrong. We won't stop until we've got every end of this case tied up. He won't—"

"Or she," I broke in. "Jack, if the police believe Katy could kill some-one, why do you keep referring to the shooter as he? This is Texas. East Texas. Plenty of women around here can handle a rifle."

"I haven't ruled that out. But I also came in here to ask you for one huge favor."

"I'm not going to quit trying to clear Katy, Jack, so don't even ask."

His face told me that I'd grasped his unvoiced request. "I need to get out there and spearhead things," he said. "But I don't want to leave you ladies alone. Will you at least wait until the guard reinforcements get here?"

"No," I said flatly. "Katy's languishing in that horrible jail cell. Every minute counts. The fastest way to clear her is to get Bucky calmed down and see if he's got some evidence that you can use to ferret out the real killer!"

"Alice, this ghost business—"

I pushed past him and walked out the bathroom door. I didn't feel like arguing that route with him right now. He had his ideas about what needed done; I had mine. Never the twain shall meet. I knew that from past experience.

Twila and Granny waited in the bedroom, Twila with her satchel of protections. Which we damned sure might need before this night was over. I heard Jack's voice in the bathroom and decided he was on his cell phone to somebody. Twila, Granny, and I stared at each other.

"What next?" Twila asked.

"I think we should search the manor house again," I said. "Like you said, Bucky's hanging around here for some reason. Maybe somehow he realizes his head is nearby." Jack strolled out of the bathroom and stood silently, listening. "We'll need flashlights," I continued. "I want to search the hidden passageways."

"No one told my men about any hidden passageways," Jack said.

"I assumed Katy had." I looked around to gather my forces and nodded at Miss Molly and Trucker, stretched out over by the fireplace. "We'll want them with us."

"You should be in bed resting," Jack insisted. "A bullet wound's nothin' to—"

"I think Katy keeps a flashlight in each bedroom, for times when the power goes out." I opened a drawer in the lady's boudoir desk and revealed a flashlight. After a test for battery strength and satisfied when the beam glowed brightly, I marshaled my troops with a hand wave and headed for the door.

"Wait a minute." Twila set the satchel on the bed and removed some necklaces made of the same quince seed we wore as bracelets. She handed Granny and me one and hung one around her neck. Then she took out a plastic bag, and I wrinkled my nose in distaste as I recognized the asafetida bags on leather throngs. But we all put one of those around our necks, also. Twila even tried to get Trucker and Miss Molly to wear one, but both my pets scrambled under the bed when she got within two feet of them.

"We'll have to rely on the white light and baths you gave them," I said. "Let's get the other flashlights."

Jack followed into the hallway, but instead of turning toward the stairwell, he dogged our footsteps as we stopped at the Blue Room first. "I thought you had an investigation to spearhead," I reminded him in Twila's room.

"I called the chief out of bed. Told him I was tied up on another end of this and gave him my cell phone number."

Shrugging, I waited while Twila found her flashlight. Then she cast Jack a considering look, laid her satchel on the bed and pulled out two necklaces for him. Jack shot back a stubborn look. "I'm not—"

"You are, if you're going with us." Twila dangled the quince seed and asafetida necklaces in his direction. "Or we'll just sit here and wait until you give up. We've got more time than you do. Suppose the chief comes out here and finds you sitting like a tea party guest with three ladies in this bedroom. You're lucky I don't insist you take a quince soap shower before we start out, so consider wearing the necklaces the minimum we'll accept."

"This is our ball game, Jack," I added. "You don't mess around in this business without protection."

"You're just lookin' for the damned head," Jack said.

"We're looking for a ghost's head," Twila said. "A newly-dead, confused ghost. Sir Gary may be able to keep Bucky occupied for a while, but we can't count on how long. Any minute Bucky could be on the prowl again. He's unpredictable, despite the fact he seems to be trying to bond with Sir Gary. Wear the necklaces or forget about coming with us."

"I can search those passageways myself," he said. "I don't need you ladies."

I laughed wryly. "You'll never find them. I'm the only one here who knows how to get to them. Where they run. And I swear, if you don't cooperate...if you try to get a search warrant and wreck the walls in this house to find the passageways, I'll fight you every step of the way."

Granny, silent until now, added with an evil grin, "I'll bet them TV news folks would like t'have a ghost story. I ain't never been on TV. Might be fun to look back on in old age."

"The judge has slapped a gag order on this investigation," Jack reminded us.

"So what's he gonna do?" Granny threw back. "Stick some nice little old lady like me in that there jail with Katy for openin' my toothless mouth?"

Jack actually glared at the dear old elderly woman for a long second before he muttered, "Shit." He swiped the necklaces from Twila's hand and hung them around his neck, grimacing at the smell. Maybe not only the smell, but also—probably—at being demoted to participant rather than head honcho by three civilians.

Twila held out her hands, one toward Jack, one toward Granny. Even though we'd called down the white light at the manor house door, we needed to reinforce and strengthen its power now. I took Granny's hand and moved into the circle, catching hold of Jack and pulling him with me. Twila clasped his free hand, and we bent our heads.

Except for Jack, who continued to stare at us. I nudged him with a sideways kick, and he finally bowed his head. Clearing my mind—as well as I could—I joined Twila and Granny in three deep, cleansing inhales and exhales. Jack joined in on the last one.

"I want all of you to imagine a white light inside your minds," Twila began in a slow, hypnotic voice. "Close your eyes and see it there...in your mind's eye." She waited a brief instant, then continued, "Now, brighten that light. Expand it. Let it engulf your body. Feel its soothing presence, its warmth." A pause. "Now, let the light flow through your body. Feel the warmth and protection. Then expand it to encompass the person on your right...the person on your left." Pause. "Let it fill this room...move out through the manor house, the grounds around it. Even beyond, until it covers everything and reaches skyward, to the powers of the Universe, seeking their blessing and protection for our quest."

We stood silently for a few moments. I'd felt the power of the white light from the very first time Twila showed it to me. Whether I called on it in a brief request or a more powerful ceremony as we were using now, it gave me confidence and courage, but also reminded me of the dangers I needed to heed.

We all marched into the hallway and down to Granny's room, where she found a flashlight for herself in a bureau drawer. That left Jack without a light, but I didn't wait for him to ask to retrieve one from the patrol car. I led the way back into the Peach Room and over to the marble fireplace. Trucker and Miss Molly crawled out from under the bed.

There was a light switch beside the fireplace, but it didn't operate any lights. I flicked the switch up, then slid the small plastic panel aside. Behind it was a knob, and I turned it. It was rusty from neglect and I had to twist it hard, but it finally moved. I pushed the right place on the fireplace—back, then a release. After a small click, the fireplace fell away from the wall a few inches. Grasping the side, I opened the door to the passageway and shone my light inside.

It was dark, of course. Spooky. Cobwebs fluttered in the interior in the slight breeze from the fireplace swinging open. The rest of my crew crowded around, Twila and Granny adding their flickering flashlight beams to mine.

The landing was about five-foot square, just large enough for two people. Wooden steps both ascended and descended. Timbers lined the walls, old and decaying. I played my beam on the steps to see if they were safe. Once in a while Katy and I had run across a rotten board that broke under us. They'd mostly been near the ground level, though, where moisture heightened the rotting process.

I wasn't sure how many people knew about the passageways. There were rumors, of course, in family history, but Katy and I had found our clues to the secreted hallways and tunnels in one of Grandmere Alicia's diaries, which we poured over late one night while visiting Miss Emmajean. We made our first entrance into the hidden secret of the manor house right here in the Peach Room and explored the passageways, mapping them in our young minds so we wouldn't get lost. We even ventured into the underground tunnel, but found it collapsed about fifty feet or so inside. We'd jealously guarded our knowledge from the slew of other family offsprings. Katy kept the diaries on a bookshelf in the library.

"Granny's going to have trouble with these stairs," Twila mused.

"No, I ain't." Granny grabbed Jack's arm. "Got me a nice strong man here to help me along. I ain't stayin' behind."

"We wouldn't think of it, Granny," I said. "You're one of us. Shall we go up first...or down?"

"Up, I believe," Twila said after a moment's concentration. "To the attic."

"There are some rooms in the basement, where the runaways were hidden. But there's also a small area up in the attic. Katy and I used to hide things we didn't want our parents to catch us with up there. We weren't real enthused about that dank basement."

Twila shone her flashlight beam up the stairwell. More spider webs, a lot of dust—but something was fishy.

"Give me that light!" Jack grabbed Twila's flashlight and played the beam on the steps. The dust that should have covered them like on the walls was missing in the middle of the steps. It lay fairly thick on the edges of the boards, but someone had very obviously brushed out something in the middle. Footsteps?

Twila picked up a bright orange feather near her feet. "This looks like it's from one of those feather dusters people use to clean hard-to-get-at places."

Jack took the feather. I expect he wanted to put it in an evidence bag, but he wasn't prepared for something like that. He thought we were on a wild goose chase—probably hoped we were. Still, I flickered my flashlight beam across his face and noticed a distinct change in his expression. His cop mode. I'd seen it before.

"You ladies are gonna have to go back. I'm declaring this area part of the crime scene."

We laughed, actually laughed at him. "I mean it," he said. "All three of you get back into the bedroom."

A silent glance passed between Twila, Granny, and me. Jack was still standing in the fireplace opening, although Granny had edged onto the platform. Her tiny body didn't take up much room, but it was a little crowded. No room for Jack. Trucker stood beside Jack, Miss Molly under his belly. From the looks of the cat, I doubted very much she'd follow us up those stairs, even with her huge friend to shelter her. In fact, she inched out to peer up the stairwell, then backtracked between Trucker's rear legs and skittered beneath the bed. Trucker whined after her, but stayed in the doorway.

Granny sighed. "Guess we best do what he says. The cat figures he's right." She turned slightly, as though to go back into the bedroom, but instead, she stuck her walking stick behind Jack's legs. I shoved him—hard—on the chest, surprising him. He tumbled into the bedroom with a growl of outrage, but before he could scramble to his feet, I swung the fireplace closed. There was another latch on the inside, and I barely got it shut before Jack pounded on the wall. Outraged at being left behind, Trucker howled one long, eerie warning before he subsided.

We waited for a few seconds, listening to Jack fumble with the switch, but he couldn't open the fireplace as long as we had it locked from this side. Katy and I had tried that.

"Open this damn thing! Right now!" Jack shouted, hammering on the wall. The thumps echoed in the confined area, but the fireplace held firm.

Twila put her foot on the first step.

"Stay close to the edges," I cautioned. "The steps are stronger there."

She eased her foot over against the wall. There was a railing, but I didn't really trust it. I urged Granny in front of me and brought up the rear as she steadied herself against the wall on one side and used her walking stick in her right hand.

It took us a while to climb—we didn't hurry, given Granny's presence. The passageway smelled old...dusty and moldy, disused and dank. I kept an ear out for scurrying sounds; I don't like rats or even mice. Spiders or snakes, either, for that matter. We came to the next landing without running across any tiny four-, eight-legged, or legless intruders.

I had to bypass my two companions to reach the wall, and found the latch on my first try. Like the one on the fireplace, it was rusty with neglect, but I forced it open as Twila illuminated it with her flashlight beam. The door swung inward with a squawk of hinges, revealing a fairly large room lined with shelves on one side. The Hollow Room, Katy and I had always called it.

I played my beam around. It appeared much the same as the last time I'd been in here, more years back than I wanted to count. In a corner stood an old pie cabinet, pin holes in the metal on the front to allow air in but keep ants and flies out of the pies or other food stored in years gone by. There was even a pile of musty old blankets against the other wall, and a couple of feather ticks rolled up. History. So much history in this room. How many people had passed through? Families, children, people with dreams of freedom and fulfilling lives. Mothers and fathers who weren't afraid of hard work, but wanted decent lives for their children despite the dangers associated with their journey. Despite the risks to their own lives if they were caught.

A dusty volume lay on a shelf, and I frowned. It hadn't been there before. Crossing to it, I opened the cover, sneezing but too interested in what it contained to do more than rub my nose.

"It's a list of the slaves who passed through Esprit d'Chene," I said in awe. "Some of them wrote their own names. Some lines have an X, and the same handwriting throughout wrote the name for the person."

"I'd think something like that would have been rather dangerous to keep around," Twila said. "If the room were discovered."

"Maybe they kept it hidden better back then. One of our relatives with a feeling for the fitness of it must have put the book up here in later years, since I've never seen it before."

"I feel a lot of pain in this room," Twila said. "But also a lot of hope."

A thump sounded on a nearby wall in the attic area, and I jumped. The book slid to the floor, and I reverently picked it up as the noise moved closer to the Hollow Room.

"Jack," I explained as I replaced the book. "He came up the attic stairs, and he's trying to find out where the area's hollowed out. But there's only one way into this room."

"Still, we better hurry," Twila said. "The pie cabinet first?" She strode over and reached for the door handle, a tremble in her hand. She hesitated, then jerked the door open.

I shone my flashlight beam on the empty shelves. "Whew. Nothing."

"Whew," Granny also breathed. "Had me a pie cabinet just like that there one when I was first married. Didn't look forward to finding a bloody head in it."

My beam floated over to the blankets and feather ticks. Jack continued to pound, his thumps more persistent as his temper probably erupted. The noise was moving away from us.

Twila and I inched reluctantly toward the blankets and feather ticks. Granny remained where she was, leaning on her walking stick, her elderly body not meant for bending down and shaking out blankets. Which we had to do. I swallowed and reached for the top blanket. Held the edge for a long second. Swooshed it up and shook it.

Nothing. Only a dust shower. I sneezed violently. And gave Jack an idea of where we were, since the next series of fist thuds pounded right beside us.

"Damn it, Alice!" he called faintly. "Come out here!" The walls on the room were fairly thick, to enclose any inadvertent sounds that would betray the occupants. But they would have had to do their part and keep quiet.

Twila picked up the next blanket and shook it. Nothing. We examined the last two with the same result, then turned our attention to the rolled-up feather ticks. One was a lot thicker than the other one—could just be the stuffing or perhaps something was rolled up inside. I grabbed for the thinner feather tick, but Twila beat me to the punch. She shook out hers—empty. I stared at the other one and tried to swallow again. My dry mouth and throat didn't cooperate.

"Want me to get that one?" Granny offered. Jack sounded like he was kicking the wall now with his western boots.

"I'll do it." I reached for a corner. When I pulled, it resisted, confirming there was something inside. Something fairly heavy. "Oh, God," I burst out as I swung the feather tick high and shook.

The baby doll thumped out onto the floor, and even Twila stifled a scream. It wasn't the head we were looking for. The baby doll's head was missing. We knew where it was—on Bucky's shoulders.

Granny said, "I s'pose some poor chile left her dolly behind."

I squatted by the doll, unable to touch it; my hands had enough trouble holding the flashlight. It was about two feet long, the body anyway. A four- or five-year-old toddler's doll rather than an infant's. It wore a white gown, tattered lace disintegrating. A pair of intricately laced ballet slippers covered tiny feet, one with a hole where a miniature toe peeked out. My light picked up something else on the dusty floor at about the same time as Twila's and Granny's.

"Someone's dusted this floor, too, like the steps. Hiding footsteps. Jack's going to kill us for ruining evidence."

"Uh..." Twila put in. "Let's don't use the word 'kill' right now, if you please."

"Okay," I agreed. "But look."

The three beams converged and followed the smeared reddish brown spots across the floor, through the disturbed dust—to a foot-high space beneath the shelves. Neither Twila nor Granny could see what I could from where I squatted.

I screamed—screeched to high heaven. Dropped my flashlight and scrambled backward, lunging to my feet and pointing, backing up until I hit the wall.

"Alice!" Jack yelled. "Damn it, what's going on?"

"Him?" Twila asked.

I could only nod and point. I couldn't see the grisly horror now, but I could still see it in my mind's eye: Bucky Wilson-Jones' head, stuffed under the shelf, eyes wide, though opaque. A surprised look on his face, neck sliced clean. Dried blood pooled on a towel beneath his cheek.

CHAPTER 31

Afterwards I found out that Sir Gary had let Jack into the passageway. The ghost lost track of Bucky somehow, came to see what we were up to, and ended up in the attic with Jack. At first he'd stayed back in the shadows, watching Jack's ineffective tirade and enjoying the show. When he heard my scream, he stuck his head inside the Hollow Room to see if we were in danger. Rapt in our horror, we didn't notice. Sir Gary visualized in the attic and led Jack back to the Peach Room, where he opened the fireplace.

None of us wanted to touch that head. We hadn't thought that far in advance—decided what to do if we actually found it. Granny did toddle over and bend down to shine her flashlight under the shelf. But she just said "huh" and straightened.

So we were all still standing there when Jack pounded up the stairs. Think what you want, but sometimes even liberated women appreciate having a strong man take charge. Each one of us heaved a sigh of relief as Jack and Trucker burst into the room.

He didn't have to ask. Twila and Granny each lifted a hand and pointed at the same spot my finger was still frozen on. Trucker sniffed and growled low in his throat.

"No," I whimpered, but it was Twila who grabbed the dog's collar and halted him.

Jack squatted and picked up my flashlight. I scooted along the wall to put more distance between myself and the grisly resting place of the conclusion of our hunt. I'd seen enough. Now we had to decide who was brave enough to tote that head to its rightful owner.

"You ladies ready to go on downstairs?" Jack asked in a far-too-calm voice. He didn't have to repeat himself. Three heads bobbed in unison, and I scurried onto the landing. Granny thump-limped out after me, but when I looked back, I saw Twila having a time with Trucker. The dog planted his feet, nose pointed at those shelves, not about to move.

"Trucker, come!" I ordered. He ignored me.

Granny thumped her walking stick. "Dog! Get over here!" He ignored her, too. "Well, I'll be," she said with a huff.

"Can we leave Tru—" I began.

"No!" Jack broke in. "Everyone out of here!" He grabbed the dog's collar. I started to warn Jack that Rottweilers have large necks, so collars slip off easily, but I didn't have to. Trucker lunged backward against Jack's hold, leaving him with the empty collar dangling.

He headed straight for the head.

Jack bounded after him and grabbed Trucker by the scruff of his neck. But not before Trucker got a paw under the shelves and batted that head across the room like a football.

Twila, Granny, and I—Jack, too—froze, our eyes following it. I don't know about Twila and Granny, but I couldn't have screamed again if I wanted to. And damned if I didn't want to. But my breath was caught somewhere inside, far removed from my vocal cords. The head rolled straight to the baby doll and rested at the neck.

That did it. That horrible picture settled in my mind with a sharp click that would haunt me forever. The lacy dress, a pair of tiny ballet slippers on the feet poking out from under the hem, a tiny toe from the slipper hole. And the ghastly head resting there as though it were the missing part of the body, albeit an incongruous one.

I grabbed Granny and practically carried her down the first few steps.

Somehow Twila slipped around us. She swept Granny up and rushed through the fireplace into the room, me right behind them. It took every ounce of fortitude I could muster not to hit the floor on my belly and crawl under that bed with Miss Molly.

Instinctively, I swung around to shove the fireplace closed, barely stopping. Jack wouldn't appreciate being locked inside the passageway. I held onto the side of the marble, breathing deeply, fingers clenched so tightly my knuckles pained and my wound throbbed. The mattress springs squeaked, and I forced my grip loose, turning as Twila sat Granny on the bed. Beneath it, Miss Molly hissed and meowed, but didn't appear.

Sir Gary did, though, in the Peach Room doorway.

"Good," Twila said with a relieved sigh. "I'd much rather deal with a ghost than dead body parts."

"I assume your search ended successfully," Sir Gary said.

"Yeah," I managed. "But now we've got to get the head to Bucky."

Jack's heavy footsteps descended. Huffing and puffing from exertion, he stepped onto the landing and dropped Trucker inside the room. "Stay!"

Trucker stayed, on his rump, ears pricked, gazing past Jack as though waiting for an opportunity. Jack tossed the collar to me, and I slipped it on Trucker's neck. Tugging the way I'd learned wouldn't dislodge the collar, I got the reluctant dog over by the wardrobe, opened the door, and grabbed his harness and leash from a clothes hook.

By the time I secured the dog, Jack had a small bamboo wastebasket. He removed the plastic liner. It was empty; I hadn't been in the room long enough to throw away any trash. Then Jack grabbed one of the pillows, jerked the case free, and tossed the pillow on the bed. He turned back to the passageway without a word of explanation.

He didn't need to. The plastic liner and pillowcase were to carry the head down the stairs with. Trucker took a tentative step after Jack, but I yanked on the leash to remind him who was in charge here. Well, in charge of him, at least.

Silence ruled. Even Sir Gary just stood in the doorway, waiting. Jack's footsteps returned, and he re-entered, cell phone to his ear, pillowcase dangling from his other hand. Twila edged to the far side of the bed, but Granny sat there, legs dangling, watching Jack with bright-eyed interest. I swallowed and backed away, but the wardrobe left me no room to distance myself farther. The case swung back and forth, the head dragging down one corner, and I searched for signs of seeping blood.

None, of course. The head had been dead and the blood dried for a while.

I hadn't been paying any attention to what Jack was saying. He disconnected the phone and stuck it in a pocket. "So, that's that," he said.

"What?" I asked.

"He's taking that head to the funeral home," Granny said. "Didn't you hear him?"

"You can't! We need to reconnect it to Bucky's soul!"

Jack rolled his eyes and shook his connected head. He shut the fireplace firmly behind him. "That's a crime scene now, like I said. I don't want anyone disturbing it until I can get some techs out here in the morning."

"I don't think you have a thing to worry about along that line," I said.

"I hope not." He carried the pillowcase to the door, and Sir Gary moved hurriedly out of his way. The ghost evidently wasn't any more enthused than the living about being in close proximity to the cargo inside that case.

Jack disappeared down the hallway. The rest of us heaved sighs mixed with relief and frustration, even the ghost.

"Now what are we going to do?" Twila asked.

"Go get the head back, of course," Granny said.

CHAPTER 32

"Wh—what? Wh—who? U—us?" I stammered. "Huh-uh. No way. We've flirted with arrest for interfering in a police investigation too much already. No way in hell are we gonna actually steal evidence!"

"We'll give it back." Granny slid toward the side of the mattress, and Twila helped her to the floor.

"Granny's right," Twila said. "There's no choice, with Jack refusing to cooperate."

I glanced at Twila. "You can't be serious about sanctioning this. We can't steal that head, even if we do plan to return it."

"Katy's in jail," Twila reminded me. "Charged with murder."

"But—"

"Weren't you listenin'?" Granny asked. "Jack said he was takin' that head to Campton's for the night. Storin' it in one of them body coolers 'til they can send it on to that place they use in Garland to do them autopsy things."

"So?" I questioned. "And no, I wasn't paying much attention. The roaring in my ears made it impossible for me to focus on anything but that damn dangling case!"

"Campton's," Granny repeated. "My granddaughter, Maxine Campton, was the JP who came out and declared Bucky dead. An' she and her husband, Claude, run Campton's Funeral Home out there on the edge of Jefferson."

"You can't ask your granddaughter to risk her position and business," I insisted.

"Watch me." Granny walked over to the bedside phone.

"Wh—who's going to handle the damn thing?" I protested. "Not me!"

"We'll worry 'bout that when we get there." Granny picked up the phone.

"Yeah, like we worried about who'd handle it once we found the darn thing!"

"Come on," Twila urged, joining Sir Gary at the door. "Let Granny make her arrangements. You need a break from this situation for a while."

I needed a permanent break from this situation, but that wasn't going to happen. Katy depended on us. I held Trucker's leash tightly and made sure the fireplace was solidly latched while Granny punched in numbers on the phone. Then I released the dog to stay with Granny and followed Twila and Sir Gary down the hall to the Blue Room. Behind us, Granny's faint "Hello" negated any hope that her granddaughter wouldn't answer—and that we'd have to pass on Granny's plan.

In the Blue Room, Twila motioned me to a chair in front of the fireplace. Someone had laid kindling and logs in the grate, and Twila took a wooden match from a silver case on the mantle and struck it against the bricks. She touched flame to kindling, and the fire crackled with small flames, which spread into a cheery blaze—a definite contradiction to my mood. The visage under the shelf—on the body of the doll—the sack dangling from Jack's hand—

Twila sat in another lounge chair. "Let's talk about Sir Gary's problem. Take our minds off Bucky and let the thoughts calm down and soak in our subconscious. We probably won't be able to go after the head for a couple hours or so."

"It'll take Jack a while to store it and get out of our way." I clapped my hand over my mouth and surged to my feet. "I can't believe I said that! No way! We can't steal evidence!"

"We're only borrowing it, Alice," Twila said in a placid voice. "Sit down."

I sat, but not because she told me to. My unsteady legs were glad to be relieved of my body's weight. "Twila, we've done a lot of things together in our lives. Things we probably should have been arrested for. But this...this —"

Twila ignored me and turned to Sir Gary. "Would you like to sit?" she asked.

"I'm fine." He leaned against the fireplace. "However, we discussed my predicament earlier and came to no conclusions."

"Alice may have a new perspective. Why don't you repeat what you told me?"

Sir Gary nodded. "It's not much more than she already knows. I recall being with a woman—not my wife, as I told Alice—during the last moments I can remember about my life."

I leaned forward. Maybe Twila was right and I needed a different path for my thoughts for a while. "Tell us who she was. It may mean something."

"I doubt it," Sir Gary said. "I was breaking off the relationship. She had an offer of marriage, to a decent man. I wanted her to accept the proposal and have a good life."

"Instead of guilty liaisons in out-of-the way rooms," I added.

"That was part of it," Sir Gary conceded.

"I wonder if there truly was another man in her life?" Twila asked. "Sometimes women will make up a story like that to see if jealousy spurs a reluctant lover into committing himself."

"There was never any question of my leaving my wife," Sir Gary denied. "And yes, there was another man. My brother."

Twila cocked her head attentively. "You didn't mention him."

"It seems we get disrupted now and then from our discussions. It was my older brother, James. The one who inherited the title. He'd lost his wife in childbirth, along with the child, his first. He came to visit me as he worked through his grief and ended up staying several months. Lucinda, my wife, liked him quite well and never complained about him being with us so long. In fact, I believe James's company was good for Lucinda, since he was quite kind to her. I, on the other hand, had trouble being in my wife's presence."

"You said her riding accident was your fault," I recalled. Lord, it seemed like weeks ago that we'd talked in the Garden Room instead of just yesterday.

Sir Gary gazed at the floor. "I bought her the mare. She loved to ride. Had been born into a horse family. I met her during a trip to a farm to furnish my own stables after my shipping company became successful enough for me to purchase a larger home with its own pond on some lovely grounds. Quite a beautiful place, and besides horses, it needed a woman to care for it."

I shot him a frown, and he hastily added, "But I did care for Lucinda. It wasn't one of those matches of convenience. Until...until the accident a year into our marriage."

"Children?" Twila asked.

"No. We were careful about that at first. Lucinda wanted us to have some time alone before we started a family. After our marriage, she took a deep interest in our stables. She desired to breed her own line of horses, and I had plenty of funds to allow her that joy." He frowned slightly. "Even though that wasn't the most...womanly occupation for her time. However, I spent hours upon hours away from home, keeping the shipping business on sound financial grounds. So I had no problem with her hobby filling her free time."

Twila and I flashed each other a look, in complete understanding as to how we felt about his chauvinistic comment, but let it slide. "So how'd you end up buying a mare on your own?" I asked. "Wasn't she in charge of that?"

"I found the mare in a cargo of horses in a ship that docked at our

269

port. Arabians. The man who'd purchased the horses died before they arrived, and the widow wanted them auctioned off. I bought the mare for looks and breeding. I didn't think to ride her first."

"But Lucinda would have wanted to ride her first thing," I mused, knowing the woman without ever having met her.

"The mare appeared docile. She tolerated the bridle and saddle without difficulty. Lucinda was terribly excited. She thanked me profusely, allowing that the mare was perfect for her breeding plans."

"We're sort of getting off the track here," Twila reminded us. She's not much of a horse person. But I was deeply interested in the story. I nodded at Sir Gary to continue.

"The mare flew into a frenzy the moment Lucinda got into the saddle. Looking back, I believe it was the riding skirt. There was a breeze that day, and part of her skirt flew up and landed across the mare's eyes. No one was holding the mare. Lucinda wouldn't allow that indignity to her riding skills."

"She was thrown," I said.

"More than that." Sir Gary glanced up to gauge our reactions just as Granny toddled into the room, Trucker and Miss Molly behind her.

"All set," she said.

"We'll talk about that in a minute, Granny," I said gently. "Sir Gary's explaining what happened to his wife right now."

Granny nodded agreeably, and I focused on Sir Gary. However, Twila politely rose and offered Granny her chair, something I should have thought of. The elderly woman limped over and took the seat gratefully, and Twila stepped behind her. Miss Molly gracefully settled on Granny's lap and Trucker touched noses with her before he lay down in front of the fire.

"You said it was more than just being thrown from the mare," I prodded.

He closed his eyes briefly, then opened them. Obviously this was painful. "The mare caught Lucinda off guard, though I'd seen her ride difficult-to-handle horses before. Yes, she was thrown. But the mare didn't quit. Screaming in rage, she pounded Lucinda with those sharp hooves, flinging her body around like a lifeless doll before I lunged forward and stopped her."

We waited breathlessly as Sir Gary controlled his emotions, then said, "But she was in a wicked rage. She snapped at me, reared and plunged. I had a pistol on my belt. I shot her. She fell, and I rushed over to Lucinda. It wasn't only her body that was mangled. One side of her face had taken the full brunt of one hoof."

"Sweet Jesus," Granny murmured.

"She'd been a beautiful woman," Sir Gary went on. "But her spine was also injured and she was in a wheelchair from then on. She never rode again. She grew embittered, angry. There was no chance of children, something that she'd wanted as soon as we decided the time was right. And whenever I looked at her from then on, I was reminded of my part in her ruined life. Reminded that I deserved all the harsh words she spoke to me. Which were, from then on, the extent of our conversations. She, of course, moved into another bedroom."

We listened to the fire snap and crackle. The drapes were open, and beyond the window the clouds had subsided in the night sky, leaving behind a blanket of stars glowing both dim and bright. Some winked as though shadows passed across them in those mega-million light years before their light meandered through the universe for our enjoyment. A shooting star flared an arc across the heavens, drawing my gaze to Centaurus, the half-man, half-horse constellation, which Greek legend said Jupiter had placed in the sky after Hercules accidentally killed him.

Who knew? Maybe Lucinda was up there now, free from pain and enjoying riding once more. I looked at Sir Gary, who was gazing out the window now. Our eyes met, and I knew he'd seen the shooting star.

"You said James was good to Lucinda," I said. "But he evidently fell in love with...what was your current mistress's name?"

"Current?" Twila frowned. She didn't like straying men any more than I did.

Granny caught our drift and shrugged. "Man's got needs. 'Specially a

271

young man. Even carryin' a load of guilt and not bein' able to gaze on a woman he once loved."

That didn't make me much more sympathetic, even though I'd spent a lot of long, lonely nights in my own bed after Jack and I divorced. But I supposed I could understand.

"Her name was Alexa." Sir Gary gazed at us steadily. "She and James met at a ball. And before you ask, no, James did not know Alexa and I were lovers. From what I gathered, he and Alexa weren't waiting for the marriage bed to consummate their relationship either."

"She was pregnant." A dreamy look on Twila's face indicated she'd tuned into long-gone vibes from a thousand miles way, centuries earlier.

"No!" Sir Gary denied. "She couldn't have been!"

"It wasn't yours." Twila still focused across the veil. "It was James's child, but she wasn't sure."

I surged to my feet and glanced at Granny. "How long before your granddaughter will let us into the funeral home?"

Granny pulled a small pocket watch from her ever-present skirt pocket and opened the cover. "'Bout another hour or so."

"What are you thinking, Alice?" Twila asked.

"Katy did a genealogical search on Sir Gary. It's probably still stored on her computer, since I'm sure she would have wanted me to see it. We might as well use the time we're waiting productively. Katy's computer's in the Master Suite."

I led my cohorts to the Master Suite. Katy kept her computer in an early 1800s wardrobe she'd converted. When I opened the wardrobe, modern technology, mixed with the age-gone-by, graceful décor Katy achieved, appeared incongruous in the historical ambiance. Uneasy about invading Katy's privacy, I powered the computer up and sat down at the keyboard. My band of followers gathered behind me.

Katy hadn't passworded her system. I clicked into the same word processing program I used and studied the folders. Easy enough; she'd labeled one "Sir Gary Gavin." I opened it and then a "Genealogy" sub-file. Her usual scrupulous self, Katy annotated several generations of English ancestors. I arrowed through until I found the ghost's birth.

"Look. Katy even did a little research on Lucinda. Oh, dear."

Sir Gary peered over my shoulder. "She died a few months after I did. Do you think the records might show what happened to her?"

Another file probably contained the information, but I glanced at Twila, who shook her head. Assuming Twila's psychic senses had retrieved that and her warning meant it wasn't something Sir Gary needed to know, I evaded lying. "I don't see anything about causes of death," and I continued, "but Alexa and James did marry. They had four sons, and one daughter."

I scanned further. "Well, I'll be. I guess you've got some pioneering genes in your family, Sir Gary. The descendants spread out all over the country. One of your great-great...ever how many generation greats...nieces lives here in East Texas. A nephew in New Orleans. It's probable that Katy and I have met them over the years."

"I'm glad to see my family line didn't die out," Sir Gary said. "Perhaps having family in the area led my wanderings here. But that still doesn't tell us what happened to me."

Something thumped downstairs, and we all stared at the door. "That might be Bucky," I said. "Will you go see, Sir Gary? You can handle him better than we can right now."

Obediently, the ghost dissolved, and Twila murmured, "It was probably just Sue Ann dropping something. Let's look at whatever you were reluctant to show Sir Gary."

I clicked on the "Causes of Death" file and paged to Sir Gary's name. And frowned, puzzled. The information only gave the cause, not the circumstances, our quest.

"Drowning?" Twila read. "But he was a sailor."

"Very few sailors back in those days knew how to swim," I explained. "But here, look. He died in Boston, at his home. He must have drowned in the pond on his estate."

"Lucinda died of pneumonia." Twila pointed at the screen. "But I'd already sensed that. And it was a fairly peaceful death, from what I gathered."

"Good," I said. "She had enough pain in her life."

273

I closed the file, not knowing how soon Sir Gary would return. Twila shut her eyes, concentrating, but shook her head. "I don't understand why I can't break through the veil and find out how Sir Gary died. I didn't have any trouble reaching back to Lucinda."

"Something's complicating it," I guessed. "We'll need to do a séance at some point."

Sir Gary materialized. "The noise was the housekeeper and her husband on the porch, repairing the windows. And your phone is ringing in your bedroom, Alice."

We all rushed to the Peach Room. It wasn't the bedside phone. I opened my briefcase and grabbed my cell phone. When I answered, a voice asked, "Granny?"

"Uh...no, this is Alice."

"This is Maxine Campton," the woman said. "My grandmother asked me to call her back on this number."

My gang of co-conspirators lined the doorway, listening. "Maxine?" Granny asked. "I give her that number, 'cause I didn't know where we'd be when she called back."

I walked over and handed her the phone.

"Hello?" She listened for a few seconds, then said, "See you in a bit," and disconnected. "We're all set. Jack's gone, and he won't be back 'til sometime in the mornin'."

I swallowed. Tried to, anyway. My gag reflex engaged as a picture of that grisly head under the shelf in the Hollow Room flashed through my mind again. A vision which Twila must have read, because she touched my shoulder soothingly. "We can go alone."

"No," I said firmly...well, somewhat firmly, since one side of my mind shouted for joy at the chance of evading this journey, but the other side told me that no way in hell would I stay behind. "We'll take one of Katy's cars, just in case Jack prowls back past the funeral home tonight. He'd recognize my Jeep."

Before we left, Trucker needed to go out. Downstairs once again, I glanced out of the Garden Room windows, looking for the guards, but didn't see anyone. *Real secure security guards.* But with Trucker by my side, I didn't hesitate. I let him and Miss Molly out, then followed into the Rose Garden. With the lights gleaming and the clear sky, there weren't many shadows to contend with.

Miss Molly didn't care much for an outdoors litter box, but she pranced daintily through the grass. She headed straight for the same rose bush she'd been so interested in before while Trucker did his business. A blasted peacock wandered out from behind the rose bush, spied the cat, and squawked with that eerie sound I loathed. Miss Molly raced at the bird, growling in cat and arching her back.

The peacock spread its multi-eyed tail, which gave Miss Molly pause, since it now appeared a much larger antagonist. I grinned, proud of her when she stalked onward. The peacock scratched dirt, flinging pieces of mulch behind it, and stood its ground until the cat slinked to within a couple feet. Then it garbled one last squawk—sounded like fear to me— and half-flew, half-scrambled off across the Rose Garden and disappeared.

Miss Molly complacently washed her fur as Trucker joined his friend. The cat finished her brief bath, rose and nosed at the disturbed mulch beneath the bush, and meowed up at Trucker. After a second, the dog started to dig.

"No!" I rushed over. "Katy'll have a conniption."

I pulled Trucker back, but Miss Molly took his place. I'd never seen a cat actually dig in the dirt, unless it was covering up leavings, but Miss Molly hadn't done anything that needed to be covered. I reached down to pick her up—and saw the corner of the package. A plastic manuscript package, dark brown, which blended with the dirt and mulch. The animals had it nearly completely uncovered, and I brushed the rest of the dirt off and tugged it free.

Bucky's manuscript. He must have hidden it on the Esprit d'Chene grounds, maybe the night he was murdered. I untied the string and pulled out the first page to confirm my suspicions. A nearly illegible scrawl on yellow tablet—something an editor would send back promptly if it crossed his or her desk—but I could read it even in the dim light. And it wasn't the formatting or preparation. The contents were what could cause a public uproar if they ever got beyond this plastic sheath.

Something else also. I shoved my hand between the manuscript pages, but didn't bother removing the videotape. I knew what was on that, also.

"Jack needs to have this," I said to my pets as I stood. They gazed up at me, and Trucker cocked his head. I blew out a resigned breath. Katy's conniption fit wasn't going to even compare to Jack's when he found out I hadn't immediately called him. No way could I get involved in another explanation just now. We had other things to do.

Pets at my heels, I went back into the house, where I showed the find to Granny and Twila in the kitchen.

"The manuscript you told me about when we had lunch," Twila guessed correctly.

Granny patted her foot. "We can talk 'bout that later. Maxine's waitin'."

I stuck the manuscript in one of the lower cabinets, then brushed my hands. "Let's go. But where's Sir Gary?"

"He said he'd stay here and keep an eye on Bucky," Twila explained. "If he shows up, Sir Gary will tell him what we're up to and, hopefully, keep him calm until we return."

We chose the Mercedes, both for comfort and dark windows. I found the keys on the wall hook, and Granny and Twila piled into the back seat with Trucker, crouching low, since I was afraid the guards would question us. I hoped my cover story would keep them from reporting our departure to Jack.. I put Miss Molly in front, then pushed the button to open the garage door.

I backed the car out, and one of the guards on the porch saw us. That's where all of them had been, I realized, helping Gabe cover up the windows. One guard strolled over, and I inched the window down slightly. "Out of cat litter. Be back in a half hour or so."

He turned away without reaching for the radio on his belt. Relieved, I continued down the drive as Twila helped Granny up to settle on the seat. A gate opener lay on the console, and I used it to slide the gate open. The guard there started toward us, but I called out, "Cat litter. Be right back," and drove on before he got close. I watched in the rearview mirror as I closed the gate. He took up his post without any indication of reporting our departure.

CHAPTER 33

Campton's Funeral Home was a former plantation manor house, white two-story-columned, with a veranda. Ancient live oaks surrounded the paved parking lot, remnants of the grounds from bygone days. Now, however, there were gift shops and a couple convenience shops lining the street, encroaching on the privacy of the stately house. A dim light burned on the veranda, no lights inside. I pulled into the parking lot, but Granny shook her head. "Go 'round back."

A drive led to the rear, where two hearses were parked, one I recognized from the day I arrived at Katy's. Or assumed I did. There wasn't much difference in the two vehicles, other than one of them looked older. I parked beside the newer hearse and killed the engine. There were more lights back here, thank goodness. The woman I'd seen in the hearse at the plantation opened the back door and flicked the lights off. She peered out and placed a finger to her lips.

The darkness didn't seem to bother Twila and Granny, who got out without hesitation. However, much as I loved prowling graveyards, day or night, I didn't care for funeral homes or that end of the death process. Plus, I wasn't one bit happy about why we were here. I followed more slowly, ordering Trucker and Miss Molly to wait. Wishing desperately that I could stay with them, I steeled myself and walked to where the other three women waited.

"Isn't this something?" Maxine said conspiratorially as I slowly climbed the steps. "Sorry I had to turn the lights off, but I don't normally leave them on at night. One of the local patrol cars might think something's wrong and stop by."

"Smart thinkin'," Granny said with an emphatic nod. "But then, you's my grandchild."

Smiling happily at the compliment, Maxine ushered us inside. Into a kitchen. And it looked as if it were in use, although I couldn't imagine how anyone could enjoy sitting down to meals in a funeral home.

"We won't have to worry about lights once we get into the embalming room," Maxine said as she led the way. "We covered those windows a few years ago. Neighborhood kids kept trying to peek in on Halloween nights."

"You don't seem bothered by the fact that we want to...borrow that head," I said, lagging behind as we passed a large viewing room. My steps hastened, and I caught up.

"I think it's exciting!" Maxine replied merrily. "Part of reconnecting a poor lost soul's body. We don't get much excitement around here. And shoot, you won't do any damage. I'm sure you'll cherish the head very respectfully, as we do our bodies."

At the end of the dark hallway, she opened a fairly heavy door. Antiseptic smell wavered out, along with the chill. Granny and Twila walked in without hesitation, while I stared up at the high, filigree-bordered ceiling for a moment, then rigidly marched onward.

And halted abruptly. Two gleaming steel tables sat beneath the bright lights, one near a stainless steel sink, with a sheet-shrouded body on it. On the far wall was a huge freezer-type door, and Maxine opened it, then noticed my frozen stance and followed my gaze.

"That's Miz Cassandra. She's at peace after the horrible pain she suffered the past few months. Claude had to go down in the basement for more embalming fluid."

I cleared my throat, a loud sound in the eerily quiet room. "Your husband...he's okay with this, too?"

"Of course. He understands about bodies needing to repose serenely."

I still couldn't cross that room. Maxine disappeared into the cooler and reemerged carrying a white foam cooler with a garish red Budweiser beer logo on it.

"I got this out of the garage after you called." Maxine handed the cooler to Granny. "I thought it appropriate for Bucky. We do believe in appropriateness. We urge the bereaved to take their time deciding on what sort of casket and service they want. It's the last thing they can do to show their respect for the dearly departed."

Granny handed the cooler to Twila, who accepted it gingerly.

"We better get going," I said, in a hurry to get out of there.

I turned and bumped directly into a large, soft belly. It took both my hands on my mouth to cut off my gasp, and I looked up, up, into the twinkling eyes of a man who stood nearly seven feet and weighed close to four hundred pounds. He chuckled and set the large cardboard box he held easily in one arm on the floor before he held out his hand. "Claude Campton. I know who you are. I admire your books a lot. They're just the thing to read and relax after a long night in here."

I shook his hand, amazed that he'd consider one of my books relaxing after a night embalming bodies. But to each his own. "Pleased to meet you."

"Say, maybe when y'all bring Bucky's head back, you can sign my books." His round face beamed with delight. "I'll get them ready."

"O—of course," I agreed. Just what I wanted. A book signing in a funeral home. But fans are fans.

"Gettin' late," Granny said. "We best hustle."

I was ready to hustle, so we left the funeral home for the parking lot. Maxine switched the lights on after reminding us she couldn't leave them for long. Twila opened one of the rear doors, but I shook my head. "That's going in the trunk!"

"Okay," she said with a shrug.

I opened the trunk and she tenderly placed the cooler inside. Leaving Twila to close the trunk lid, I slid in and started the car, waiting impatiently while she and Granny settled in. Maxine turned out the lights, and I pulled out of the parking lot and headed for Esprit d'Chene. The instant I left the town proper behind and started down the back roads, I sped up. The sooner this was over with, the better. The actual ceremony when we connected Bucky's missing part didn't bother me, just all this cloak and dagger preparation.

Granny tapped me on the shoulder. "You's got that pedal awful close to the metal."

Her reminder of my speed on the lonely country, wildlife-filled night roads came nearly too late. The emu stood in the road just around the bend I'd sped through, and I slammed on the brakes. Thank goodness for anti-lock! The car skidded to a halt a foot from the bird, and it lifted its head on its snake-like neck and fluffed out its stubby gray wings without moving. Opened its mouth, and though I couldn't hear, probably hissed at me.

"Good God," Twila said. "What's an ostrich doing out here?"

"Ain't no ostrich, it's one a'them emus," Granny said. "Must've jumped a fence somewheres."

The bird bent its neck and pecked furiously at the hood. That brought Trucker up from his sprawl, and Miss Molly alert on the passenger seat.

"Emu?" Twila asked.

"Yeah," Granny explained while I waved my hand at the windshield and blew the horn. "Folks was farmin' them for a while. But the market kinda died."

The bird decided pecking its displeasure wasn't enough. It leaped onto the hood and bent to stare through the windshield, totally disregarding the car's frantically blaring horn. It had large, brown eyes with long lashes. Deep gouges marred the car's paint from the claws on the feather-tufted feet.

"Get out of here, bird!" I yelled. The eyelashes blinked, then it pecked the windshield. I instinctively pulled back, glaring at it, as Trucker roared his displeasure right in my ear and I surged forward against the steering wheel, eyeball to eyeball with that blasted bird. And jerked backwards again. Shit, I felt like I was on a rocking horse!

Miss Molly decided the floorboard was a safer haven from the monstrous bird.

"Damn it, Trucker," I yelled. "Shut up. Twila, grab him!"

She wrapped her arms around the dog and pulled him close, soothing him into silence. "There, there, Trucker boy. That nasty ole bird can't get at your mommy."

"Two bad we ain't got the patrol car," Granny mused. "Si-reen might scare it off. You don't wanna get out there and try to run it off. Heard them things can be dangerous."

So had I, and I wasn't about to confront that nasty beak outside the car.

"I think we've got another problem," Twila put in. "I heard something thump loose in the trunk when you slammed on the brakes."

Three sets of wide, stricken eyes met in the rearview mirror.

The emu stood upright, arched its neck, and fluffed those stumpy wings again. Then it turned its back on us, wiggled its rump, and sat down smack dab on the hood.

"Oh, for heaven sakes," I muttered. "Now what?"

"The poor thing's probably chilled," Twila said. "The hood's warm."

"Something in the trunk's gonna start warming up if we don't get out of here!" I spat.

"Drive on," Granny ordered. "It'll jump off when the car starts movin'."

"How am I supposed to see? It's fat rump is in my line of vision!" I blared the horn in one last attempt to scare the bird off. The emu cranked its head around and blinked at me. Then rose to its feet.

"Thank goodness," I said. "It's leav—"

It splat a gob of guano on my windshield, a huge, runny gray and white mess that slid down the window and pooled on the wipers. Then it settled back on the hood.

"Ick," Twila said all too calmly for my state of mind.

Gagging, I searched the console switches for the windshield washer. There, the same place as my Jeep, on the blinker handle. I sprayed the glass, but the wipers came on at the same moment and smeared the mess back and forth. The wipers settled back well before the windshield was clear.

"Huh," Granny said. "Didn't help much."

I turned the washer switch again. Again. Katy was going to love the condition of her car when we got her out of jail! The washer fluid cleaned the spot directly in front of me, but the leavings ran down the left side of the window where the wipers didn't reach. And I still couldn't see past that blasted bird.

"You're gonna haveta drive on," Granny repeated. "Here. Me and Twila will he'p you." Before I could admonish them, the two opened their windows and stuck their heads out.

"Go on," Twila said. "We'll guide you."

Nothing else for it. I took my foot off the brake and eased the gas pedal down. The car moved forward, and I tried to remember which direction the road went beyond the emu. Straight, I thought.

"Right," Twila said. "Steer to the right." I did. "No! Not that far! Straight, go straight now!" I straightened the wheel.

"Left!" Granny yelled, waving her hand inside the car. I did.

"No! Your other left!" Twila shouted. I jerked the wheel the opposite way. Glanced out the side window into a deep water-filled ditch a foot away and slammed on the brakes again.

"This isn't working!" I glared at the emu sitting unconcerned on the hood.

"You's gonna haveta go faster to shake him off," Granny said. "Go on. But pay attention to what we're sayin'."

"We're going to end up in the ditch," I said as reasonably as I could, given the fact I was speaking through clenched teeth. "If that happens, we'll have to call a tow truck, and who the hell knows how long it'll take for them to get out here this time of night! And—and—"

"—and how long it will take our cargo to thaw out," Twila mused when I sputtered to a halt. And before I realized what she was up to, she flung open the door. "Sic 'em, Trucker."

The dog sicced. He bounded out with a deep growl that reverberated in the air. Miss Molly leaped back onto the passenger seat and set her front paws on the dash to watch the show. Which was a pretty good one, if you discounted the fact that I was going to have to get both a wash and paint job on the Mercedes before I let Katy set eyes on it. Trucker lunged around to the side of the hood and, honestly, gave the emu a chance. He roared and barked for several seconds, but the bird just ruffled its feathers and settled back down.

Trucker crouched, then launched himself onto the hood. He hit the emu full force, and the bird screeched. Claws digging, it slid off the hood.

But the damn bird swiveled around and confronted the dog in the middle of the road, the headlights outlining the fracas like spotlights. The emu screeched, then jabbed its beak at the dog. Trucker ducked, and bravely flew through the air again. He hit the emu broadside, and they both tumbled to the pavement.

The emu had finally had enough. It scrambled up and loped into the woods, stubby wings flapping and cries hanging in the air. Unfortunately, Trucker was hot on its trail.

I threw open my door and jumped out. "Trucker! Get back here!" Other than my voice, all I could hear was crackling brush and a chase-bay from my dog that would have made a pretty sound, had we been on a fox hunt.

I yelled again, "Trucker! Here, boy!" And managed a piercing whistle.

The baying stopped, but the brush crackles continued, fading off into the distance. The emu screamed one last time, then utter silence. Total darkness beyond the headlights. Tangled briars and underbrush on the side of the road, an impenetrable mass for a human to negotiate. In the car, Granny and Twila sat wordless. Only Miss Molly moved.

She strolled across the console and jumped out the door. Pacing to the edge of the road, she meowed plaintively. Noises in the brush responded to her plea. Unsure whether it was dog or fowl, I edged toward the driver's seat and grabbed the door, prepared to fling myself inside. I ended up with a handful of emu guano and furiously rubbed my hand against my leg, still worrying about what would emerge and perhaps attack my cat.

"Uh—" I said softly. "Here, kitty, kitty."

Miss Molly tossed me a glance, but didn't move. The brush parted...and my dog pranced out, tongue lolling. I sighed with relief as the two of them casually strolled back to the car. I picked up Miss Molly, cuddling her in one arm, stroking Trucker with my other hand. He waggled his stubby tail, panting and slobbering, and I petted him for a long while, murmuring praises, before the three of us got back in.

Twila and Granny made a fuss over Trucker, also, as I drove on down the road, carefully this time, very, very carefully. More like I had the car out for a walk than a drive. By unspoken mutual consent, we didn't mention what had to have been on all three of our minds. Who was going to open the trunk?

CHAPTER 34

Mr. Quick was at the gate when I pulled up. I used the electronic opener and drove on in, the cop eyeballing the damage to the car. He strolled toward us, and I rolled the window down a gap. "We just ran to the store."

"You slide in a ditch?" He flicked his head at the hood. "Smells like swamp water. You okay?" I let him draw his own conclusions, erroneous as they were, and just nodded. "Miss Sue Ann an' Gabe went on home. Said to let you know."

I drove on. Two of Katy's guards were patrolling nearby. Probably the others were scattered. I opened the garage door and eased the Mercedes into its slot. It had the same type timer as my Jeep, and after I shut the door and killed the engine, the lights remained glowing. We sat there in silence. Finally, the headlights went out and the darkness closed in.

"Shit," I muttered. "There must be a button on the opener to turn on the garage lights." I picked the opener back up, but it was useless to try to examine it in the dark. Fumbling at the dash to try to turn on the car's interior lights, I got the wipers first, then the air conditioner.

"Just open the car door or turn the key on," Twila said reasonably.

Disgusted for not thinking of that—half of me understanding why my brain was rattled—I opened the driver's door. There, just as I thought, a button on the opener for lights. But I didn't need to push it. The lights came on, framing Jack in the doorway connecting the garage to the manor house. He slouched against the jamb, gaze fixed on me, face deadly stone.

"Oops," Twila said with an uneasy giggle.

"Shit," I whispered, which was becoming my favorite word. "Now what?"

"Mebbe he just came by for a cuppa coffee," Granny said. "We'll tell him we're outta coffee and he'll have to come back in the mornin'."

If we'd just gotten casually on out, perhaps we could have pulled that off. However, each second that ticked by with us just sitting there likely expounded Jack's suspicions and heightened our guilt. Whatever caper he thought that guilt pointed to. He couldn't know about our trunk cargo. Could he?

"Make a run for it," Granny ordered. "Open the garage door again and hightail it!"

That idea had strong appeal, but what stopped me was that Jack would no doubt be right on our bumper in a matter of minutes. The bumper behind the trunk. The trunk with—

"I'm not up to *Dukes of Hazard* tonight," Twila said. "Let's just get out and tell him we're going to bed. We'll wait until he leaves."

Suiting action to words, she opened her door, and Granny followed. I swallowed and picked up Miss Molly, setting her out to run whatever interference she could. Jack had always liked the cat. Trucker bounded out, and the two of them wandered straight to Jack. Who ignored them both, other than moving aside so they could enter the manor house.

I had sense enough to take the keys with me as I slid out. Without those, Jack couldn't get in the trunk. I followed Granny and Twila, echoing their cool greeting to Jack. He stepped into the garage and let them pass, but barred the door to me with his arm.

"Heard you run outta cat litter," he said. "Miss Molly's box looks full to me."

"She's particular," I said adamantly. "I have to keep it extremely

287

clean, or she'll leave her droppings outside the box." That, at least, wasn't a lie.

Before I realized what he was up to, Jack snatched the keys from my fingers. "I'll get the litter out of the trunk."

"No!" all three of us screamed, Granny and Twila filling the doorway, faces drawn with apprehension. That alone had to have told Jack what we'd been up to, but I struggled to grab the keys back anyway. He held them over his head, that stone expression on his face set as flint-hard brown eyes flicked over each one of us.

"Look, Jack," I said as calmly as I could manage considering the jitters in my belly and the overloaded upheaval of my mind. "We're going to bed. I just wanted the litter here in the morning to change the box. I'll get it tomorrow, when I need it."

"You never was that good of a liar, *Chère*." Jingling the keys, he strolled toward the Mercedes's trunk.

I rushed past him and flattened myself across the trunk, arms spread and buttocks nestled against the lock. "Do you have a search warrant?" Hell, it was the only thing I could think of, although I realized the moment it left my mouth it was definitely the wrong thing.

"Have it your way." Jack handed me the keys, and I breathed a sigh of relief—too soon. He ambled around to the passenger door, opened it, reached in, and flicked open the glove box. Pushed the trunk release button. Behind me, the trunk lid clicked.

Hell, I could have shoved it closed again. Should have. But I didn't even think. I scrambled away like the trunk had burned my ass and raced to my cohorts. Stubbed my toe on the doorstep and tumbled straight into Twila's arms with an "oomph" that echoed hers. We staggered, but caught ourselves and whirled behind Granny. Jack leaned on the car roof, staring at us quietly. "What do you suppose I'm gonna find in that trunk?"

The trunk lid hadn't opened completely, although a gap showed between it and the fender. It creaked open another inch, and Jack walked along the car. But instead of going all the way around, he stuck his hand in the gap. Slowly, he eased it upward. And jerked his hand free a bare instant before the trunk lid slammed closed with a resounding thump!

Face darkening with thunder, Jack glared around the garage. "All right, you damn ghost! Where are you?"

Sir Gary obediently materialized behind the trunk. He and Jack locked eyes, and Sir Gary serenely lifted his hand, index finger and thumb extended, and blew on it as though clearing away gun smoke. Then he pointed his finger gun at Jack and said quietly, "Bang."

Jack didn't flinch, but all three of us did. Shouldered together there in the doorway, I felt each of us shudder. Jack and Sir Gary weren't more than two feet apart, both of them over six feet of confrontational male. Women are supposedly the peacemakers of the two sexes, but none of us made a move to step between that battle of wills.

Sir Gary leaned negligently on the trunk lid. "Look, we can play...what do you modern mortals call it? Mexican standoff?" Jack nodded his head an inch in response, jaw set grimly, and Sir Gary continued, "We can play that, or you can get it through that set mind of yours that there is something larger than you're used to dealing with here. You know, in another life, I believe the two of us could have been friends."

Jack relaxed a tad. "Depends on which side of the law we each lived on in that life."

Sir Gary chuckled. "I have seen much progress over the past centuries in your laws, but there have been mistakes made, also. I wandered through those years alone, confused, and misunderstood when I did try to end my misery by making a mortal aware of my predicament and asking for assistance in something I didn't quite understand myself. Not to say that I didn't probably compound my troubles at times, when I antagonized some of the people I met. I do admit that I have somewhat less patience with people who cannot comprehend my existence than perhaps I should have. But I doubt very much that I would have been tolerant myself, had I crossed paths with a soul of my status during my lifetime."

Jack relented a little more and slouched against the fender. "Well, I didn't believe in ghosts, still have trouble acceptin' this. But either I've gone totally crazy, or we're really standin' here havin' this discussion."

The two men actually grinned at each other, and we women relaxed in the doorway. Still, none of us spoke a word, aware of the charged atmosphere.

"Katy's uncle believed in me, saw me clearly," Sir Gary went on. "But he considered me dangerous, I presume. I guess I went about seeking his help the wrong way. The night I lost my patience and tried to force his assistance, we rather had it out. I'm not sure who lost that battle. He left, but I was alone again. Until Katy moved in."

"Just what sort of battle was it?" Jack asked. He looked truly interested.

"Oh, chains and moans, shouts and threats on my part. I learned my lesson, because I did quite a bit of thinking about my errors after he left. Then I met Katy. And although I have enjoyed my...existence more with the understanding I've experienced from her and my latest acquaintances..." He glanced at us in the doorway, then back to Jack. "...I'm tired and I wish to travel on."

Jack nodded. "I don't believe I'd enjoy wanderin' through time. I don't like even thinkin' about it. But the point is, I have a job to do, and I can't allow tamperin' with evidence in a crime investigation. That's enough to get my ass fired, prevent me from ever workin' in law enforcement again."

Sir Gary considered that, then said, "But...think of what you are foisting onto Esprit d'Chene if you do not allow these ladies to complete their ceremony. Another disgruntled spirit here, another soul lost in time."

"Where's this soul at the moment?" Jack asked.

"I have told him of the quest to return his head to him and complete his soul. I have his agreement not to cause any trouble for the moment, since he appears as anxious as I am to end this half-existence we share. But I cannot be responsible for what he will do, should I not honor my assurance."

Jack deigned to glance at us. "And after you complete this...this...?"

"We'll do a ceremony," I answered quietly rather than in a confrontational manner, hoping to maintain Jack's calmer attitude. "And we should have a few moments to talk to him before he crosses over. Ask him who killed him."

I could see the battle going on inside Jack's mind. His eyes darkened, his shoulders stiffened. He glanced at the trunk. "So I'm right about the head bein' in there."

He didn't phrase it as a question, but Twila answered him anyway. "It's necessary."

"How did you manage to steal it?"

Granny ruffled up like a banty hen, and then before I could stop her, said, "That's where I come in. But I ain't tellin' you how I did it without my lawyer present."

Granny's spunky retort thawed the atmosphere, and Jack actually laughed. Shaking his head, he looked at Sir Gary. "Where's Bucky waitin'?"

"In the maze. With all the bobbies around, I couldn't think of any other place where there would be the privacy Alice and Twila will need."

"Why not in the house? I can order the men—"

"No," Twila interrupted. "The maze is exactly right. Rituals like we need to do have been performed outdoors for centuries. We'll have the help of the Universe forces available much better outdoors."

"Didn't realize this ghosthuntin' business included Druid beliefs."

"The rituals are combinations of all sorts of beliefs," Twila explained. "Druid, Wiccan, even portions of Christian religious doctrines." She shrugged. "Lore even indicates that portions of the Easter celebration, as well as other Christian holidays, descend from centuries-old Druid rituals. We do whatever we feel will work."

"But first y'all have to get into the maze without the guards stoppin' you," Jack said, and I realized that he'd finally accepted the necessity of the ritual.

"That should be fairly easy," Sir Gary told Jack. "After all, you are in charge. They'll follow your directives, should you order them to forgo their duties in one area and direct their attention elsewhere."

"Yeah," Jack said with a nod. "Well, let's get on with it."

My relief evaporated like steam on a sidewalk on a hot July day in Texas the instant I realized what we had to do next. Twila, Granny, and I stared as one at the trunk.

"Uh...we'll meet you in the maze," I said. "You two can...bring...the rest of Bucky."

"Y'all can't go to the maze until I rearrange the guards," Jack said. "I'll do that, and you can bring..." He glanced at the trunk with an evil grin that I wanted to slap off his face. "...bring everything you need with you."

He sauntered around the Mercedes. I swear I saw him and Sir Gary exchange winks, but it was such a quick motion I could have been mistaken—until I saw the lingering dimple in Sir Gary's cheek. Jack strolled to the doorway, paused, and then moved onto the step. The three of us backed out of his way and let him in.

The doorway led into the kitchen, and Jack nonchalantly picked up an apple from the bowl of fruit on the table, tossed it in the air, then took a huge bite on his way into the Garden Room. The crunch mingled with the sound of chuckles from Sir Gary.

"I need to get my satchel." Twila took off across the kitchen.

"I'll he'p you." Granny thump-limped after her, leaving me alone, the demand for them to get their asses back there caught somewhere below the lump of panic in my throat.

I grabbed the door jamb and gazed pleadingly at Sir Gary. "Are you going to leave me alone, too?"

"I seem to recall from our first meeting that you are quite an independent lady," he mused. "You don't seem to need much assistance from others." I gulped, but relaxed when he continued, "But without you, I would not be feeling that perhaps my long journey can finally end. You brought me assistance, even though you did it somewhat against your will." He bowed in my direction. "I am at your service, Miss Alice."

I didn't have to give him any orders. He wiggled his finger at the trunk, and the tumblers clicked. It slowly slid open, and Sir Gary murmured, "Well, my friend"—not to me, to the trunk interior—"seems it is time for you to become joined again."

"Is he...it...uh...there's a cooler in there," I stuttered.

Sir Gary wiggled his finger again, and things moved around in the trunk. He bent down. It appeared that he didn't use his powers. Instead, he seemed to gently cup the head in his hands and place it inside the cooler. A second later, he straightened and levitated the cooler onto the floor. The lid was secured, the red plastic handle upright, ready for someone to pick it up.

"I shall leave the trunk up," he told me. "It needs to dry."

The cooler floated off the floor, across the garage, toward me, Sir Gary strolling behind it with his finger poised. I swallowed my distaste and grasped the handle when it floated within reach. Then turned back into the kitchen to see Twila and Granny waiting for me, Twila with her satchel of protection, Trucker and Miss Molly at her feet. Sir Gary joined us, and we walked into the Garden Room to examine the Rose Garden through the windows. Jack stood alone, and he motioned us outside. One by one, we filed out the door.

The night remained clear, a three-quarter moon low in the east, stars shimmering in a cloudless sky. The Milky Way brushed its path across the darkness. I had no idea what time it was, but it had to be getting close to sunrise. Yet the silver-gray that precedes dawn hadn't yet intruded on the night.

Twila set her satchel down and spread it open. "We need to remove our protection."

"Why?" Granny asked.

"It's necessary," Twila told her. "It can't interfere with whatever happens."

I handed over my necklace and bracelets, and Granny reluctantly dropped hers in the satchel. When Twila looked at Jack, he shook his head. "Left all that junk in the patrol car."

We made our way to the center of the maze on the oyster-shell-covered path, our footsteps the only sound. Somewhere in the distance an owl hooted plaintively, and the faint bark of either a dog or coyote answered. We walked slowly, both in deference to Granny's gait and respect for the coming ritual. And to honor the contents of the cooler.

I used the time to prepare myself mentally, as I supposed Twila did. We'd never done anything remotely similar to what we planned. Many times we'd assisted lost souls cross through the light, one of the most satisfying feelings I've ever experienced. However, those souls were...complete souls, eager to end their confusion and lonely existence. First we had to complete this soul, and although I had no idea what that would entail, I trusted Twila implicitly.

As Sir Gary said, Bucky waited for us in the middle of the maze. Sitting cross-legged on the ground, he glanced up with his doll head, eyes wide in anticipation. Sir Gary glided over beside him. "I kept my word."

"Yep." The doll mouth spread into a grin. "And I sees you brought plenty of help." But then he swiveled his head toward Jack. "Didn't know you was gonna bring a cop, though."

I tried to discern whether Jack could see Bucky. Since his gaze was zeroed on the spot where Bucky sat, I thought maybe he did. But he could have been looking at Sir Gary.

"Can you see him?" I asked quietly.

"Just Sir Gary," he answered. "Bucky's over there with him?"

"Yes." I handed the cooler to Twila and read the command in her eyes when she bent her head in Jack's direction. I pulled him back toward the path we had just walked up. "Listen, Jack, whether or not you can see him, you need to know that it's extremely important not to have any negative thoughts interfering with our ritual. We can probably accomplish it anyway, but it'll take longer and be more complicated if we have to overcome even one person's disbelief."

He heaved a sigh and nodded agreement. That's when Tildy stormed up the path behind us. Before I could react, she caught Jack by surprise and shoved him between the shoulders. Raised the pistol in her hand and screamed at Bucky, "I thought you was dead!"

The pistol fired with a flash of light and a roar so close to my ear that it deafened me.

CHAPTER 35

I dropped in reaction, but kept my eyes open, in fear that Tildy would turn the pistol on one of us next. Granny raised that walking stick with an ease I wouldn't have thought possible for someone her age. She thunked the end of it down on Tildy's wrist, knocking the pistol loose the same moment Jack tackled Tildy and she went down with a screech of mingled pain and rage. She grabbed for the pistol, but Granny flicked it away with her stick.

I scrambled backward like an upside-down crab as Jack wrestled with the deranged woman. Trucker roared and surged forward, looking for an opening to protect Jack. Granny stood over them, walking stick raised, waiting for an opening to whack Tildy again. Twila thrust the cooler into my arms, and I instinctively grasped it as she hurried over to Granny. Miss Molly leaped on top of the cooler, back arched, tail flicking. Her tail caught me in the mouth, and I swept her down beside me, her claws dragging across the lid and me spitting out cat hairs.

"Let Jack handle it," Twila said to Granny. "You've already helped enough."

"I'd like to get one more crack in," Granny said, but Jack and Tildy rolled away from her in the grass and shells. I'd never seen a woman with that much strength against a man.

Jack ended up on top at last, pinning Tildy's arms over her head and shouting, "Behave yourself, damn it! You're under arrest!"

"Hmmm," Granny mused. "Wonder what he's chargin' her with. Shootin' a ghost?"

Tildy bucked and twisted, trying to bite Jack's arm. At least she had her clothes on this time, a pair of jeans and T-shirt, my jacket, a wicked pair of pointy-toed cowboy boots. Her heels beat the ground. She didn't say anything intelligible, just screamed bloody murder.

Then she successfully bit Jack, and he jerked in reaction. She twisted loose and aimed a kick at his crotch. Lucky for Jack, he anticipated the blow. He jerked back, then lunged on her again, swung her around, and pushed her head into the grass, garbling her screams.

"Get me something to tie her with!" he demanded.

"We don't have anything with us!" I yelled back.

Twila crouched and opened her satchel. "Yes, we do." She drew out a loop of gold tassel that I recognized as curtain braid, a souvenir from one of our adventures. As she hurried over to help Jack, I clutched the cooler in my arms so tightly the foam cracked. Hastily I set it down, noticing that Miss Molly claws had opened a gap as I'd dragged her off the top. I secured the lid, then glanced around for Sir Gary and Bucky.

I stared at the two ghosts. Sir Gary sat on the ground now, Bucky with an arm around his shoulders, his doll head bent close to Sir Gary's handsome face. I knew neither one of them had been shot— they were already dead. But something was definitely bothering Sir Gary. He rubbed his eyes and shuddered, then cupped his face in his hands.

Concern on her elderly face, Granny started toward Sir Gary, and I joined her. Keeping a close eye on Bucky, since I'd never been this close to him, I knelt in front of Sir Gary while Granny hovered over us. "What's wrong?" I asked.

"He says he 'members," Bucky told us when Sir Gary didn't answer. "Don't know what he 'members. Tildy was shootin' at me, so I wasn't listening real close. S'pose she still ain't forgive me for not payin' her child support."

"You didn't pay for your young'uns?" Granny growled. "Ain't right!"

"I was meanin' to," Bucky whined. "That's what it was all about."

Sir Gary dropped his hands and blinked. "I...I...she didn't mean it." His voice was so soft I could barely make out his words.

"She sure did," Bucky said. "Tildy don't shoot lessen she means to kill."

"How on earth did she recognize you?" I asked Bucky, the question in my mind overriding the concern I had for Sir Gary.

He shrugged, the doll head wobbling as though losing its grip. I inched backward as he said, "Woman knows her man."

Sir Gary rubbed his eyes. "My sight...I can't see. That's how it happened. My own death. It wasn't deliberate. She only meant to scare me. To show me how angry and hurt she was. I didn't think she would actually pull the trigger of the dueling pistol."

"What are you talking about?" I asked. Concentrating so hard on Sir Gary, I'd lost track of what was going on over across the maze. But when Twila and Jack moved in to join our group, I looked over to see Tildy nowhere in sight.

"We laid her back down the path," Twila said in response to the question in my eyes. "Don't worry. She's not going anywhere trussed up like that and tied to one of the bushes. We gagged her, too."

Bucky chuckled. "Tildy ain't gonna like not bein' able to talk."

"She can talk to her lawyer," Jack said.

"But the guards?" I asked, worried about interference with our ritual.

"One of them came running," Jack explained, "but couldn't find us in here. I heard him, though, and yelled out to order them to watch the house."

Sir Gary blinked his eyes rapidly. "My sight...it's coming back. And my memory."

None of us spoke while we waited for Sir Gary to continue. Somehow I knew that all of this was part of what we had set out to do. All interconnected.

"It was the flash of the pistol that woman used," Sir Gary mused. "I recall the same bright glare from before. It all started when we were alone in the house, except for a servant or two busy elsewhere. After my discussion with Alexa. She and I talked in the study while James saw to a loose wheel on the buggy so he could take Alexa home. I assumed we had privacy, although our discussion grew somewhat heated. Later, I realized we'd been overheard."

"By your wife?" I asked quietly, wondering what the pistol flash had to do with his drowning.

"Yes. I thought she was reading in the parlor, as she did for hours on end. But after Alexa and James left, I went in search of her and found her in the Game Room, sitting at the card table with a deck of cards spread out before her. There was also a bottle of whiskey on the table, and a nearly empty glass. She'd taken to drinking, and I could smell it on her now and then, even over her perfume. But she'd been secretive about it up until that point.

"She didn't apologize for the glass when I looked at it. She said she was bored and that she would love to get some air. I didn't notice anything different about her demeanor, except she appeared more composed than I had seen her in a long while. Perhaps it was the whiskey, but she wasn't slurring her words, so I don't believe she was drunk.

"She was already prepared to go out, a shawl around her shoulders and a blanket on her lap. So I pushed her chair outside, where she asked if I thought it would be too much trouble to get down to the pond. I was agreeable to anything she wanted, filled with guilt and remorse after my fight with Alexa, wondering how things had gotten into such a state."

Bucky patted Sir Gary on the shoulder. "Women kin do that to a man."

Granny muffled a harrumph, but Twila nudged her to silence, as enthralled as the rest of us in Sir Gary's tale, her face rapt.

"I placed her near the edge of the pond and wandered a few feet away, nearer the bank. It was deep at that end, shallower on the other side. She'd purchased some swans and geese after we first moved in, and

I watched them floating on the water. Then she spoke to me in a deadly quiet voice, telling me to turn around."

Sir Gary closed his eyes briefly, then opened them. "She had one of my dueling pistols aimed straight at my chest. Besides being a horse-woman, Lucinda was a dead shot. Before her accident, she loved riding on hunts. I stared at the pistol, knowing I probably deserved whatever she had in mind, but never truly believing she would shoot me."

"But she did?" Twila asked. "That can't be true. Your death was by drowning."

Sir Gary continued as though he hadn't heard her. "When I looked into her eyes, I saw she had every intention of pulling that trigger. She said, 'I have lived with the disgrace and dishonor of your infidelities for too long. Now you bring your wenches into my home. And you cuckold your own brother! A man worth a dozen of you!' Then she screamed, 'I'll not have it!'

"I lunged for the pistol, but she pulled the trigger. Now I realize she only meant to scare me. There wasn't any ball in the pistol. But the flash of gunpowder blinded me."

Sir Gary fell silent, then continued, "My God, I remember the pain. The horrible agony. I stumbled back...into the pond." He shook his head. "I can't swim, you know. And there was no one there to help me. Lucinda was pinned in her chair and even had she been able to make her way back across the lawn to call a servant, it would have been too late. I could hear her cries even through my pain and struggles. But since I couldn't see, I had only her voice to guide me toward the bank. A bank I couldn't reach, because my water-clogged boots pulled me under."

"An undeliberate murder," Twila whispered.

"Yes," Sir Gary replied. "She cried out how sorry she was. That she didn't mean it. She only meant to frighten me. I assume she chose to do this down by the pond to keep the servants from overhearing, but that choice led to my death."

"I believe," I said in a near-whisper, "that your confusion and wandering stem from your realization of how you hurt Lucinda. You needed to forgive her, have her forgive you. But it was too late once you turned back through the light."

Sir Gary nodded. "Where I need to ask for...and hopefully receive that forgiveness now, is with Lucinda. I need to go where she is."

"Well," Bucky grumbled. "I ain't likin' the thought of bein' on this side with Tildy still after my ass neither. Y'all give me back my head, and me an' Gary here'll get where we belong."

CHAPTER 36

We gathered in a circle that included the ghosts. Jack gently helped Granny down, and nearly sat on Bucky. Granny jerked his arm and scooted over to give him more room. As unintentional designated guardian of the cooler, I placed it inside the circle before I sat down beside Granny. Trucker and Miss Molly stretched out behind me, Trucker with his nose on his paws and the cat cuddled against him.

"Before we start," Jack reminded me, "you said you were going to ask Bucky something."

"Well, we intended to wait until the end of the ritual, but...what do you think, Twila?"

She was still on her feet, waiting to seal the circle, and she said, "I think he's cognizant enough with the doll head. Bucky, was it Tildy who murdered you?"

We waited breathlessly, but Bucky only shrugged. "Could've been, I s'pose. She'd've done it, iffen she got a chance. She was that pissed at me. But I donno who it was. Last I 'member, like my buddy here, was bein' in the water. Well, not exactly. I was layin' on the concrete, lookin' at the rest of me in that there water. Guess my head was, anyways."

"Shit," Jack grumbled. "All this and you didn't see who killed you?"

"Nope," Bucky said, unconcerned. "Guess whoever done it snuck up on me. I was gonna go in there and jerk Miss Goody Two-Shoes Katy outta bed and make her promise to talk to my daddy. But I never got the chance. Somebody got me on the way to the back door."

Frustrated, I glanced at Twila, but she shook her head. "I can't read what happened either. We'll do a séance later, after they cross over. Maybe Bucky will know more then."

"Whatever y'all want," Bucky said, glancing at the cooler. "Right now, you made me a promise, an' I think I've waited long enuf."

"One more thing," I insisted. "Well, two. Someone poisoned the sugar in the kitchen."

"Weren't me," Bucky denied. "I weren't in no shape to plan somethin' like that."

"What about the stuff you buried in the Rose Garden? What was the purpose of your blackmailing Katy?"

"It was for the kids," Bucky insisted, that whine in his voice. "Kids change a man. I didn't know Tildy was pregnant when we split up, but them twin boys are mine, no doubt. Tildy's momma got them now." He wobbled his head back and forth. "Truth be known, neither me or Tildy was worth a flip as a mama or daddy. But I figgered if I could get back in Daddy's good graces, the boys would have a decent life. He's got all that there money."

"Ever think of gettin' a job and takin' care of them boys yourself?" Granny fumed.

"I was gonna do that," Bucky insisted. "If the other didn't work out."

Twila glanced skyward at a barely perceptible lightening in the darkness.

"Can we get on with it?" Bucky demanded.

"We need to," Twila agreed.

Jack started to rise, but Twila inclined her head in a command to stay where he was. For a second I thought he might ignore her, but finally he relaxed.

"Seems we don't have my rope I normally use to enclose a circle, so we'll have to make do with just a ritual closing." She turned and paced clockwise around us, past Sir Gary and Bucky, Jack and Granny, murmuring softly as she went. "Earth, air, water, and fire. We call upon the forces of the Universe to aid our quest this night."

She returned to her place beside me and sat down. "The circle is now sealed. I ask that no one break it until I open it again." She took a deep breath. And opened the cooler. Laid the lid aside and said, "Join hands."

Around the circle, our hands joined. Twila with Sir Gary and me, me with her and Granny, Granny with me and Jack. Sir Gary and Bucky joined hands, but Jack had his right hand on his leg. An awestruck look crossed his face when his hand lifted. We could see Bucky holding it, but Jack only shivered as though chilled, his gaze frozen on his suspended hand.

"Relax, Jack," I said. "We need peace and calm here."

Jack shut his eyes and sat unmoving. Twila asked us to clear our minds, her soothing voice an aid to the cleansing of unrelated matters from our thoughts. We drew in deep breaths and blew them out, three times. The world around me receded and my concentration focused on the circle and the task at hand.

"We're here to put one soul to rights," Twila said. "And to ask the help of the powers of the Universe, whoever, whatever, and whichever they may be, to open a pathway through the lights for both these souls to journey home. I ask that all of you in our circle concentrate your thoughts on our quest."

She allowed the silence to linger for several moments. Jack kept his eyes closed, but I glanced around to see everyone else focused on Twila's face. She sat there serenely composed, eyes with that inward look I probably had on my own face whenever I led a ritual. But this one was all Twila's. The powers needed were beyond my scope as a relative amateur compared to her years of experience.

She glanced at Bucky. "You need to remove the temporary head you've been using."

Jack's hand clunked to the ground as Bucky let go to reach for his head. Jack's eyes flew open, and he stared at what he saw as an empty space at his side. But when Bucky lifted the head off his shoulders and laid it down, took his hands away, Jack's face whitened. I knew he saw the head now, but to his credit, he didn't disrupt the circle.

"Sir Gary," Twila said quietly. "Will you do the honor?"

Sir Gary pointed at the cooler. His index finger curved, and ice slid. Ever so slowly, the plastic bag containing the head rose as Bucky's head-less body silently waited. Twila reached forward and removed the plas-tic, tossing it on the ground beside her. I squeezed my eyes shut, but they refused to cooperate and slit open to peruse the grisly countenance from the Hollow Room. Instead, there was a serene look on the face beneath the matted, stringy hair. The eyes opened and stared back with a gleam of anticipation.

Sir Gary straightened his finger, curved it again, and the head floated through the air, slowly, ever so slowly, then settled on Bucky's shoulders.

"So mote it be," Twila whispered.

"So mote it be," Granny and I replied together.

Jack just sat there stunned. "Where...where did it go?"

"Just wait," Twila said.

Complete now, Bucky grinned in delight. "Feels good."

"Will you both please rise?" Twila said to Sir Gary and Bucky.

They did, but Bucky's head didn't rise with him. It tumbled to the ground and rolled over by Jack's feet. Jack gazed at it, then looked to his side where Sir Gary and Bucky waited, Bucky now complete, with his own head on his shoulders.

"Uh—" Jack began.

"Shhhh," Twila said. "Shhhh. We have more to do." She removed a white candle in a crystal holder from her satchel, then a container of jasmine oil. The scent spread as she rubbed oil on the white candle. Next she removed a packet of matches and lit the candle.

"White is for the light," she whispered, "which leads through the veil, where our friends and ancestors wait to welcome us. I call upon the powers of the Universe to send us the light, to send us a door through the light, so these two souls can complete their journey."

For a moment nothing happened. Then the air stilled with silence so profound you could almost hear it. A wide beam that always reminds me of moonlight whenever I see it flowed down from the sky, and a deep peace stole through me. Sir Gary and Bucky faced the light as it settled a few feet from them. It brightened and widened, then split to above Sir Gary's height.

"I guess this is it," Sir Gary said. "I want to thank you for everything."

"Me, too," Bucky joined in. "We'll see y'all sometime."

Sir Gary chuckled and wrapped his arm around Bucky's shoulders. "Yes, we'll see y'all...sometime. Tell my lady Katy goodbye for me." Trucker whuffed and Miss Molly murmured a plaintive meow. "Goodbye to you two, too," Sir Gary said.

The two of them strolled forward, through the opening. "Think they got anything to drink over here?" Bucky asked.

"I surely hope so," Sir Gary replied. Then we could hear nothing else. The door closed, and the light faded. Rather than withdrawing, one moment it was there, the next, not.

"So mote it be," Twila repeated, and Granny and I echoed her words one last time.

"Be happy," I added.

"I think they're gonna have a grand old time," Granny said. "Now, he'p me up. We got things to do."

"Let me release the circle first." Twila rose and turned the opposite way this time. She slowly walked around us, murmuring, "We thank you, all the powers, for your aid this night. For your help in allowing two lost souls to rest in peace." Back at my side, she nodded. "The circle's open. We need to take care of earthly matters now."

I helped Granny up. Jack sat a while longer, staring at the head in front of him. Trucker stretched to his feet, his gaze trained across the circle where the ghosts had disappeared. Then he and Miss Molly padded down the path that led out of the maze.

Finally Jack sighed and got up. He picked up the plastic bag, then squatted by the head. Gently he shoved it inside and placed it back in the cooler when Twila carried it over.

"We don't know a damn thing more than we did before," Jack growled.

"I think one of us here knows quite a bit more," Twila said, eyes twinkling.

"I was talkin' about the investigation," Jack said.

"You've still got Tildy to question," I put in. "But I doubt very much she's gonna admit killing Bucky. Or if she could have. Someone unfamiliar with Esprit d'Chene couldn't have gotten inside to take that sword. Or hidden the head in the passageway afterward."

"We needs to get that head back to Maxine." Granny toddled off down the path, her walking stick punching in with each step.

And suddenly I was terribly afraid I might know who killed Bucky Wilson-Jones. To my distress, when my eyes flew to Jack's and latched there like our gazes were glued, I saw realization spread over his face.

CHAPTER 37

Dawn broke as Jack and I walked out to the patrol car behind the guard company van, hidden from sight. Vivid orange and dark maroon streaked the sky, scattered cloud underbellies dark gray. A new day; one I wasn't looking forward to. Jack had already secured the cooler in the trunk and Tildy in the back seat, still trussed, although he'd removed her gag. Twila and Granny stayed behind, although Granny did so under protest, even though she had been so tired she could hardly lift her walking stick. We got in, snapped our seatbelts, and Jack drove off. Tildy kept quiet, although now and then she sniffled.

We drove to the funeral home first, and Jack sat with Tildy while I returned the cooler to Maxine. I'd hoped it was too early for them to be up, but sure enough, my books were spread on the kitchen table. Claude had a grin of anticipation on his face and a cup of coffee in his hand.

"Sure am gonna be pleased to actually have your John Henry on my books," he said. "Wanna cup of coffee?"

"No, that's all right." I signed his books, trying not to show my impatience. After all, fans expect a certain sense of appreciation when they ask for an author's autograph. After the last book, I smiled and stood. "There you go."

"'Preciate it." Claude picked up one of the books reverently and opened it to the flyleaf with my signature. The awe on his face made me glad I'd taken time to fulfill his request.

"You come back now any time you need our help," Maxine said, patting my arm as she walked me to the door. "And tell Granny she best visit before she goes home."

Finally I escaped. Jack drove on into Jefferson and parked at the jail, squeezing in between two other cars already there.

"Could I see Katy?" I asked.

"Come in and we'll see what's up," he said, the first words he'd spoken since we left the plantation. He helped a defeated Tildy out, and she bowed her head and walked ahead of him, a dejected picture rather than a spitting, snarling woman. Being taken toward a jail cell will do that to most people.

Jack ushered Tildy into the street-side building rather than back to where Katy was housed. Officer Smith sat at one of the desks, but I gave a start of recognition when I saw the other man.

"Why, hello, Alice," he said with a huge smile of greeting. "This is a nice change in a day that started off like it wasn't going to be one of the better ones."

Jack pushed Tildy over to Officer Smith and muttered an order to start the booking procedure. I smiled at Cory, though a picture of how I must look flashed in my mind: covered in grass and dirt stains, my hair straggling, since I hadn't bothered to brush it before I left the plantation. My makeup case had remained unopened ever since I arrived at the plantation. To top it off, I suddenly remembered that I hadn't paid any attention to renewing my underarm deodorant in far too many hours and recalled the emu guano on my jeans.

But still, I smiled. If he could smile at me the way I looked, it was the least I could do.

"What are you doing here?" I asked.

"Brought my brother in. He's a lawyer."

"He's with Katy?"

"Yeah. He called me when his car wouldn't start, and we got here an hour or so ago. How are you holding up?"

"I'll do," I said. But even the interest in his eyes couldn't thaw the ball of dread in my stomach as I thought of where Jack and I would have to go next.

Cory poured two cups of coffee, returning to offer me one and pull out a chair for me. I sat and cupped my hands around the paper container, breathing in the caffeine aroma. "Have you talked to your brother yet?"

"He's been with Katy ever since we got here. But you can bet he'll get her out of jail as quick as he can. He's a pretty good attorney, considering the fact that all he was interested in growing up was coon dogs and fishing."

"I don't guess I'll be able to see her then," I said, sipping at my coffee.

"Not right now." Jack stuck out his hand to Cory. "Jack Roucheau."

Cory shook hands. "Ah, Alice's *ex*-husband. Cory Stevens. And I think you should know right up front that I intend to get to know your famous former wife a lot better."

Jack glanced at me and said, "She's well worth knowing. But you'll have to wait a while. We've got somewhere to go."

That knot of dread in my stomach tightened like a lump of congealed oatmeal. I set my coffee on the desk and rose. "Jack's right. But please do call me."

"Bet on it," Cory replied.

I walked ahead of Jack, out the door, over to the patrol car. Had I a choice, I would have gone into The General Store and lost myself in the knickknacks and tourist regalia, but it wasn't open. I stared across the car at Jack. "Where are we going?"

"You know, *Chère*. Get in the car if you want to ride along."

I didn't. I'd rather have stripped my clothes off right then and there and done a book signing naked in the middle of the street. Jack slid in and started the engine. Steeling myself, I joined him and slammed the door.

"You could have brought your coffee," Jack said as he backed out.

Yeah, but I wouldn't have been able to drink it. That one sip set like vinegar in my mouth. "What will they charge Tildy with?" I didn't really care, but it was another focus.

"Not shootin' at a ghost." He chuckled. "We'll keep that out of it. I told Smitty to book her on attempted assault and resistin' arrest. He'll get a search warrant as soon as the judge is awake. I've got a feelin' we'll find the rifle that fired that bullet at you stashed in her house."

"The senator?"

His lips thinned as he turned left at the stoplight. "Heard he's already on his way back to D.C. Emergency hearing. It'll be a couple days before we release Bucky's body."

I slumped, so tired and sleepy my eyelids kept drifting closed. But not for long. They popped open every time. Jack and I needed to talk, but I couldn't think how to open the conversation.

Jack finally said, "It was probably an accident."

"What do you mean?" I sat up, unable to stifle a flicker of hope. "We...Jack, please tell me where we're going, without my having to tell you where I think."

The corner of his mouth flickered in a half-smile, overshadowed with regret in his brown eyes. "Your Uncle Clarence's house."

"That's what I was afraid of. But...an accident?"

"I doubt he'll get off on anything less than manslaughter. After all, he did kill him." Jack turned down the side road leading to my uncle's house. "The way I see it, he thought he was protectin' Katy. Probably thought Bucky was Sir Gary, and he was lopping off the ghost's head. And with his age and health, maybe we can talk the judge into probation or house arrest."

"He must have worn bedroom slippers. They're like moccasins, and that's why he didn't leave any tracks in the grass. But his cane disturbed the oyster shells around that tire track."

"Yeah. Had to be someone who knew the manor house. Knew those passageways and how to get in there and hide the head."

"Katy probably told him about the passageways. But why did he even bother?"

"Strain. Stress." Jack shrugged. "Who knows? People do strange things when their mind's all screwed up in a situation like that. I've seen it time and time again. How'd you feel if you thought you were takin' a swat at a ghost, but you cut off a real person's head instead?"

"I'd probably flip out and babble until the men in white coats came," I admitted.

Jack pulled into Uncle Clarence's drive. "I'll go in alone, *Chère*."

"No." We got out and I joined him. "Why didn't he come forward when Katy was arrested?"

"He doesn't even know she's in jail. It all happened within the last few hours."

"Seems like days. My mind's really fogged time-wise."

"What I don't understand is why your grandpere's sword," Jack said as we climbed the veranda steps. "That particular weapon."

I halted. Uncle Clarence stood in the doorway, back straight, cane propped beside him. He was already dressed for the day, a dapper figure in a neat white suit, black string tie, and a red handkerchief poking out of his breast pocket. His hair was still shower-damp, but combed.

"Ah've been expectin' you," he said quietly. "Katy's friend Irene called me an hour ago and said Katy was in jail. She didn't do it. Ah did. But it sounds as though you've already figured that out."

"You got any coffee on, sir?" Jack asked.

With a regal nod, Uncle Clarence picked up his cane and led us through the house. The kitchen was cluttered, but a fresh pot of coffee set on the warmer. Like a good little Southern woman, I motioned the men to the table and fetched coffee for all of us.

Uncle Clarence waited until we each had coffee before he spoke again, as though he were continuing a nonexistent prior conversation. "As to the sword, it was exactly because it was a ghost I was after that I chose that particular weapon. It was in my possession for years, while Cat and Ah were together. She told me once that the sword had seen history, had magical powers to protect its owner, Jean Leveau. It was the only thing Ah could think of to destroy that ghost and keep him from botherin' Katy."

"But Katy wasn't afraid of Sir Gary," I said.

"Not at first," he admitted. "But Ah knew what that spirit was capable of. Ah was afraid he was resortin' to type when Ah heard Katy was askin' you to come help. Ah went lookin' for him that night, not wantin' Katy to know Ah was around, 'cause Ah thought she might have some misguided sympathy for that rascal. And when Ah saw him sneakin' toward the house like he was up to no good, Ah took the opportunity to stop his clock." He sighed and his bushy eyebrows lifted. "Only it wasn't *his* clock Ah stopped."

"Bucky doesn't look anything like Sir Gary," I said.

"Ah didn't realize that 'til after Ah'd already swung that sword. Done the damage. That there ghost played hide'n seek with me, and Ah never got a good look. Not that Ah wanted to."

"Bucky was blackmailing Katy again," I told him.

His eyes darkened. "I know."

"It was you on the answering machine tape, wasn't it?" I mused. "That sound...you must have been in a bar. The jukebox started to play. That country song that starts off with a train whistle. Later that night, Katy was discussing what to do about Bucky's blackmail attempts with you and the fact that someone had killed him. What would happen if anybody found out."

"That swamp rat was no good. It was bad enough he didn't take care of his woman and kids. Ah got the right man after all."

"I'll pretend I didn't hear that, sir," Jack said, then looked at me. "You never did explain what that blackmail business was all about. Have you got any evidence?"

I thought of the manuscript and videotape in the kitchen cupboard, wishing I'd taken time to hide them better. As soon as I got back to Esprit d'Chene, I planned to destroy both of them.

"*Chère?*" Jack prodded.

"You said I wasn't a very good liar, Jack. Let's just say it's all water under the bridge. Or a closed door in the light, better left unopened unless it's needed for something good."

He nodded reluctantly. Maybe some day I'd tell him; maybe not. These wouldn't be the only secrets buried in southern soil.

"Best leave," Uncle Clarence said. "Ah don't want Katy in that cell one more minute."

"We've got an attorney already waiting there, Uncle Clarence." I hugged the dear old gentleman tightly when he stood, and received a tight, desperate embrace in return.

EPILOGUE

In the Master Suite, I grabbed the last page from Katy's printer, shuffled it in with the rest, then stuck all five hundred and twenty-three pages in the padded envelope. I slapped on the Fed Ex label, sealed the tape...and answered my cell phone.

"Alice," my editor said. "We're backed up, so I'm letting you know that if you want a while longer to work, feel free not to rush. I won't be looking at it for a while."

I pulled the phone away and stared. For three days I'd fought fatigue to finish that damn book while Twila squired Granny and Katy around, "touristing" amid celebrating Katy's return and that Uncle Clarence would be placed on probation. And truth be known, this book was still my best effort yet. How dare she put off reading this wonderful story?

I glanced at the Fed Ex package, waiting for one of those sexy drivers to pick it up and handle it with their usual negligence, not realizing what a precious cargo it contained. Damned if I'd wait...yet...well, that last chapter could be tightened...

"Alice?" the phone said.

I jammed it against my ear. "I do appreciate not being rushed. I guess I would like to go over it once more."

"Oh, I'm positive it's as free from any editing need as always," she said, mollifying my disgruntlement easily with words of praise. "I've also decided to take early maternity leave. I can get caught up on some of my work at home, without the distractions of endless meetings. I wanted to thank you, too, for the beautiful mobile. It's exactly right for the baby's room décor. How did you ever think of it?"

I relaxed and smiled. I knew how long she'd wanted a child, putting off the decision until she could juggle her career and still be a good wife and mother.

"Enjoy the rest of your pregnancy. Next time I'm in New York, I'll want to see the baby."

"Of course," she replied. "I'll talk to you soon."

"Take care. Goodbye."

I laid the cell phone down, popped my disk out, and strolled out of the bedroom to change clothes in the Peach Room. In deference to my deadline hell, Katy deferred the celebration party until this evening. Jack told us that Tildy made a deal after the search warrant turned up the rifle she'd used. In return for a confession, she would serve ten years in the Gatesville, Texas, women's prison. She admitted planning revenge on Katy after seeing her and Bucky at the Holey Bucket. Knowing what day Sue Ann did the grocery shopping, she injected the poison into a bag of sugar in the housekeeper's cart—shades of the Tylenol poisonings. She'd been the woman at the convenience store, but the guards foiled her when the poison didn't work. Hell hath no fury, and Tildy sought revenge on anyone associated with Katy and Esprit d'Chene. Personally, I thought she should have extensive psychological counseling, also.

Senator Wilson-Jones took convincing that it was in his best political interest not to insist on a full-blown trial for Uncle Clarence. Jack informed us what turned the tide. Both Tildy and Uncle Clarence were willing to reveal the involvement of ghosts in Bucky's murder. Tildy wanted the senator to pay Bucky's lost child support to her mother. I guess she did have a streak of buried motherhood. Maybe the senator would be a decent grandfather. Age and mistakes can mature a person. Uncle Clarence and his lawyer threatened to use the ghosts as defense tactics. Senator Wilson-Jones shuddered at what that would do to his career and agreed with the DA that probation was the best route for Uncle Clarence, given the little time he had left.

I destroyed the manuscript and videotape, burning them both in Gabe's trash barrel one night. My friendship with Katy forged even stronger when I realized how she'd tried to protect me at the risk of her own reputation and freedom. Well, of course I scanned the darned manuscript before I destroyed it! My writer's curiosity wouldn't be stifled. My name appeared as often as Katy's in that poorly-written piece of tripe, but the explosive contents mattered more than the grammar mistakes. As the last page curled into ash, burning paper odor mingled with melting plastic, Twila stepped out of the shadows. We fixed icy mint juleps in the dimly-lit kitchen. Several of them, truth be known, but we damned sure deserved every one.

I still didn't know for sure who that new ghost was at my house, but I suspected it was a spirit instead. I left the Peach Room and headed down the hallway. At the bottom of the stairwell, I detoured by the Great Room and winked at Grandmere Alicia's portrait. I swear, it winked back, but it could have been a trick of the light.

For once I found all three of my friends in the kitchen, but they were preparing to leave again. Snacks and boxes scattered around, and Katy glanced up with a smile.

"Alice! Uncle Clarence found some crawfish for the party. The men are over there getting things ready." She slid me a sly grin and winked. "I invited Cory, too, and he's bringing soft drinks and beer."

"We got the rest of the food fixed," Granny said. "Got you bread puddin', knowin' how that there's your favorite dessert."

My stomach lurched, but I smiled back at them.

Twila leaned down to stroke Trucker. "You can have the mudbugs. Your uncle promised me fried 'gator tail."

Katy carried a box toward the garage door as I picked up Miss Molly. "Hope you're making mint juleps," I called after her.

"I am," she replied as she juggled the box and opened the door. Then, "Alice! What on earth happened to the Mercedes?"

AFTERWORD

Like Alice, I'm an author and also a ghosthunter. I see ghosts. I talk to ghosts. My own real-life Aunt Twila, Belle Brown, dragged me down the fascinating trail in search of ghosts years ago, and since then, she and I have shared many spooky/scary/thrilling adventures. We also hunt ghosts with friends who love prowling haunted houses and graveyards as much as we do. Several paranormal residents share my one-hundred-year-old home with my husband and me, and even my animals seem to see and interact with the ghosts or spirits at times.

Some of the ghosts Aunt Belle and I "met" during our quests told us wonderful stories about their lives. As fascinating to us as actually speaking with ghosts was the research, which confirmed the lives of these souls. Writer friends who were both scared spitless and captivated by the tales I told them in e-mail urged me to write my stories, and thus the idea for the *Dead Man* series, tales in which the ghosts actually participate in the investigations of their own deaths.

Six Gun, Texas, is a fictitious town, but some of the stories in the series are based on actual conversations with ghosts; some are the product of my own weird imagination. Or perhaps, tales of adventures that I would enjoy being a part of...although on this side of The Veil! Feel free to guess which are which, and I hope you enjoy the stories as much as I enjoy writing them. Also, although many of the protective devices I use in the stories are gleaned from research and actual experience, I wouldn't suggest you try to handle any ghosts you encounter on your own. Indeed, tread carefully into the paranormal dimension...as well as these tales. Things truly *do* go bump in the night, as well as the day, and sometimes dreams are actual reality.

T. M. Simmons
Author/Ghosthunter

DEAD MAN HAUNT
A DEAD MAN MYSTERY, BOOK 2

Such a grand piece of decay. Brimming with ghosts!

From across the street, Twila and I stared at the once-magnificent hotel and released twin sighs of yearning to explore the decrepit structure. It rose above us U-shaped, multistoried, and numerous broken windows shattered any sense that the façade sheltered anything other than wrack and ruin. Atop, a bell tower crowned the edifice, rising alone into the early morning, cloud-spotted April sky. A wide veranda graced the front, where in times gone by natty gentlemen and flapper ladies— or non-ladies—strolled when not partaking of the mineral baths or hidden-room gambling.

Though I'd been here once before, experience taught me that in Twila's company even more fantastic weird happenings would transpire. Her psychic powers far surpassed the fledgling abilities I possessed, since she'd been chasing ghosts years longer than me. The possibility of encountering past residents in her company, more than the building's wonderful history, fired my anticipation for another one of our shared adventures.

Oh, yeah, that and the fact that Patrick had already intrigued us with tales of his life in the hotel's heyday. Former life, really, since he now abided in the afterlife.

Twila raised her camera and snapped several pictures to begin the record of this adventure, and beside her, Patrick materialized briefly. Could a ghost cry, I'm sure tears would have rolled down Patrick's cheeks at the sight before him, even though in his time men characteristically hid their emotions. Come to think of it, so did men today, like my ex-husband, Jack, except when he was pis...angry at me.

Damn...darn! Now I even censored my thoughts so I wouldn't have to pay into Granny's trip kitty!

Patrick stoically gazed at the building he had called home-away when he lived, then faded back into his own realm.

"Gosh damn," Twila mused, since she wasn't part of the trip-kitty pact. "I wish that ghost would put some clothes on when he visualizes. He's so hot, he even makes a long-married woman pant and remember those days when sex took precedence over sanity."

I giggled. "He forgets sometimes."

"Or maybe he knows how much *you* like to ogle that fantastic body." She nudged me and winked.

I grinned in remembrance. "That day in the men's dressing room, over there in the hotel basement? The first time I met Patrick? Jeez Louise. He'd just stepped out of the shower. Had a white towel thrown around his neck. All that naked muscle and dribbles of water crawling down that tanned skin..."

"You've mentioned that several times. If I didn't know better, Alice, I'd swear you were half in love with a ghost."

"Infatuated, maybe," I admitted. "Not in love, but a definite possibili-ty...infatuation. I've seen your eyes bug out when our friend appears, Twila. Ten seconds after you met Patrick at my house yesterday, you forgot he couldn't consume and offered him a Jack and Coke."

"Well..." she mused. "Maybe fifteen seconds. After I got my breathing under control and could think."

* * *

Available in Paperback and eBook from Your Favorite Bookstore or Online Retailer

About the Author

T. M. Simmons lives in a haunted house on the edge of the East Texas Piney Woods, which she and her husband share with a variety of pets and paranormal residents. In between writing cozy mysteries and other stories, she delights in scaring herself silly during otherworldly encounters and visits haunted building and graveyards during both dark and full moons. Her husband goes along sometimes to protect her from the bumps in the night, although he's been know to spy a ghost and retreat rather than confront. She also pursues paranormal entities with her own real-life Twila, Aunt Belle Brown, and they are Lead Investigators of the Supernatural Researchers of Texas paranormal investigative team. SRT's motto is, "Leave Peace Behind," and the team seeks to leave peace for the people who are dealing with troubled hauntings, as well as for the ghosts. Simmons is extremely willing to discuss her experiences with anyone she can corner.

Sign up here for the T. M. Simmons newsletter and receive a copy of *Thrall Bound, a Short Story;* only available to newsletter subscribers.

https://ghostie3.wixsite.com/index1

www.iseeghosts.com

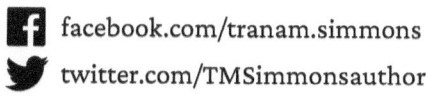

facebook.com/tranam.simmons

twitter.com/TMSimmonsauthor

www.ingramcontent.com/pod-product-compliance
Lightning Source LLC
Chambersburg PA
CBHW030638020726
47493CB00006B/1774